The Secrets of Wilson House

Robin Perks

ISBN: 978-0-473-73798-6

For my family, both at home and extended

CONTENTS

ACKNOWLEDGMENTS

A heartfelt thank you to Miblart for their exceptional work in creating a cover that beautifully captures the essence of my story.

I deeply appreciate Julie Perks, whose tireless proofreading polished every word in this book to perfection. Your dedication was invaluable.

Thank you all for being part of this incredible journey.

CHAPTER 1: THE INHERITANCE

Ethan slammed the last of his belongings into the cardboard box, muttering curses under his breath. He had given more than fifteen years to this company, dedicating himself to building some of the most iconic landmarks in the city. And this was his reward— the proverbial golden handshake. A euphemism for betrayal, a pat on the back before the shove out the door.

"Economic hardships," they said. "The property market has taken a downturn. It's nothing personal, Ethan." Nothing personal? He wanted to laugh. Of course it was personal. How could it not be? The job had been more than a paycheck; it was his identity, his pride, and his future. Now, a handful of polite corporate platitudes had stolen all of that.

"What the hell am I supposed to do now? Nobody is hiring architects. It was supposed to be a career for life," Ethan muttered to no one in particular. His words hung heavy in the air of the now-sterile office space, stripped of the personal touches he'd accumulated over the years.

"I'm sure you'll bounce right back," an intern sneered, snapping him out of his thoughts.

"Oh, go to hell, you bloody idiot!" Ethan said.

"That's out of line!" the intern said, his face flushing red.

Ethan said nothing. He clipped the intern's shoulder on his way to the elevator, never breaking stride.

As the elevator hummed downward, Ethan shifted his weight

from foot to foot, his grip tightening around the box in his arms. A muscle twitched in his jaw. His reflection in the mirrored walls stared back at him—tight-lipped, eyes shadowed with something heavier than anger. He exhaled sharply, but it did nothing to ease the knot coiling tighter in his chest.

The elevator dinged. Cold fluorescent light flooded in, casting harsh lines across his clenched fists. He swallowed hard, his throat dry. The strain of the mortgage, the bills, Claire's hopeful smile—it wrapped around him, suffocating, heavier than the box he carried.

Ethan reached his car, his movements rigid. He hurled the box onto the back seat, its contents spilling across the floor. Slamming the door, he set off a nearby car alarm—the shrill noise blending with the chaos in his head. He collapsed into the driver's seat, gripping the wheel, his chest rising and falling in ragged bursts.

He pounded the steering wheel, then started the engine and drove away for the last time. As he merged onto the city streets, he stole one last glance in the rearview mirror. The office building loomed, its glass facade catching the late afternoon sun—suddenly small, meaningless.

"To hell with you all," he muttered, knuckles whitening on the wheel.

The red glow of the afternoon was fading into a deep indigo as Ethan pulled into the driveway of their upper-class home. Their house, once a symbol of success and stability, now stood before him like a ticking time bomb of debt. Its manicured lawns, slick with droplets from the sprinkler system, seemed out of place—a pristine façade masking the chaos within.

Ethan lingered at the wheel, staring at the shadowy silhouette of the house. He needed to compose himself before going inside. Neither Claire nor the kids deserved his frustration. Outside, crickets droned, unaware of his despair.

With a heavy sigh, he collected his box of belongings, stepped out of the car, and made his way to the door. The faint glow of light spilled through the living room window, and he could already hear the muffled sounds of an argument inside. Not the peaceful refuge he had hoped for.

The moment he stepped into the house, a whirlwind of childish uproar swept over him.

"I told you not to touch my stuff, Ben!" Olivia screamed. His sixteen-year-old daughter, usually quiet and reserved, was furious. Her younger brother, Ben, stood his ground with a defiant look that only an eleven-year-old could muster.

"I didn't break it!" Ben shot back. "You left it where anyone could step on it. That's your fault, not mine!"

"It's *ruined*, you little…!"

"Enough!" Ethan barked. Both kids froze and turned to him, wide-eyed.

"Welcome home to chaos, my love," Claire said, appearing at the doorway to the kitchen with a tired smile. She walked up to him, kissed him on the lips, and then pulled back, studying him. "What's wrong? What happened?"

Ethan let out a slow, uneven exhale, steadying himself. "I've lost my job."

Claire paled, the colour draining from her face as she sank into the nearest chair. Her hands gripped the armrests as though bracing for impact. "Why?"

"Economic downturn. Apparently, it's nothing I did. The market's slow… there's no work for architects right now. At least, that's what they told me." He trailed off, unable to say more.

Claire's chest tightened, heat rising in her skin as uncertainty coiled around her with a heavy, relentless pull. Her mind raced with the daunting realities they faced—mounting bills, never ending responsibilities, and the ever-growing list of expenses. She reached for Ethan's hands, her grip tight, as if anchoring herself to him might somehow steady the storm swirling inside her. "What are we going to do?" she asked. "The mortgage, the school fees, groceries—how are we going to manage it all?"

Ethan said nothing.

Claire sat for a moment, staring at the floor as though searching for answers in the wood's grain. "Okay… okay, hear me out," she said, holding Ethan's hands. "Maybe this is a sign."

"A sign?"

Claire nodded. "I want to show you something."

She led him into the kitchen, where an open file lay spread across the counter. Claire grabbed the papers and held them out to him, her hands trembling.

"What is this?" Ethan asked, frowning as he paged through the documents. The language was dense and formal, but one word caught his attention: 'inheritance.'

"Someone in my family left me a property—Wilson House. It's an old mansion up near Hollow Creek. The paperwork came through today. I've been struggling with whether to keep it and add it to our list of worries or... well, maybe it could be something more."

"A mansion? Where is this coming from? Who left it to you?"

"It was my aunt, I think. A lawyer tracked me down this morning to fill me in. The place is enormous, Ethan—eight en-suite rooms. We could turn it into a small bed-and-breakfast. It could be our chance to start over."

"Claire, this sounds... crazy. Couldn't we just sell it? Use the money to pay off this mortgage?"

"We can't."

"What do you mean, we can't?"

"There are conditions. We can't sell the house. We have to live there. Otherwise, the inheritance is void."

Ethan let out a short, humourless laugh and shook his head. "This is insane. Who leaves a house like this with strings attached?"

"I don't know," Claire said, "but maybe it doesn't matter. This could be the fresh start we need, Ethan. We could put this house on the market, pay off what we can, and move to Wilson House. It's not ideal, I know, but it's *something*. It's hope."

Ethan stared at her, weighing the desperation in her voice against the gnawing uncertainty in his gut. He flipped through the documents one last time, the pages rustling in the quiet kitchen.

"What the hell!" he said, forcing a half-smile. "Let's do it."

Claire's face lit up, her excitement breaking through the tension that had gripped the room. She threw her arms around him. "This will work," she said. "It has to."

As Ethan held her, staring over her shoulder at the pile of papers, a faint unease settled in his chest. Somewhere deep in his gut, something told him that this would not be the fresh start Claire believed it would be.

Three months later, Ethan stood in the empty living room, the lingering scent of Claire's rosemary candles the only trace of their time here. The house—once filled with life and laughter—now felt hollow, as if they were dismantling a part of themselves. Olivia hovered near the window, gazing beyond the picket fence, while Ben traced his fingers over the empty bookshelves.

"I'm going to miss this place," Olivia said.

Ethan sighed, forcing a smile. "New beginnings, Liv Wilson House could be an adventure."

Claire entered, dusting off her hands. "It's just a house—we'll make it our own."

With one last glance at their old home, Ethan grabbed the last box and stepped outside.

With the house sold; The plan was to use the meagre profit they had made from the sale to renovate the mansion. They had not yet seen the property in person and were relying on instinct and trust in their lawyer, Penelope Marsh, who had assured them it was a worthwhile venture. Despite the uncertainty, Claire was eager to dive into the project. With her extensive experience as a freelance illustrator specialising in historical artwork, she felt certain the mansion would inspire her creativity in ways she had never experienced before.

The kids were bubbling with excitement about this new chapter in their lives. Olivia, in particular, saw it as a chance to start over. At her last school, she struggled to make friends and classmates bullied her about her academic achievements. This move felt like a lifeline, a fresh opportunity to start anew. Even Ben, with his usual restless energy, seemed eager for the adventure ahead, though he couldn't resist peppering the car ride with his usual stream of odd questions and comments.

Miles stretched behind them as Ethan focused on the road, gripping the wheel while his children sang loudly and off-key along to the radio. Outside, the night closed in around them, the headlights cutting through the darkness in thin, wavering beams. For the first time since losing his job, he felt a glimmer of hope, a sense that maybe they could make this work. Yet, lurking beneath his cautious optimism, was an unshakable sense of impending doom.

"Dad, can I get an earring?" Ben asked, tugging at his earlobe.

"Over my dead body!" Ethan said, adjusting the rearview mirror to glance at Ben. A faint smile undercut his stern tone.

"I'll give you one," Olivia said. "We just need some ice and a needle."

Ben recoiled and covered his ear, his face twisting into a dramatic grimace. "Are you crazy?"

Claire offered a faint smile, her thoughts drifting to another time and place. "I remember the stories my mother used to tell me about my aunt who lived in that old mansion. She would describe it as if the house itself were alive—like it had a presence, a personality all its own. It was different, she'd say, unlike any other place she'd ever known. But she never explained why. It was always just… different."

Olivia and Ben had stopped laughing, their amusement fading into silence as their full attention shifted to Claire's words. But Claire didn't continue the story. She paused, distant, as if the pull of the memories held her back—leaving them suspended in quiet anticipation.

Shuddering, Ethan returned his attention to driving. Out of nowhere, a young woman appeared in the middle of the road, illuminated by the car's headlights. Time seemed to slow as Ethan slammed on the brakes, the squeal of tyres piercing the air. The sudden stop threw Olivia and Ben forward against their seatbelts, while Claire's hands shot out to brace herself against the dashboard. The car veered to the side, tyres skidding on loose gravel. Ethan wrestled with the steering wheel, but the vehicle spun uncontrollably before coming to a jarring stop just inches from a tree.

For a moment, there was only silence, broken by the faint ticking of the car's cooling engine.

"Oh, my word… I hit her," Ethan said, his face ashen. His hands trembled on the steering wheel as the realisation sank in.

"Who?" Claire fumbled with her seatbelt in panic, glancing back to check on the kids. "Who did you hit?"

Before Ethan could respond, Olivia unbuckled her seatbelt and bolted out of the car. "Daddy, help!" she screamed.

Ethan scrambled out of the car and ran toward Olivia, his heart pounding. "Oh, no… oh no…" he said, the words tumbling from his lips as he raced to her side.

Olivia was standing at the edge of the road, her slender frame silhouetted by the headlights. She pointed to the ground, trembling. "Daddy, it's hurt. Do something."

Ethan froze as his eyes fell on the creature lying on the asphalt. It was a deer, its body twisted and broken. Its entrails glistened under the harsh light, spilled out onto the road. The animal let out a low, agonised moan, its chest rising and falling in shallow breaths. Olivia's tear-streaked face turned to him, her eyes wide with pleading.

"Where is she?" Ethan said, his head snapping around the darkened road. "Where's the girl?"

Olivia blinked at him in confusion. "What girl? Daddy, you hit the deer. It's dying. Please, help it."

Ethan shivered. He looked again, scanning the road and the surrounding area for any sign of the person he was certain he'd seen. But there was nothing—just the broken deer and the cold, empty night.

His stomach churned as he knelt beside the animal. Its eyes, glossy and unfocused, seemed to plead with him for release. He felt helpless, torn between the surreal certainty of what he'd witnessed and the undeniable reality before him.

"Dad, do something!"

Ethan swallowed hard, his hands trembling as he reached out to the deer. But his mind was elsewhere, haunted by the image of the young woman who had vanished into the night.

The next few hours of the drive up to Wilson House were uncannily quiet, each family member lost in their own thoughts. The rhythmic hum of the tyres against the road and the occasional rattle of loose objects in the car created a strange sense of calm. Ben had slumped against the window, fast asleep, his breath fogging up the glass. Olivia stared out at the passing dark landscape, her mind still replaying the agonised cries of the deer. A single tear traced down her cheek, though she quickly wiped it away, not wanting anyone to notice.

Ethan's hands were white-knuckled on the wheel, his eyes locked on the winding road ahead. He tried to push aside the unsettling event of earlier, but couldn't stop thinking about it—the young lady he thought he saw, the sound of the impact, the deer's broken body. It had felt so real. Too real.

The GPS chimed, shattering the silence. "Take the next left. Your destination is ahead."

Ethan followed the mechanical voice's instructions, the car's tyres crunching on gravel as he turned onto a narrow, forgotten road. Thick trees loomed on either side, their gnarled branches intertwined above like skeletal fingers, blocking out the moonlight. The headlights only just seemed to penetrate the blackness, the beams swallowed up as if by a living thing.

"You have arrived at your destination," the GPS announced with finality, then fell silent.

Ethan brought the car to a stop, craning his neck to look out the windshield. Up ahead, caked under years of growth and decay, hung an old wooden sign. One of its chains had snapped, leaving it tilted at an unnatural angle. Moss and mildew encrusted the wood, but Ethan squinted and could just make out the faded lettering: *Wil...House.*

"Are we there?" Ben said, rubbing his sleepy eyes as he sat up.

"I think we are," Ethan said. "Unless the GPS is broken, and that sign is wrong."

He pressed on the accelerator, and the car crept forward, its tyres crunching over dirt and fallen leaves. The road stretched out like a tunnel, the overgrown trees arching so low it felt like they might scrape the roof of the car. The headlights threw distorted shadows on the trunks, twisting and curling like dark spectres.

"Isn't this exciting?" Claire said, making everyone jump.

"Exciting?" Olivia said, peering out into the darkness. "It's more like creepy. But... I kind of like it." There was a faint smile on her lips, as if the gloom was helping her forget the haunting image of the deer.

"Do you think it's haunted?" Ben said, his earlier drowsiness replaced by curiosity. He had wriggled out of his seatbelt and perched in the middle, between Ethan and Claire, his wide eyes searching for a glimpse of something—anything—beyond the trees.

"There's no such thing as ghosts."

"How do you know, Dad?" Ben said. "Didn't you see one tonight?"

"That's not funny, Ben," Claire said, though she bit back a smile. She turned in her seat, trying to give him a stern look, but it only half succeeded.

Before long, the overgrowth broke apart, the claustrophobic tunnel of trees giving way to an open clearing. The sight that awaited them made everyone fall silent.

The mansion loomed before them, a hulking silhouette against the dark sky. Its massive, three-story frame was a testament to another era, a late nineteenth-century relic that once might have stood proud, but now exuded a sense of abandonment. Ivy crawled up its stone walls, choking the structure like a slow-moving parasite. The front driveway curved into a circle around a dry, crumbling fountain, its basin cracked and filled with dead leaves. The mansion's windows stared back at them, dark and empty, like the hollow eyes of a corpse.

Ethan pulled the car to a stop, the engine idling as the family stared out through the windshield in stunned silence.

"Whoa," Ben said, his earlier bravado gone.

"Is this it?" Olivia asked, awestruck and apprehensive.

Claire leaned forward, pressing a hand to the dashboard as she took in the sight. "It's incredible," she said with a note of uncertainty. "It's like stepping back in time."

"We're going to need help," Ethan said.

His mind raced with the sheer scale of work ahead of them—the overgrown grounds, the crumbling stone, the countless repairs.

"Or maybe an exorcist," Ben said, half-joking but unable to tear his eyes away from the looming structure.

Ethan cut the engine, and the sudden silence felt deafening. For a long moment, no one moved. The mansion seemed to wait, anticipating their arrival.

"Come on," Claire said, breaking the stillness. She smiled, though there was a trace of doubt in her eyes. "Let's go see our new home."

The family exited the car, their eyes transfixed by the building, its shadow stretching across the overgrown lawn under the pale light of the moon.

"I need to pee," Ben said, shifting from foot to foot in a little dance.

"Come on, let's go find a bathroom," Claire said, taking Ben by the hand as though he were a toddler again.

"Are you nuts? I'm not going in there!" Ben said, pulling his hand away and staring up at the dark windows like they would stare back.

"So where do you plan on living then? This is our new home, Ben," Ethan said with a chuckle.

"Oh, yeah," Ben said, taking his mum's hand again, something he rarely did anymore at his age. "It would have been better if we arrived in the daytime."

They ascended the cracked stone steps to the terrace. A massive wooden door stood before them, its surface scarred and weathered but still imposing. Claire pulled out an old iron key from her purse, its jagged edges glinting in the light of her phone. With a satisfying *click*, she unlocked the door and pushed it open.

The heavy wooden door creaked as it swung inward, revealing a vestibule cloaked in darkness. Claire stepped forward, her phone's light casting long, eerie shadows that danced across the walls. A second door lay ahead, and she pushed it open as well, revealing a small hallway that led into a grand staircase hall. The air inside was cool and perfumed, smelling of aged wood and polish.

Ben clung to Claire's arm, his earlier bravado replaced by wide-eyed apprehension. "It smells weird," he said.

Ethan ran his hand along the wall, searching until his fingers found a series of switches. He flipped them downwards, and one by one, chandeliers and sconces blinked to life, bathing the hallway in a warm, golden glow.

"Oh, wow!" Olivia and Ben said in unison, their earlier apprehension replaced with awe.

Ethan stood frozen for a moment, taking in the sight before him. The polished marble floors gleamed under the lights, leading to a grand spiral staircase that ascended to the upper floors. Intricate mouldings adorned the walls, and the antique and elegant furnishings were in extraordinarily good condition. It stood in striking opposition to the dilapidated exterior they had seen.

"Oh, it's beautiful," Claire whispered, marvelling at the sight. "I didn't expect it to be so… intact."

"I'll grab our sleeping bags from the car," Ethan said, still unaware that the house came fully furnished.

As Ethan stepped outside, the quiet hit him like a wall. The garden, wild and untamed, seemed to swallow all sound. There were no chirping insects, no rustling leaves—just an oppressive, unnatural silence. He shivered and said, "What kind of place is this?"

He headed to the car, his footsteps crunching on the gravel path. Halfway there, he tripped over something solid and swore. Looking down, he saw an old stone ornament—a dolphin—half buried in the weeds. He kicked it aside, but froze as a red glow pulsed near the side of the house. For a split second, it blinked like an eye, then vanished.

Adrenaline surged through him as he reached into the car's trunk. He grabbed a tire iron and moved toward the source of the light.

"Who's there?" he said, searching the blackness of the night as the words hung in the stillness.

"Wahoo! What the heck?" a man yelped, stumbling back in shock.

Ethan jumped back, almost dropping the tire iron. In the dim light, he saw a large man stumble backward, his hands raised.

"Mr Wallace? Mr Ethan Wallace?" the man said, tossing his cigarette to the ground with a trembling hand.

Ethan lowered the tire iron, his heart still pounding. "Yeah. Who the hell are you?"

"I'm sorry, sir. Really sorry," the man said, holding his hands up as if to calm Ethan down. "I'm with the moving company. We got here early and parked the truck around the back. My guys and I were going to sleep in the truck overnight and start unloading in the morning. I didn't mean to scare you."

Ethan exhaled, realising the red glow he'd seen was from the man's cigarette, now discarded on the ground. He let out a nervous laugh; the tension draining from his body.

"You scared the hell out of me," Ethan said. "It's so damn dark out here."

"Back at you, sir," the man said with a sheepish grin "Didn't mean to freak you out. I'll let my team know you're here. And… sorry again."

"It's fine. Glad you made it. But next time, maybe give me a heads-up before lurking in the shadows."

The man chuckled and nodded. "Will do, Mr Wallace. Have a good night."

Ethan watched as the man disappeared around the side of the house, shaking his head at the absurdity of the situation. He grabbed the sleeping bags from the trunk, glanced once more into the pitch-black night, and headed back to the house, the unsettling silence following him every step of the way.

He stepped back into the house, but before he could gather himself, Ben's voice sliced through the quiet. "Dad, you have to see this." He grabbed his hand and pulled him forward.

Ethan, still shaken but comforted by his son's eagerness, allowed himself to be led. Ben guided him into a large room just off to the right of the hallway. As they stepped inside, the space opened up to reveal an impressive billiard table that immediately caught his attention. The table, though aged and worn, stood solid, its presence commanding the room. Despite the faded and torn green felt, the intricate woodwork and craftsmanship hinted at the table's former grandeur. Individual wooden racks along the walls stored cues, their lacquered finishes gleaming softly under the warm glow of old incandescent lamps. The room's quiet charm captivated him, and he felt it was a forgotten relic of a bygone era.

"Wow," Ethan said, running a hand along the table's edge. "This thing must be over a century old."

"It's cool," Ben said, but his eyes weren't on the table. He was staring at the paintings that lined the walls, a crease forming between his brows. "But… Dad, look at these."

Ethan turned his attention to the artwork and felt a chill creep up his spine. The paintings were dark and macabre, each depicting a hunter standing triumphantly over a slain animal. The details were grotesque—the bloodied faces of the hunters smeared with the crimson of their prey, their eyes glaring with an almost feral intensity. One painting showed a man standing over a deer, its lifeless eyes staring out of the frame. Another featured a bear, its massive form crumpled at the hunter's feet, its fur matted with blood. There was a surreal, almost otherworldly quality to the scenes that made them unsettling.

"Who would hang these in their home?" Ethan said, shocked by the barbarism.

"Maybe mum's aunt was into hunting?" Ben said.

"Not likely," Ethan said, his eyes narrowing as he studied the signature on one painting. It was illegible, more like a scrawl than a name. He made a mental note to investigate further once they settled in.

"Oh, Ethan!" Claire said, stepping into the room and breaking the tension. She twirled in place, taking in the high ceilings, the antique fixtures, and the grand windows covered in heavy, dust-laden drapes. "I think this will work. It's more than I dreamed it would be."

Ethan forced a smile. "It's got potential, that's for sure." But his mind lingered on the unsettling artwork.

Later that night, the family gathered on the second floor in one of the larger bedrooms. They spread out their sleeping bags on the hardwood floor, leaving the beds untouched until they unpacked their linens from the moving truck the next morning. The room was spacious, with a grand canopy bed looming in one corner and an ornate fireplace opposite it. Paintings lined the walls, depicting serene landscapes and pastoral scenes.

As they settled in, the quiet of the house weighed on them. The occasional creak of the floorboards and the faint rustle of the wind against the windows kept them on edge. Olivia lay on her back, staring at the intricate plasterwork on the ceiling, while Ben clung to his flashlight like a talisman.

"Do you think the house has a name?" Olivia asked, breaking the silence.

"It's called Wilson House," Claire said, brushing her hair out of her face as she adjusted her sleeping bag. "It's in the deed."

"Sounds like the name of a haunted place," Ben said, burrowing deeper into his sleeping bag.

"It's just a name," Ethan said, though he couldn't shake the uneasy feeling that had settled over him since their arrival. He glanced at the bedroom door, which they'd left ajar, and thought he saw a shadow flit in the hallway beyond. He chalked it up to exhaustion and closed his eyes, willing himself to sleep.

As the house settled into the stillness of the night, a faint sound echoed through the halls—a soft, rhythmic tapping, like footsteps on the wooden floors. Olivia sat up, her eyes wide.

"Did anyone else hear that?" she said.

Ethan opened his eyes. "It's just the wind," he said, but his attention remained fixed on the darkness beyond the room door.

Claire reached over and squeezed his hand. "Welcome home."

A loud banging on the front door jolted Ethan awake. He sat up, his heart racing. He couldn't remember falling asleep, which had been deep and dreamless—almost unnatural. Disoriented, he blinked at the unfamiliar surroundings of the grand bedroom. Sunlight streamed through the tall, dusty windows, bathing the ornate walls and furniture in a golden glow that softened their once ominous appearance. The room looked almost cheerful now, stripped of its nighttime foreboding.

Ethan glanced around, expecting to see Claire and the kids, but the room was empty. His brow furrowed. Muffled voices emanated from downstairs—Claire's voice, calm and conversational, and another he didn't recognise. A sudden burst of laughter from Claire put him at ease, but curiosity gnawed at him. Who was at the door this early?

He slipped out of the sleeping bag; the fabric crinkling in the still room, and got dressed. Checking his watch, he realised with surprise that it was already ten in the morning. He'd slept like the dead. As he buttoned his shirt, the tantalising smell of bacon wafted up through the house, making his stomach grumble. Combined with the soft glow of sunlight and the faint sounds of life from below, the house felt inviting. Almost... homely.

Ethan ran a hand through his dishevelled hair and headed downstairs. The grand wooden staircase creaked beneath his feet as he descended, its ornate banister gleaming in the sunlight. Turning to the kitchen, tucked behind the stairwell, he stepped into a scene that felt both surreal and domestic.

Claire stood by the stove, flipping strips of sizzling bacon, the sounds of crackling grease punctuating her cheerful conversation. Across the counter sat a woman Ethan had never seen before;

elegant and out of place in their current situation. She wore a tailored suit and was paging through a thick sheaf of papers.

Claire glanced up as Ethan entered, a warm smile spreading across her face. "Good morning, sleepyhead. You're up just in time. Ethan, this is Mrs Penelope Marsh—the lawyer I told you about. She's here to go over the legal documents."

Penelope looked up from her papers, offering him a polite, professional smile. "Good morning, Mr Wallace. It's a pleasure to meet you."

"Morning," Ethan said, still a little groggy. He rubbed his face before extending his hand. "Nice to meet you as well. Claire mentioned there were some… conditions we needed to know about?"

Penelope nodded, her smile turning tight-lipped, as if she'd had this conversation more than once. "Yes, though nothing out of the ordinary for an inheritance of this nature. Most of the stipulations pertain to maintaining the integrity of the property."

She glanced down at her notes, then continued. "The conditions are: you are required to make this house your primary residence, keep the current maintenance worker employed, and preserve the original artwork by keeping the paintings where they are. Permit no modern art or renovations that might change the home's character. And you must not sell the house under any circumstances."

Ethan exchanged a glance with Claire, who had paused mid-motion with the spatula. "That's… quite a list," he intoned. "We'll have to keep the maintenance worker employed? We can't afford that right now. Claire and I are both—well, unemployed."

Claire agreed, offering a faint, regretful smile as she dished up the bacon and eggs. "It's just not realistic for us to keep on staff."

Penelope appeared unfazed. "There's no need for concern," she replied, flipping to another page in her documents. "The inheritance includes a fund allocated to cover his salary for the next ten years—longer, depending on the economy."

Ethan blinked, speechless. "Wait, you're serious?"

"Yes, Mr Wallace," Penelope said.

Claire let out a low whistle, shaking her head in disbelief. "Well, that's unexpected," she said, a small grin tugging at her lips. "Ten years of staff covered? That changes things."

Ethan couldn't suppress a quiet laugh of astonishment. He muttered, "No shit...", as he processed the sheer magnitude of what had just been revealed.

The kitchen fell quiet, save for the soft hiss of the gas stove and the sounds of the kids exploring the house. For the first time, Ethan let himself exhale, allowing the edges of their strange new reality to settle around him. Maybe this place wasn't the burden he'd feared. Maybe—just maybe—it was something else entirely.

Ben startled them all as he burst into the kitchen, sliding across the polished floor in his socks like a runaway train. "Whoo! I love this house—it's awesome!" he said, grinning from ear to ear. "Dad, why are so many of the doors locked?"

"Probably to keep grubby little fingers like yours from touching everything," Ethan said, smirking as he slid a plate of food toward his son.

Claire leaned against the counter. "Why *are* so many doors locked?" she asked, turning to Penelope. "Any idea?"

The lawyer adjusted her glasses and offered a small shrug. "I'm afraid I don't have the slightest clue. You'd need to ask your handyman. It's possible he is carrying out repairs or maintenance in some rooms."

Claire turned to Ethan, resolute. "Well, we're unlocking them all today. This family has no secrets—and this house shouldn't hold any either."

A deafening crash reverberated through the house, sending a sharp vibration shuddering through the walls and floors. The sound was so sudden and violent it might have been a bomb going off.

Ben was the first to react, tearing down the hallway at full speed, his socks skidding on the polished marble floor. "Ben, wait!" Ethan said, but the boy was already gone. Cursing, Ethan followed.

When he reached the source of the noise, the sight that greeted him stopped him in his tracks. A wooden dresser lay in ruins on the marble floor, its splintered pieces sprawled across the tiles like the aftermath of an explosion. Shards of glass from the shattered mirror lay scattered everywhere, catching the sunlight streaming through the ornate dome of the staircase above. The light fractured into thousands of tiny reflections, dancing across the room—beautiful and dangerous all at once.

Ben stepped forward while looking up to see where it had fallen from.

"Whoa there, buddy!" Ethan said, stopping Ben in his tracks with an outstretched arm. Ben's attention shifted to the floor's scattered shards as he held Ethan's arm. "You don't want to cut your feet on that glass. What were you thinking?" Ethan said.

Ben's wide eyes stared at the wreckage in awe. "What *happened*, Dad?"

Before Ethan could answer, a commotion echoed down from the second-floor balcony. Muffled shouts of panic and apology rang through the air like guilty bells.

"Sorry, Mr Wallace!" A tense call came from above. "We were trying to manoeuvre the dresser around a table up here on the balcony, and we—we lost our grip on it. It just… slipped. We are so sorry. Is anyone hurt?" The man wiped sweat from his balding head, his face flushed with fright.

Ethan glowered at the balcony. "You could have killed someone down here!"

His voice reverberated through the open stairwell, echoing off the high walls and ornate railing like an accusation. Silence followed, except for the faint crunch of glass beneath his boots as he stepped back. The tension hung heavy in the air, amplifying the contrast between the sunlit beauty of the space and the sharp reminder of its hidden dangers.

Ethan exhaled, trying to steady his temper as he looked at Ben, whose eyes remained fixed on the destruction. "Stay here," he said, lifting Ben and setting him down on the edge of the hallway where the glass hadn't reached. "Don't move until I've cleaned this up, okay?"

Ben nodded, subdued.

Ethan cast another glance at the balcony. A dark unease prickled at the edges of his thoughts. The house, with all its grandeur and beauty, was feeling… temperamental. First the locked doors. Now this. He shuddered, a sense of unease washing over him as he wondered what other dangers lurked, unseen.

"Oh, no… is *that* my dresser? The one you gave me for my birthday?" Olivia cried, emerging from the reception room where she had been investigating the vast library of dusty, leather-bound books. Her face paled with dismay at the sight of splintered wood and a shattered mirror spread across the marble floor.

Behind her, a man stood biting a pipe between his yellow teeth, his expression calm despite the chaos. "I'm afraid that dresser is beyond repair. Though I can bring in another from storage. There's one that used to belong to Miss Eliza—still in excellent condition, if I recall."

Startled, Olivia let out a small gasp and spun around. Samuel stood there, having materialised from nowhere. Dressed in an old, worn handyman's uniform, he was a thin, wiry man with sharp features and dark eyes that held a quiet knowing. His sudden appearance made Olivia's heart skip a beat.

"Who's Eliza?" Olivia asked, frowning as she steadied herself.

Samuel thoughtfully tilted his head. "Miss Eliza Wilson—one of the original residents of this house. Quite the spirited young lady."

The words struck Ben like a jolt of electricity. He straightened up, his pulse quickening as the fragments of his dream rushed back to him.

"I think I dreamt of her last night," Ben blurted. He turned to Olivia. "It was so real. I saw this weird, blue shimmer—like I was looking through wavy glass. And beyond it, there was a girl. She looked a little older than you."

Olivia blinked, startled by his sudden declaration. "What are you talking about?"

"It was her—Eliza. Someone called her name, but it was weird, like they were speaking through a tin can or something. It didn't feel like a normal dream."

Curious, Olivia crossed her arms, her scepticism momentarily forgotten. "You saw her? In the dream?"

"Yeah," Ben said, nodding emphatically.

Samuel froze for a moment before chuckling." Miss Eliza went missing in 1810. If it really were her, you'd be dreaming of a lady who'd be over two hundred years old by now."

Claire stepped forward, eyeing the stranger suspiciously.

"Excuse me," she said, her posture stiffening with caution, "but who are you?" She glanced at Ben with a faint sigh. "And Ben, please stop making up stories."

Samuel turned his attention to Claire, sporting—a thin, crooked smile that revealed a missing front tooth. "My apologies, madam. I didn't mean to startle anyone. Name's Samuel. I am the grounds and handyman here. Been keeping this place ticking for some time now. I was just on my way to sort out the electrics in the den when I heard the commotion." He extended his rough, calloused hand toward her as he stepped further into the room, the crunch of broken glass beneath his boots punctuating the silence.

Claire hesitated before shaking his hand. There was something old-fashioned about his demeanour—too polite, too practiced, as though he belonged to another time.

"I'm *not* making up stories," Ben said. He kicked at a broken piece of wood, his brow furrowing. "I *saw* her in a dream."

Samuel's attention lingered on Ben for just a second longer than necessary, though he said nothing further. Instead, he turned back to the broken dresser and let out a small, reflective sigh, as though it was not the first time such accidents had occurred in the old house.

"Well," he said, wiping his hands on a rag from his pocket, "I'll bring up that dresser for you, Miss Olivia. The one from Miss Eliza's old room—it's quite beautiful. Almost as though it's waiting to be used again."

He turned and walked to the hallway with an unhurried gait, the echo of his boots carrying through the house long after he was gone. Claire watched him go, her unease deepening.

"Where did *he* come from?" she said.

Olivia, still frowning, knelt to examine the broken fragments of the mirror, as though searching for something within them. "Sometimes I feel like there's someone here... watching us."

"Don't start," Claire warned. She glanced at the shattered mirror, then up at the grand staircase. For the first time in the bright daylight, the house seemed darker—its secrets lurking just beyond reach.

"Well, I must say," Penelope said with a dramatic sigh, "this has all been *quite* the eventful morning. A bit too exciting for my taste, if I'm honest." She gave a nervous laugh, her polished demeanour cracking. "Thank you for signing the last of these papers. I'll ensure you receive copies—likely by tomorrow."

Claire offered a polite smile, though her eyes lingered on the broken glass still scattered across the floor. "Thank you, Penelope, for taking the time to come all the way out here with those. I know it couldn't have been convenient." As she spoke, she reached out, stopping Ben with a firm hand in front of his chest just as he stepped forward. "Ben, watch your feet!"

He froze, his toe hovering inches above a jagged shard of mirror glinting in the sunlight. "Honestly boy!"

"Sorry, Mum." Ben stepped back, his eyes still fixed on the wreckage.

Penelope adjusted her glasses and peered over at the scene, tutting. "Children and sharp objects," she said with a faint shake of her head. "Never a good combination. That mirror didn't survive the day, did it? A pity, though I suppose it was bound to happen in a house like this." She paused. "This place... it's beautiful, of course, but it carries something with it, doesn't it? A kind of presence. A heaviness, if you will. One must wonder what stories these walls could tell."

Claire glanced at Penelope, surprised by the remark. "Heaviness?" she echoed, unsure whether she agreed. The house sometimes felt oppressive, but she wasn't ready to admit it—not aloud, at least. "It certainly is full of history," she said, her hand resting on Ben's shoulder.

Penelope gave a knowing smile, her eyes flicking to the towering staircase and the darkened hallways beyond. "History, yes," she said. "Though history often comes with its share of secrets, doesn't it? I'll leave you to uncover those for yourselves." She gathered her bag and smoothed her gloves, her every movement deliberate and practiced. "Now, if you'll excuse me, I'll see myself out before something else crashes to the ground."

Claire chuckled, though the laugh felt hollow. "Let me walk you to the door," she offered.

Penelope held up a hand. "No need, my dear. I know the way. Besides, it seems you have your hands full," she said with a pointed glance at Ben, who was now inspecting the remains of the broken dresser with far too much enthusiasm.

Penelope hesitated for a moment as she reached the doorway, her eyes scanning the room once more. "Be careful in this house— old places like this… well, they have a way of holding onto things. Memories. Some good. Others…" Her voice faded, a shadow lurking behind her thoughts. Then, with a brisk nod, she straightened. "Take care, Claire. Call if you need anything."

With that, she turned and made her way out, her heels clicking against the marble floor, the sound fading as the grand front door creaked open and then shut behind her.

Claire exhaled, her hand slipping from Ben's shoulder as a heavy silence settled over the room. She glanced down at her son, who remained fixated on the scattered shards of glass at his feet.

"What's so fascinating, Ben?"

Ben shrugged, his brow furrowing as he struggled to find the right words. "It's just… weird," he muttered, his focus never leaving the fragments on the floor.

Claire tilted her head. "What's weird?"

"Well… I've never heard the name Eliza before. Not until today. And just this morning, I had a dream about her."

"Are you sure? Maybe you heard her name before and just don't remember? These things have a way of sticking in the back of your mind."

Ben shook his head firmly, goosebumps prickling his skin. "No, Mum. I'm sure. I've never heard any stories about her. The first time I heard her name was this morning when Samuel mentioned it." Pausing, he spoke in a near whisper. "But I dreamed about her *before* he said it. Isn't that… weird?"

Claire frowned, pondering his words. "Dreams can be strange. Sometimes your brain picks up on little details you don't even realise you noticed. Maybe you saw her name on something around the house, like a plaque or one of the paintings?"

Ben shook his head again, more emphatically this time. "No," he said with conviction. "It wasn't just a name. I *saw* her, Mum. She was standing there, through this weird blue shimmer—like glass or water. And then someone called out to her, but their voice sounded… strange. Like it wasn't really here."

"Ben, dreams can feel incredibly real, but they're just that—

dreams. You've been spending time in this old house. Maybe your imagination is piecing things together."

Ben looked back at the broken shards on the floor, his toes brushing against one of the jagged pieces. "I don't think it's just my imagination. It's more than that. I *know* it is."

For a moment, neither of them spoke. Claire reached out and gently took his hand, pulling him away from the sharp fragments. "Come on," she said. "Let's clean this up and leave the past where it belongs."

Claire couldn't help but glance over her shoulder, her unease growing. If Ben truly hadn't heard of Eliza before Samuel's mention, how could her name have appeared in his dream? She shook the thought away, but the doubt lingered, as persistent as the wind outside.

CHAPTER 2: SETTLING IN

After a long and exhausting first few days, they had finished unpacking most of the boxes. Yet, the belongings that had once filled every corner of their previous home were barely noticeable in the vast, cavernous rooms of the old mansion. They cleared the grand staircase hall, once cluttered with debris, remnants of disuse and the shattered dresser; now, it gleamed under the light streaming through the stained-glass dome above. It was as though the house was breathing again, revealing its forgotten grandeur.

Considering their usual sibling squabbles, Ben and Olivia claimed their bedrooms with little argument. Ben's room was next door to his parents' spacious main bedroom, while Olivia had chosen a bedroom tucked away in the far corner of the house, as though seeking a sense of independence in the sprawling estate.

Ben was in awe at the size of his new room. It was larger than his old bedroom and playroom combined, complete with a walk-in closet that felt more like a secret hideaway and a private bathroom that made him feel like a king. He had already begun filling the shelves with his books, action figures, and gadgets, though they looked almost laughably small in the vast space. The tall windows, draped in heavy velvet curtains, cast dramatic shafts of light across the floor, making the room feel like something out of a storybook.

Meanwhile, Olivia found her room enchanting. The centrepiece was the bed—a grand, four-poster masterpiece draped with faded but intricate lace curtains that looked like they belonged in a princess's castle. She couldn't help but run her fingers along the carved posts, marvelling at the craftsmanship.

Her attention shifted to Eliza's dresser, the one Samuel had brought up from storage. It was magnificent: a sturdy, ornate piece of furniture with rich, dark wood that shimmered in the golden light from her windows. Delicate carvings of flowers and vines adorned its surface, and its many drawers seemed to invite her curiosity. As she slid them open, she discovered hidden compartments—perfect for storing her jewellery, little trinkets, and perhaps even a diary. She smiled as she thought about the secrets the dresser must have kept over the decades, hidden away in this old house.

Compared to her old dresser, which now lay in splinters, this one was in a different league. Truth be told, she felt almost relieved that the old one had shattered. It appeared fate had conspired to give her something so much more beautiful and fitting for this enchanting, mysterious home.

Her fingers trailed over the smooth wood of the dresser as she let out a contented sigh. For a moment, she felt like she had stepped back in time, as though Eliza herself might walk into the room at any moment to reclaim her belongings. The thought sent a faint shiver down her spine.

She glanced out the tall window. She could see the sprawling grounds beyond, cloaked in the amber glow of the sun. This house was strange, yes, and full of secrets, but it was also hers now. And a small part of her couldn't help but feel like it had been waiting for her all along.

Ben's small collection of clothes and shoes looked sparse in the massive walk-in closet. He stood back and admired the vast space for a moment before his natural curiosity kicked in. The mansion was full of secrets; he was sure of it. Maybe the closet, with its strange nooks and crannies, was hiding something, too.

He began tapping the walls, listening for the hollow sound he'd learned from TV shows about secret rooms and trapdoors. But his efforts were in vain. The walls weren't the thin drywall like from their old house—drywall you could punch a hole through if angry enough. These were cold, solid stone. Cutting or prying his way through would be impossible.

Frustrated but undeterred, Ben turned his attention upward. His eyes followed the wooden shelves climbing all the way to the ceiling, each one promising endless possibilities. With a grin, he hoisted himself up onto the lowest shelf and began climbing like it was a jungle gym, using his wiry frame to manoeuvre higher and higher until he was resting on the very top shelf. He leaned back, a thrill running through him.

"This is an *excellent* hiding spot," he said, picturing all the games of hide-and-seek he'd win now.

Something on the opposite side of the closet caught his eye. Was that... a loose plank? His heart raced. Treasure, maybe? Or something even cooler?

He jumped down with practiced ease, landing on the wooden floor with a thump. Without hesitation, he scrambled up the other side, scaling the shelves like an expert climber. The top shelf wobbled under his weight, but he didn't care. His fingers grasped at the edge of the supposed plank, but as he worked it loose, he realised it wasn't a plank at all. It was part of the wall—an uneven, removable piece of stone tucked into the architecture.

Ben pried the piece loose, revealing a small, dark opening. His pulse thundered in his ears as he squinted, trying to make out what was inside. It was too dark to see anything, so without hesitation, he stuck his hand inside.

The air in the opening felt colder, like the chill of a forgotten space untouched for years. He groped blindly, searching for something—anything—hidden inside. Then, all at once, his fingers brushed against something warm and soft.

Ben froze. Every hair on his body stood on end. It felt like... fingers.

With a sharp yelp, he yanked his hand back and lost his balance, toppling off the shelf in a flurry of limbs. He hit the floor hard; the impact knocking the wind out of him. For a moment, he lay there, stunned and gasping, his chest heaving as he tried to comprehend what had just happened.

Claire called through the doorway, her tone demanding. "Ben! What are you doing in there?" The rustle of sheets and the rhythmic fluffing of pillows followed, punctuated by the creak of the giant bed frame.

Ben groaned, still sprawled on the closet floor. "Nothing, Mum!" he said, pushing himself into a sitting position.

Claire's footsteps paused for a moment, as if she were deciding whether to investigate. Then she sighed and went back to wrestling with the sheets.

Ben inhaled unevenly. Whatever it was, it hadn't come after him. It couldn't be that dangerous... right? His limbs trembled as he climbed the shelves again, fear battling with curiosity.

The dark opening loomed before him, daring him to try again. He plunged his hand inside, determined to prove it wasn't just his imagination. His fingers touched something solid—not smooth and warm this time, but rough and textured. Carefully, he pulled it out.

A book.

Ben held it up to the light, his heart still pounding as he examined the cover. The book was old—ancient, even—its leather worn and cracked at the edges. Faded golden lettering glinted in the dim light. He ran his fingers over the embossed name on the cover.

Eliza.

Ben's skin prickled, and a wave of unease tightened his chest as the memory of his dream rushed back without warning.

He stared at it, wide-eyed, his earlier fear forgotten in the rush of discovery. His mind raced with possibilities. Did Eliza hide it there? What secrets might it hold? And more importantly... why did it feel like someone—or something—had been waiting for him to find it?

He flipped through the diary, scanning the faded handwriting. The words held little interest for him—old-fashioned musings and entries about daily life. But then he paused on a page that caught his interest. There, sketched in precise detail, was that of a desk. A small "X" enclosed in a circle marked a hidden panel beneath it. His eyes widened as recognition dawned.

"Eliza's dresser!" he said aloud, clutching the diary. Without wasting another second, he bolted out of his room and down the hall to Olivia's room. He burst into her room without knocking.

"Hey, squirt! Knock before you come in!" Olivia yelped,

jumping in surprise. She had been lounging on her bed, flipping through an old book she had selected from the library.

"Olivia, look!" Ben said, holding up the diary like a trophy. "I...I found her book! Her diary or something!"

"Wait, what?" Olivia sat up, her irritation replaced by curiosity.

"Come on, let's show Mum and Dad!" Ben said, bouncing on his heels.

"No, hold on a second..." Olivia's eyes narrowed as she reached for the diary. "Let's see if it holds any secrets first. You know, before the adults ruin the fun."

Ben hesitated before relenting, his excitement too great to argue. He flipped to the page with the drawing and jabbed his finger at it. "Look! This might be under Eliza's dresser!" he whispered, as if someone might overhear and steal their discovery.

Olivia's eyes lit up as she studied the diagram. She jumped off her bed, all annoyance forgotten, and pulled out the chair tucked under the dresser. Kneeling on the floor, she craned her neck to peer beneath it, her fingers feeling along the smooth underside of the wood.

"Anything?" Ben asked, crouching beside her and peering under the table, excitement lighting up his eyes.

"Hold on..." Olivia said, squinting as her hand brushed against something in the corner. Her fingers traced the faint outline of a circled "X," as the diary depicted it.

"I found it!" she said excitedly.

"Push it!" Ben said, startling her so much that she bumped her head against the underside of the dresser.

"Ben! My nerves." Olivia rubbed her head and shot him a glare. But she couldn't hide the grin tugging at the corners of her mouth.

Steeling herself, Olivia pressed the small marking upward as Ben leaned in. For a moment, nothing happened. Then, with a soft *click*, a hidden compartment folded down from beneath the dresser.

The siblings exchanged a wide-eyed look before Olivia reached in, her fingers brushing against something cold and metallic. She pulled it out and held it up to the light.

It was an old key. Tarnished and heavy, its ornate design hinted at its age and importance.

"Whoa…" Ben said, his eyes gleaming with wonder.

"What do you think it unlocks?" Olivia asked, turning the key over in her hands.

"Only one way to find out," Ben said, grinning from ear to ear.

For a moment, the two of them stared at the key, their minds racing with possibilities. Whatever secrets this house held, they had just taken their first step toward uncovering them.

"I think my room must have been Eliza's," Ben said, a thrill sparking in his fingertips as he turned the old key over in his hand. Its intricate design seemed to trigger his imagination with every glance.

"Yeah, maybe. I think mine belonged to a boy," she said, pointing to a small tin soldier perched on a high wall shelf, its sword gleaming in the light.

"A boy? Do you think he was her brother?"

"Maybe. We can figure that out later. For now, let's see if we can find what this key unlocks."

Determined, the two set off on their mission, scouring every corner of the sprawling house. They tested the key in countless doors, cupboards, and chests—on every floor, in every hallway, and even in the attic—but none of the locks would budge.

They stood at the top of the staircase, their enthusiasm dimming as they exchanged a glance. There was only one place left: the basement.

Ben swallowed hard, and Olivia hesitated. Both had avoided the basement since they arrived. It was a place of shadows, strange noises, and a persistent, musty smell that seemed to seep up from under the house.

"Do we have to?" Ben asked.

Olivia gave him a determined look, though her own nerves were betraying her. "Come on. We've tried everywhere else. It has to be down there."

They descended the creaking wooden stairs, each step groaning underfoot. The air grew colder as they reached the bottom, the smell of damp earth and mildew growing stronger. A single dim bulb cast eerie shadows on the old musty walls, making every object loom larger and more menacing than it was.

"It smells like something died down here," Ben said, wrinkling his nose.

The basement was a cluttered maze of old furniture, trunks, and forgotten relics from generations past. The faint hum of the water heater filled the air, and the pipes groaned, their sounds echoing in the confined space.

Olivia shivered. "This is creepy."

Somewhere in the shadows, something rustled. Ben instinctively reached for Olivia, gripping her arm tight. "What was that?" he whispered.

He stood frozen beside her, his wide eyes scanning the shadows. The air in the basement was thick and damp, clinging to their skin like an unwelcome second layer. The musty scent of old wood, mildew, and something else—something stale and metallic—grew stronger with every step they took. Olivia swallowed hard, forcing down the unease rising in her throat.

Their footsteps echoed against the stone floor as they moved deeper into the basement. They tried the key on an array of old cabinets and wooden trunks, their fingers trembling as they fumbled with rusted locks and warped handles. Every creak of wood, every faint shuffle in the darkness behind them, sent nervous glances over their shoulders.

A sudden gust of cold air swept past them, carrying with it the faint scent of damp earth and something long forgotten. Olivia shuddered. "Did you feel that?"

Ben nodded, rubbing his arms as goosebumps prickled his skin. "Where's the wind even coming from?"

They moved cautiously; the silence pressing heavy around them. As they rounded one of the towering shelves stacked with dust-covered relics, a sudden, ear-splitting crack shattered the quiet.

The ancient hot water cylinder groaned and rattled violently, sending a shockwave through the basement. Olivia yelped, stumbling backward into Ben, who clutched her arm, his face pale. The pipes overhead shuddered in protest, rattling like bones in a crypt. For a moment, neither of them moved, their hearts hammering in unison.

Ben swallowed hard and forced a shaky laugh. "Just the pipes."

Olivia wasn't so sure. Her eyes darted to the farthest corner of the basement, where the darkness seemed almost too thick—too solid. She tugged on Ben's sleeve. "Come on," she said, her tone assertive. "We've seen enough."

Without waiting for his agreement, she pulled him toward the stairs, their pace quickening with every step. The shadows seemed to press closer, and the faint creaks and groans of the old house followed them, as if whispering secrets meant only for the walls to hear.

As they reached the top of the stairs, Ben cast one last glance over his shoulder. For a split second, he thought he saw something shift in the darkness—just beyond the reach of the faint light. But Olivia yanked him through the door, slamming it shut behind them with a resounding thud.

"Never again," Ben muttered, panting as he leaned against the door. Olivia didn't argue.

Ethan approached from the kitchen, tool-bag in hand. "What's up with you two? You look like you've seen a ghost," he said, glancing down at his breathless, wide-eyed children—and couldn't help but grin. He remembered being young and terrified of basements himself. "What's got you so worked up?"

"There's something *down there*!" Ben said, glancing over his shoulder.

Olivia straightened, brushing imaginary dust from her blouse. "The water heater made this awful noise, that's all," she said, forcing a casual shrug. "It's just… it's creepy down there, you know?"

Ethan laughed, finding their reactions both amusing and endearing. "Ah, the infamous basement fear. It gets everyone, even adults sometimes," he said. Then he grew serious. "I want you to be careful in the basement. There are too many things that could hurt you—sharp tools, exposed pipes, and maybe even rats."

"Rats?" Ben said.

Olivia shuddered at the thought, her face twisting in disgust. "Ugh."

"That's right," Ethan said with a mischievous grin, bending to meet their eyes. "And not just any rats. These are the size of small dogs."

"Yeah, right, Dad." Ben said, his eyes narrowing as if he were trying to gauge his dad's sincerity.

Ethan smirked. "See for yourself, then."

"Not happening!" Ben shot up the stairs, two at a time.

Olivia followed close behind, muttering, "Not a chance."

Ethan laughed as he watched them retreat, shaking his head. "Lesson learned," he said to himself, turning back to whatever he had been doing.

For now, the key—and the mystery of the basement—would have to wait.

Night was falling, and the family was acclimating to the peculiar noises and temperament of the old mansion. The sudden cracks and creaks of its ancient wooden floors no longer startled them as they had during their first days. Instead, the sounds had become part of the house's personality—a steady reminder of its age and history. As day turned to night and night into day, the shifting groans of the house seemed like the slow breathing of a giant at rest.

A hooting owl had made its home in a nearby tree, serving as Olivia's nightly companion. Its rhythmic calls were oddly comforting as she lay in her enormous bed. Tonight, however, she had other plans. Brimming with excitement, she slipped out of bed and made her way to the library on the third floor—a treasure trove of books she and Ben had stumbled upon earlier that day. She had spent hours imagining the treasures hidden within, eager to explore what mysteries the shelves might hold.

Downstairs, Claire and Ethan were enjoying the crackling warmth of the fireplace in the grand living room. Ben sat cross-legged on the plush rug, engrossed in building an elaborate structure with old wooden blocks he'd discovered in one of the attic trunks. At first, the lack of television and internet connectivity had been a source of frustration for all of them, but that had faded. Now, living without technology felt like a blessing in disguise. It had brought them closer together, forcing them to engage with one another and the strange, enchanting world of the mansion. This new perspective allowed the children, especially, to experience life as it was in the past.

Olivia climbed the grand staircase, the old incandescent lamps lighting the dimness of the third floor. The library door stood ajar, as if it had been waiting for her. She pushed it open and stepped inside, wonder stealing her voice.

The room was vast, with floor-to-ceiling bookshelves stretching up to meet a domed ceiling painted with a faded mural of cherubs and clouds. Dust motes danced in the golden glow of an antique chandelier, and the faint scent of old paper filled the air.

There were leather-bound volumes with gilded spines, faded tomes with handwritten titles, and even some of the property maps rolled into a wooden chest in the corner. It was more a library; it was a time capsule, a preserved relic of another era.

Her eyes wandered to the far wall, where several life-sized portraits hung in ornate gilded frames. The largest one drew her in. It depicted a young girl, perhaps just a year or two older than Olivia herself. She stood beside a sleek black horse, the sprawling mansion in the background. She had braided dark hair, and her piercing blue-green eyes seemed to follow Olivia as she moved. The girl's dress flowed in elegance around her, and a quiet intelligence played across her features, as if she were guarding secrets she wasn't quite ready to share.

Olivia stepped closer. The craftsmanship of the portrait was exquisite, every detail brought to life with stunning precision. She reached out, her fingers brushing the heavy frame as she searched for a name. Her eyes fell on a small brass plaque affixed to the bottom of the frame. The name engraved on it sent a chill up her spine:

"Eliza Wilson," Olivia said.

Shuddering, she stared into the painted eyes of the girl. It was as though Eliza were looking back at her—not from the past, but from somewhere far closer.

Olivia dashed downstairs to the living room, her heart pounding and the image of Eliza vivid in her mind. Claire and Ethan paused mid-conversation, their attention snapping to their daughter, who seemed out of sorts.

"Ben, the room with all the books—were you in there before today? You know, when we were exploring?" Olivia asked.

Ben frowned, as though she'd accused him of something. "No... You mean the one upstairs? No, I haven't."

"You said once that you saw Eliza in a dream?"

"Yeah," Ben said with a shrug.

"Okay," Olivia said, narrowing her eyes. "She had long blonde hair, didn't she?" She was testing him, planting a false memory.

"No," Ben said, screwing up his face in concentration. "It was brown—or black. No, dark brown."

"And how tall was she? Your height, right? Like ten or eleven years old?"

Ben shook his head. "Nope. She was tall—maybe older than you. I already told you. Oh, and she was wearing something, like a badge or a pin. It had wings."

"A dragonfly brooch," Olivia said, her face draining of colour.

Claire frowned. "Olivia, what's going on? Why are you encouraging Ben's stories?"

Olivia turned to her parents, trembling. "Mum, Dad, I need to show you something."

She led her family upstairs, her footsteps quick and eager, though her heart fluttered with hesitant excitement. She wasn't sure what to make of everything she had heard—or felt—but something compelled her forward. When they reached the library, she pushed open the door and gestured for them to follow her inside.

"This library still amazes me," Ethan said as he stepped into the room, admiring the towering shelves filled with books and furnishings that seemed untouched by time. "I swear I hadn't noticed it before. In fact, I could have sworn this room was a lot more empty than the last time I looked. Must be confusing it with another floor," he added, scratching his head as a frown of bewilderment crossed his face.

Olivia ignored Ethan. Her attention was already on Eliza's painting. Pointing, she approached the framed figure. "This is her?"

Ben stepped closer, his eyes narrowing as he studied the painting. The hairs on his neck prickled. "Yeah, that's her," he murmured, haunted by the girl's face. "But... her hair wasn't tied up like that. It was loose—long." A chill entered his voice as goosebumps spread across his skin. "Oh, bloody hell... did I see a ghost?"

"Language, young man!" Ethan said, though he seemed more distracted than stern. "And no, ghosts do not exist. It was just your imagination." The dusty shelves drew his attention away from the conversation, his fascination with the library overtaking his thoughts.

Olivia wasn't about to let it drop. "How do you explain the brooch, then?" she said, pointing first to the dragonfly brooch depicted in the painting and then to the name etched into the plaque beneath it. "And look at her name—right there!"

Claire crossed her arms, trying to maintain her composure. "Ben could have come across another picture of her elsewhere in the house. You know how portraits can be; they turn up in every room of these old places."

"Perhaps," Olivia said, glancing over her shoulder as if expecting the ghosts of the past to leap from the shadows. "But I haven't seen another painting of her anywhere—not one."

Ben's face flushed with frustration. "I am so confused. She wasn't a painting, and she wasn't see-through or floating, either. She looked real, but like in another room behind glass. Why won't anyone believe me?"

"I do!" Olivia said, her words spilling out before she could stop herself.

Ben's stare softened with surprise as he looked at her. "You do?"

Claire let out a sigh and opened her mouth, but Ethan beat her to it, stepping between the two siblings. "Alright, enough of this. It's late, and we're all tired. I think it's time for bed now. We can discuss this again in the morning when we're all a bit more rational."

"Dad, I'm sixteen," Olivia protested with indignation. "It's too early for bed!"

Ethan raised an eyebrow. "Sixteen or not, this conversation isn't going anywhere tonight. Off to bed, both of you."

The siblings exchanged a glance—Ben's defiant and Olivia's resigned—but neither argued further. Olivia cast one last, lingering look at Eliza's portrait before following the others out of the library. The old electric globes wavered like candlelight, making the painted figure's eyes seem almost alive.

The pipes in the walls groaned, a deep, mournful sound, as if protesting their own existence. Ethan glanced at the walls with a weary sigh. "I'm going to clear out that basement tomorrow and get that damned hot water cylinder replaced. We should use some of the money from the house sale for a more modern gas heater. This old thing is on its last legs."

Claire nodded thoughtfully. "We'll just have to be extra careful with our spending. Don't forget, we still need to get those rooms ready for guests. They have to meet the standards if we want to open on time. How long do you think it'll take before we see any profit?"

Ethan rubbed the back of his neck, looking pensive. "I'm guessing at least a year—maybe longer."

Claire exhaled, her lips drawn into a thin line of worry. "I hope we can stretch the funds that far." She managed a smile as she wrapped an arm around Ethan's waist. "We'll make it work. We have to."

"It makes you wonder, doesn't it? How Ben knew about that brooch—and all those details about Eliza," Claire murmured, lost in the young girl's painting. The soft glow of the chandelier's few remaining working globes across the canvas, bringing an almost lifelike quality to Eliza's serene expression and the delicate folds of her dress. There was a wistful air about her, as though she held secrets she dared not share.

Claire whisked her fingers over the frame. "It's like he knew her. But how could he? Eliza's been gone for over a century."

Ethan groaned, breaking the spell of her thoughts. "Oh no, not you too!" he said, a playful grin spreading across his face as he pulled Claire into his arms.

"What?" A half-smile hid the defensiveness in her tone.

"You're buying into all that ghostly nonsense," Ethan said, laughing. "Next thing I know, you'll be insisting we hold seances in the dining room."

Claire chuckled, leaning into him. "I know it sounds silly, but it's strange, isn't it? He described the brooch in perfect detail. And that story about Eliza… it feels too real."

Ethan kissed her forehead. "Strange? Sure. But let's not get carried away. Ben probably saw the painting before and just forgot."

Claire stared thoughtfully at the painting, a small smile on her lips. "Maybe," she said dubiously.

"Don't forget how Ben came up with that whole elaborate story about his imaginary friend," Ethan said, smiling. "You were so convinced he was being stalked by someone real. I thought you were ready to call the police!"

"I guess he does has an overactive imagination."

"Overactive? That kid could write novels with the stories he spins. Remember how he even described what the *friend* looked like? Right down to the scar on his cheek and the way he walked with a limp?"

Claire nodded. "It was so detailed," she said, almost wistfully. "Too detailed. That's what made it so eerie. Sometimes I wonder where he gets it all from."

Ethan reached over and gave her hand a reassured squeeze. "He's just a kid with a vivid imagination. Nothing sinister about it. Besides, it's part of what makes him so unique."

Claire looked toward the window, its darkened glass mirroring the room's warm light. "I suppose you're right," she said. "Still, there's something about the way he tells these stories… as if he's drawing from something real."

Ethan waved it off with a light laugh. "Claire, you're overthinking it again. Next thing I know, you'll be telling me his imaginary friend was Eliza's long-lost brother or something."

Claire laughed, but the thought lingered in her mind, stubborn and unsettling.

CHAPTER 3: THE SHIFT

Ben jolted awake, his heart pounding and fists clenched around the crumpled sheets. Something had woken him—a noise, faint and unplaceable. The house lay silent, the oppressive stillness amplifying every creak and groan. Glancing toward the large windows, he saw an almost-full moon cast an eerie silver light across his room.

He realised, with a frown, that he'd forgotten to close the curtains before bed. He had always been wary of the dark expanse beyond the glass at night time, half-convinced that someone— some crook or worse—might lurk out there, watching him from the shadows. His stomach tightened at the thought.

Ben lay still for several minutes, straining to hear anything unusual. His ears picked up nothing but the faint ticking of the grandfather clock in the hall below. Unsure of what to expect, he considered footsteps, a whisper, perhaps?—but the silence only made the unease grow.

Swinging his legs out of bed, he felt the cold floor against his bare feet. He padded to the window and pulled one of the heavy curtains closed with a quick, nervous motion. Just as he reached for the other, his eyes caught movement outside, near the fountain.

Two figures stood in the pale moonlight.

Ben froze, his blood running cold. The men turned their heads and looked up at the window. One of them pointed at Ben.

A surge of panic overtook him, and he stumbled backward, his mind racing. Without thinking, he darted to his walk-in closet, heart thudding in his chest. Quietly entering, he shut the door and climbed onto the shelf, his secret hiding place.

Trembling, he breathed, "Idiot. Why didn't I just wake daddy?"

The thought gave him a moment of courage, and he considered making a dash for his parents' room. But before he could move, he froze.

Footsteps.

They were faint at first, but unmistakable. Someone—or something—was in his bedroom.

He wedged himself deeper into the hiding place, his pulse roaring in his ears. His whole body trembled as he strained to hear every nerve on edge. The soft rustling sound of movement came again, closer this time, followed by the faint creak of his bed as if someone had sat down.

A chill ran through his body, his eyes wide and unblinking as they stared into the darkness.

Minutes felt like hours as he waited, heart pounding in a relentless rhythm. Eventually, the sounds faded, and the stillness returned.

Ben didn't dare move. He stayed in his hiding place, rigid and silent, until exhaustion won over terror and his eyelids grew heavy. Sleep came, pulling him under as the frightening memory of that pointing figure haunted his dreams.

Ben's dreams were a chaotic blur. He was outside the house, locked out, pounding on the front door. Something relentless chased him, its icy presence closing in. He shouted, pleaded to be let in, his fists slamming against the wood as the chill of its presence drew nearer. Just as he felt its cold, clammy hand clamp down on his shoulder, he woke with a jolt.

Ben panicked, his heart racing as if it might burst from his chest. He felt like he was falling, his limbs flailing. His right arm hit the wall with a sharp pain, while his left met only empty air. Disoriented, he realised he was still on the top shelf of his hiding spot. Then, the memory of why he was there came rushing back.

Ben climbed down, his movements slow and deliberate. Something felt different. His fingers brushed against unfamiliar fabrics. Clothes? But these weren't his. Had his mum started using this space for extra storage? Confused, he felt around until his hand found the closet door.

As quietly as he could, Ben eased it open just a crack.

The room beyond was his, and yet, it wasn't.

A dancing candle cast shifting shadows across unfamiliar furniture. The bed was wrong—an ornate, wooden frame with heavy quilts—and the wallpaper, too, was unlike anything he had ever seen. Fear and bewilderment gripped him, his heart racing.

"Am I still dreaming?" he whispered.

Steeling himself, Ben tiptoed out of the closet. His bare feet brushed against a thick woven rug as he moved to the bed. Someone was sitting on the other side, their back to him, staring out the window.

For a fleeting moment, he thought it might be Olivia. But no— this figure was taller, thinner, and not his mother. As the person shifted, the dim light caught their profile.

It was Eliza.

Ben froze. His hand shot up to his mouth to stifle a gasp, but he was unsuccessful.

Eliza turned, her wide eyes locking onto him. Her words trembled with unsteady authority. "Who are you? What are you doing in my room?"

Panic surged through Ben. He stumbled backward, his heel catching on the rug as he fell to the floor. Scrambling, he crushed himself against the wall, his chest heaving.

Eliza moved with purpose, but without a hint of threat. She approached him, her hands raised in a gesture of reassurance. "Don't be afraid," she said. "I'm not mad. I just want to know who you are."

Unable to speak, Ben could only stare.

Eliza stopped a few paces away, tilting her head as she studied him. She noted his strange garments—so unlike anything she had seen before—and his bare feet, no shoes. They looked pink and clean, not the rough, dirt-streaked feet she'd expect of an ordinary orphan. Was he a runaway who had somehow snuck into the house to do what? Hide? Pilfer?

"Are you lost?" she asked, curiously. "Where did you come

from?"

Ben's lips parted as if to speak, but no words came. He didn't know how to explain what was happening—not to her, not even to himself.

Ben whispered, "Are… are you a ghost?"

Eliza tilted her head, surprised by the question. Then she laughed, the sound light and melodic. "A ghost? You mean like a dead spirit?" she asked with a playful smile. "Heavens no, I should hope not!"

Ben nervously took her hand as she extended it to him. Her skin was warm and soft, nothing like the cold, ethereal touch he'd always imagined ghosts would have. His trembling eased as she guided him to the bed.

"Here," she said, draping a heavy quilt over his shoulders. "You're shivering."

Ben shook more from fear than cold, but the warmth of the quilt and Eliza's soothed presence calmed him. His fear ebbed, replaced by a growing sense of curiosity. If this was a dream, it was unlike any he'd ever had—it felt too vivid, too real.

Eliza sat beside him, her posture graceful and composed. Softly, she asked, "Now, can you tell me who you are?"

He swallowed hard, trying to collect his thoughts. "I'm Ben," he said. "I live here. This is my room… only…" He looked around, taking in the quivering candlelight, the antique furniture, and realising there was nothing modern. "It looks so different."

Eliza watched him curiously. "This is my room," she said, a faint frown forming. "Are you sure you're not mistaken? Do you have a fever?"

Eliza felt his forehead. It was cool to the touch.

Before Ben could respond, the sound of laughter erupted from downstairs. The joyous noise carried up through the floorboards, and one booming laugh made Ben recoil.

Eliza noticed his reaction and placed a reassuring hand on his arm. "Don't be afraid," she said. "That's just papa and his friends. They're having one of their drunken gatherings. Although…" Her tone turned serious. "It might be best if you avoid my papa. He doesn't look kindly upon orphans."

Ben's heart sank at her words. Shaking his head, he said, "I'm not an orphan. I live here. I have parents... I have..." His words thinned as he struggled against the rising knot of despair, realising how impossible it would be to explain his presence.

Eliza studied him with growing concern. "You're not an orphan? Then... where did you come from, Ben? And how did you get into my room?"

Ben opened his mouth to answer, but found himself at a loss. He glanced at her; her question hanging in the air, and for the first time, he wondered how he had somehow crossed into a world that wasn't his own.

"Come, you look ashen and tired. You can sleep in Julian's room tonight—he won't breathe a word of it," Eliza said, taking Ben's hand. She led him through the staircase hall, her candle casting ghostly shadows on the unfamiliar faded wallpaper.

Eliza stopped at a door tucked away in the far corner and knocked once before opening it.

"This is Julian's chamber," she said, pushing the door open.

Ben hesitated at the threshold. "But this is my sister's room," he said, confused.

Inside, a boy, smaller than Ben, scrambled to his feet. He had a mop of blond hair styled in a way Ben thought odd and was crouched over a regiment of tin soldiers arranged in precise lines on the worn wooden floor. A rocking horse stood sentinel near the window, and in the corner, a chest brimming with wooden blocks caught Ben's eye. He instantly recognised them—they were the same blocks he had played with earlier that day in the sitting room, he was sure of it.

"Who are you?" the boy asked, his eyes darting from Eliza to Ben.

"This is Benjamin," Eliza said, ushering Ben inside. "Let him sleep on the spare bedstead tonight. He's lost. Papa will punish us both if you tell him."

The boy frowned, but nodded. "I'm Julian," he said.

Ben regarded him, perplexed. "It's Ben," he corrected. A puzzled look crossed his face as he asked, "Why are you in a dress?"

Julian bristled, straightening his posture. "It's not a dress. It's a nightgown," he said, his chin lifting with indignation.

Eliza turned to Ben, her lips curving with quiet amusement. "You most certainly aren't from around here, are you? You've got the strangest accent I've ever heard."

Ben felt a sudden rush of unease. He glanced back at the hall, half-expecting to see the familiar world he knew waiting beyond the door. But there was only the gentle glow of Eliza's candle, the heavy silence of the house, and the occasional booming laughter from downstairs.

"I'll come and check on you in the morning," Eliza said as she adjusted the candle in her hand. The warm glow illuminated her face, making her look kind. "In the meantime, stay here. Julian can loan you some of his clothes, though I'm not sure they'll fit well—you're quite taller."

Julian's face lit up, his eyes sparkling with excitement. "I have some! Remember, Eliza? When Papa brought those clothes from London last spring?" He turned to Ben, a bright eagerness lighting his face. "Most of them are too big for me. Papa said I could wait and grow into them, but you can wear them!"

Ben couldn't help but smile at Julian's enthusiasm. The boy's energy was infectious, and for a moment, the strangeness of his situation faded into the background. "Thanks, Julian. That's… kind of you," Ben said, glancing between the two siblings.

Julian beamed, already moving toward a tall chest of drawers in the room's corner. "Wait until you see them! There's this navy jacket with brass buttons and some trousers."

Eliza chuckled at that, shaking her head. "All right, Julian, don't overwhelm him. He's had a long night. Let him rest." She looked at Ben, something about him warming her heart. "Try to sleep, Benjamin. You seem to have had quite an ordeal, and you'll need your wits about you in the morning."

Ben nodded, his unease returned as Eliza turned to leave. The candlelight followed her to the door, shrinking the room's shadows to a faint, wavering outline.

Ben was almost certain this was all a dream.

"Goodnight," she said before closing the door behind her, leaving Julian and Ben in the dim glow of a single oil lamp.

Julian's eyes narrowed as they fixed on the strange object strapped to Ben's wrist. He leaned in, his curiosity unrestrained, and pointed a small finger at it. "Benjamin, what is that peculiar bangle?"

Ben instinctively shielded his smartwatch the moment he noticed Julian staring at it. For a moment, he hesitated, unsure how to explain. Then a shimmer of hope sparked in his mind. *This could be it—proof. Proof I'm from the future!* His heart raced as he lifted his wrist to show Julian. The excitement drained from his face. The screen remained dark. No glow, no sounds, nothing. The battery was flat, or worse—it failed to work in this place.

"It's... it's a watch," Ben said, disappointed. "It does heaps of things—tells the time, plays music, tracks stuff. But the battery is flat."

Julian tilted his head, frowning. "Flat? What do you mean?"

"The battery—it's what makes it work. Without it, it's just... useless," Ben said, letting his arm drop to his side.

Julian leaned in even closer, his nose inches from the black face of the watch. "A watch that plays music? What kind of sorcery is this? And what is this 'battery' you speak of? Is it some kind of magic stone?"

Ben sighed, realising just how strange his words must have sounded. "No, it's not magic. It's... uh..." He paused, searching for a way to explain. "It's like... a tiny container of power, making things run without winding them up."

Julian gasped, his eyes wide with amazement. "You mean it carries power, like thunder in a jar?"

Ben couldn't help but chuckle at the analogy. "Kind of, yeah. But right now, it's 'thunder' is all used up."

Julian sat back on his heels, unsatisfied. "Can you fix it? Make it work again? I want to see this... music-playing magical bangle."

"I can't. It needs charging, and I don't have the right equipment here. I don't even know if it would work... in this time." Ben fell silent, the full impact of his words dawning on him.

"It sounds like something from a fairy tale," Julian said. "But if you say it's real, I believe you, Benjamin."

Ben looked at Julian, surprised by the boy's earnestness.

Julian grinned, his earlier enthusiasm returned. "If you're from a place where things like that exist, then maybe you'll fix it. Until then, I suppose I'll just have to trust you're telling the truth."

Ben smiled, though his thoughts were far away. He hadn't just lost proof of where—or *when*—he came from. He'd lost a small piece of the world he knew, and the realisation left him feeling even more out of place in this strange house, full of secrets.

"I'm hungry. Are you hungry? Come on, let's sneak down to the kitchen and get some food—maybe even steal some ale," Julian said, his eyes twinkling with mischief as he leaned closer to Ben.

"Eliza said we should stay here," Ben said, fidgeting with the hem of his sleeve.

"Come on," Julian said, grabbing Ben's hand with a grin. "Where's your adventure gone to?" He pulled Ben to the door before he could protest further.

As they crept down the oil lamp lit corridor, Julian glanced back, observing Ben's attire with interest. "You are wearing strange garments," he remarked.

"They're my pyjamas," Ben whispered as they approached the staircase. "I guess kind of like your... um... nightgown."

Ben followed, his mind racing. Was this happening? If it was just an elaborate dream, it was the most vivid one he'd ever had. And yet, if it wasn't... the thought of never seeing his family again crept in, icy and unwelcome. He shoved it aside for now.

They reached the kitchen, its warmth and noise enveloping them at once. The air smelled of roasted meat, fresh bread, and something sweet that made Ben's stomach growl. The kitchen staff bustled about, balancing trays laden with food and pitchers of ale and wine, their movements efficient and practiced.

Most of the servants paid little attention to the two boys as they weaved through the chaos, though a few muttered annoyed comments when they came close to colliding with the pair.

Julian's eyes locked on a large serving table piled high with cakes, pastries, and other tempting treats. He reached out, fingers brushing against the edge of a decadent-looking slice of plum cake, when a mammoth hand slammed down next to his.

"And what do you think you're doing, young master?" boomed a woman with broad shoulders and a face as stern as it was kind. She burst into laughter at the startled look on Julian's face, her laugh a rich, rolling sound that filled the room.

"Can we *please* have a piece?" Julian said, clasping his hands in mock innocence. "Please…"

The woman's stern facade softened, and a fond smile tugged at her lips. "Oh, very well," she said, reaching for a knife. "But that's too small a piece for the both of you. Here—two slices, one for each of you. And don't you dare tell your papa I gave it to you!" She winked as she handed them their spoils.

Julian grinned, stuffing a piece onto Ben's plate before the woman's smile turned curious. She studied Ben for a moment, her brow furrowing. "Who's this boy with you? I don't remember seeing him here before."

"Benjamin," Julian said. "He's staying the night."

The woman raised an eyebrow but didn't press further. "Very well. Away with you both, to your chamber before your papa gets wind of this," she said, shooing them away.

Julian thanked her with a cheeky grin, and they slipped out of the kitchen, their laughter hushed as they hurried back down the hall.

"Wait here," Julian said, pressing Ben against the wall near a shadowy corner. He disappeared back into the kitchen, leaving Ben clutching both slices of cake, his heart pounding at the prospect of being caught.

Moments later, Julian reappeared, his grin even wider as he held up a large, sloshing beaker. "It's ale," he said with a knowing smile.

Ben stared at the beaker, caught between laughter and disbelief. "You're mad," he said, shaking his head, but a grin tugged at his lips despite himself.

Julian shrugged, his mischievous smile unwavering "Come now, if we are to get into trouble, we might as well make it worth our while!"

Back in the room, the boys wasted no time diving into the cake.

"This is the best cake I've ever had," Ben said between mouthfuls, his words muffled as he devoured the soft sponge and cream like a starving man discovering dessert for the first time.

Julian wasn't far behind, his cheeks stuffed like a chipmunk. "Mmm, it is rather good, though I daresay Cook's ginger biscuits might still have the upper hand," he said, crumbs falling down his nightgown.

By the time they finished, their plates were spotless, and the boys sat cross-legged on the floor, licking the last sticky remnants off their fingers. For a moment, they shared a satisfied silence, the empty plates like victorious trophies.

Then their eyes drifted to the beaker of ale.

"Let us have a sip each, shall we?" Julian said, his grin wide with mischief.

"You first," Ben said, leaning back with a smirk. He was enjoying this dream.

Julian picked up the beaker, holding it like a prized treasure. He raised it to his lips as if performing on stage, then tilted it back and took a gulp that was far too large for someone his size.

Triumph and regret warred on his face. He slammed the beaker down, gasping, "It tastes frightful! Like stale bread mixed with an old shoe!"

Ben burst into giggles. "Why would you drink that much if it's so bad?"

"Because I am courageous, Benjamin," Julian said, puffing out his chest. Then he winced. "Courageous and possibly poisoned."

Ben wiped his eyes and picked up the beaker. "All right, my turn." He took a cautious sip, trying to ignore the way Julian's face still contorted in disgust.

The liquid hit his tongue like an unwelcome guest—bitter and warm. He forced himself to swallow, gulping down more than the younger boy had in a show of boldness, and grimaced. "Hmm... delicious," he said, dripping with sarcasm as he shoved the foul-smelling beaker away.

Julian cackled. "You are a dreadful liar, worse even than Eliza when she swears she did not take the last biscuit!"

Ben laughed along. The room spun, and he leaned back against the bed. "This stuff's awful. Who honestly enjoys drinking it?"

Julian shrugged, reaching for another sip despite his earlier critique. "Papa drinks it all the time. Perhaps it is something one must simply endure until it becomes tolerable—like turnips."

Ben raised an eyebrow. "Or school."

They both dissolved into laughter, Julian spilling another drop of ale.

But as the giggles faded, Ben felt his head grow heavier, the room seeming to blur at the edges. "Julian... I think..." he started, his words slurring.

That was the last thing he remembered.

Ben stirred, his limbs heavy and unresponsive. Opening his eyes felt like a struggle, his head spinning with a faint buzzing and a spiralling white light at the edges of his vision. The buzzing in his ears slowed, the fog cleared, and the room came into focus.

Something wasn't right.

He was lying on the floor, the wooden boards cool beneath his back. For a moment, he thought he was still in Julian's room. But as he blinked, he noticed the electric fixtures above him, their sharp, modern lines replacing the smoky oil lamps he'd fallen asleep beside. His heart leapt as he realised he was back in Olivia's room, but at the same time, a shock ran through him—had he been sleepwalking?

The morning sunlight streamed through the curtains, casting warm patches on the floor. One bright square of light fell on his legs, making him aware of a sticky left over mess of plum cake clinging to his pyjamas.

Ben's heart raced as he stared at the stains, his face flushing with fear and confusion. The taste of ale lingered on his tongue. How could this be real? Somewhere downstairs, the rhythmic thud of hammering echoed through the house—maintenance work, loud and persistent.

Ben sat up, his head still spinning, and spotted Olivia sitting on her bed. She was staring at him with a mixture of curiosity and disbelief, her dark hair tousled from sleep.

"Why are you in my room? Did you sleep here last night?" she asked.

"I… I was in…" Ben said, rubbing his temples. "I had a strange dream."

Olivia raised an eyebrow, sliding off her bed to get a closer look. "What have you been eating?" she asked, eyeing the sticky stains on his pyjama shirt. Her nose wrinkled as she leaned in, and then she froze. "Wait, a second… is that beer? You've been drinking beer!"

Ben flinched, shaking his head. "You don't understand… I was with Julian. He stole the beer from the kitchen and dared me to drink it."

Olivia crossed her arms sceptically. "Who is Julian? Don't lie, Ben. You drank some of Dad's beer, and now you're in serious trouble!" Without waiting for an answer, she turned and bolted from the room.

"Wait, Olivia!" Ben called after her in dread, but she was already gone.

Ben wanted to run, to hide, to escape the impossible reality closing in around him, but he sat frozen on the floor, his mind reeling as the enormity of what had happened bore down on him.

Minutes later, Ethan came into the room, his tool belt slung low on his hips and sawdust clinging to his clothes. Worry etched itself into his features. Behind him, Claire followed, her face sharp with disapproval. Olivia trailed behind, looking less angry now and more genuinely worried.

"Ben, what's going on?" Claire asked, stepping closer. The smell of alcohol was unmistakable. She leaned in, her nostrils flaring. "That's beer. Stale beer. Ben, where did you get it? Who gave it to you?"

Ethan frowned, cleaning his hands with a rag. "He didn't get it from me. I haven't bought beer since I lost my job. Ben, this is serious. Who gave you beer?" His grip on the rag tightened, shoulders stiff with a worry that went beyond the drinking— concerned about who might have handed alcohol to a child.

"Mummy, I fell asleep, but when I woke up, I was in my room... except it wasn't my room anymore. It was Eliza's room. Everything was different—the walls, the furniture, even the smell. I went to her brother's room, and then we went to the kitchen and had cake and ale—he called it ale, but it tasted strange, like nothing I've ever had before. I thought it was all just a dream, but then I woke up here, in Olivia's room. And Mummy, this room—it was Julian's room in my dream. It was his room!" Ben's words tumbled out in a frantic rush, trembling with confusion and urgency. He paused only to catch his breath, his wide eyes darting to the stains on his clothes. He stared at them, his hands clutching the fabric as if trying to make sense of the impossible. "How... how did this happen? How did the stains get here if it was just a dream?" He looked up at his mother, searching for answers she couldn't possibly have.

Claire crossed her arms tightly over her chest as she stared at Ben. Her son sat on the floor, his knees drawn up to his chest, his face pale and streaked with tears. The sticky remnants of cake clung to his pyjamas, and the faint smell of beer lingered in the air. Her stomach churned—not just at the thought of someone giving her child alcohol, but at the wild story he was spinning.

Her anger flared. Ben had done nothing like this before. He wasn't the type to sneak around or lie, not like this. She wanted answers—needed them—but the more she pressed, the more he insisted on this impossible tale. Her frustration bubbled over, sharp and hot. "Ben, stop it," she snapped. "Just stop with these stories. You need to own up to what you've done and stop covering it with wild lies. Or tell me if someone forced you to drink!"

Ben flinched, his eyes widening as fresh tears spilled down his cheeks. "I'm not lying, Mummy, I promise, I'm not."

Claire's chest tightened at his small and broken sound. She wanted to believe him, wanted to wrap him in her arms and tell him everything would be okay. But how could she? His story made no sense. Yet the fear and confusion in his eyes were too powerful for her to ignore.

"Ben—I need you to tell me the truth. Who gave you the beer? Who gave you the cake?" She paused, watching his face for any hint of recognition. "Was it someone in the house? Someone outside? Please, sweetheart, just tell me."

"It was Julian. He's just a boy, Mummy. He used to live here a long time ago. I don't know how I got there, but it was real. It was real."

The desperation in his voice was unmistakable, and for a fleeting moment, Clair wondered if he truly believed what he was saying. Could he have…? No. It was impossible. Time travel wasn't real. Ghosts weren't real. Still, his pleading eyes made her unsure of herself.

She crouched down in front of him, taking his hands in hers. "Ben, I want to believe you. I do. But you have to understand how this sounds."

Ben's lower lip quivered, and he looked away, his shoulders

slumping in defeat. "I know," he whispered. "But it's true."

Claire's heart ached. She wanted to yell at him, but also hug him tight. The conflict tore at her, leaving her feeling helpless and frustrated. Looking over her shoulder, she saw Ethan in the doorway, his face a mask of anger and worry. He didn't believe Ben either, she could tell. But what if...?

No. She couldn't let herself go down that path. There had to be a logical explanation. There had to be.

"We'll figure this out, Ben," she declared, steady despite the turmoil inside her. "But for now, you need to stay in your room and think about what happened. And no more stories, okay? Just the truth."

Ben nodded, his eyes downcast. Claire reached out and brushed a tear from his cheek, her touch gentle despite the storm of emotions raging inside her. For a moment, she allowed herself to linger, her hand resting against his face as she fought the urge to pull him into a hug. But then she stood, her resolve hardening, and walked out of the room.

In the hallway, she leaned against the wall. Her hands trembled as she clutched her face, trying to steady herself. What was happening? Her son—her sweet, honest son—was lying to her, and yet...

She couldn't shake the look in his eyes. The desperation. The certainty.

What if he wasn't lying?

Ethan was furious. He wasn't angry at Ben—he was angry at whoever had the audacity to give his son alcohol. The thought churned in his stomach, burning with rage. He stormed downstairs, his boots thudding on the floorboards, and found Samuel leaning against a ladder in the hallway, wiping his forehead with a dusty rag.

Without a word, Ethan grabbed him by the collar and shoved him against the wall with a force that rattled the nearby picture frames. "Did you give my son alcohol?"

Samuel's eyes widened, and he raised his hands in defence. "No... no!" he said, shaking his head.

A sharp tang of whiskey on his breath was undeniable, and Ethan's grip tightened. "Then what the hell have *you* been drinking?"

"Whiskey, okay? Whiskey!" Samuel said, struggling against Ethan's tightening grip. "But I don't keep any here."

Ethan glared at him, his jaw clenched hard enough to make it ache. He could smell the alcohol wafting off Samuel, his words slurred just enough to make Ethan doubt him. But there was no proof—only suspicion. With a growl of frustration, he shoved Samuel aside.

Samuel stumbled but didn't retaliate, his hands trembling as he adjusted his shirt. "I didn't give him anything, I swear," he said as Ethan stormed off.

Olivia, silently observing from her bed, eyed her brother with sceptical unease. Something about his trembling voice, the way his tears fell, tugged at her. She wanted to dismiss his story as nonsense, but the way he spoke about Julian… it sent an icy shiver down her spine.

She wrapped her arms around herself, the hairs on the back of her neck stood on end. Somehow, she believed him—or at least believed *he* thought he was telling the truth.

"Ben," she said, as hammering resumed downstairs. "What… what happened last night? What did you see?"

Ben looked up at her, his red-rimmed eyes filled with desperation. "I saw Julian," he said. "He was real, Olivia. I promise. I thought he was just a dream until now."

Olivia didn't respond, but the icy feeling in her chest didn't fade. If Ben was telling the truth—or even if he wasn't—there was something strange about this house. Something she didn't want to think about too hard.

Olivia noticed something in the shadowy corner of her room. It hadn't been there before—she was sure of it. There, standing proud as though it had always belonged, was a rocking horse. But not just any rocking horse—an antique, its craftsmanship unmistakably old, yet impossibly untouched by time. The deep mahogany gleamed as if freshly polished, the paint unblemished, not a single crack in its surface. Its mane, a pristine white, looked newly woven, and the leather saddle bore no signs of wear. Everything about it was perfect—too perfect. Yet, despite its flawless condition, it seemed someone had plucked it from another time and placed it here.

"Ben," Olivia whispered, her eyes fixed on the rocking horse. "Do you know who put that in my room? Was it Daddy?" She pointed at it, her hand trembling.

Ben's head whipped around, and when his eyes landed on the object, he froze. His face shifted from confusion to awe, and then to something Olivia couldn't quite place—fear, perhaps, or wonder.

"It's... it's Julian's!" Ben scrambled to his feet, staring at the rocking horse with wide eyes. "It was in his room last night. I swear it was. I remember seeing it by the window!"

Olivia stared at him, her stomach twisting in knots. "Ben, what are you talking about? How could it be Julian's? Did you... did you bring it in here somehow?"

Ben shook his head. "No—it must have come back with me!"

Olivia stepped closer, her unease mounting. She crouched, running her fingers over the smooth wood, expecting to feel the rough imperfections of age but finding none. It was ancient, yet untouched—as if time had skipped it. Then, beneath the saddle, her fingertips brushed against something carved into the wood.

"What is it?" Ben asked, inching closer.

Olivia squinted at the faint carving, her heart skipping a beat as she made out the name. A chill ran down her neck as she spoke it aloud. "Julian."

"I told you!" Ben said, clapping his hands with such force that the sound hurt his ears. "It's his. It was in his room. It came back with me, Olivia. I don't know how, but it did!"

Olivia straightened, her face pale. "Ben, this doesn't make any sense. Things don't just... appear. This is impossible."

"But it's real!" Ben stepped closer to the rocking horse. "What if other things came back too? What if... what if Julian's still here?"

Olivia shivered at his words, an icy dread settling over her. She glanced at the door as though expecting Julian to step through it. "We should tell Mum and Dad," she said hesitantly.

Ben shook his head. "They won't believe us. They already think I'm lying."

Olivia hesitated, her mind racing. She didn't understand what was happening, but one thing was clear—Ben had experienced something strange, something otherworldly. How had he just appeared out of nowhere? And how had this toy horse materialised so suddenly?

There was something electric in the air now, a charge to the house she had never felt before, and it unsettled her deeply. The house, she realised, held secrets far stranger than she had ever imagined—secrets that seemed to stir, waiting to reveal themselves. It was as if the house itself was waking up.

CHAPTER 4: THE BASEMENT

A few days had passed since the strange events, and the tension in the household had eased, though a lingering forbidding remained just beneath the surface. Even Ben was wondering if it had all been nothing more than a vivid dream—a trick of his imagination fuelled by exhaustion and perhaps too much sugar.

Claire, determined to put the incident behind them, had insisted that Ben spend more time outdoors. "Fresh air will do you good," she had said, shooing him out the back door with a gentle nudge. "And stay away from those old paintings. You don't need any more ideas for your wild stories."

Ben wandered the sprawling gardens, their once-manicured hedges now overgrown and untamed. The centrepiece was an old fountain, its stone basin chipped and moss-covered. The water had long since dried up, leaving behind a bed of cracked stone and a few stubborn weeds growing in the crevices.

At first, Ben had sulked, annoyed at being sent outside like a punishment. But as the days passed, he enjoyed the quiet solitude of the garden. He imagined knights and battles among the twisted rose bushes and scaled the low stone walls, pretending they were fortress ramparts.

Today, he sat perched on the edge of the dry fountain, poking at the moss with a stick. The sun filtered through the dense canopy of trees, casting dappled light across the ground. Somewhere nearby, a bird chirped, its melody blending with the gentle rustle of leaves in the breeze.

Still, no matter how hard he tried to lose himself in play, the thought of Julian lingered in the back of his mind. He'd replayed that night over and over, questioning every detail. The rocking horse, the cake, the beer—it had all felt so real. But was it possible it had just been a dream?

He sighed, tossing the stick into the fountain basin. "Maybe I made it all up," he said to himself.

As if in response, a faint gust of wind swirled through the garden, brushing past him like a whisper. Ben froze, glancing around. It was just the wind, he told himself. But the sensation left him with a peculiar feeling, like he wasn't alone.

He stood and dusted off his hands when the old oak tree at the far end of the garden caught his eye. Its twisted branches seemed to beckon him, and he felt an odd pull to explore. Shrugging off the strange feeling, he set off toward it, his footsteps crunching on the gravel path.

Reaching the tree, he noticed something he hadn't seen before—a faint carving high in the bark. Though the wood had swelled and cracked over time, the letters remained weathered yet stubbornly intact. Leaning in closer, he ran his fingers over the rough grooves, feeling the history etched into its surface.

Julian.

His heart skipped a beat.

Ben stumbled back, his thoughts racing. Could it be a coincidence? Or was it another sign that his "dream" had been something more? The cool breeze stirred again, ruffling his hair, and for a moment, he thought he heard a faint laugh—childlike, distant, and familiar.

"Julian?" Ben said, trembling.

The garden felt suspended in time, the hush almost tangible.

Ben shook his head and backed away from the tree, his pulse quickening. "It's just my imagination," he said aloud, trying to convince himself. But as he turned and hurried back to the house, he couldn't shake the feeling that the garden was watching him, holding secrets he wasn't ready to uncover.

On the sun parlour's chaise lounge, Olivia sprawled, bathed in the warm afternoon sunlight streaming through the tall windows and pooling around her like liquid gold. The room smelled of warm cloves and zesty orange, a comforting blend that mingled with the faint sweetness of dried rose petals and the earthy depth of cedar. In her hands was an old novel, its pages yellowed and its spine creased with age. It was a love story, predictable but comforting, and she had been losing herself in its gentle escapism.

The diary Ben had found beckoned to her, but fear kept her from opening it. What if it angered the spirits she half-believed still lingered here? She tried to refocus on the novel, but her eyes skimmed the same sentence for the third time. With a frustrated sigh, she set it down and reached for the diary. Her fingers hesitated as they brushed the worn leather cover. "It's just an old book," she said to herself, though the words felt hollow.

She flipped it open to the place she had last marked, somewhere in the middle. The pages were dense with looping handwriting, the ink faded but still legible. The handwriting was elegant but erratic in places, as though the author had written in a hurry or under duress.

She ran her fingers over the page, feeling the slight indentations left by the pen. Her heart pounded as she read, the words pulling her in with an almost magnetic force:

April 15

A most perplexing event continues to haunt my thoughts and cast a shadow over this household. My brother's companion, who arrived so suddenly and vanished just as swiftly, remains an enigma beyond my understanding.

I believe him to be a poor orphan, seeking shelter from the bitter night, for I found him in my chamber—wide-eyed and trembling, his strange garments unlike any I have seen. Pity, not anger, filled my heart, and I resolved to offer him kindness, to spare him the cruel fate that awaits so many without home or kin.

Julian took to him at once, as though they were long-lost friends. They laughed and played, unshackled by the woes of the world, held together by an unseen thread of kinship.

And now, he is gone. Poor Julian is heartbroken, his days spent gazing out the window, longing for his return. I, too, am troubled—who was this Benjamin? Where did he come from, and where has he gone? His manner, his garments, so peculiar, so unlike our world. I dare not speak it aloud, yet I cannot shake the feeling that he was not of this place or time. I dare not speak these thoughts aloud, for others would dismiss them as the fanciful imaginings of a young lady. But in my heart, I wonder: Was Benjamin an orphan, or was he something far stranger?

Whatever the truth, I can only hope that he is safe, wherever he may be, and that one day he will return to ease my brother's aching heart.

Olivia's pulse raced. The name *Benjamin* leapt off the page, sending a chill through her. She looked up from the diary, her eyes darting to the backyard visible through the parlour windows. There was Ben, poking around the old fountain with a stick, oblivious to her unease.

Olivia's hands trembled as she closed the diary, pressing it to her chest. Her mind raced, questions swirling faster than she could keep up with. Was it possible? Could Ben's strange experiences— his tales of Julian, the rocking horse—be connected to the entries in this diary?

She glanced back out the window, her brother now crouched near the tree at the garden's edge. A sense of urgency gripped her. Whatever was happening, whatever secrets this house held, they were deeper and darker than she had imagined. And somehow, Ben was at the centre.

Olivia shot to her feet when she saw the way Ben froze, his eyes fixed on something etched into the bark of the old oak tree. His pale face and tense posture made her uneasy, and she decided it was time to resume her investigation of the house—this time with him by her side. If there was any truth to the strange events, perhaps they could piece it together.

Reaching into her jacket pocket, she withdrew the mysterious key they had found weeks earlier. The cool metal felt heavy in her palm, laden with secrets yet to be uncovered. Today would be the day, she decided. They would find the missing room—the one that seemed to exist only in whispers.

Her instincts told her to start in the basement. Ethan had installed new light fixtures there, and a modern gas heating system replaced the old, intimidating boiler. Though forgotten junk— dusty trunks, old furniture, and the occasional cobweb—still cluttered the basement, it was no longer the stuff of nightmares.

She headed to the back door, where she found Ben standing stiffly, his face pale and his eyes staring at the tree. He looked as though he had just seen a ghost.

"Ben, what is it?"

"Nothing," he muttered, shivering as he looked at the tree.

"Ben, when you had your… experience—you know, with the beer—"

"I don't want to talk about it!"

"Just listen to me for a moment. What name did they use for you?"

"I don't know what you mean?"

"You know, did they call you Ben? Or something else?"

"Why are you asking me that?"

"I think I may have figured something out."

"What?" Ben asked. He glanced over his shoulder, his mind drifting to the name Julian, carved high in the tree.

"I'll tell you once you answer me," Olivia said. "What name did they call you?"

"Ben, I think…"

"Are you sure?" Olivia's confidence wavered as she tried to hold on to her theory.

"No, wait, it was Benjamin. They kept calling me Benjamin. I tried to correct them, telling them it was just Ben, but they didn't listen. So I gave up."

At his words, Olivia let out a small, excited yelp, startling Ben.

"Come in here." She sat him down on a wicker chair across from her.

"Why are you suddenly so interested?" Ben asked.

Olivia leaned forward. "What else can you tell me? Anything you remember—anything at all."

"Are you just going to make fun of me again or say I've got an overactive imagination?"

"No, I promise. I want to know everything. Leave nothing out. Please, Ben."

Something in her tone convinced him. Ben recounted the events, starting from the moment he met Eliza. As he spoke, Olivia listened, her eyes darting between his face and the diary resting on her lap.

Two details stood out: the moment Eliza found Ben in her room, and the mention of him being an orphan. Ben chuckled as he retold that part, finding it funny in hindsight. "Me, an orphan? Can you believe that? They *really* thought I just wandered in looking for treasures or something."

But Olivia wasn't laughing. Her grip on the diary tightened, her knuckles white as she processed his words.

"Thank you, Ben," she said when he finished. Then, opening the diary to the bookmarked page, she read aloud.

Ben listened, his face draining of colour. The words she spoke were familiar, mirroring parts of his own story almost exactly. His reaction only confirmed what Olivia was suspecting: his experience wasn't just an overactive imagination.

By the time she finished reading, the air between them felt heavy. Ben stared at her, his lips parted as though he wanted to speak but couldn't find the words. A few moments passed as the pair tried to comprehend it.

"Do you believe me now?" Ben said.

Olivia nodded, her earlier scepticism replaced by a chilling certainty. "I think there's more going on in this house than we ever realised," she said. "And I think we're just beginning to understand it."

Ben leapt to his feet, pointing out of the sunroom's large windows. "There, look!"

Olivia jumped up, startled by his urgency. Following his outstretched hand, spotting two men standing near the overgrown hedges at the edge of the property. One of them was pointing at the house, his arm sweeping in wide motions as if explaining something. The other held what looked like a camera, the long telephoto lens glinting in the sunlight as it pointed at the house.

"What are they doing?" Olivia said.

"I don't know, but I've seen them before," Ben said, then bolted to the staircase hall.

He sprinted upstairs, shouting, "Dad! Daddy!"

Upstairs, Ethan was in the middle of installing new shelves on the third floor, a drill in one hand and a pencil tucked behind his ear. At the sound of Ben's frantic calls, he froze, a chill running through him. He dropped the drill onto the workbench and rushed to the stairs.

"Ben, what is it?"

"There are men in the garden. I think it's the same men I saw a few nights ago—they were looking up at my room!"

Ethan's face grew stern. "Stay here!"

"Dad, don't let them get away!"

Ethan burst out the back door, his boots pounding against the ground as he sprinted through the garden. The men were still there, but the moment they saw him, their heads snapped around like startled animals.

"Hey! What are you doing here?" Ethan said, his face flushing a deep shade of red.

For a split second, the men froze, their faces obscured by the distance and shadows cast by the trees. Then, as if by some unspoken agreement, they turned and bolted, disappearing into the dense undergrowth at the edge of the property.

Ethan chased after them, his frustration mounting with each step, but they were too quick. By the time he reached the spot where they had been standing, all that remained was a faint trampled path through the bushes.

He scanned the area, his body tensing, eyes narrowing as he took in the evidence of their presence: faint footprints in the soft earth, a few broken twigs, and a cigarette butt still smoking near the hedgerow.

Olivia anxiously watched her father from the back door of their house. Beside her, Ben paced, his stomach tied in nervous knots.

Ethan returned with a grim look on his face. "They got away."

"They had a camera, Dad," Olivia said. "It looked like they were taking pictures of the house."

"Why would they do that?" Ben asked. "Do you think they are robbers?"

Ethan frowned, his mind racing. "I don't know. But if they come back, I'll make sure they don't get away again."

"What if they're after... the house?" Olivia said, glancing at the upstairs windows.

Ethan nodded. "Maybe. But I'll find out. You two stay inside for now. And if you see them again, you fetch me right away—understood?"

Ben and Olivia nodded, their unease palpable as they watched their father head back inside, his jaw set with determination.

As the door closed behind them, Olivia said, "Do you think they're connected to… everything else?"

Ben didn't answer, but his mind was already racing with possibilities, none of them comforting.

Claire stepped in from the front terrace, wiping her hands on her gardening apron. Dirt smudged her palms. She had been near the old fountain, studying its cracked basin and considering its restoration. Her thoughts had been on practical matters—pipes, pumps, and the stubborn moss that clung to the stone—until the tension inside the house pulled her back in.

"What's all the commotion?" she asked, taking in the nervous energy radiating from the trio.

"Some men were out near the garden. They were taking photos of the house. Ben says he thinks it may be the men he saw a few nights ago." Ethan said.

Claire froze, her grip tightening on the trowel. "A few nights ago? Was that the same night you… you know…" she trailed off, not wanting to say the words aloud.

"Yes," Ethan said, confirming what Claire had dreaded.

Claire looked at Ben. "Why didn't you tell us about them? Were they the ones who gave you alcohol?" Her words came sharper, quicker, as if trying to catch up with the surge of fear rising in her chest. The thought of strangers—grown men—near her child sent a chill through her.

Ben looked down at the floor, squirming. "I forgot to tell you about them," he said. "You wouldn't have believed me, anyway."

"Ben, were they the men that gave you alcohol?" Claire asked.

Ben's head shot up, and he groaned in exasperation. "No, Mum!"

Claire straightened, lips pursed. A look passed between her and Ethan. He shrugged, but his face stayed serious.

She took a calming breath. "Then who were they?"

Ben threw up his hands. "I don't know! They were just standing outside, looking at the house, like today. I thought it was weird, but I didn't know who they were or why they were there."

Olivia opened a window, letting in a gust of fresh air that

smelled of damp earth. "They had a camera. It looked like one of those professional ones, with a huge lens. They weren't just *looking* at the house—they were studying it."

Claire's eyes widened, and she turned back to Ethan. "Could they be surveyors, do you think?"

"I don't know. But if they've been here more than once, it's obvious they're up to something."

"And why was no one told about this earlier?" she asked, her frustration bubbling up.

Ben flinched, but stood his ground. "I didn't know it was important!"

Claire sighed, her shoulders slumping. "This is feeling bigger than us," she muttered, almost to herself. She glanced at Ethan. "What do we do now?"

"We keep an eye out. I'll set up something—cameras, motion lights, whatever we need. If they come back, we will know about it."

"And the kids?" Claire asked, her eyes flicking to Ben and Olivia.

"They stay inside," Ethan said. "For now, at least, until we know what's going on."

Ben groaned but didn't argue. Olivia stared out the window, fixated on the garden where the men had stood. "I think they're looking for something," she said.

Claire and Ethan exchanged another glance, their worry deepening. Whatever was happening, it was no longer just about their family or the house—it was about something far more mysterious, and far more dangerous.

Trying to forget the men, Olivia turned to her brother and put her arm over his shoulder. "Come on, sport, let's go explore." The casual gesture made Ben grin and lifted Olivia's spirits, too. It was rare for them to feel this connected, and in that moment, their shared curiosity bound them even closer.

Claire caught the moment and smiled. Whatever strangeness had taken over their lives in the past weeks, it was bringing the siblings closer together—a silver lining amidst the tension.

"Be safe, you two," Ethan called out. "If you go into the basement, be careful. There are loose planks and nails down there."

"We will, Daddy!" they said in perfect unison, earning an amused chuckle from Claire.

As they headed for the basement entrance, Olivia pulled the brass key from her pocket and held it up in front of her chest, giving Ben a mischievous wink. She shielded it from their parents' view, her confidence sparking excitement in her younger brother. Ben smiled, feeling closer to Olivia than he had in a long time.

The siblings descended the creaky basement stairs. Unlike the dark and foreboding space it had once been, the basement now gleamed under the glow of the new neon lights Ethan had installed. The harsh brightness made it feel almost clinical, banishing the shadows that had once made the place so intimidating.

"Do you think there's a door down here?" Ben said.

"I don't know," Olivia said, weaving her way through rows of shelves filled with forgotten treasures. "There might be. It's like a museum down here," she added, brushing her hand against a dusty stack of books as she passed.

Ben rounded the corner of the last shelf, stacked with old clothes and bedding, and found only the back stone wall. Its jagged surface of rocks and mortar looked as ancient as the house itself. He sighed in frustration.

"Oh, drat it. There isn't a door here," he said, leaning against the cold, unyielding stones.

Olivia, trailing behind him, stifled a laugh. "What did you say? *Drat it?*"

"Yeah, I don't know. It's something Julian said when he spilled some… err… ale."

"Since when do you talk like an old-time tavern keeper?"

Ben opened his mouth to retort, but before he could, his attention snapped to a scuttling movement on the wall. A small cockroach, its shiny brown body glinting, skittered upwards. With a reflexive flick of his foot, Ben kicked at it. His shoe struck the wall, and a faint, hollow sound echoed. The stone shifted a few millimetres inward.

Ben stepped closer. "Look… do you think there's something behind the wall?"

Without waiting for her response, he pressed his hands against the stone, wiggling it back and forth, trying to loosen it. The coarse edges scratched his fingers, but he didn't care.

"Move over!" Olivia shoved him aside and knelt to examine the stone. Her fingers probed the edges, looking for a grip. When pulling didn't work, she gave it a hard push, and with a low, grating sound, the stone slid inward. It toppled out of sight with a muffled thud, disappearing into the darkness beyond. A musty, earthy smell wafted out, mixing with the faint hint of something metallic.

"Uh-oh," Ben said. "Dad's gonna be mad…"

"Mad about what?" came a voice from behind, sudden and sharp.

Ben and Olivia jumped, grabbing at each other for support. Whirling around, they found Ethan standing there, his face half-hidden in the neon-lit shadows, a mischievous smirk tugging at his lips.

"Daddy! Don't *do* that!" Olivia said, clutching her chest. "You scared the living daylights out of us!"

"What are you two up to back here?" Ethan asked, stepping closer and eyeing the hole in the wall. "What's that?"

Ben and Olivia exchanged nervous glances, but neither said a word. The faint glimmer of curiosity—or was it unease?—stirred in Ethan's eyes as he leaned in, his hand reaching for the opening.

Ethan pulled a flashlight from his tool belt, the beam slicing through the shadows as he directed it into the dark recess beyond the loosened stone—his usual calm giving way to a sharp, determined focus. He crouched, running his hands along the edges of the wall, scrutinising the structure.

"This isn't a support wall," he said. "Ben, go get me a pickaxe. There's one out back near the stairs."

"Yes, Daddy." Ben, vibrating with excitement, sprinted to the basement stairs, taking them two at a time.

Olivia stayed rooted to the spot, her heart thudding in her chest. "Are you going to break it down, Dad?"

"Yes. There's something back there."

Moments later, the sound of Ben's hurried footsteps echoed as he returned.

"Careful, Ben," Ethan said, taking the tool from him with practiced ease. He turned it over in his hands. Before he began, he glanced down at the two children, who had edged closer, their wide eyes glued to his every move. "Back up. Both of you, if this wall collapses, you could be hurt—or worse."

Ben and Olivia shuffled backward, their eyes never leaving the wall. They stopped just short of disappearing behind the rows of shelves, positioning themselves where they could still watch without being in the way.

Ethan gripped the pickaxe, bracing himself. With a sharp, deliberate motion, he drove the tool into the stone, the sound of metal striking rock ringing out in the confined space. Dust puffed into the air, illuminated in the dim light like tiny motes of gold. He pulled back and swung again, each strike reverberating through the room.

The kids watched, their excitement mounting, as Ethan chipped away at the old stone. Bits of old mortar and rock crumbled to the floor, the hole widening with each powerful swing. The air grew heavy, smelling of earth and stone.

"Daddy, do you see anything yet?" Olivia said.

"Not yet, but we're getting close."

The wall groaned under the force of his blows, a low, eerie sound that sent shivers down their spines. Ethan paused for a moment, wiping sweat from his brow with his sleeve. His eyes flicked toward the hole, and for just a second, something shifted in his face—was it surprise? Or something else?

The kids watched in tense silence, waiting for him to speak. But without a word, he raised the pickaxe again and swung, determined to uncover whatever lay hidden behind the ancient stones.

Ethan jumped back just in time as much of the wall crumbled, collapsing under its own weight and shoddy construction. The sound of falling stones reverberated through the basement, and a cloud of dust billowed out, filling the air with the acrid scent of ancient mortar. Coughing, Ethan waved the dust away from his face and took a step forward to examine the breach.

It was clear to Ethan that this wall hadn't been part of the original house. Its uneven stones and crude mortar screamed afterthought—a hurried effort, likely meant to conceal something long forgotten. Ethan ran his hand along the jagged edge of the opening, testing the stability of the remaining structure. Satisfied it wouldn't collapse further, he turned and beckoned to the kids with a wave of his hand.

Olivia and Ben came running, their excitement uncontained. The faint glow of the basement's fluorescent lights dimly illuminated the revealed space. It cast long, eerie shadows over the steps leading downward to a wooden door at the bottom.

Olivia's eyes widened. "It's the door! It *has* to be!"

Ben nodded, his face alight with excitement. "Yeah! This is it!"

"What door?" Ethan asked.

Olivia fished something out of her pocket—a large, ornate brass key—and handed it to her father. "We found this key, Dad. We've been trying to figure out which door it belongs to. This has to be it. It's the only one left in the house we haven't tried."

Ethan turned the key over in his hands, its intricate engravings catching the dim light. His puzzlement faded into determination. "Well, come on then, what are we waiting for?"

The kids followed, their earlier bravery now tempered by the growing eeriness of the scene. Somehow, they felt safer with Ethan leading the way. He reached the wooden door, its surface worn. After a moment's hesitation, he tried the handle. He found the door locked. With deliberate precision, he slid the brass key into the lock. The mechanism clicked with a satisfying *clunk*, and the door creaked open.

Ethan shone his flashlight around, its beam cutting through the darkness. The room was sparse—almost disturbingly so. In one corner was a narrow bed, its frame rusted and its mattress long decayed. A small table and a single wooden chair sat near the centre, covered in a thick layer of dust. In the far corner, a bucket sat in eerie stillness, its purpose sending a chill down Ethan's spine.

But what drew all their eyes was the skeletal figure sprawled on the floor near the bed. The remains, clothed in a tattered, disintegrating dress, were human. The skull lolled at an unnatural angle, and the empty sockets seemed to study them.

Ben clutched Olivia's arm. "Is that a *real skeleton*?"

Olivia's face went pale as her eyes landed on the table. "Oh, no… is that a dragonfly brooch?"

Ethan stepped closer, his unease growing with every detail his flashlight revealed. "Someone locked this poor soul down here. They must have died from hunger, neglect… maybe worse."

"Daddy," Olivia whispered, clutching her chest. "I think… this might have been Eliza."

"What do you mean, Eliza?" Ben said. "No! It can't be! She was happy! She didn't…"

Ethan turned to his son, alarmed by his reaction. "Ben, calm down. Son, listen to me. This all happened a very long time ago. It's alright."

Ben shook his head, backing away from the scene.

Ethan sighed, placing a hand on Olivia's shoulder. "Olivia, take your brother upstairs," he said. "Now. Neither of you are to come back down here. I'm going to call the police. It doesn't matter how old these remains are—this was a human being, and the authorities need to know."

Olivia nodded, taking Ben's hand and leading him upstairs. Sorrow and dread filled Ethan as he watched them go. Turning back to the room, he looked once more at the remains, a chill running down his spine.

There were questions now—too many to count. But one lingered above the rest: *Who was Eliza, and why had someone gone to such lengths to bury her story here, in the darkness?*

CHAPTER 5: SECRETS

Ethan got a formal report from the authorities after several weeks. The forensic tests provided some answers but left other questions unresolved. They explained the remains were around 200 years old. However, one discovery stood out—DNA analysis revealed a direct connection to Claire's family line. The news sent a ripple of shock and intrigue through the household.

Claire sat at the dining room table that evening, the document spread out before her. She turned the pages, her eyes skimming over the cold, clinical language. Words like *female, malnutrition,* and *likely confined* sent shivers down her spine. Yet it was the connection to her family that gripped her the most. Somewhere, tangled in the roots of her ancestry, was a woman whose life had ended in tragedy and whose identity remained a mystery.

The dragonfly brooch lay on the table beside the report, its delicate wings catching the fading light. The police had catalogued it before being returned to the family. Now Claire held it, running her fingers over its intricate design. The craftsmanship was exquisite, though tarnished with age, and she wondered how it was in that cold, lonely room beneath the house.

Later that evening, she stood in front of Eliza's portrait. The painting hung in the sitting room, an elegant yet haunting depiction of a young woman with striking eyes and a serene expression. Claire stared at the brooch and then at the portrait, her mind buzzing with questions.

"Was it you?" she asked.

Somehow, the thought that the remains could belong to Eliza wasn't far-fetched. The timeline fit, and the dragonfly brooch seemed like an undeniable link. From the start, Olivia and Ben believed it. Claire had first dismissed it as youthful speculation, but now, standing here with the evidence in her hands, the possibility felt unavoidable.

Her heart grew heavy as she tried to imagine what might have transpired all those years ago. What could have led to such a grim fate? Had Eliza been wronged, betrayed, or forgotten by the world above while she languished in that basement?

The thought was unbearable. Claire clenched the brooch in her fist, her nails pressing into her palm. She felt a pang of guilt, as if she were complicit in a family secret that had gone unspoken for generations.

"I don't know what happened to you, but I promise—I won't let anyone forget your story."

Behind her, the faint sound of footsteps startled her, and she turned to see Olivia standing in the doorway. The girl stared solemnly at the brooch in Claire's hand.

"Mum, do you think Eliza was… hurt? Like, by someone in our family?"

"I don't know, sweetheart."

Olivia nodded, stepping closer. "I hope we can figure it out. I'll keep reading her diary, Mum. Maybe there's something in it—some clue that could tell us what happened."

From the doorway, Ben peeked around the corner, his face curious. "Maybe… I can go back in time again, somehow, and warn her."

Claire turned to him, her brow furrowing. "Oh, Ben. It was just an elaborate dream you had. It's not possible to go back in time."

"But, Mum!" Ben said, stepping into the room. "What about what Eliza wrote in her diary? About the boy—Benjamin? She mentioned his name! What if it was me? What if I'm supposed to help her?"

"Stop it, Ben," Olivia said. "Listen to Mummy. There's no such thing as time travel."

"What if I was really there? What if I could go back and fix things? Maybe I could stop whatever happened to her!"

"Ben, enough," Claire said, taking his hands in hers. "It's just a coincidence. The name Benjamin was common back then; It means nothing. I need you to stop thinking this way—it's not healthy."

"But, Mummy, it felt so real. When I woke up, I could still smell the oil lanterns and feel the cold stone floors. It wasn't just a dream—I know it wasn't. What about the cake and the ale?"

Claire's heart ached at the desperation in his voice. She wanted to reassure him, to dismiss his fears, but she didn't know how to explain everything that had been happening. The brooch, the diary, the remains—it all felt like pieces of a puzzle she couldn't quite fit together.

"Listen to me, both of you," she said, standing and turning to Olivia as well. "We need to focus on what we *can* understand. The diary is a good start, Olivia. But Ben, you need to let go of this idea of going back in time. It's not possible."

"But—" Ben said, his face flushing with frustration.

"No 'buts," Claire said, cutting him off. "We have to stay grounded. There are enough mysteries here already without adding more confusion."

Olivia glanced at Ben. "Mummy is right, Ben. Let's just focus on what we know for now. If there's something in the diary that can help, we'll find it. Together."

Ben hesitated, his shoulders slumping in defeat. "Fine," he said, kicking at the carpet. "But I'm not crazy."

"No one's saying you're crazy," Claire said. "You have a big imagination, and that's a wonderful thing. But sometimes, imagination can trick us into believing things that aren't real."

Ben didn't respond, staring at the floor.

Olivia wrapped an arm around her brother's shoulders. "Come on, let's go see if there's anything new in the diary. Maybe Eliza left us more clues."

Ben looked up, conflicted. He nodded, letting his sister guide him out of the room. Claire watched them go, her heart heavy. She turned back to the table where the dragonfly brooch lay, its delicate wings catching the light. As she reached for it, her hand brushed the metal, and a strange, almost electric sensation coursed through her fingertips. She snatched her hand back, startled, a gasp escaping her lips.

"Imagination," she said to herself. But as she looked at the brooch and then at Eliza's portrait on the wall, she couldn't shake the feeling that there was something more at play—something the house was trying to tell them.

Since moving to this magnificent, yet strange, house, something had changed between Olivia and Ben. What had once been a casual sibling relationship—cooperative when necessary, distant when not—had transformed into something stronger, something unbreakable. The house, with its secrets and shadows, had become a binding force, drawing them together in ways they never could have expected. They were now inseparable, united by their shared mission to uncover the mysteries of their new home.

They headed upstairs to Olivia's room, a cosy space filled with her books, sketches, and trinkets. It was her sanctuary, a quiet haven where she could retreat from the strangeness of the house. But to Ben, it was something far more significant. He was certain it had once been Julian's room.

Olivia settled onto the floor at the foot of her bed, crossing her legs as she opened the diary to the last place she had read. The worn leather creaked in her hands, and the faint smell of aged paper filled the room. Ben flopped onto the plush rug, lying on his tummy with his chin propped in his hands. For once, he seemed focused, his usual fidgeting replaced by an almost solemn anticipation.

As Olivia scanned the page, Ben recalled with a light, certain tone, "This is where Julian and I ate the cake and sipped the ale he stole. He said he was ten, but he was smaller than me—shorter. He was wearing this long night-robe. At first, I thought it was a dress. It was weird."

"Ben, listen to this..." Olivia said, and read:

April 16
This day, my heart is both uplifted with love and burdened by sorrow. My father has forbidden me from ever meeting Alexander again, declaring him unworthy of my station. He brands him a commoner, a man of no title nor

71

noble lineage, yet how can such matters hold sway when his heart is purer and truer than any gentleman I have known? Alexander is honourable and kind, virtues that Papa refuses to acknowledge. And he is handsome beyond words, with eyes that lay bare my soul and a smile that steadies the unsteady world.

Despite Papa's command, I met Alexander by the riverbank this afternoon, concealed from watchful eyes. His embrace was so gentle, so full of love, that I felt the breath leave my chest. He spoke of dreams—dreams of a life where we might be together without fear or shame. Yet as I listened, my heart broke, for I know such dreams are impossible while my father holds my fate in his grasp.

But in our moment of love and passion, I fear I have committed an error from which there is no retreat. I carry now a secret—a new life, conceived in our love. I cannot bring myself to speak of it, not even to Alexander. How can I? To tell him would risk pulling him into the storm of disgrace that is sure to follow. My father would never pardon such a scandal, and I tremble to imagine the punishment he would inflict should he discover my shame.

Alexander, if he knew, would be proud, I think. He would take my hand and vow to protect me, defying even my father's wrath. But what could he do? Papa wields all power, and I fear he would sooner destroy Alexander than allow us to marry. The mere thought sends a chill through me.

Today, Alexander gave me a token, a small pin shaped like a dragonfly, fashioned by his own hand. It is the most exquisite thing I have ever owned, delicate and imbued with his spirit. I hold it now as I write, running my fingers over its fine edges. It reminds me of him—strong and unyielding, yet free in ways I can only dream of. And yet, as much as I treasure this gift, it weighs upon me, for it cannot lighten the secret I hide from him.

What am I to do? If Papa learns of my condition, I fear he will cast me out, or worse. I would shame my family, and my life would change forever. Yet how can I bear this silence, this deception, when every part of me longs to confess the truth to Alexander?

I am filled with dread. I fear my father's fury, the judgment of the world, and above all, losing Alexander. If only I could undo what has been done, or if society were kinder to women who love without regard for titles and wealth.

For now, I must keep my secret hidden as the dragonfly pin beneath my bodice. I shall pray for the strength to endure, though my heart is heavy with fear and uncertainty.

Olivia looked up from the diary, her face pale, her hands

trembling as she gripped the fragile pages. "The brooch," she said. "Alexander made it for her. She... she was pregnant."

Ben's eyes lit up with curiosity, sitting up straight on the plush rug. "That's so cool! Was she going to have a baby?"

Olivia shot him a sharp look. "Ben, it wasn't cool. Not back then. If you weren't married and had a baby, it was an enormous problem. People would have judged her. Worse, her family could have disowned her, or even—" She paused, not wanting to frighten him. "It was just... terrible."

Ben's smile faded, but his curiosity only grew stronger. "Oh," he said, then added with urgency, "Read on. I have to know what happened next."

Olivia hesitated, her eyes dropping back to the diary. The elegant, flowing handwriting was so unlike her own, yet something in every word seemed to settle deep within her. The story unfolding on these pages wasn't just a relic of the past—it was alive, raw, and devastating.

Eliza had written how afraid she was. Her father had forbid her from seeing Alexander, and she didn't think she could tell him. She was so scared of what her father would do if he found out. She thought it would bring shame on her entire family.

Ben leaned closer, his eyes wide. "What about Alexander? Did he find out? Did they run away together or something?"

"I don't know yet, Ben. Back then, it wasn't easy. Some families controlled everything—especially for women. If Eliza tried to run away, her father could have had her tracked down and brought back. He might have done something terrible to Alexander, too."

"That's so unfair—they just wanted to be together. Why couldn't people just let them be?"

"Because back then, people cared more about rules and appearances than love. Especially people like Eliza's dad. He didn't care what made her happy—only what made the family look good," Olivia said.

"That's stupid. Do you think Alexander ever knew she was having his baby?"

"I don't know. But if he didn't... I hope he found out—he deserved to know."

She turned another page, her hands trembling. The faint, musty scent of the diary filled the room as both siblings leaned closer to the story, desperate to uncover what happened next. The shadows on the walls seemed to deepen, as if the house itself was listening, waiting to reveal its secrets.

"Something bad is coming. I can feel it," Olivia said.

"Read it, Olivia—we have to know!"

Trembling, Olivia continued her story.

April 19

Today, I confessed to Alexander the truth I have carried alone these many weeks. The words spilled from me before I could think better of it, and I watched his face, dreading what I might find there. But he laughed—a sound so full of joy it startled me—and swept me into his arms, spinning me until the room blurred. He kissed my cheeks, my forehead, my nose, murmuring that this was the happiest day of his life. For a moment, my fears melted away, and it was only us, and the life we have created.

But then he grew serious, declaring he would go to Papa and ask for my hand. My heart seized with terror. I begged him not to, for I know Papa would sooner kill him than allow such a match. And what Papa might do to me, I cannot bear to imagine. Alexander vowed he would not let anyone harm me, not even my father. He spoke of running away together, to his family's farm, where we could live freely and raise our child in peace. His words were a balm, yet my heart is torn.

How can I leave Mama and Julian? My sweet, loving brother—he is my light, my joy. The thought of never seeing him again is a wound too deep to fathom. Yet to stay would mean ruin for us all. Alexander says he will make the arrangements, that I must trust him. And I do, but the path ahead is fraught with peril.

I must hide this diary now, for if it were found, all would be lost. It holds my deepest fears, my hopes, my heart. I pray for courage—for both of us—and for the strength to leave behind the life I have always known.

Dread filled Ben's wide eyes as he sat up. "Her dad killed her, didn't he?"

Olivia's heart skipped a beat at his words, but she forced herself to stay calm. "Ben, we don't know that. We don't even know for sure that it was Eliza down there."

She was trying to convince herself as much as him, but the

words felt hollow. The diary's revelations, the brooch, and the remains they had found in the basement all painted a grim picture that was hard to ignore.

"It must have been her! What about her brooch? That's the same one we found down there. It has to be hers!" He paused, pleadingly looking at her. "Don't stop, Olivia. Read on. We have to know what happened."

She hesitated, the diary's fragile pages trembling in her hands. Her fingers lingered on the edge of the next page, and for a moment, she wasn't sure she could continue. What if the truth was too terrible? What if Ben was right? Could their family's history hold something so dark?

"Olivia, please."

Olivia nodded, swallowing the lump in her throat. "You're right," she said, more composed now. "She deserves to have her story told. Let's find out what happened."

Ben leaned in closer as she read aloud, bringing to life the words of a long-lost past.

April 20

What a cruel and desolate day this has been! My heart aches with fear, for I had hoped to meet Alexander by the riverbank once more, to feel the comfort of his embrace and hear his promises of a brighter future. But fate, or rather my father, has intervened.

This morning, as I attempted to slip away unnoticed, Papa stopped me at the foot of the stairs. He did not shout, nor did he strike me, but his silence was far worse. He looked at me with such dreadful, unyielding disappointment, his eyes alight with something between fury and disdain. He said not a word, only pointed to my chamber, his meaning unmistakable. I dared not defy him, though every fibre of my being screamed to do so.

How did he find out? I can only imagine that in Alexander's joy and eagerness, he must have confided in someone, perhaps a friend, perhaps even a servant, who then carried the news to Papa. I cannot blame Alexander for his excitement, for he was so elated at the thought of our child and the future we might share. But now, that joy has brought ruin upon us both.

Later, from my chamber, I heard raised voices drifting up from the drawing room. Mama was pleading with Papa, while his bellowed response shook the walls. I heard him speak of shame, cold and unyielding. Mama wept, though her words were muffled. It is a sound I shall never forget, her sorrow, so much like my own.

I thought of climbing out of my window tonight, of escaping into the darkness to find Alexander and run away with him. But my window is far too high, and I lack the strength to brave such a perilous descent. Besides, what if I were to fall and harm the little one? The very thought fills me with terror.

But perhaps the worst torment of all is the silence. Alexander has not sent word in days, and it is so unlike him. He is steadfast, always finding a way to reach me, no matter the obstacles. Yet now, there is nothing. No notes, no whispers of his plans, not even the faintest sign that he still waits for me by the riverbank. What could have happened? Has Papa done something to him? Has he been warned away? Or worse, has my beloved been harmed?

Oh, Alexander, where are you? What is to become of us? I pray with every breath for your safety, for your love to remain steadfast, and for some way, any way, for us to be together again.

For now, I must endure, though my courage wanes. I can only hope that tomorrow will bring some sign, some glimmer of hope amidst this endless darkness.

Ben's heart ached for Eliza. The thought of her suffering alone, trapped and afraid, filled him with anger and sadness. He hated she had to endure such cruelty.

He crept closer to Olivia, sitting beside her and leaning into her for comfort. Without a word, she wrapped her arm around him, pulling him close in a protective, reassuring embrace.

She turned her eyes back to the fragile pages of the diary. "Let's see what happens next," she said, steady despite the knot of unease in her stomach, and continued to read.

April 29

I have not had the will to write these past days, for my heart aches so profoundly that even the act of lifting this quill feels burdensome. Alexander consumes my thoughts—my Alexander—from whom I have heard nothing. The silence is a torment greater than words can convey, and I fear the worst. What has become of him?

This may be my last entry before I must hide this diary away. Papa's plans to lock me in the dark basement behind the rows of wine seem to near fruition. He has already stationed a servant outside my chamber door to guard me, as though I were some criminal or madwoman to be restrained. The man is unaware of my true condition and bewildered by the harsh treatment I receive. How could he know? Papa has forbidden me from speaking of the life growing within me to anyone—not even to my dear Julian.

Oh, my sweet brother. His cries echo through the house in the dead of night, and my heart breaks anew each time I hear him. He does not understand why Papa has forbidden him from seeing me. We have been inseparable since his birth, and now the poor boy is beside himself with worry. If only I could hold him, whisper to him I am still here, still his loving sister. But I cannot, for the servant outside my door would report any such interaction to Papa.

The days grow darker, and with them, so does my hope. I feel like a bird trapped in a cage, its wings clipped, unable to fly. What future awaits me in that cold, desolate basement? What will become of my child once it is born? Will they allow me to hold my baby, look into its innocent eyes, and feel the joy of its existence? Or will someone discard it like some shameful secret to be forgotten?

All I can do now is pray. I pray that God, in His infinite mercy, will forgive my inequities and protect the life within me. Though my actions may have been born of love, I know they defy the laws of propriety and duty. Yet, I cannot believe that this child, conceived in love, is a sin. Can the Lord not see the purity of my heart, even as the world condemns me?

I pray too for Alexander. If he is alive, I pray he finds the strength to reach me. If he is not… oh, I cannot bring myself to complete that thought.

The hour is late. I must hide this diary in haste. If these pages were to fall into Papa's hands, I shudder to think of the consequences.

If this is my last entry, let it be a testament to my love for Alexander, my devotion to Julian, and my hope for the life within me. May these words survive even if I do not.

"The next page is blank!" Olivia said, clutching the fragile diary against her chest. Next to her, Ben pretended to understand while trying to comprehend.

For a moment, neither of them spoke, the silence in the room broken only by the faint creaks of the old house around them. Ben pulled away, his saddened face transforming into one of fierce determination.

"I need to go back," he said. "I have to help her. Or at least warn her."

Olivia wiped a tear from her face and looked at him, her heart aching at his desperation. "Oh, Ben," she said. "How do you think that would even be possible? Time travel isn't real." She paused, her words catching in her throat as she remembered the strange things that had already happened in the house. "It's not possible to…"

"It took me before," Ben said. "The house somehow did it. I don't know how, but I know I was there. Julian and Eliza need me. If I can figure out how to go back, maybe I can stop Eliza from dying."

Olivia hesitated, her mind racing as she tried to find the right words. She wanted to comfort him, to make him feel safe, but his determination scared her. "What are you going to do, Ben? How would you even try?"

Ben's hands curled into fists at his sides. "I'll do what I did the first time," he said. "I'll fall asleep on the top shelf in my cupboard."

"Ben, what if it doesn't work? Or what if it *does*, and you get stuck back there and can't come home?"

"I don't care!" Ben said. "Eliza doesn't get to come home, does she? She's stuck—forever! If I don't help her, who will?"

Olivia stared at him. She wanted to tell him to stop, to think, to be safe—but she didn't know what was right anymore. The house seemed alive with secrets, its mysteries unfolding in ways she couldn't explain or control. Maybe, just maybe, Ben *could* find his way back.

She reached out, placing a hand on his arm. "If you're going to try," she said, "promise me you'll be careful. And… and if anything feels wrong, you'll come back. Go to the same place you were when you last came back, in my… Julian's room. Don't stay there too long, Ben. Please."

"I promise," he said, though the weight of what he was about to do strained every word.

Olivia wrapped her arms around him and hugged, holding on for a moment longer than usual. "I'll be right here," she whispered. "No matter what happens."

Ben pulled away and headed for the door, his footsteps echoing softly down the hall. As he disappeared, Olivia sat back, clutching the diary. She prayed—not just for Ben, but for Eliza too, and for the slim chance her brother could change the course of history.

In the room's stillness, the house creaked, as if it were listening.

Ben went to the large living room, where Claire and Ethan were relaxing after a long, tiring day. The warm glow of a lamp bathed the comfortable space in a gentle, welcoming light. Claire was curled up on the couch with some old house documents she had found in the library, while Ethan leaned back in his armchair, flipping through a magazine. The quiet hum of contentment filled the air, broken only by the occasional rustle of a page being turned.

Ben paused in the doorway, watching his parents for a moment. The sight of them sitting together, so peaceful and at ease, filled his heart with overwhelming love.

Without saying a word, he approached his mother first, wrapping his arms around her in an embrace. Claire looked up in surprise, documents slipping from her lap as she felt his arms squeeze around her with an intensity that was both unexpected and endearing.

"Goodnight, Mummy. I love you," Ben whispered as he buried his face against her shoulder.

Claire's heart melted at his words, and she pulled him closer, pressing a kiss to the top of his head. "I love you too, baby," she said, brushing her fingers through his hair. "What's this for? Not that I'm complaining."

Ben did not answer, just gave her one more squeeze before letting go. He turned to his dad, who was watching with a curious smile.

"Goodnight, Daddy," Ben said, stepping up to him and wrapping his arms around him. "I love you."

Ethan blinked in surprise, surprised by the sudden show of affection. He hugged his son back. "I love you too, buddy. Very much," he said, glancing over at Claire with a little shrug of confusion. She gave him a small, knowing smile.

As Ben pulled back, Ethan placed a hand on his shoulder. "Everything okay, champ?" he asked.

Ben nodded. "I'm fine, Daddy. I just love you is all."

Claire rose, took hold of Ben's hands, and asked, "Are you sure, darling?"

Ben smiled, a small but genuine smile that made Claire's heart ache with love. "I'm sure, Mummy," he said. "I just wanted to tell you… because I do. A lot."

Claire pulled him into another hug, unable to help herself. "We love you too, Ben. So much," she whispered.

Ethan joined them, ruffling Ben's hair with a tender smile. "More than you know," he added.

For a moment, the three of them stayed like that, the quiet of the room now filled with a warmth that seemed to wrap around them like a blanket. It wasn't often that Ben was so openly affectionate, and it was a moment both parents treasured.

Claire and Ethan watched Ben go as he left the room and made his way upstairs, their hearts full.

Ethan reached for Claire's hand. "He's a good kid."

"The best."

Neither of them knew what had prompted Ben's sudden outpouring of love, but in that moment, it didn't matter. What mattered was the bond between them, strong, carrying them through the mysteries and challenges their family faced.

As Ben climbed the stairs to his bedroom, grim determination battled nagging uncertainty within him. He knew, deep in his heart, with what he was about to do, it needed to be said and done. If the house somehow pulled him back into the past again—if it transported him into Eliza's world—he could not guarantee his return. The thought chilled him, but it also strengthened his resolve.

He couldn't bear the idea of leaving without telling his parents how much he loved them. It wasn't something he said often; the words felt too big, too important, to just toss around. But tonight, with everything pressing on his mind, he realised how much they needed to hear it—and how much he needed to say it, and hear it back.

When he hugged his mother, when he told his dad he loved him, it felt like a knot in his chest had loosened. The warmth of their love, the comfort of their presence, gave him the courage he needed. And now, as he stepped into his room, he felt ready— ready to face whatever came next, no matter how uncertain or dangerous it might be.

He glanced around his room, taking in the familiar sight of his bed, his desk, and the little trinkets scattered across the shelves. Would he see them again? Would he wake up here tomorrow, or would he find himself in the shadowy halls of a long-lost time? He didn't have all the answers—he didn't even know if this would work—but he couldn't ignore the pull he felt, the strange sense of responsibility growing inside him. Eliza's story, Julian's laughter, and the struggles they faced called to him.

Lying back on his bed, Ben stared at the ceiling. "Take me back," he whispered. "If I'm supposed to help, then take me back."

He knew he needed to retrace his steps, to recreate every moment as it had been the last time he'd slipped through the veil of time. If there was a way back, this had to be it. His heart raced at the thought, driven by determination as he pushed forward.

He changed into his pyjamas, the familiar fabric comforting against his skin. He hesitated for a moment, looking around his room one last time, the shadows cast by the dim moonlight stretching across the walls. Would this be the last time he saw it like this? Shaking off the thought, he padded barefoot on the cool floor to the walk-in closet.

The closet was dark, the fresh scent of recently washed clothes and wood filling the confined space. He stepped inside, closing the door behind him with a soft click that seemed to echo louder than it should have.

Ben glanced up at the top shelf, the place he had climbed up to the first time it happened. It seemed smaller now, less like the mysterious hiding place it had felt before, and more like an ordinary shelf. But he knew this was where it had occurred. He grabbed the edge and hoisted himself up, the muscles in his arms straining as he manoeuvred into place.

Once on top, he wriggled back, pressing himself as close to the wall as he could, the cool surface of the wood against his spine grounding him. The enclosed space was tight, the air still, but it felt safe in a strange, unexplainable way.

Now to wait, he thought, his mind racing with fragments of the diary's words, the images they conjured swirling in his head. He replayed them like a mantra, trying to hold on to the connection he felt to Eliza and Julian, to the strange pull that seemed to draw him closer to their time.

He closed his eyes, his breathing steadying. The strain of the day pulled at him, his exhaustion making it harder to keep his eyes open.

In his mind, the diary's words lingered as sleep overtook him. He thought of Eliza's fears, Julian's laughter, and Alexander's promises. He thought of the life they had lived so long ago, and the life they might still live if he could only help.

Before he knew it, the darkness of the closet gave way to the darkness of sleep, and Ben drifted off, his body relaxed but his mind still reaching for the past.

CHAPTER 6: THE PAST

Ben flailed, his arms and legs thrashing as though he were falling. The sensation jolted him awake, his heart racing as he struggled to orient himself. Clinging to the edge of the shelf, he steadied himself, his eyes wide in the darkness.

Did it work? He strained to hear any sounds that might confirm he had travelled back in time—voices, footsteps, or even the faint rustle of fabric. He climbed down from the shelf, his outstretched toes contacting the cold closet floor as he felt his way down in the dark.

Although the air smelled faintly of perfume, it felt heavier somehow, and cooler against his skin. He reached out, running his hands against the shelves where Eliza's clothes had been last time. His hand met only the smooth, empty wood. His heart sank, disappointment crashing over him like a wave.

"It didn't work." Ben felt defeated.

He opened the closet door just as a brilliant flash of lightning lit up the room, momentarily blinding him. Seconds later, a thunderous growl of thunder shook the house, its deep vibrations resonating through his body. Ben froze, his hand gripping the doorframe, listening as the storm raged outside.

Darkness again enveloped the room as he made his way back across it. Climbing into the familiar safety of his bed, he pulled the covers up around him. But as soon as he settled, a strange sensation crept over him. The sheets felt different. They weren't the usual soft cotton he was used to. These were smoother, almost slippery, like silk. His brow furrowed as he ran his hands over the material.

Another lingering flash of lightning lit the room, casting sharp, fleeting shadows against the walls. Intricate patterns, ones he recognised from before, carved the bedposts. The curtains were heavy and embroidered, not the simple ones that belonged in his room. His heart raced.

With each bolt of lightning that followed, the room revealed itself further. The ornate dresser with its polished mirror. The faint outline of a vanity table laden with unfamiliar objects. A tall wardrobe with its gilded handles.

"This isn't my room," Ben whispered. "It's… hers. It's Eliza's room."

Ben sat up, his hands clutching the silk sheets as he stared into the darkness, waiting for the next flash of lightning to confirm what he already knew. He was back. Somehow, he had returned to Eliza's world. Fear and excitement battled within him, making his hands shake uncontrollably. "I'm here," he whispered, his words swallowed by the deep rumble of thunder that followed.

He swung his legs over the side of the bed, his bare feet touching the cool floor. Whatever lay ahead, Ben knew one thing for certain: this time, he wouldn't waste a moment. He would find Eliza.

Shadows consumed the room, cloaking it in total darkness— except for a faint orange glow of light beneath the door. It was hard for Ben to see anything in the unfamiliar room. He remained seated at the edge of the bed, the only sound his shallow breaths and the distant groan of thunder as the storm moved on.

He wondered what time it was and if everyone else in the house was asleep. His hand groped along the bed table, searching for something useful—matches, a candle, or even a lighter—before the realisation struck him. Those things might not even exist yet.

"How on earth am I supposed to light a lamp?" he said in frustration.

The light outside the door drew his attention again. He wondered who it could belong to, the faint glow casting shadows that seemed alive in the stillness. Curiosity and fear wrestled within him.

He crept to the door, his heart thudding louder with each step, and turned the knob. The door creaked as he opened it, just enough to peek into the hallway.

The light was coming from a lamp perched on a small table at the top of the staircase. Its flame dim, casting long, eerie shadows along the walls and ceiling. Ben scanned the hallway, his eyes darting from one corner to the next, searching for any sign of movement.

Seeing no one, he stepped into the hallway, his movements careful. He retrieved the lamp, the warm glass comforting in his hands. The light illuminated his surroundings just enough to reveal the intricate woodwork of the bannisters and royal looking wallpaper.

He paused, uncertain of what to do next. Should he go down to the basement to see if Eliza was there? Or should he try to find Julian and let him know he was back? His thoughts swirled with indecision.

A guttural sound shattered the silence. "Julian... is that you?"

The deep, imposing tone echoed from the main chamber, right next to where he stood, its authority filling the house and freezing Ben in place. He clutched the lamp tighter. His instincts screamed at him to run, to hide—maybe back to the closet on the top shelf where he'd first arrived.

But something else stirred within him—something braver. Before he could stop himself, he called out, "Yes... er... Papa."

The words felt strange on his tongue, but they hung in the air, drawing an immediate response.

"What in heaven's name are you doing out of bed at this hour? Explain yourself at once!" the man boomed, carrying an authority that made Ben's knees feel weak.

"I... was thirsty, Papa." He remained frozen, the lamp trembling in his grasp.

There was a pause, heavy and suffocating, before the man commanded, "To bed with you, this instant!"

"Yes, sir." Ben turned and hurried down the hallway, his heart pounding like a drum in his chest.

He reached Julian's bedroom, the familiar door offering a

strange sense of safety. He slipped inside and placed the lamp on a small table near the bed. The room was quiet, the faint sound of the storm outside struggling to penetrate through the thick walls as the storm drew distant.

Ben stood near the edge of the bed, his hands shaking as he replayed the encounter in his mind. The imposing voice—Eliza and Julian's father—had seemed even more intimidating than Ben imagined. It was clear this was a man used to being obeyed, his presence casting a shadow over the house itself.

Ben wondered what he would do next. For now, though, he needed to stay quiet. Stay hidden. And most of all, stay brave.

A small body stirred in the enormous bed, shifting under the blankets. Ben froze, his excitement giving way to confusion. In his rush to lie low after the encounter with Eliza's father, he had forgotten where he was.

Julian pushed himself up, the blankets sliding off his slight frame. He looked sleepy and dishevelled. He blinked at Ben, his eyes squinting in the dim light of the lamp.

"Benjamin?" His eyes widened as recognition dawned, the sleepiness melting away and replaced by pure astonishment. "Benjamin!"

Ben smiled, raising a hand in a small wave. "Hi, Julian."

"It's you!" Julian said. "I thought... I thought you were naught but a dream, or my imaginings. But you're real! You've come back!"

Julian embraced Ben, a comforting warmth filling Ben's chest at Julian's genuine joy. "I'm real," he said. "And I came back because I needed to. There's something important I have to do."

Julian pulled back, his small, unworked hands gripping Ben's arms as he looked up at him with wide, shining eyes. "Do you mean to say... for Eliza?"

"Yes. For Eliza. And for you too."

"You'll help her, won't you? You'll see to it she's safe?"

"I'm going to try. I don't know how yet, but I'll figure it out."

Julian smiled. "I always knew you were special. When you were here last, I told Eliza you were a guardian angel sent to watch over us..."

Ben's throat tightened at Julian's words, but he forced a smile. "Well, I don't know about that, but I'm here now, and I'm not going anywhere until we figure this out."

Julian's eyes fluttered closed, his breathing evening out as sleep overtook him again. Ben sat for a moment, watching the boy's peaceful face. He felt a deep sense of responsibility settle over him, heavier now than ever.

He fought to stay awake, remembering his last sleep in this room; something had transported him back to his own time. He had come back for a reason, and he needed to see it through. He glanced around the room, his eyes settling on a pair of shoes stored beside Julian's small wardrobe. They were peculiar things—funny-looking shoes with great big buckles on them. Ben grabbed them and slid them onto his feet, but they were far too small, pinching his toes. Wincing, he decided it would be best to go barefoot. It would be quieter that way, too.

He waited for what felt like hours, listening to the creaks and groans of the old house. Occasionally, he would hear faint sounds from downstairs—inaudible murmurs and footsteps—but the house soon fell silent. He hoped this meant Julian's father had fallen asleep.

Ben picked up the lamp, ensuring the oil was still good, and went to the door. The dim light cast shifting shadows on the walls as he crept into the hallway. His feet made no sound on the cool wooden floors as he tiptoed to the main stairwell. The air was heavy with stillness, broken only by the faint crackle of the lamp's flame.

Step by careful step, he descended the grand staircase, each creak beneath his weight making him stop and listen. When he reached the basement door, he hesitated for a moment, clutching the lamp. He calmed his racing thoughts, then pushed the door open.

The basement was colder than he expected; the chill seeping into his skin as he stepped inside. It smelled damp and musty, redolent with stale wine and cold stone. Rows of neatly packed wine racks stretched into the shadows, wholly unlike the cluttered, modern basement he was used to.

As Ben made his way deeper into the basement, something small and furry darted across his toes with a sharp squeak. He jumped, stifling a gasp, and almost dropped the oil lamp in surprise.

"Get a grip, Ben," he whispered to himself.

At the far end of the basement, his lamp illuminated the faint outline of a staircase leading down to the door. Ben recognised it as the same one he, dad and Olivia had uncovered in the future. His hands shook as he descended the stairs, the pale light casting eerie shadows on the walls.

When he reached the door, he knocked and pressed his ear to the wooden surface, listening intently. For a moment, there was only silence. Then a whisper cut through.

"Who's there?"

Her words were weak, but a glimmer of hope remained. Ben's heart soared.

"Eliza!" he cried, throwing himself against the door, hugging it as though she could feel his presence. "It's me! It's Ben!"

There was a pause, followed by a soft, trembling gasp. "Benjamin?"

"Yes! Yes, it's me! I am here to save you. Where's the key, Eliza? Tell me where it is!"

Eliza's reply came, tinged with fear. "Papa keeps one with him, and the servant carries another. Oh, Benjamin, you must go! If he finds you here, he'll... he'll have you whipped for certain. Please, go home at once!"

Ben leaned his forehead against the door, his mind racing. "I'm not leaving you," he said fiercely. "I'll get the key. Just... just hold on, okay? I'm going to save you."

"You oughtn't have come," Eliza whispered desperately. "He'll harm you, truly. You don't understand the danger he poses."

"I don't care. You're not staying down here. Not like this."

Eliza fell silent for a moment, then said, "You're so brave— braver than any soul I've ever met."

"I'll be back, Eliza. Stay strong. I won't let him win."

As the echo of her quiet sobs reached his ears, Ben turned and made his way back up the stairs, his mind racing with plans. He would find the key—no matter what it took.

He ascended the stairs out of the basement, his legs trembling as he made his way back up the main stairwell to the imposing main chamber. The house was silent save for the distant rumble of thunder, the storm outside casting distant fleeting flashes of light through the tall windows. Each creak of the wooden floor under his feet felt deafening.

At the entrance to the main chamber, he placed the lamp on the floor, its glow barely lighting the interior. Swallowing hard, he tiptoed inside.

A massive four-poster bed, draped with heavy, luxurious curtains, dominated the chamber. Lord Ambrose and Lady Isadora lay beneath the thick covers. Ambrose's snoring was loud and guttural, the sound reverberating through the room like the growl of a slumbering beast.

Ben's eyes darted to a chair where Ambrose had draped his clothes, the rich fabric catching the faint light. *The key has to be there,* he thought, clinging to the hope that his search might be quick and uneventful. Moving as silently as he could, he crept to the chair, his hands trembling as he reached into the pockets of the coat hanging over it.

The first pocket was empty. His fingers searched the second pocket—a tin of snuff. He cursed, his pulse pounding in his ears. As he straightened, his eyes caught the glint of a key on the bedside table.

It rested beside a beaker of water and a small stack of papers. Ben swallowed hard, his mouth dry. The table stood next to the snoring Ambrose. The thought of getting so close to the man—and the risk of waking him—made Ben's stomach churn with fear. But he had no choice.

Step by careful step, he inched toward the table, each movement feeling too slow. He reached out, his fingers brushing the cool metal of the key. He tensed, lifting it carefully from the table.

The key caught the rim of the glass beaker, tipping it off balance. Ben lunged to grab it, heart lurching as his fingers brushed the smooth surface—only to fumble and lose his grip. The beaker toppled in a slow, sickening arc, spilling water down his arm and chest before clattering—and cracking—onto the wooden floor. The sound was deafening in the room's stillness.

Ben froze, clutching the key as his eyes darted to the bed. Ambrose stirred, a spattering of water droplets landing on his face.

The man's snoring stopped, replaced by a sharp inhale.

"Egad!" Ambrose said, sitting up in bed, his face contorted in confusion and rage.

Ben's instincts took over. He dropped to the floor, scrambling to roll under the bed, but it was useless—there was no space for even the smallest of children. The shadow of the big man loomed over him before he could think of another plan.

"Boy!"

A powerful hand seized Ben's arm, lifting him off the floor as though he weighed nothing. The key slipped from his fingers and clattered to the ground. Ambrose's face loomed inches from Ben's, his features contorted with raw fury and stark disbelief. "What in blazes are you doing in my chamber, boy?"

Ben's mouth opened and closed, but no words came out—fear overtaking him as he dangled in the air. He struggled, but Ambrose's grip was unyielding.

Lady Isadora sat up in bed, her hair a mess, her breath hitching as panic seized her at the thought of Ambrose's fury. "Ambrose, what's going on?" she asked, voice trembling with terror at the punishment he might inflict on the orphan boy.

"I caught this little wretch sneaking about!" Ambrose said, his patience wearing thin as he scrutinised Ben. "Julian's companion, is he not? Benjamin, if I recall?"

Ben's mind spun. He wanted to explain himself, to escape, but every thought seemed jumbled and useless. He trembled as he stammered, "I… got lost… I was looking for water…"

Ambrose's eyes bore into him. "Do not dare lie to me, boy! What mischief are you about? Speak the truth at once!"

Ben's fear threatened to consume him, but somewhere deep inside, a spark of courage glimmered. He wasn't sure what would happen next, but one thing was certain—he had to protect Eliza at all costs.

"Papa… he speaks the truth." Julian stood at the chamber door, trembling but steady enough to be heard across the room.

Ambrose glared at his son in the doorway. Julian clutched the edge of the doorframe, his tiny frame dwarfed by the grandeur of the chamber. His wide, pleading eyes flicked to Ben, still dangling in Ambrose's grip like a rag doll.

"I forbid you boys from entering my chamber! Is that understood?"

"Yes, Papa," Julian whispered.

"Yes, sir," Ben said, trembling under Ambrose's imposing presence. He looked at the floor, spotting the brass key, half of which now lay beneath the bed table, just out of reach.

Ambrose's scowl deepened as his eyes swept over Ben, taking in the strange clothes he wore, lingering on the unfamiliar pyjama top and pants. "What manner of ridiculous garments are these?" he demanded, suspicion lacing his words. "Where do you hail from? Speak, boy! What is your family name?"

Ben's mind raced. He struggled to think of a name that would seem plausible. He blurted out his own name. It only made sense. "Wallace, sir. My name is Ben... er... Benjamin Wallace."

Ambrose's grip loosened around Ben as he considered the name, his head tilting slightly. "Wallace. Hmm. I know no Wallace." His piercing eyes narrowed again, his suspicion undiminished. "You will take me to your family at first light."

Panic surged through Ben like ice in his veins. He didn't have a family in this time, and any lie he concocted would fall apart under Ambrose's scrutiny. Desperate, he blurted, "I'm... I'm orphaned, sir."

Ambrose's face twisted into a scowl as he released Ben, dropping him into a puddle of water. Ben slipped but quickly scrambled to his feet, standing at attention.

"Since when do you consort with orphaned boys, Julian?" he said, turning his attention back to his son. With disdain, he rubbed his robe, as if purifying himself.

Julian hesitated, his hands clutching each other. "He's... he's my friend, Papa."

"Your friend?" Ambrose sneered, his lip curling as he looked back at Ben. "I don't like this, Isadora. Orphans steal. They lie. They bring naught but trouble."

Lady Isadora's hand trembled as she brushed a strand of hair from her face, her voice tight with dread. "Please, Ambrose," she said, eyes flickering toward him, "let the boys return to their beds. It's late, and I—I fear you've frightened them more than enough for one night."

Ambrose's scowl deepened, and his eyes snapped back to Ben. "Begone with you, boy. If I catch you in my chambers again, I'll have your hide. Do you understand me?"

"Yes, sir. Sorry, sir."

Julian stepped forward, taking Ben's hand in his small but firm grip. "Come along," he whispered, tugging him to the door.

Ben glanced over his shoulder as they hurried out of the room, his eyes flicking to the brass key still lying on the floor. His heart sank, knowing he could no longer retrieve it.

They ran to Julian's chambers. Julian turned, worry and determination etched on his face. "What on earth were you doing in there?"

"I... needed the key for Eliza. I was going to help her."

Julian's eyes widened, and he glanced down the hallway, as if expecting Ambrose to come storming after them. "You're mad, Benjamin," he whispered. "But you're brave too."

Ben gathered his composure, his pulse still unsteady. "I couldn't just do nothing," he said. "I'll figure out another way."

Julian nodded, his hand still gripping Ben's. "We'll think of something. But for now, we must stay here. Papa won't take kindly to finding us still awake."

Ben awoke the next morning on the spare bedstead. The mattress, wrapped in unfamiliar fabrics that smelled of straw and age, was softer than he was accustomed to. The golden light of dawn streamed through the tall windows, casting a warm glow across the room. He blinked, his mind foggy, and pushed himself up on his elbows.

He couldn't remember falling asleep. The last thing he recalled was whispering hurried plans with Julian. Ben had resolved to stay awake, to be vigilant, but now here he was, groggy and disoriented, unsure how long he had been asleep.

For a moment, he thought he might have returned to the present, that Olivia would walk through the door any second with one of her teasing remarks. But as he looked around, reality set in. The room was far too ornate; the walls adorned with tapestries, and there were no electrical fittings.

Julian was sitting on the edge of his own grand bed, already dressed in clothes that made him look like a prince from an old storybook. His dark waistcoat bore golden filigree embroidery, and his pristine white shirt tucked into polished breeches. A small lace cravat peeked out from his collar, and he wore fitted stockings. Delight shone in his eyes as his feet, decked out in shiny buckled shoes, hung inches from the ground.

"You're still here. I thought you would vanish again, as you did last time."

Ben blinked at him, pushing himself up. Julian's enthusiasm was contagious, and despite the heaviness of the situation, Ben smiled back. "Yeah," he said, rubbing the sleep from his eyes. "I'm still here."

"When I awoke and saw you, I feared you'd faded away again, like a spectre. But you're real, aren't you? Not just a figment of my mind?"

"I'm here—no ghost, no dream. Just me."

Julian beamed and hopped down from the bed. "I'm ever so glad. You do not know how worried I was. After you left last time, I thought perhaps you didn't wish to stay. Or... maybe I'd driven you away."

Ben shook his head, his smile fading. "No, Julian. It wasn't like that at all. I didn't want to leave. I didn't even know I was going to. It just... happened."

Julian frowned in thought, then smiled again. "Well, you're here now," he said. "And this time, you'll stay, won't you? At least for a little while?"

Ben paused, pulling at the woven blanket covering his legs. "I'll stay as long as I can."

Julian nodded, satisfied with the answer. "Good, because I've so much to tell you! So many things have happened since you went away."

Ben couldn't help but grin at Julian's eagerness, his earlier worries pushed aside for the moment. "Then you better talk," he said. "I'm all ears."

Julian laughed, his youthful energy filling the room as he began recounting the events that had unfolded in Ben's absence

Just then, the large matronly cook burst into the chamber, her round face flushed and her hair coming loose from its bun. She thrust a bundle of clothes into Ben's arms—breeches, a grubby white shirt, a coat, and a pair of well-worn brogues. "Get yourself dressed, boy!" she ordered, low but urgent. "I know the garments may be a tad large—they're my son's—but they'll fit you well enough for now. There's no time to argue."

She glanced at the doorway. The sound of heavy boots echoed from somewhere down the hall, sending a jolt of fear through Ben. The woman's hands fluttered in agitation, as though she longed to help him but dared not linger.

"Now hurry," she said again, rising in urgency despite her struggle to keep it hushed. She looked back, worried. "Make haste, boy. If he—" Her words broke off, and her throat tightened.

Ben swallowed hard, his fingers trembling as he fumbled with the shirt. Whatever was coming, it wasn't good, and the cook's anxious urgency made it clear he had no time to waste.

"Cook, what's the matter?" Julian asked. He cast a nervous glance at Ben, who was pulling on the oversized breeches.

"There's no time to explain," she snapped. "Come, we must go at once."

Without waiting for Julian's response, she grabbed Ben's arm, pulling him forward with surprising strength. He stumbled as he worked to get his foot into the last of the heavy brogues, but he didn't protest. Somehow, he knew—perhaps from the sharp urgency in her manner or the fear flashing in her eyes—that she was there to help.

She led him at a near run, her grip firm and unrelenting. Down the narrow servant's staircase they went, the old wooden steps creaking underfoot, and into the warm, bustling kitchen. The smell of stew, rich and savoury, hung in the air, a jarring counterpoint to the tension crackling around them. For the briefest moment, Ben's stomach twisted with hunger, but there was no time to linger. With a determined tug, the cook pulled him to the back door without stopping. The morning sun was just beginning to rise as she threw open the door, flooding the yard with soft, golden light. There, standing amidst the dewy grass, was a large, sturdy horse. Its breath came in visible puffs in the cool morning air, and its muscular frame shivered with anticipation. The rider, a few years older than Ben, sat astride the horse, his youth belied by his experienced posture and determined stare.

The cook didn't hesitate. With a strength that seemed impossible for her size, she scooped Ben up as though he weighed nothing and hoisted him onto the horse's broad back. "Hold tight, boy!" she commanded, her voice cutting through the stillness of the morning. The horse, snorting and pawing at the ground, was eager to be off. The rider adjusted himself in the saddle, one hand gripping the reins and the other steadying Ben.

Julian hesitated, his face pale. "What's happening? Cook, where are you sending him?"

She turned to him, her face fierce and resolute. "There's no time for questions," she said. "If you care for him, you'll trust me. Now go!"

She slapped the horse's flank, and the animal surged forward with a powerful leap, its hooves thundering against the dirt path. Ben clung to the rider as though his life depended on it, his heart pounding in his chest as they made their way over the hills into the morning light, the mansion disappearing from view behind them.

"Where... are you taking me?" Ben said, trembling as he clung to the rider for dear life. The wind whipped past them, and the rhythmic pounding of the horse's hooves echoed in his ears.

They galloped at full speed for what felt like miles. After a long while, the rider slowed the horse to a trot, granting both the animal and its passengers a brief reprieve.

"I'm Daniel," the boy said, glancing back at Ben over his shoulder. "The cook—Martha—is my mother." There was a protective edge to his words. "Lord Wilson was fixin' to send you to his coal mine. My momma knows all about those wretched places. She told me to get you out of there and take you to the Whitfield farm. They'll look after you."

Ben swallowed hard, his throat tightening. "But... I can't leave. I have to go back—I have to save Eliza." His chest ached as he held back tears. The mansion was his only way back to his family, but more than that, he couldn't abandon Eliza.

Daniel pulled back on the reins, slowing the horse further. A look of sceptical curiosity crossed his face as he glanced at Ben. "Best you lie low for now," he said. "Ambrose Wilson ain't right in the head. He hates commoners and orphans—a right awful man.

If you go back, you'll end up exactly where he wants you." He tilted his head. "Wait… what did you mean about Eliza?"

"She's locked in the basement," Ben said in desperation.

Daniel shook his head, frowning. "No, that ain't possible. They sent her away to the city, to work. That's what my momma told me."

"No, no, you're wrong. Lord Ambrose locked her in there because…" He hesitated, unsure if he should reveal the secret. But he couldn't hold it back. "Because she's… you know… going to have a baby."

Daniel let out a loud, incredulous snort. "What? That's daft! She's without a companion."

"No! She loves a man called Alexander, but he's gone missing. Lord Ambrose is keeping her locked up—he doesn't want anyone to know about her baby."

Daniel turned in the saddle to face Ben, his eyes narrowing. "How do you know all this?" he asked. "Sounds like something out of a folktale to me."

With an earnest look, Ben met his stare. "I'm telling you the truth! I overheard things… I've seen things. Please, believe me."

Daniel paused, considering Ben's words. "Alright," he said at last. "I'll take you to the Whitfields', like Momma said. But tell her everything you've told me. If it's true, she'll know what to do. She always does."

He snapped the reins, urging the horse back into a gallop. The animal surged forward, its hooves pounding against the dirt road once more. Ben clung to Daniel, his heart racing—not just from the speed of the ride, but from the growing urgency of his mission. Somewhere behind them, in the shadows of the mansion, Eliza was waiting. He just hoped they weren't too late.

***

Olivia pulled her knees to her chest, clutching the old diary as though it might anchor her to sanity. The room was silent, save for the faint ticking of the clock on her nightstand. She stared at the clothes on the floor—Ben's pyjamas. The sight twisted her stomach. He hadn't materialised back into her room with them, like before. This time, he was… gone.

Her mind flashed back to that first night Ben had returned, his face pale and his breath tinged with the sharp, yeasty smell of beer. No one believed his wild and disjointed story about the past, the mansion, and a girl named Eliza. Even she hadn't believed him, not truly. Her parents had been furious, convinced someone had given him beer and that his story was just a poor excuse to cover up whatever trouble he'd got into.

She could still hear the sting of her father's words: *"Ale? Time travel? Do you think we're fools, Ben? Just tell us the truth!"* And her mother's tearful disappointment: *"Why won't you just admit it, Ben? Who gave you the ale? We're not mad; we just need you to be honest!"*

Ben had stood firm, insisting on his story with a desperate conviction that had only made him seem guiltier in their eyes. Olivia had watched, torn between wanting to believe him and the impossibility of what he was saying. A part of her had even laughed along with their parents, teased him about his "time-travelling adventures." Now, the memory made her stomach churn with guilt.

This time, it was different. His pyjamas—abandoned and out of place, were undeniable proof that something strange was happening. Olivia felt certain, deep in her bones, that the past had trapped him.

Her heart twisted at the thought. Where was he now? Was he safe? Did he even know how to return? The thought of him being lost—stuck in a time she couldn't reach—made her chest tighten. She gripped the diary, its cracked leather binding pressing into her palm. The entries she'd read earlier that day swirled in her head.

Her eyes shifted to her bedroom door, an awareness of her parents settling over her. What would she tell them? Should she tell them Ben was trapped in the 19th-century? That the story they had dismissed as an ale-soaked fabrication was real? She could already picture their faces: her father's furrowed brow, her mother's tearful, pleading eyes. They would never believe her— not after the last time. But this *was* the truth. She knew it now, as surely as she knew her own name.

Tears slipped down her cheeks as she whispered into the stillness, "Ben, where are you?"

But even as the heaviness of grief settled over her, a spark of determination grew. Ben needed her. If he was in the past, as impossible as it seemed, he was depending on her to figure out how to bring him back. She couldn't let herself give in to despair—not this time.

Olivia opened her eyes and glanced at the diary again. Somewhere in its brittle pages lay the answers—or at least a clue. She wiped her tears with the back of her hand and pushed herself to her feet, clutching the diary. She would keep reading, researching, digging into the mansion's history until she brought her brother home.

Outside, just beyond the old mansion gardens, Olivia spotted movement beneath the sprawling oak trees from her second-story window, the same two men they had seen earlier; the ones taking photos of the house. A chill ran through her as she realised they were in the graveyard, crouched over the old, weathered gravestones.

The men moved as if on a mission, wiping away dust and pulling back tangled overgrowth to expose the inscriptions beneath. One of them carried a notebook, jotting down notes while the other snapped pictures with a camera. They didn't look like tourists, and their presence stirred an uneasy feeling in Olivia's gut.

Her hands trembled as she clutched the old diary, but she couldn't tear her eyes away from the scene. She watched as one man knelt beside a broken gravestone, brushing away dirt. The urgency in her chest grew, and she placed the diary on her dresser, spinning toward the door.

"Daddy!" she shrieked, panicked.

Ethan came running, his face tight with worry, with Claire following close behind. "What is it?" he asked, his eyes scanning her face.

Olivia pointed at the window. "They're back."

Ethan's fists clenched as he moved to the window. His eyes narrowed at the sight of the men in the graveyard, still engrossed in their mysterious work. "I've got them this time," he muttered. Without hesitation, he turned and charged out of her room.

"Ethan, wait!" Claire called after him, but he was already

heading down the stairs.

Claire spotted Ben's pyjamas crumpled on the floor. "Olivia," she said, uneasy. "Where is your brother?"

Olivia opened her mouth, but the words caught in her throat. How could she explain Ben wasn't just missing—he was trapped in the past?

"He…" She swallowed the lump in her throat. "He's… not here."

"What do you mean, not here? Olivia, where is Ben?"

Olivia's mind raced. She glanced at the diary on her dresser, her thoughts tangled. If her parents wouldn't believe Ben's story the first time, why would they believe hers now? But the look in her mother's eyes—equal parts fear and hope—told her she couldn't hold the truth back much longer.

Before she could respond, the sound of the front door slamming shut echoed through the house, followed by Ethan shouting something outside. Olivia darted to the window again, watching as her father strode across the yard to the graveyard. The two men looked up, startled, as Ethan called out to them.

Claire came to the window, her eyes narrowing as she watched Ethan confront the strangers. "Stay here," she said to Olivia, before hurrying out of the room.

Olivia stood frozen for a moment, torn between staying put and following her parents. Her gaze drifted back to the diary, its cracked leather binding catching the light of the sun. Something told her the men in the graveyard weren't just curious historians or photographers. They were searching for something—something tied to the mansion.

She scooped her brother's pyjamas off the floor; the cotton crumpled like a shed skin, and clutched them tight against her chest. If she squeezed hard enough, maybe—just maybe—Ben would flicker back into them, whole and real. She pressed the fabric to her face, breathing in the faint trace of him. "Oh, Ben, what have we done?"

CHAPTER 7: A PRISON IN TIME

"How old are you?" Daniel asked, casual as the horse settled into a comfortable trot.

"I'm eleven, almost twelve."

Daniel turned his head, eyeing Ben with a raised brow. "You look older. You're quite tall—and brave, I'll give you that—but you're also daft," he said with a smirk, noting how the boy's height almost matched his own, even though Daniel was fifteen.

Ben remained silent, staring ahead, the enormity of everything that had happened pressing down on him.

A few miles later, Daniel spoke again. "Here we are—the Whitfield farm."

"Wait," Ben said, panic creeping in. "How do I get back to Eliza... to the mansion?"

Daniel slowed the horse, glancing over his shoulder at Ben. "You don't. This is your home now," he said. He motioned to Ben's clothes. "And keep the garments—they're my old ones. Might as well use them."

Before Ben could respond, a tall, slender young woman stepped out from the farmhouse, her auburn hair tied in braids that framed her sharp, kind features. She had a welcoming presence, and her smile was warm as she waved them over.

"Good day. I'm Maggie," she said, standing at the foot of the farmhouse steps as Daniel pulled the horse to a stop.

Maggie reached up to help Ben down from the horse. "You

must be Benjamin," she said, her kind eyes scanning him before turning to Daniel. "We shall take good care of him. Do give my regards to your mother, won't you?"

"Will do," Daniel replied, tipping his head. He turned the horse and, with a quick glance back at Ben, rode off down the dirt path, leaving him in Maggie's care.

"Welcome home," she said, taking Ben's hand, and led him toward the farmhouse steps.

Ben hesitated, glancing around the rustic property. The worn wood of the porch creaked beneath their feet as Maggie opened the door, and the smell of fresh bread and bacon made Ben's stomach rumble. Inside, the farmhouse was cosy and lived-in, with mismatched furniture and a fire crackling in the hearth.

"Is this your farm?" Ben asked, his eyes wide as he took in the simple but inviting interior.

Maggie laughed, a light sound that filled the room. "Goodness, no," she said, shaking her head. "The farm belongs to Mr and Mrs Whitfield. You shall find them quite agreeable—they're kind, generous souls who took me in some years ago. I'm an orphan, much like yourself."

"I'm not... oh, never mind," Ben said, his shoulders slumping.

Maggie squeezed his shoulder. "I know it's difficult," she said. "But you're safe here, Ben. That's what matters most at present."

Ben nodded, though his heart still ached. Safe or not, he couldn't shake the thought of Eliza locked in the mansion—or his own family waiting for him in another time. But for now, he had no choice but to follow Maggie's lead.

Maggie guided him through the house. "Let's get you settled. You'll find it quite delightful here—I assure you."

Ben followed her, his mind swirling with questions, but a small part of him hoped she was right. For now, at least, he had somewhere to call home.

In the kitchen, Sarah Whitfield was cooking breakfast. She turned from the coal stove when Maggie and Ben entered. "Oh, just look at you," she said. "Such a dashing young lad!" She threw her arms open without hesitation, pulling him into a quick, motherly hug.

Ben stiffened at first, unused to the sudden warmth and

affection, but there was something so genuine about Sarah's attitude that he couldn't help but relax, if only for a moment.

"You must be famished," Sarah said, stepping back and giving him a quick once-over. Her eyes softened as she took in his oversized clothes and the faint look of exhaustion on his face. "Maggie, sit him down. The poor dear needs a proper meal!"

"Sit down," Maggie said, pulling out a chair for him. "Mrs Whitfield's cooking is simply the best—better than anything you've ever tasted, I daresay."

Ben hesitated, glancing from Maggie to Sarah and then at the pan on the stove. His stomach growled, betraying him, and Sarah chuckled.

"Well, that settles it," she said, turning back to the stove. With brisk, practiced movements, she flipped a few thick slices of bacon onto a plate, followed by a generous scoop of scrambled eggs. "Let's get you something to fill that belly of yours."

As Sarah set the plate in front of him, she rested a hand on his shoulder, giving it a gentle, reassuring squeeze. "There you are, love. Eat up. You're safe here, and we shall take good care of you."

"Thank you," Ben said, cutting into the bacon. For a moment, he allowed himself to savour it, the tension in his body beginning to ease.

Just then, a flurry of movement came from the doorway as two young children burst into the room.

"Mama!" called a girl with messy blonde pigtails and an infectious grin. A smaller boy followed close behind her, his round face and button nose framed by a mop of curly red hair.

"Oh, here we go," Maggie said with a laugh. "Lily and Samuel, meet Benjamin."

Lily, the ten-year-old tomboy, darted over to the table, her curious eyes fixed on Ben. "You're new!" she declared with excitement. "Are you staying with us? Do you like chickens? We've loads of them!"

"Give him a moment, you two," Sarah said. "The poor lad's barely sat down, and you're already bombarding him with questions!"

"It's all right," Ben said, managing a small smile as he glanced at Lily and Samuel. "I—I like chickens."

Lily beamed. "Splendid! I'll show you the coop after you've eaten. We've one hen that lays the grandest eggs. She's my favourite."

"Mine too," Samuel added, stepping out from behind his sister and inching closer to Ben.

Sarah exchanged a knowing look at Maggie, her smile warm as she watched the children interact. "It seems you've already made a few friends, Benjamin."

Ben nodded. For the first time since arriving at the farm, he felt a trace of something he hadn't felt in a while—hope. It wasn't home, and it wasn't his family, but maybe, just maybe, this place could be a safe harbour until he figured out how to set things right.

"Who do we have here?" a young man said as he stepped through the back door. His tall frame filled the doorway for a moment before he crossed the room, leaning down to give Sarah a kiss on the cheek. Without waiting for an invitation, he dropped into a chair at the table next to Ben, studying him.

"This is Benjamin," Sarah said. Then, with a pointed look, she added, "Henry, I wish you'd wash those hands before sitting at the table." She shook her head in exasperation.

Henry grinned, holding up his palms in mock surrender. "Ah, right, my apologies, madam. But don't fret—a bit of dirt adds flavour to your cooking." He winked at Ben, who couldn't help but crack a small smile despite himself.

Henry leaned back in his chair. "So, Benjamin, what's your tale?"

Before Ben could respond, Maggie swooped in, swatting the back of Henry's head with her hand. "Henry, let the boy eat first!"

"All right, all right," Henry said, rubbing the back of his head, but still chuckled. "Can't fault a man for being curious."

Ben hesitated, his spoon halfway to his mouth. The room felt heavier, as though everyone's attention had shifted to him. "Well, I was… I am friends with Julian," he began. "But his sister, Eliza…" He trailed off, the words sticking in his throat. "Never mind."

Henry's demeanour shifted. His playfulness melted away, replaced by a focused intensity. Something in Ben's words had struck a chord. He leaned forward, his hands resting on the table.

"What about Eliza?"

Ben looked up, unsure of how much to say. "Do you know Alexander?" he asked, hoping Henry might hold some answers. Henry looked to be about the same age Ben imagined Alexander might be, though Ben had only heard about him through fragments of a forgotten historical diary.

Sarah's worried look met Henry's, a silent query exchanged between them.

Henry stood up quickly, scraping the chair against the floor, the wooden legs tipping over with a loud clatter. "What do you know about Alexander?"

"Henry, stop!" Sarah said. "You're frightening the boy." She moved to Ben's side, her presence a calming counterpoint to Henry's sudden outburst.

She took Ben's hands in hers. "Benjamin, Henry isn't angry with you. He's merely concerned. You see, Alexander is his friend."

"You know Alexander?" Ben's eyes widened as he clutched Sarah's hands. "I must speak to him—it's important!"

Henry's jaw tightened, and he paced the room, his hand running through his tousled hair. His earlier calm was gone, replaced by a simmering tension. "Alexander's been missing for weeks. No one knows where he is. And now you appear, speaking of him and Eliza—how do you know them?"

"I overheard some things at the mansion. Please, I don't mean any harm—I only wish to help."

Maggie stepped forward, placing a hand on Henry's arm. "Do give him a chance, Henry. He's just a boy. If he knows something, we ought to listen."

Sarah, still at Ben's side, squeezed his hands. "Benjamin," she said, "we all care a great deal about Alexander. If there's anything you can tell us, it could help. But you needn't be afraid. We'll sort this out together."

Ben nodded, his heart pounding. The warmth of her touch bolstered his courage. "Eliza told me. She said Alexander disappeared—and that Lord Ambrose knows something." He carefully avoided mentioning the parts he had learned from her diary.

The room fell silent. Henry's face was dark with worry. "Lord

Ambrose—if he's involved..." he said.

Sarah stood. She squeezed Ben's shoulder. "That's enough for now! Benjamin's been through quite enough today. Let's allow him to rest and eat. We'll speak more when he's ready."

"No, please, I want to speak now," Ben said. He pushed the remnants of his meal away from him, his appetite gone, though for the first time in what felt like ages, a glimmer of hope sparked in his chest. "I cannot explain how I know or where I came from, but Eliza needs our help."

Sarah's eyes narrowed, concern etched across her face. "Eliza doesn't need rescuing—she's living with her aunt in London now. At least, that's what Lady Isadora told me."

Ben shook his head. "She's still at the mansion."

Maggie frowned, leaning against the back of her chair. "That cannot be right," she said. "She used to visit us often—bringing things for the children and the farm. She loved coming here, but she stopped some time ago. I assumed it was because she moved away."

Ben's throat tightened. "He locked her in the basement, because she..." He looked down at the table as he struggled to find the courage to continue.

Sarah leaned forward. "What is it, dear? You can tell us."

"Because... she has a baby growing inside her."

A heavy silence descended upon the room, the impact of Ben's words palpable.

"That scoundrel," Henry said, his face dark with rage. "We ought to go at once and free her!"

"Stop!" came a commanding voice from the doorway Robert Whitfield entered the room, wiping his hands on a rag. "Rushing in like that would ruin us. It would ruin this farm and everything we've built. Do you understand?"

Henry turned to him. "Ruin us? She's locked up, Father! We cannot simply stand by and do nothing."

"Acting recklessly will only make matters worse—for her and for us. Ambrose has the means and the power to crush us without a second thought. Is that what you want? To risk everything for the sake of those who depend on this farm?"

Henry's frustration boiled over, and he swept the half-eaten plate of food off the table, sending it crashing to the floor. Ben and the other children jumped in fright, their eyes wide with fear.

"Enough!" Robert stepped forward, firm. "No one is suggesting we do nothing. But we must sit down and think this through—not charge in like fools."

Sarah stepped in, attempting to ease the tension. "Benjamin, this is my dear husband, Robert. Robert, meet Benjamin."

Ben stood and extended his hand, which Robert shook, visibly surprised by the boy's poise and manners. "Lad. You seem wise beyond your years, bearing a burden no child should have to carry. But this isn't something you can solve on your own. Let the adults handle this. Do you understand?"

Ben hesitated, his fingers gripping the edge of the table as he nodded. "I just… I don't want her to suffer anymore."

Robert placed a hand on Ben's shoulder. "And neither do we. But we must be prudent about this. If what you're saying is true, then Eliza needs us to act without drawing Ambrose's suspicion. Otherwise, we'll only make things worse."

Maggie moved to pick up the broken dish, her face troubled. "We must do something, Robert. Her life is in danger, and we cannot simply abandon her."

"We shan't, but we'll do it properly. No rash decisions, no unnecessary risks. For now, we plan."

Henry muttered something and sat back down, his frustration still simmering beneath the surface.

Sarah, sitting beside Ben, patted his hand. "You did the right thing by telling us. We'll sort this out together. You're not alone, Benjamin."

Ben nodded, though his heart remained heavy. He glanced around the table at the Whitfields, their faces tense. He was no longer alone in this fight—and perhaps, together, they would save Eliza.

Lily, with her bright, curious eyes and the wisdom that sometimes came with being a child who had seen too much, reached out and placed her delicate hand on Ben's. Her fingers were warm and soft, and though the gesture was simple, it carried a surprising depth of comfort and understanding.

"Don't worry, Ben," she said. "We'll help you. You'll see. Mama always says we take care of family."

A lump rose in his throat. He blinked, hoping she wouldn't notice tears threatening to spill over. "Thanks, Lily," he said.

Lily nodded, as if his gratitude was unnecessary but appreciated all the same. Then, with the ease only a child could manage, she smiled and said, "If that wicked man comes after you, don't fret. I know all the best hiding places round here—Samuel and I use 'em when we play. You'll be safe with me, I promise."

Ben let out a small laugh, a sound that felt foreign but welcome. It was the first time he'd laughed in what felt like forever. "I'll keep that in mind."

Lily beamed, pleased with herself, and gave his hand one last squeeze before letting go. The moment passed, but the warmth lingered, settling in Ben's chest like a small sparkle of light in the darkness that surrounded him. For the first time since this strange journey began, he felt a tiny spark of hope.

Later that morning, after Sarah had rummaged through the chest of hand-me-down clothes and outfitted Ben with more appropriately fitting garments—a sturdy cotton shirt, rough-hewn trousers, and boots that didn't threaten to fall off his feet with every step—she sent him outside to join Lily and Samuel.

The late morning sun bathed the farm in a soft, golden light. The air was crisp but warming, and Sarah watched from the kitchen window as the three children made their way to the chicken coop. Lily led the way, chattering enthusiastically, a wicker basket swinging from her hand. Samuel trotted along beside her, clutching a smaller basket, his eyes darting to Ben as if inviting him to join in.

Ben faltered at first, his posture rigid as he followed them into the yard. But it didn't take long for Lily's infectious energy to draw him out of his shell. Soon, they were crouched together near the coop, reaching under clucking hens to retrieve warm eggs, their laughter carrying across the farmyard in the bright morning air.

Sarah leaned against the sink, a smile tugging at the corners of her lips as she listened to the sound of Ben's laughter—a bright, beautiful sound she hadn't expected to hear so soon. There was something about it that warmed her heart, reminding her of how a child's joy could shine through even the darkest of circumstances.

From her vantage point, she could see Lily showing Ben how to handle the eggs without cracking them, her small hands moving with practiced care. Samuel, meanwhile, darted around the coop with a small broom, sweeping up stray feathers and bits of straw.

As Sarah watched, her smile faded, a thoughtful look settling in its place. She couldn't stop her mind from wandering back to the questions that had lingered since Ben arrived. Who was he? Where had he come from? He was polite and well-spoken, with an odd accent, but there was an air of mystery about him she couldn't ignore.

Most troubling of all was the intimate knowledge he seemed to have of the Wilson family—knowledge that went far beyond what any ordinary boy would know. His words about Eliza and Alexander, about the mansion and Ambrose, echoed in her mind. How could he know such things?

Sarah turned from the window, her hands resting on the edge of the sink as she tried to comprehend it all. She'd seen her share of hard-luck cases—children who had come to the farm with nothing but torn clothes on their backs and stories too painful to share. But Ben was different. There was a quiet intensity about him, a blend of compassion and purpose that didn't match his young age. "Who are you, Benjamin?" she murmured to herself.

Ben was standing now, his face lit up as Lily gestured dramatically, likely recounting one of her grand tales. Samuel tugged at Ben's sleeve, pointing at the barn, and the three of them took off running, their laughter ringing out once again in the late morning stillness.

Sarah sighed, pushing her questions aside for the moment. Whatever Ben's story was, it was clear he needed this—a chance to be a child again, if only for a little while. She would let him have that, and she would give him time. But she resolved to understand his mystery, not out of suspicion, but out of a growing sense of responsibility and care.

That night, as Ben lay on his bedstead in the boys' room with his hands clasped behind his head, a thousand schemes danced through his mind. He contemplated the way forward, trying to piece together how he could help Eliza.

Sam was sleeping in a bedstead next to him, his chest rising and falling. He had drifted off dreaming of their day's adventures, unaware of the turmoil churning inside Ben. The soft creak of a door opening downstairs broke the silence. Ben's ears perked up as he heard murmured chatter and the sound of someone being welcomed in. Then came a familiar tone—Daniel's voice.

Curiosity tugged at him. Ben slipped out of bed, careful not to wake Samuel. He tiptoed across the wooden floor and crouched at the banister. From there, he could see the sitting room below, lit by the glow of fire crackling in the hearth. Shadows danced on the walls as the flames licked at the logs, casting the figures of the adults into moving silhouettes.

It was Daniel, all right, and standing with him was his mother. Robert and Sarah were there too, their faces grave as they listened to Martha speak.

"The boy was telling the truth," Martha said. "After Daniel told me about their conversation this morning and Eliza's possible imprisonment, I refused to believe it. I couldn't imagine Lord Ambrose capable of such cruelty. But I had to see for myself."

She paused, her hands gripping the back of a chair. "I slipped into the wine cellar to investigate and caught sight of a servant leaving a deeper chamber. I hid until they passed, and then I saw her. Poor Miss Eliza... The servant was replacing a lamp and carrying a bucket of... well, let's just say it didn't smell pleasant at all."

Ben's knuckles turned white as he gripped the balustrade, his palms sweaty and his heart racing. His stomach churned at the thought of Eliza locked away, suffering in the dank, hidden chamber.

"That blackguard!" Robert said. "How do we get her out without starting a war?"

"We'd need someone to sneak into the servants' quarters and retrieve the key. It'll have to be my son, Daniel—he's small enough to slip through the hidden wall passageways at night."

Robert glanced over at Daniel. "Do you know what to look for?"

"I believe so," Daniel said, nodding, "but if not, I can take all the keys—one of them is bound to fit."

Before Robert could respond, Ben stood up and interrupted from the stairs, descending into the room with quiet determination. "I know what the key looks like. I'm skinny enough to fit through the secret passageways, too. Let me help."

Surprise and worry showed on the adults' faces as they looked at him.

"Benjamin, you ought to be in bed already," Sarah said, her tone softening as she placed a hand on his shoulder. "And no, I cannot allow you to put yourself in harm's way."

Daniel put his arm over Ben's shoulder. "We can do it—both Benjamin and I. Besides, I know all the house's secret passages, even the ones Lord Ambrose doesn't know about. Benjamin knows what the key looks like."

"Stop calling that scoundrel 'Lord'!" Robert said. "He doesn't deserve the title. He's a cruel man and deserves to be locked in that room instead of Eliza."

Martha placed a calming hand on Robert's arm, though her own face was tense with worry. "As much as I hate the idea of putting the boys in danger, Ben has a point. They're small enough to fit in the passageways without being noticed. If we plan this carefully, it could work."

"I can show Ben the passageways tomorrow so he can get familiar with them. We'll make sure we know the routes before the real thing."

Sarah looked torn, her gaze shifting between Ben, Daniel, and the other adults. "I don't like this—they're just boys!"

"They're also our best chance," Robert said. "If we don't act, who knows how much longer Eliza can endure in those conditions?"

Martha nodded. "I shall ensure the boys are careful, Sarah. But Eliza needs us. If we don't help her, no one will."

"I can do it. I can't let her stay down there," Ben said.

Sarah's face softened. She took Ben's hands in hers. "You're brave, Benjamin, but promise me you'll be careful."

"I promise."

A silent agreement formed between the adults as they

exchanged nods. The plan wasn't perfect, but it was all they had. The room grew quiet, the only sound the steady crackling of the fire, as each of them contemplated the dangerous road ahead.

Robert placed his large, calloused hands on the backs of both Ben and Daniel. "You lads are the bravest boys I've ever had the privilege to know. To set aside your own safety and comfort for the sake of another takes a courage many grown men lack. I am proud—truly proud—to know you both."

Daniel straightened a little, puffing out his chest, touched by the rare praise from Robert. He gave a small nod, though his usual confidence seemed tempered by the seriousness of the moment.

Ben felt something different. He looked up at Robert, their eyes locking. The words warmed him, filled him with a sense of honour he hadn't felt before. But at that moment, Ben couldn't bring himself to feel brave at all. The familiar tightness of fear curled in his stomach.

He glanced down, staring at his feet as the enormity of what they were about to do loomed over him. It wasn't just the danger that scared him—it was the uncertainty. Suppose someone caught them. What if their attempts were unsuccessful? What if he couldn't save Eliza, and she remained locked away in that terrible place?

Ben tried to stop his hands from trembling—he didn't want Robert or Daniel to see how scared he was, how much doubt churned within him.

"You all right, Benjamin?" Daniel asked.

Ben forced a nod, his throat dry. "Yeah," he whispered.

Robert's large hand cradled Ben's neck. "It's all right to be frightened, lad. Courage doesn't mean you're not afraid. It means you act despite your fear. And that's what you're doing."

Ben nodded. The words didn't erase his fear, but they gave him something to hold on to—a tiny ember of strength in the face of his growing doubt.

Robert straightened and patted the boys' backs. "Now, let's get to work. If we're going to do this, we're going to do it properly. No room for mistakes."

Daniel grinned, nudging Ben's arm. "Come on. You heard the

man—time to show just how brave we are."

Ben forced a small smile, though his fear hadn't gone away. Deep down, he knew Daniel was just as scared as he was. But somehow, that thought made it a little easier to take the next step.

As the two boys turned to the table where Martha was sketching the layout of the mansion's hidden passages, Ben composed himself. This was about Eliza, about doing what was right. He couldn't let her down.

CHAPTER 8: DESPAIR OF THE PRESENT

"What the hell are you doing on my property?" Ethan demanded, surprising the two men. One of them was crouched by an old, moss-covered gravestone, brushing off dirt, while the other had a camera slung around his neck, mid-way to taking a shot.

The taller man, wearing a rumpled tweed jacket and glasses, sprang up, lifting his hands in a placating gesture. "I am sorry, sir. We should have approached you first. We're with the Historical Society of Strange Phenomena. My name is Theodore Marlowe, and this is my colleague, Vince Colby." He gestured to the younger man, who saluted, his camera dangling against his chest.

Ethan ignored the man's extended hand. "Why did you run the last time I saw you? And what is your business here?"

Vince adjusted the strap of his camera. "Sir... yes, we ran because we thought you were carrying a weapon. We've been shot at before while investigating this property, so we didn't want to risk it."

"Well, that wasn't me. We've only been here a short while," Ethan said, his expression hardening as he added, "And why the hell were you looking into my son's bedroom window a few weeks ago?"

At this, both men exchanged a confused glance, their brows knitting together. Theo cautiously adjusted his glasses "Your son?"

"Yes, my son! What were you doing looking into his window?"

113

"We thought... well, we thought the house was vacant. When we saw the boy, we were... surprised." He trailed off, glancing at Theo for support.

Ethan's eyes narrowed. "Thought what?"

Theo cleared his throat. "We, uh... thought he was someone else."

"What the hell is that supposed to mean?"

"Sir, this is going to sound strange, but the boy... he looked like someone from a painting we've studied. An ancient painting from the late 19th-century, depicting a child associated with this property. We thought..."

"You thought he was some kind of ghost?" Ethan said disdainfully.

Vince opened his mouth to answer, then hesitated, looking both apologetic and uneasy.

Theo stepped in again. "Mr...?"

"Wallace." Ethan said.

"Mr Wallace, we are serious researchers, I assure you. Our work may seem unusual, but we've been studying this property and its history for years. We've uncovered countless reports of strange occurrences here, going back centuries. We meant no harm by our presence."

Ethan's jaw tightened. "Look, we're dealing with something far more important than your so-called research. I'd appreciate it if you left us alone. By the way, have you seen my son?"

Vince's face softened, his earlier nervousness replaced by genuine concern. "Your son's missing?"

Ethan had had enough. "Please leave!"

"Of course, Mr Wallace, we'll leave. But if there's anything we can do to help..." Theo reached into his pocket and pulled out a card, "please contact us. We're not just researchers—we want to help uncover the truth."

Ethan hesitated before taking the card, glancing at the words printed on it: *Historical Society of Strange Phenomena.* His face remained stern as he crammed it into his jacket without speaking.

Vince lingered for a moment. "If your son's disappearance has anything to do with the strange history of this property... we might be able to help. Please, think about it."

Ethan didn't respond, his silence making it clear the conversation was over. He turned on his heel and walked away, leaving the two men standing by the gravestones.

Theo exhaled, adjusting his glasses as he glanced at Vince. "That could have gone better."

Vince nodded, his face still troubled. "Yeah… but I think there's more going on here than he's letting on."

The two men exchanged a meaningful look before heading off the property, leaving the gravesite—and the mystery—behind, for now. Ethan watched them from a distance, his thoughts racing as he tried to piece together what they had said. The mansion's past, the strange painting, and their apparent recognition of Ben—it all gnawed at him, adding yet another layer to the already overwhelming puzzle of his son's disappearance.

"What did they want?" Claire asked as Ethan approached the back door, his face set in a scowl.

"Nut jobs. Ghost hunters," Ethan said, brushing past her into the kitchen. He dropped his hands onto the counter, gripping it as he let out a frustrated sigh. "Have you found Ben yet?"

Claire shook her head. "I don't know where that boy is."

Ethan straightened. "I'll search the grounds. You keep looking through the house. He's probably just exploring."

Without waiting for her response, he turned and strode to the nearby sheds.

Claire stood in the doorway for a moment, wringing her hands. She didn't like splitting up—it made the house feel emptier, the situation even more dire—but she had no choice. She turned back into the house and began searching again, her voice echoing through the hallways.

Clair's tone grew more urgent with every passing moment. She checked closets, peeked under beds, even opened the pantry. But with each empty space she uncovered, her heart sank further. Dread washed over her when she noticed his bed—placing a trembling hand on the covers, her fingers brushing over it as though searching for some sign.

"Oh, God…" she said. "He's been missing since last night."

For a moment, she stood frozen, her thoughts spiralling. How had she not noticed sooner? She had assumed he was somewhere on the property, safe, but the untouched bed told a different story—one that filled her with a terror she couldn't suppress.

Her panic rising, Claire turned and bolted out of the house, shouting for Ethan.

He came running from the sheds, his face alarmed. "What? What is it?"

"He's been gone since last night," Claire said, stumbling toward him. Tears brimmed in her eyes, and her hands gripped his jacket. "Oh, God, Ethan... we have to call the police. What if someone took him?"

Ethan's face hardened, though she could see the fear darkening his eyes. He placed his hands on her shoulders, trying to steady her. "Claire, don't jump to conclusions. We'll search every inch of this property first. He could still be hiding somewhere, or he might have wandered off. Let's not panic yet."

"Not panic? Our son is missing, Ethan! Missing! He's been gone all night! What if—" She choked on her words, unable to finish the thought.

Ethan pulled her into a brief but firm embrace. "I know, I know, Claire. But let's not waste time. You check the woods in front of the house—I'll cover the fields."

Claire nodded, wiping at her tears. "Fine—but if we don't find him soon, we're calling the police."

Ethan nodded.

Later, after a thorough search through the woods, Claire returned to the house. She headed straight to Ben's room, hoping against hope to find him there—perhaps curled up on his bed, or sitting on the floor surrounded by his toys, lost in some game. But the room was just as she had left it, the bed untouched and the air still. The sight of it made her chest tighten.

Swallowing back the rising panic, she turned and made her way to Olivia's room. As she stepped inside, she froze. Olivia was sitting on her bed, clutching Ben's pyjamas to her chest, her slight frame shaking as tears streamed down her cheeks.

"Olivia," Claire said, crossing the room in an instant. She sat beside her daughter and put an arm around her. "What is it? What's wrong?"

Olivia looked up at her mother, her face streaked with tears. "I think he went back in time, Mum. I think Ben's gone back."

"Oh, Olivia. Stop it. Just stop with that nonsense. Time travel is not possible. Please, tell me the truth—do you know where he is?"

Olivia held the pyjamas closer, her tear-filled eyes unwavering. "I think he's here, Mummy," she said. "But not in our time."

A chill ran up Claire's spine, her daughter's tear filled insistence sending an inexplicable shiver through her. It wasn't the first time Olivia had spoken about Ben disappearing into the past, but Claire had dismissed it, writing it off as a child's imagination, a way to cope with her brother's absence. But now, faced with Olivia's tearful certainty, Claire couldn't shake the unease creeping over her.

She pulled Olivia closer, stroking her hair. "Honey, we need to work together on this. Think carefully—did you see anything strange around the grounds last night? Anything at all?"

Olivia sniffled. "No... but I heard noises outside, near the trees. It was late, and I thought maybe it was just animals, but now I'm not so sure."

"What noises?"

"Footsteps, and voices. I couldn't tell what they were saying, but it sounded like men talking. I wanted to tell you, but I was afraid."

Claire's heart raced. Men? Could it have been the strangers Ethan had confronted earlier, the ones claiming to be ghost hunters? Could they have been involved in Ben's disappearance?

She kissed the top of Olivia's head, trying to steady herself. "It's okay, honey," she said, though her trembling words betrayed her growing unease. "You're doing the right thing by telling me now. We'll figure this out. I promise."

As Olivia nodded, Claire's mind whirred with possibilities. The boy the men claimed to have seen weeks ago, the strange noises near the trees, and Olivia's insistence about time travel—it was all too much to make sense of. But one thing was obvious: she wouldn't stop until she found her son.

With renewed determination, Claire stood, giving Olivia a reassuring squeeze. "Stay here for now, sweetheart. I'm going to talk to daddy and check the grounds again. If you remember anything else, anything at all, you come find me, okay?"

Olivia nodded, wiping away her tears as she breathed in the scent of Ben that still lingered on his pyjamas.

Claire left the room, her heart heavy and her mind racing. As she descended the stairs, she couldn't shake the chill that lingered in Olivia's words. If Ben wasn't here *now*... then where on earth—or in time—could he be? No, she refused the childish belief that her son was *time travelling*.

The police car's tyres crunched on the gravel driveway as it pulled away. Claire stood at the front door, her arms wrapped around herself as if to shield against the cold, though the chill came more from within than without. The past few hours had been gruelling, and the air in the house still felt heavy with tension.

Ethan appeared beside her, running a hand through his hair, his face etched with frustration. "Well, that was pointless!"

"They're just doing their jobs," Claire said, uncertain if she believed her own words.

Ethan sighed, leaning against the doorframe. "Yeah, well, asking if he's on drugs or someone's hurting him... it's not helping me find him."

Claire caressed his face. "They have to ask those questions, Ethan. They need to rule everything out and don't know Ben like we do."

Ethan placed his arm around her waist. "You're right. But it doesn't make it any easier."

Inside, Olivia sat on the stairs, clutching the old diary. She had been listening, her heart sinking as she replayed the questions the officers had asked. They didn't believe her parents—she could tell. They thought Ben had run away or was hiding somewhere nearby. The way they'd glanced at each other when Ethan mentioned the "wackos" from the Historical Society of Strange Phenomena said it all.

Olivia wanted to tell the police that Ben hadn't disappeared, but that something had pulled him into the past. But every time she opened her mouth, she imagined the sceptical expressions on their faces, and the words died in her throat.

"Olivia?" Claire's call broke her thoughts, and she looked up and saw her mother and father stepping back inside, their faces worn with exhaustion.

"They didn't believe you, did they?" Olivia said.

Claire exchanged a glance with Ethan, then said. "Honey, the police are doing everything they can, but they need more information."

Olivia continued. "They think Ben ran away."

"They're exploring every possibility. But they're wrong! Ben wouldn't just run off—we know that," Ethan said.

Olivia hugged the diary tighter. "What about those men—the ones from the Historical Society? What if they know something about what happened to Ben?"

Ethan frowned. "I told the police about them. I gave them every detail I could, but they didn't seem to take it seriously. They probably think those guys are just harmless eccentrics."

"But what if they're not? What if they saw something or know something about the house? Ben's been missing since last night, and no one's listening!"

Claire sat beside Olivia and put a hand on her knee. "I know it's hard. We'll keep looking, and the police will too. But we have to stay calm, okay? We'll figure this out."

"You're not listening to me. Ben's not here, Mum. He's not anywhere near here. He's... he's in the past. I know it sounds crazy, but I *know* it's true."

Claire hesitated, her hand falling away as she glanced at Ethan. His face was tense and unreadable. "We're not dismissing you, sweetheart, but right now, we need to focus on finding him here," she said.

Olivia looked away, her grip tightening on the diary. Her parents' worry and doubt bore down on her, yet she couldn't shake the certainty that her brother was out of reach—not because he ran away, but because time held him captive.

As her parents continued their search, Olivia remained on the stairs, her mind racing. She couldn't tell the police, and her parents were sceptical. She had no choice and had to find out more on her own.

Her eyes fell to the diary in her lap. Somewhere within its pages lay a clue, something that would lead her to Ben.

Later, Ethan was crouched on the wooden floor of the study, threading the last of the cables through a narrow hole in the baseboard. The faint scent of old wood and dust filled the air as he worked. Samuel knelt beside him, tightening the last screws to secure the satellite router to its stand.

Ethan had resisted this moment for weeks, determined to keep the house free from modern technology. He had wanted to embrace the simplicity of their new life here, away from the constant notification alerts and emails. But with Ben missing and no answers in sight, he couldn't afford to be stubborn anymore. He needed every resource at his disposal.

"There," Ethan said, standing up and brushing his hands off on his jeans. He reached for the power cable and plugged the computer in for the first time since they'd arrived. The machine whined to life, its screen glowing in the dim room.

Samuel watched him for a moment, his wiry frame silhouetted against the window. "Keep an open mind, Mr Wallace," he said. "You need to."

Ethan frowned, looking sceptically at the man. "What does that mean?"

Samuel smiled, but the intent behind it was impossible to read. "If you listen… you can hear the house talk."

"The house talk—what are you on about?"

"Every old house has its stories. This one, though… this one has more than most. You've felt it, haven't you? The way the air feels heavier in certain rooms? The way the floor creaks even when no one's walking on it?"

"It's an old house. They creak, they groan. That's not news."

"Maybe. Or maybe it's trying to tell you something. This place has a past, Mr Wallace. A past that doesn't enjoy being ignored."

Ethan let out a frustrated sigh, turning back to the computer. He wasn't in the mood for cryptic riddles or local folklore. "Right. Well, thanks for your help, Samuel," he said, dismissing the man as he began typing in the network setup instructions.

For a moment, Samuel lingered, his eyes seeming to absorb something unseen by Ethan. "Just keep your mind open," he said again, softer this time. "You never know what you might learn."

He turned and left the study, his footsteps fading down the hall. Ethan shook his head, muttering to himself as he focused on the screen. But as he worked, Samuel's words nagged at the back of his mind.

The house was quiet—too quiet. The kind of quiet that felt deliberate, as if the walls were listening. Ethan brushed the thought aside, chalking it up to his own nerves and exhaustion. As he got the internet running and the computer hummed to life—first time since the move—he couldn't help glancing at the doorway where Samuel once stood. The man's cryptic comment about the house stayed with him, a seed of unease he couldn't quite shake. And somewhere, as if carried by the draft that always seemed to blow through the house, a soft creak echoed. Ethan froze, his fingers hovering over the keyboard. The sound was subtle but distinct—like footsteps. He glanced behind him. The hairs on his neck stood on end, but the doorway was empty. He shook his head, letting out a short laugh. "It's an old house," he said, then returned to his work. But the unease lingered, wrapping itself around him like the unseen shadows of the house's secrets.

Upstairs, Olivia paged through the old diary. "Speak to me, my dear brother. Let me know if you are okay, please."

***

The boys cautiously made their way through the cramped passageways hidden behind the stone walls. Ben glanced at Daniel after accidentally stepping on his toes. "Sorry," he said. "Where are we now?"

"Eliza's chamber," Daniel whispered in hushed excitement. "Just a bit further, and there's a panel that opens into her closet."

As they crept forward, Ben spotted what he was after, tucked high on a wooden strut embedded in the wall. "Look! There it is," he said, pointing upward. "It's Eliza's diary! Help me get it."

Daniel crouched down and cupped his hands to give Ben a boost. "Very well, but make haste," he said with urgency.

Ben stepped into Daniel's hands, and with a grunt of effort, Daniel hoisted him up. Reaching out, Ben's fingers brushed against the worn leather cover of the diary. As he gripped it, a warm, soft hand slipped in from the other side of the wall, rubbing over his knuckles. He pulled back in horror, slapping his hand over his mouth, muffling a startled gasp. He thought he heard a boy's cry—shrill with fright—then a thud, and sudden, deafening silence.

"What is it?" Daniel asked, steadying Ben as he clambered down.

Ben landed beside Daniel, gripping the diary tightly. "Did you hear that?" he asked, trembling.

"Hear what?"

"A kid. I think I heard another kid in the closet... and I swear someone touched my hand when I reached for the diary."

"I heard nothing. Perhaps it was merely your fancy," Daniel said, glancing at the hidden panel leading into Eliza's closet.

Ben clutched the diary, his mind racing. He remembered the strange sensation of someone's hand touching his own when he first found the diary in his own time. Could it have happened again? And if so... who?

"I need to write something in the diary," Ben said.

Daniel frowned, still perplexed but nodding in agreement. "Let us make haste, then," he said, motioning to the panel. "But be quick about it."

Daniel knelt and pushed against a section of the wall, revealing a hidden panel near the floor that led into Eliza's closet. The opening was narrow, but just wide enough for them to squeeze through.

"Bloody hell." The panel's existence amazed Ben.

Daniel was less impressed. "Why are we here? We ought to explore the servants' passageways—that's where the key is, I daresay."

"I told you, I need to write something in the diary," Ben said again, crawling through the panel into the closet, afraid he might run into the boy he had heard earlier.

Daniel sighed but followed, passing the small oil lamp through the opening before squeezing in himself. The faint glow of the lamp did little to illuminate the room beyond as they stepped into Eliza's chambers.

It was midday, and sunlight streamed through the windows, softening the room's edges. Ben and Daniel exchanged a glance, both hoping that neither Lord Ambrose nor Lady Isadora would turn up from the adjoining chambers.

Ben opened the diary to a blank page, running his fingers over the fragile paper. "I need a pen," he said, glancing around the room.

"A pen?" Daniel asked, raising an eyebrow. "Do you mean a quill?"

Spotting one on Eliza's bedside table, Daniel picked it up and handed it to Ben.

Ben frowned, turning the quill over in his hands. "It's broken, I think," he said after trying to write in the diary.

Daniel chuckled, shaking his head. "Wherever are you from? You must dip it in the inkpot."

Retrieving a small inkpot from the table, Daniel dipped the tip of the quill and handed it back to Ben.

Ben attempted to write, only to release a frustrated groan as the first stroke left a large blot of ink on the page, smudging his thumb. He wiped his hand on his trousers.

"You'll get the hang of it," Daniel said, a faint smile tugging at the corner of his mouth, his eyes warm with amusement.

Ben tried again, this time producing somewhat legible writing. It wasn't as elegant as Eliza's neat, flowing script, but it would do.

Soon after, Ben closed the diary, satisfied. "Let's put it back where we found it and head to the servants' passageways."

Daniel nodded, giving Ben a look that was half approval, half exasperation. "You're a peculiar one, Benjamin," he said as they returned the diary to its perch.

Ben smiled but stayed silent, his mind racing to figure out how to retrieve the key.

***

Olivia turned the fragile, yellowed pages of the old diary, her fingers trembling. She nearly skipped the ones stuck together, assuming it was just age or a spill. But a faint blot of dried ink caught her eye, seeping through the edges. She had no memory of these pages. Carefully, she pried them apart, mindful not to tear the delicate paper. Ink smudges blurred the text, distorting the words. She tilted the diary toward the light, squinting as the letters gradually became legible.

Her eyes grew wide with astonishment as she made out the faint, uneven words on the page. There, amidst the faded ink and smudges, were the words that sent a jolt of electricity through her:

"Oliv... tell mum and daddy that I... still busy and... Eliza. Love you all, Be..."

There, preserved alongside the message, was the unmistakable print of a small thumb, smudged in black ink.

Olivia's hands flew to her mouth as a strangled gasp escaped her. Tears filled her eyes as she stared at the page, her heart pounding. It was Ben. It had to be Ben. His thumbprint? His handwriting—somehow it was all here, left for her to find.

"Oh my goodness," she whispered, excitement trembling through her. "Ben... it's you."

Her astonishment turned to overwhelming relief and joy. She jumped up from her bed, clutching the diary to her chest, and overcome with laughter and tears, she said, "Thank you, Ben! Thank you!"

She didn't stop to think or question how it was possible. All that mattered was that Ben had found a way to reach her, to tell her he was still out there somewhere.

Olivia called for her parents, her shouts echoing through the house as she bolted down the stairs.

Claire appeared first, stepping into the hallway with a look of alarm. "Olivia, what is it?"

Ethan came in from the kitchen, his face etched with concern. "What's going on?"

Olivia skidded to a halt in front of them, clutching the diary tightly as tears streamed down her cheeks. She thrust the book at them. "It's Ben! He's alive! He left me... he left us a message—look!"

Claire and Ethan exchanged a bewildered glance before focusing on the diary Olivia held out.

"Slow down," Ethan said. "What are you talking about?"

Olivia opened the diary to the ink-stained page, pointing at the faint writing and the thumbprint. "Right here! It's his handwriting—I know it is! He wrote to us, and he said... he said to tell you he's still busy and with Eliza!"

Claire stifled a gasp as she leaned in closer, her eyes scanning the page. "Oh my word," she whispered. "Ethan, look."

Ethan frowned, his scepticism warring with the undeniable evidence before him. He took the diary, holding it closer to the light. The faint message and the smudged thumbprint stared back at him, as real as the air they were breathing.

The writing was ancient and the same ink appeared to be used as in the other diary entries; however, it was undeniably Ben's handwriting. "This... this can't be possible, can it?"

"It *is* possible," Olivia said. "Ben's alive, and he's trying to talk to us! We have to help him, Mum, Dad—we have to rescue him!"

Claire reached for the diary, her fingers brushing over the ink-stained page. "Ben. Oh, my sweet boy..."

Ethan's jaw tightened as he stared at the evidence, his mind racing. He didn't understand how it was possible—none of it made sense—but one thing was clear: they couldn't ignore it. "All right, if this is real... then we need to figure out what it means. And we need to do it now."

Olivia nodded, her determination shining through her tears. For the first time since Ben disappeared, she felt like they were closing in on the answers they needed.

"Let's verify this before assuming. I'll call a friend of mine—a forensic detective—and ask him to see if this fingerprint matches Ben's. We'll need something with Ben's fingerprints on it to compare."

Claire's eyes lit up. "His water bottle! It's next to his bed!"

Before Ethan could say anything, Olivia bolted to the stairs.

"Olivia, wait!" Ethan called after her. "Don't touch it on the sides—grip it from the top nozzle only. We don't want to smudge anything."

"Got it!"

Ethan pulled his phone out of his pocket and snapped a clear photo of the thumbprint in the diary, adjusting the angle to capture the faint lines as clearly as possible. "I'll send him this photo, along with the bottle, for comparison, but will need to be careful about how I frame this. I can't tell him our son left a fingerprint in a centuries-old diary."

Claire frowned. "What will you say?"

"I'll tell him it's for a school project Ben's doing. Or make up some story about him experimenting with fingerprinting for science class. It'll sound innocent enough, and he won't think twice about it."

Claire nodded, though her worry didn't ease.

Just then, Olivia returned, carefully holding the glass water bottle by the top nozzle, as instructed, and handed it to Ethan.

Ethan took the bottle and inspected it for new smudges. "Good job, Olivia," he said, his tone softer than usual. He placed the bottle on the kitchen counter, next to a plastic bag he had retrieved for transport.

"Will it work, Dad?"

"It should. If the prints on this bottle match the one in the diary, we'll know for sure."

"And then what?" Claire asked.

"Then we figure out the next step," he said. "One thing at a time."

Olivia and Claire nodded, their eyes fixed on the diary.

Ethan grabbed a pen and jotted down a quick note to accompany the evidence, folding it into a clean envelope. He placed the water bottle in the plastic bag and sealed it, double-checking that everything was secure.

"Okay," he said. "I'll take this into town first thing tomorrow and send it to John. With any luck, we'll have some answers soon."

As he spoke, Olivia glanced back at the diary, her fingers brushing over its cover. She wasn't sure if a fingerprint test would bring them closer to Ben, but for the first time since his disappearance, they were doing something concrete—something that might help.

"I hope he hurries," Olivia said.

Claire put an arm around her daughter, pulling her close. "Me too," she whispered.

Ethan stood by the counter, his hands resting on the sealed bag, staring at it as if it held all the answers they needed. He removed the card he received earlier from the strange men. "I can't believe I'm going to do this." Then dialled the number listed on the back.

CHAPTER 9: ALLIES IN THE SHADOWS

"Mama, your diagram of the walls was wrong over here. Me and Benjamin got stuck." Daniel jabbed his finger at the map of the mansion's secret hallways.

"Benjamin and I!" Martha said.

Daniel scrunched his face in confusion. "I beg your pardon?"

"It's 'Benjamin and I,' not 'me and Benjamin'. We may be commoners, but we are not without pride." Martha straightened her posture, her chin lifting slightly.

Daniel rolled his eyes, his lips pressing into a thin line. Across from him, Ben smiled, a muffled snort escaping before he clamped a hand over his mouth.

Robert studied the diagram thoughtfully. "Have you considered concealing them behind the shelving in the pantry? If you smuggle them there, they might then sneak into the servants' quarters in the early hours."

Martha shook her head, her brow furrowing. "Nay, remaining hidden for too long would pose a great risk of discovery. The walls are a far safer option."

Daniel leaned over the table, tracing a section of the map with his finger. "What about here? The dumbwaiter's got a panel that comes off, and it leads to the passageways behind the walls. Can't remember if it goes all the way to the servants' rooms, though."

Martha's eyes lit up as a memory came back. Without warning, she swept Daniel off his feet and hugged him, making his cheeks turn red. "That's it, my clever boy! It goes right to their quarters—I used to play in those very walls when I was a girl. Just watch out for the spiders, mind you."

Ben gulped. "Spiders?"

"Oh, yes. The old walls are full of 'em. But don't fret, they're harmless... most of the time," Martha said with a laugh, her eyes twinkling.

Ben exchanged a worried glance with Daniel, who grinned. "Well, Benjamin, if you're lucky, maybe you'll even meet the queen spider."

"Hilarious," Ben said, rolling his eyes, a hint of a smile forming.

Robert cleared his throat to get everyone's attention. "Spiders aside, this might work. If the dumbwaiter leads to the walls in the servant rooms, it's our best bet."

Ben frowned, looking confused. "Why can't we just walk into the servants' quarters and take the key? Seems like the easiest way."

Martha grimaced, shaking her head. "Oh no, dear boy. That's far too dangerous. Old Grisham'll catch you the second you step near the door. His office has a big window that looks right at the servants' quarters. And the door? It's got a bell that rings every time someone goes in or out. Grisham hears everything. He's a nasty one, always watching, always waiting to catch someone out of line."

Ben screwed up his nose. "Who is this Old Grisham, anyway?"

Daniel leaned in, lowering his tone. "He's the head butler," he said. "And he's Ambrose's right-hand man. If Grisham catches you, he won't think twice about dragging you straight to Ambrose. Trust me, you don't want that."

Ben's stomach churned at the thought. Ambrose's name alone was enough to send a shiver down his spine. "Alright," he said reluctantly, his mind racing. "The only way is to sneak through the secret passageways, then."

Martha nodded, determination etched on her face. "Then it's settled. We'll get everything ready today and make our move at dusk."

Later, as the sun dipped below the horizon, offering respite from the oppressive heat of the day, Daniel's steed thundered toward the Wilson mansion. The horse's hooves churned up the dry earth, carrying the boys on their urgent journey.

When they got to the stone wall that marked the boundary, Daniel dismounted and secured his horse between the trees. He motioned for Ben to follow. They moved to the back of the house, concealed by darkness and bushes. Twice, voices nearby made them freeze and hold their breath until the coast was clear

When they reached the back door, Daniel knocked four times. Ben crouched low, pressing himself into the thick hedge.

The door creaked open to reveal Martha. Her eyes widened as she saw them. "Quickly, inside!" she said, glancing down the hallway. "The servants are all in the dining room, helping serve dinner. We haven't much time."

Daniel nodded and led the way through the kitchen, motioning for Ben to follow. "I know where the dumbwaiter is," he said confidently.

"Wait!" Martha said, staring at their feet. "Your brogues—give them to me! You'll need to go barefoot to stay silent."

"Oh, right!" Daniel kicked off his brogues. Ben did the same, handing them to Martha, who tucked them behind a cupboard for safekeeping.

The boys hurried through the kitchen and down the corridor. At the end of the hall, Daniel stopped in front of the dumbwaiter and slid it open. He reached inside, his fingers searching the cool, uneven stone until they found a hidden handle. With a determined tug, he opened a small panel, revealing a narrow passage just large enough for them to squeeze through.

"Come on," Daniel gestured for Ben to go first. Ben climbed in, twisting his body to fit through the cramped opening. Once both boys were inside, Daniel reached back and slid the panel shut, sealing them in the dark space.

The air was thick and stale. Daniel smacked his forehead, the sound sharp in the silence. "I can't believe it," he said.

"What's wrong?" Ben whispered.

"We forgot the lamp."

Ben let out a slow, exasperated sigh.

"I'll go get it. Stay here." Daniel wriggled back through the panel.

Left alone, Ben stood in the oppressive blackness, listening for any sound. The silence crowded his ears, broken suddenly by a deep, scolding shout. "You! Boy! What are you doing in the dumbwaiter?"

Ben's chest tightened as his blood ran cold. "Oh, no!"

He inched back to the trapdoor, his hands groping for the edge. When Daniel didn't return, he tried to push it open, but it wouldn't budge. Whether locked or jammed, it held firm. He calmed himself, closing his eyes and breathing slowly and deeply, as Claire had shown him.

"Think. There has to be a different way to escape," he murmured into the oppressive darkness. He moved carefully, his bare feet brushing against the gritty stone floor as he shuffled to his left. After a few steps, his hand touched a corner. The space split into two paths.

"Left or right?" He hesitated, trying to remember Martha's drawing. The image surfaced—faint and incomplete—but he chose the right-hand passage, convinced it was the way. Turning sideways, he squeezed into the narrow wall cavity, the rough brick scraping against his shoulders as he slid through the tight space.

He frowned, wondering if Daniel would have been able to fit through. A ripple of doubt tugged at him, but he pressed on, one slow step at a time, hoping the passage would lead somewhere safe.

Ben froze, every muscle locking in place. A faint, rhythmic, and unmistakable sound emerged from the darkness he had just left. Something stirred in the black void. The hairs on the back of his neck stood on end. Someone, or something, was there.

"Who… who's there?" he asked, wondering if his mind was playing tricks on him.

With a rising sense of panic, he pushed forward. Each step sounded louder than expected, almost like the silence was stressing his movements. He pictured the beast his mind had conjured, crouched just inches away, ready to pounce.

Then, something caught his shirt. The sudden tug sent a bolt of panic through him. Was it just the jagged edge of the stone, or was something gripping him, pulling him backward into the darkness?

Ben's heart raced. He yanked at his shirt, desperate to free himself, but the hold was unbreakable. His chest tightened as fear clawed at his throat. He planted his heels on the gritty floor and gave a fierce pull. Resisting the urge to scream, he pushed himself onward, slipping free from the confines of his shirt. He shuffled as fast as the narrow space would allow, his shoulders scraping against the rough walls. The blackness was unforgiving, and he didn't dare slow down, afraid of whatever might still be behind him.

Ben's next step found only air. His stomach lurched as he tried to pull himself back, but gravity seized him. With a jarring plunge, he fell, the impact softened by a rancid pool that swallowed him with a wet, sickening slosh.

He flailed, his hands skimming the viscous surface as he scrambled to stand. The stench hit him, sharp and overwhelming, clawing at his throat. Gagging, he fought the urge to vomit, pressing his hands to his mouth. The foul liquid reached his waist, clinging to his skin like a putrid second layer.

Wading through the slime, he realised the enclosing walls had vanished. The air broadened, heavy and stifling, though the darkness had eased. His feet slid on the slick bottom as he struggled forward, each step slow and laboured.

Ahead, a thin sliver of light pierced the gloom. He focused on it—the glow a fragile promise of escape. His body shivered, the cold biting deep into his muscles and making his movements clumsy.

Ben pressed on, teeth chattering, determined to reach the light before the darkness swallowed him whole.

Light spilled from a door at the top of the slippery stairs, and to Ben's delight, it stood open. He hadn't seen this house section before—navigating the dank room, passing a pile of coal in one corner and wood in another. A trail of wet footprints marked his ascent of the narrow steps to the passage near the servants' quarters corridor. Fear had faded, replaced by frustration, cold, and anger.

Ben stopped right outside Grisham's office. The large window overlooking the entrance to the servants' quarters loomed ahead. He crouched low, pressing his hands onto the wooden floor, and crawled past the window, careful to keep his silhouette out of view.

He needed to get back to the kitchen. But to get there, he had to pass by the office—a risky endeavour, let alone in the dead of night with the man himself likely still awake. Ben took a deep breath, steeling himself. He had no choice.

Just beyond the window, at the entrance to the office, his eyes fell on a board of keys mounted to the wall. The polished wood gleamed faintly, and among the assortment of keys dangling from their hooks, one stood out—the key he had been searching for. His heart leapt at the sight, and his fingers twitched with anticipation. It was so close, almost within reach.

Ben rose slowly, his back pressed against the open doorframe, and peered around the edge. The room was dimly lit by a single oil lamp. Grisham sprawled in his high-backed chair, his head tilted back, mouth slightly agape. A half-empty bottle of rum and a cloudy beaker sat on the desk in front of him, the sharp smell of alcohol lingering in the air. The man's chest rose and fell in the steady rhythm of deep sleep.

Ben hesitated for a moment, his pulse quickening. He glanced down at his soaked breeches, the water pooling at his feet. Tensing, he stepped inside, his feet making no sound on the polished wood. He moved with painstaking slowness, each step deliberate, his eyes darting between Grisham and the board of keys.

He faced the board and, with measured care, lifted the heavy key from its hook, his breath shallow as if even that might wake the head butler.

"Daniel?" Grisham's breath was thick with sleep, slurred. "What are you doing here, boy?"

Ben's blood turned to ice. He didn't dare move, his back still turned to the man. Grisham shifted in his chair, the leather creaking as he fumbled across the desk, knocking over the beaker with a dull *clink*.

"Thought I told you I'd deal with you in the morning," Grisham muttered, burping loudly. "Playing in the dumbwaiter at your age—disgraceful. Ought to know better."

Ben's mind raced. He swallowed hard, trying to steady his voice. "Yes, sir," he replied, imitating Daniel's deeper tone. He kept his face turned away, his body tense as a coiled spring.

Grisham grunted, his movements sluggish as he leaned back in his chair. "Get out of here, then. And don't let me catch you again, or you'll regret it."

Ben didn't need to be told twice. He slipped out of the office and didn't stop until he was well down the corridor. Only then did he allow himself to exhale, his chest heaving as adrenaline coursed through his body. He glanced down at the key clutched in his hand, a triumphant grin spreading across his face despite the lingering fear. He couldn't believe his luck.

But he wasn't out of danger yet. The kitchen was still a fair distance away, and the halls were far from empty at this hour. He pressed himself against the wall, listening for the telltale sounds of footsteps or voices. When he was certain the coast was clear, he darted forward.

Finally, he reached the kitchen. The familiar scent of bread and herbs wafted over, and he allowed himself a small sigh of relief. He was almost there. Almost safe.

A servant helping Martha clean the kitchen looked up in shock at Ben, who was standing in the doorway, shirtless, shivering and wet. "Oh dear, boy!"

Martha grabbed a large towel and wrapped it around Ben. She led him to the steps outside the kitchen, where Daniel was waiting.

"What happened to you?" Daniel stared at Ben, a stunned silence stretching between them.

Ben pulled the towel tighter around himself. "You don't want to know." Then, with a faint grin, he stuck his hand out from under the damp fabric, revealing a large brass key. "But look what I found."

Daniel's eyes widened as he leaned closer. "You found it— where?"

Ben told him the story, and to expect a stern talking-to from Grisham.

Daniel's curiosity gave way to a chuckle. "Do you suppose it's the right key?"

Before Ben could respond, Martha appeared, narrowing her eyes at Ben's slime-streaked legs and soaked towel, her voice cutting through the exchange. "Take the boy back to the farm to change into dry clothes!"

Daniel pinched his nose between two fingers and took a step

back. "And perhaps a bath while he's at it," he said, grimacing in mock disgust.

Ben rolled his eyes but couldn't suppress a faint smile. "Yeah, yeah. Laugh it up. At least I found something useful while you were off—what? Eating stew and cake?"

Daniel smirked. "Touché. Let's just get you home and cleaned up before you stink up everything."

After the soothing comfort of an old-fashioned bath in a metal tub and a hearty meal, Ben sank into a deep sleep. The day had been both thrilling and exhausting, filled with unfamiliar sights and strange, unspoken tensions. At eleven years old, he was well past his usual bedtime, his energy spent from the whirlwind of events. As he drifted off, his thoughts turned to his family in the present, their faces vivid in his mind.

In his dreams, the line between past and present blurred. He saw his mother's warm smile, his father's steady hands, and Olivia's knowing glance. For a moment, he thought he was back home, the unfamiliar mansion and its secrets nothing more than figments of his imagination. But whispers and faint laughter crept in, reminding him that safety was an illusion—and the mansion's secrets might follow him.

Ben woke to the rich aroma of sizzling bacon, imagining he heard Olivia calling him. Yet, the sound of distant chickens and Lily's cheerful humming grounded him in the moment.

Startled, he sat up, his heart pounding. His attention snapped to his breeches draped over the back of a wooden chair. He jumped from the bed, searching his pockets. A wave of relief washed over him as his fingers closed around the brass key. Gripping it, the cool surface calmed his racing mind.

"Mama said you could help me get some eggs for breakfast from the coop." Lily stood in the doorway with an expectant grin.

Ben hesitated, his thoughts racing. "I... need to go back. I need to save Eliza." His eyes fixed on the key as though they might whisper the answers he needed.

Lily tilted her head, undeterred by his urgency. Her hand slipped into his with surprising determination. "First, you need food for strength. Come on." She gave him a gentle tug, her bright smile leaving little room for argument.

Ben faltered but allowed her to guide him. He knew she was right; he'd need every ounce of strength for what lay ahead. They headed toward the chicken coop—yet his thoughts remained fixed on Eliza and the secrets buried in the basement.

Sarah's heart weighed heavy as she leaned against the kitchen doorway, watching Ben and Lily dart around the chicken coop. Despite her worry, she laughed as an irate rooster flapped and chased Ben, still in his nightshirt. The boy struggled to balance the basket of eggs, attempting to prevent them from tumbling to the ground.

"Just a wee boy." Sarah shook her head. "He doesn't deserve this responsibility."

"I agree," Robert said. "We'll get the key from Ben. I'll find another way to free Eliza."

Together, they watched as Ben tripped and landed with a thud in the mud. Lily sprang into action, shouting at the rooster and kicking at it with surprising bravery. Then, unable to resist, she launched herself at Ben, dissolving into a fit of giggles as they both tumbled into the muck.

By the time the children returned to the kitchen, their basket was full save for one cracked egg. Mud streaked Ben's face and nightshirt, and smudges from the scuffle marked Lily's hands. Their laughter was infectious, lifting the sombre mood in the house.

The kitchen soon bustled with life as Sarah plated eggs, bacon, and fresh bread. The family gathered around the worn table, their chatter filling the space. Ben took his seat, his eyes darting to Robert, who studied him with quiet intensity.

"Hand over the key, boy!" Robert's tone left no room for argument. "Henry and I will sort out a way to free Eliza today. You'll stay here and help Caleb with the cows."

Ben looked sheepish. The brass key was more than just a tool to free Eliza—it was his link to his family in the future, his only chance to return. He crafted a lie.

"I… hid the key," he said, avoiding Robert's piercing stare. "I'll go get it."

Robert's eyes narrowed, suspicion crossing his face, but he didn't press further. Instead, he gestured to the plate of food. "Sit down and eat first."

Ben sat, his mind racing as he picked at his food. He had to keep the key safe and make his move before Robert or Henry discovered the truth.

After breakfast, dressed in old but clean clothes, Ben slipped out the back door to the horses. His heart raced as he approached Caleb's steed, already saddled and grazing near the fence. The animal's size intimidated him, but he steeled himself, recalling the basics Daniel had taught him about riding. With a grunt of effort and a clumsy swing of his leg, he mounted, gripping the reins as the horse shifted beneath him.

"Hey!" Caleb looked up from the fence he was repairing. "What are you doing?"

Ben remained silent. He gave the horse an awkward nudge with his heels, and it lurched forward. His movements were unsteady, his body stiff as he struggled to keep his balance, but he didn't slow. The pounding of the horse's hooves matched the frantic rhythm of his thoughts.

Guilt twisted in his chest, heavy and unrelenting. He was stealing from the very people who had taken him in, shown him kindness, and offered him a place to belong. The betrayal was heavy on his heart, but he put it out of mind. He had no choice.

Ben was certain of one thing: he had to free Eliza himself. Something deep inside told him the mansion's grip on him would never loosen unless he was the one to act. He feared failure would trap him forever in the past, leaving him separated from his family. Determined, he rode for the mansion.

He found a hidden spot near the mansion and tethered the horse to a sturdy branch. "I'll be back for you later."

He crept through the sprawling back garden, weaving from cover to cover. His eyes scanned the towering walls as he considered how to slip inside without being seen.

The shout of a young boy broke the quiet. "On guard!"

Ben froze and peered over the hedge, searching for the noise. He saw Julian with a stick raised like a sword. "Julian?"

Julian turned. "Benjamin!" He ran to him and wrapped his arms around him. "What on earth are you doing here?"

"I need to get into the basement where Eliza is," Ben said, pulling the brass key from his pocket. "I have the key."

Julian's eyes widened. "You do? How'd you manage that?"

"It was hanging with the other keys in Grisham's office "

"There's a way in through the coal room. It connects to the basement with a secret passage."

"Coal room? I think I was there last night, but it smelled awful. There was this rotting mess I fell into—what was that stuff?"

"The old wine press. It's gone rotten, and Papa told the servants to clean it weeks ago, but they never finished."

"We're avoiding that, right?"

"Of course, not through there. I'll take you another way. Come on," Julian said, pointing to a coal chute at the side of the house. Ben followed as they approached the mansion, keeping low and quiet.

"How'd you end up in the winepress, anyway?" Julian asked, his nose wrinkling at the thought.

"It's a long story. I was trying to find my way through the passages in the walls when I accidentally fell in."

"That must've been horrid."

"It was. And freezing cold."

Julian stopped by a heavy chute door, running his hand along its edge. "Here we are. Help me with this," he said, gripping the handle.

Ben stepped beside him, his hand closing over the handle next to Julian's. Together, they pulled. The metal groaned, and the door slid open, revealing a dark shaft beyond.

"Wait here," Julian said, brushing dust from his hands. "I'll fetch a lamp from inside."

Ben crouched behind the open door, his heart thudding in his chest as he scanned the garden for any sign of movement. The wide-open space around him amplified every sound, exposing him. He tucked his knees closer to his chest, making himself as small as possible.

When Julian returned, he called out loudly, "Benjamin? Where are you?"

Ben stood, his head poking over the edge of the door. "Shush!

I'm here," he whispered.

Julian shook his head and handed Ben the lamp before stepping into the chute. "Come on. Let's move before someone spots us."

Dust billowed around them as the boys slid down onto the hard coal below. Ben scrambled to his feet, gripping the lamp in one hand. He brushed at his clothes with his free hand, but the effort only smeared the black soot further across his shirt and arms.

"This way," Julian motioned to a low doorway on the far side of the room. "Keep the lamp steady and away from the dust—it's dangerous."

Ben nodded, holding the lamp higher as he followed. The faint light revealed a cramped opening leading into another room. He ducked through; the stench hitting him immediately—a foul, sour odour that made his stomach turn. Recognition struck him like a blow.

"This is where I fell last night," Ben said, his face grimacing with disgust.

Julian stopped at the edge of the large, sloping stone basin, his face grim. "The pressing pool," he gestured to the stagnant water below. "It's filled with runoff now."

Ben raised the lamp, its dim glow illuminating the murky pool. Decaying debris floated on the surface—broken planks, smashed barrels, and tattered scraps of cloth. The stench of decay and fermentation was overwhelming, and Ben stepped back, the memory of his fall fresh in his mind.

"It's revolting." Ben's stomach churned. "No wonder it was so horrible. I couldn't see anything in the dark."

Julian gave him a quick, inscrutable look. "We're not going in there," he stepped around the edge of the pool. "There's another way. Over here."

He stopped in front of a wooden panel embedded in the wall. "This is it," Julian pushed the panel. It shifted with a low groan, then clicked open, revealing a narrow passage.

Ben stepped closer, the lamp's light casting uneven shadows on the damp walls of the corridor. The air inside was cooler, carrying the faint scent of earth and mildew, a sharp contrast to the stench of the pressing pool.

"This leads to the basement." Julian crawled through the

narrow opening and into the passage. He turned to Ben. "Stay close."

Ben glanced up at the ceiling above the pool, his eyes catching on a familiar sight. His shirt hung from a rusted nail near the narrow opening he had tumbled through the previous night. A wry smile tugged at his lips.

He shook his head, a soft laugh escaping as he thought back to his panicked flight. He had convinced himself a monster was chasing him in the darkness. But as he stared at the shirt, a sense of foolishness overcame him.

Still, his smile faded as the memory resurfaced. That presence—deep, steady, and suffocating—clung to his mind like a shadow. He shivered despite himself—trying to reason it away. "It had to be the wind." Yet even as he said it, doubt crept in, tightening around his thoughts. The sound hadn't seemed natural, like the gentle rustle of air through cracks. It had been close, deliberate, and almost alive. Ben tore his attention from the passage and refocused on Julian, determined to push the unsettling question aside—for now.

He crawled through the door into the narrow passageway, the floor blanketed with a layer of undisturbed dust. Each step sent tiny puffs into the air, making it clear this route was rarely, if ever, used. After walking a little way in, Julian stopped and pushed on a panel near the floor. With a soft creak, it swung open, revealing a small gap. He squeezed through, and Ben followed.

Ben emerged into a familiar space and paused, his eyes adjusting to the oil lamp-lit enclosure. "Yes, I recognise this." He stepped to the door at the back of the room and descended more stairs. The brass key was heavy in his hand as he slid it into the lock. With a firm turn, the mechanism clicked, and the door swung open.

Ben recoiled from the fetid air, a miasma of rot and dampness. Inside, Eliza sat on a narrow bed, her face pale but her eyes wide with disbelief.

"Eliza," Julian rushed forward, throwing himself into her outstretched arms. "I thought you were in London. I've missed you so much. Benjamin told me you were down here."

Eliza kissed the top of his head and hugged him tightly, tears streaming down her face. "Oh, my dear sweet brother, you shouldn't be here. If Papa finds you—" she pulled back to look at him.

"I don't care!" Julian cried. "Why has he done this—why?"

Ben stood near the doorway, his throat tight as he watched the reunion. He wiped at a tear that slipped down his cheek, unwilling to interrupt the moment.

Then a loud clunk echoed through the basement. Eliza's eyes widened as she pushed Julian back. "Quick, hide!"

The sound of approaching footsteps spurred Julian to dart from the room, to the hidden passageway, and back through the narrow opening. Ben turned and saw shadows moving across the dimly lit walls, accompanied by the faint clinking of bottles.

"Go!" Ben reached for the secret door panel and closed it behind Julian. He knew there wasn't enough time for his own escape.

"Benjamin, no!" Julian's muffled cry came from the other side.

Ben ran back to the room and Eliza. Her look of horror froze him in his tracks. She was staring past him; her face was pale and frozen. The hairs on Ben's neck prickled as he turned slowly. Standing in the doorway, arms folded and eyes narrowed, was Ambrose. His imposing figure filled the space, his gaze shifting from the open door to Ben. His face was stony and calculating, like he was trying to understand how the strange boy got there.

"I—," Ben started, but Ambrose raised a finger, silencing him.

"Orphan boy." Ambrose spat the words with disdain. "You are a complicated one." He stepped forward, his boots thudding against the stone floor. With one hand, he shoved Ben into the room, forcing him toward Eliza. Before Ben could react, Ambrose swung the door shut and locked it with a resounding click.

Ben stood frozen, his hands braced against the rough wood of the door. He couldn't believe what had just happened.

Eliza placed a trembling hand on his arm, pulling his attention back to her. The dim light of the single oil lamp cast her face in a ghostly orange glow. "You silly boy," she said, a tear rolling down her cheek. "You brave, but silly… silly… boy."

Ben's eyes met hers, the gravity of their predicament rooting him in place. The foul-smelling air closed in around them, and the faint sound of Ambrose's footsteps receded, leaving them in heavy silence.

"Oh, no... oh no..." Gasping for air, Ben trembled with blind panic, his eyes reflecting terror.

"Shh," Eliza pulled him into a comforting embrace. She held him close, stroking his hair with a gentle hand. "It's all right. Calm yourself."

"What are we going to do?" he said.

Eliza hesitated uncertainly. "I don't know. I've been here for so long. Surely Papa won't leave you here with me—"

Ben broke away from her, his panic driving him to action. "I have to find a way out! There must be a way out of here!" He darted to one corner of the room, running his hands along the damp, icy walls. He tapped on the stones, searching for any sign of weakness or a hidden passage. Moving to the floor, he crouched and searched for trapdoors, loose panels, anything that might lead to escape.

As he moved to the door, he pressed his ear against it. A muffled sound reached him, faint at first but growing louder. His brow furrowed as he concentrated. "What's that?" A low rumble echoed from beyond the door, the sound of heavy rocks toppling onto each other. Voices followed—indistinct but unmistakable— along with the metallic clink of tools and the grating scrape of stone against stone.

Ben gasped, his eyes widening in horror as the realisation hit. He spun to face Eliza, a frantic whisper escaping his lips. "He's walling us in!"

Eliza froze, her hands clenching the edge of the bed. The colour drained from her face as her mind caught up with his words. "No," she shook her head as though denying it would make it untrue. "He wouldn't—"

"He is!" Sweat beaded on Ben's forehead. "I heard it. He's sealing us in—forever."

The crushing reality of their predicament settled over them both. Ben stood motionless, his thoughts racing, while Eliza clutched her trembling hands to her chest. The rumbling continued, each sound another nail in the coffin of their hopes for freedom.

CHAPTER 10: THE MYSTERY DEEPENS

Dr Theodore Marlowe and Vince Colby finished arranging the strange devices, their wiry appendages snaking outward to connect with various measuring points. Patterns of data danced on a large monitor, captivating Theodore as his eyes darted between the shifting graphs.

Ethan stood back, watching the two men work, a knot of doubt tightening in his chest. Had he made a mistake in trusting them? Olivia leaned in closer, her face lit by the apparatus. Wonder sparkled in her eyes as she took in the intricate web of technology.

Curiosity overrode Ethan's hesitation. He bent forward, squinting at the equations cascading down the screen. The lines of data seemed endless. "What are you measuring?"

Theodore's face lit up. "Quantum fluctuations. We're monitoring real-time updates on particle behaviour. If we detect a fluctuation, we measure for corresponding changes in the gravitational field. That would suggest the presence of a wormhole—a bend in space-time itself. At least, that's the theory." He gestured at the room. "Your house is the only place we've observed anything like this. We're grateful you're allowing us to measure it."

Ethan's frown deepened. "That's a lot of science talk. In what way does this contribute to bringing our son back?"

Theodore's expression shifted, becoming more serious yet no less animated. "We believe your son is living in the past—on a parallel timeline to this one. Events that have already happened in that timeline are fixed—they can't be changed. But your son, being displaced, is different. If he were to wander near a wormhole, and if the conditions aligned just right, it may be possible to bring him back." He tapped a series of commands on a keyboard and pointed at the screen. "The key is finding that wormhole. It's the bridge connecting here to there."

Hope and disbelief warred on Ethan's face as he listened to the explanation. Olivia's eyes remained glued to the luminous data, her hand reaching for his as if she could will an answer into existence.

Vince turned to Olivia. "Where did Ben vanish? And where did he reappear?"

The grinning face of ET on Vince's t-shirt—a cowboy hat perched on the alien's head—felt absurd against the gravity of the moment. Olivia bit her lip, stifling a laugh that had no place in the current atmosphere. "He appeared out of nowhere in my room. But he didn't say where he disappeared from. I think it was his room." Without waiting for a reply, she led Vince down the hall, Ethan and Claire trailing behind.

Vince swept a handheld measuring device across the space as they entered Olivia's room. The device was silent, its glowing screen casting an eerie blue light over his face. His movements stopped where Olivia had found Ben's pyjamas crumpled earlier. "Got it!" he blurted out excitedly, startling them.

"What?" Ethan asked, stepping forward.

Vince's fingers trembled as he pointed to the display. 'There's a gravitational anomaly here—a wormhole entrance. The field pulses are faint but distinct."

The sound of pounding footsteps broke through the tension. Marlowe burst into the room, his chest heaving. "The instruments downstairs just lit up like a Christmas tree. We might be capable of amplifying the field, maybe even coax the wormhole to reopen."

Claire's heart leapt—a sensation she hadn't felt in weeks. "If we can do that, how do we bring Ben back?"

Marlowe looked at Vince before answering. "Ben needs to be in this room, or its 19th-century equivalent. If time runs parallel between worlds, his return to the exact spot where we last saw him depends on his presence there when the wormhole reactivates."

A sudden burst of static erupted from Vince's device. Amid the crackle, Ben's laughter broke through, clear and haunting. "*You are crazy...*" The sound faded as abruptly as it had come, leaving only the faint echo behind.

"That was Ben!" Claire's hands shot out, gripping Vince's wrists. "Get him back—please!" Her fingers curled against the cold metal as if sheer force of will could bridge the impossible gap between them.

Vince's face paled. In all their research, they'd theorised, hypothesised—but never proven. Until now. "What we heard... It might be a residual frequency, an echo caught in the fluctuations. A remnant of the past bleeding into the present."

Claire's grip didn't waver. "It wasn't just an echo. It was *him*. I know it."

"We'll try. But we have to wait until nightfall. That's when we would expect Ben to be in position," Vince said.

Marlowe fought to contain his excitement as he left the room with renewed determination. The family had witnessed something tangible—something real. Perhaps now, he thought, their scepticisms would fade.

He headed to Ben's room, his scanner set to the same frequency as Vince's. He swept it over the bed, the walls, and the floor. Nothing. Frustration gnawed at him as he moved to the en-suite bathroom. Still nothing. He turned to the door.

His eyes caught sight of the large walk-in closet. Though doubtful, he approached and aimed it inside. The device emitted a high-pitched whine; the meter spiking into the red. "So this is where you were when you journeyed to the past, Ben." Marlowe stared into the dim space as if it held the answers.

Cool night air, streaming in through open windows, chased away the summer's heat as pale moonlight fell across the floor. The men finished arranging an intricate array of giant magnets and coils around the hotspot, aligning each piece with meticulous precision. As they secured the last connection, Vince straightened and gestured to the far side of the house. "To be safe, everyone needs to move away from the anomaly."

Marlowe sat at the main terminal downstairs, his hand hovering over the control panel. His fingers brushed the button, tracing its edge as if to reassure himself it was there. His pulse pounded in his ears as he clutched the side of the table, the faint whine of the cooling fans droning in the background. They calibrated the device to increase gravitational fluctuation as soon as anything interrupted the anomaly by stepping into it from the 19th-century. Marlowe tightened his jaw, the pressure of their theory pressing on his chest as he prepared to act at the slightest sign of interruption.

He was dozing in his chair when the monitor suddenly lit up, showing a burst of activity. His eyes snapped open as he scanned the readings, waiting for the measurement to reach its peak. The moment the numbers aligned, he hit the button.

The house groaned and shuddered, as though seized by an earthquake. Furniture rattled, and a low rumble filled the atmosphere. Vince shouted for the family to stay put as he ran to Olivia's room. He reappeared in the doorway a few moments later, his face devoid of colour. "It worked—it's Ben."

Claire's heart surged with hope. She sprinted to the room, her tears blurring her vision. But as she crossed the threshold, her body froze. Sitting on the ground, clutching a tin soldier with trembling fingers, was not Ben. The pale, slender boy was smaller and younger than Ben. His blonde hair clung to his damp forehead, and his wide, terrified eyes scanned the room. He was shaking so violently it seemed as if he might shatter.

Claire staggered back. "It's not Ben," she said, the hope within her crumbling in the face of disbelief.

Olivia knelt beside the boy, her movements gentle. As she reached out, a jolt of recognition struck her. The boy's face matched the descriptions Ben had given and the ancient paintings she had seen throughout the mansion. She draped her arms around his small, quivering frame. "It's okay, Julian," she whispered, combing her fingers through his hair. The boy turned to her, his eyes brimming with fear, but he didn't pull away.

As the others crowded into the room, the air hung heavy with confusion and unease. Sweat beaded on Vince's brow as he frantically tried to make sense of recent events. The anomaly had worked—something had materialised. But it wasn't Ben.

Julian's lips parted as though he might speak, but no words

came. His gaze shifted to Vince, then to Claire, before settling on Olivia. The tin soldier slipped from his grasp and clattered to the floor. Julian's trembling intensified, and Olivia tightened her embrace, whispering assurances that no one else could hear.

Vince placed his hands on his head. "We need answers—this changes everything we believed to be true!"

Olivia led Julian by the hand to Ben's room. The boy's wide eyes darted around, taking in every detail. He studied the wallpaper, the wooden floors, and the banister of the staircase as they passed, a spark of recognition dawning in his face. He paused, his fingers tightening on Olivia's hand.

"This is…" Julian turned his head, looking down the hall, his lips trembling as he searched for words. "I know this place. It is… it is my home. Is this but a nightmare?"

Olivia faced him. "It was your home, Julian," she said. "A long time ago."

Julian stared at the hallway, his eyes darting to the doors, the walls, and the ceilings. "But it's not right. The lights… the pictures…" He trailed off as he gestured toward a framed photograph hanging on the wall—a black-and-white snapshot of the Wallace family, their modern clothing an alien sight to him. His confusion deepened as he noticed the electric fixtures glowing on the ceiling and the sound of a high-flying airliner.

Olivia squeezed his hand. "Things have changed over time, but it's still the same house. It's just… newer."

Julian shook his head, his blonde hair falling into his eyes. "It's not newer—it's wrong," he said, trembling. He looked down the hallway again, pausing at a door that seemed familiar. "My mama's chamber should be there," he pointed. "And my papa's study… but it looks different." He turned to Olivia, his eyes narrowing. "What's happening to me?"

Olivia reached out, brushing a strand of hair from his face. "Julian, this is still your home, just… in another time. You've travelled to the future, and things aren't the way you remember. But you're safe here, and we'll help you understand. I promise."

She led him into Ben's room, a space devoid of the tangled wires and glowing screens that had overwhelmed him earlier. The quiet, simpler atmosphere seemed to ease him, though he still glanced around at the unfamiliar furnishings. He hesitated by the bed, touching the fabric of the quilt with tentative fingers.

"This wasn't here," he said. "None of this was here."

"No, it wasn't. But we're here now, Julian, and we'll help you make sense of it all."

Julian sank to the floor, his small frame shivering as he wrapped his arms around himself. He felt strangely at home and yet a stranger in the room, a perplexing blend of his past and present realities. He stared at the window, distant, as if trying to piece together the fragments of his fractured reality.

Outside the room, Claire and Ethan lingered, confused. They had hoped to see Ben, only to find a boy from another century— a boy whose presence confirmed the impossible. The rhetoric they had dismissed as madness was now undeniable science, made real by the pale, trembling child they had only ever seen in the aged paintings adorning the library and halls.

In the quiet, Olivia sat beside Julian, her presence a small anchor in the chaos swirling around him. She placed a comforting hand on his shoulder. "We'll figure this out together."

Julian turned his head, his eyes locking onto hers. Though fear still shadowed his face, there was a glimmer of something else— perhaps hope, or at least a shadow of trust. He stood and walked over to a framed school picture hanging on the wall. "It's Benjamin!" he said, his eyes wide. "I understand now. Benjamin told me he was from the future—this is what he meant. He's from here."

Olivia rushed to his side, her pulse quickening as she followed his finger to the photograph. The image of Ben smiling like a dork in his school uniform seemed to take on new significance. "Yes… yes…" She turned to Julian, her brow furrowing. "Where is he now? Do you know where he is?"

Sorrow clouded Julian's blue eyes as they met hers. "Papa has locked him in the chamber with Eliza," he said, as though the words themselves pained him.

Olivia's knees buckled, and she sank to the floor, her hands pressing against the polished wood. "Ben returned to stop this from happening. Now he is in danger."

Julian crouched beside her, his slight frame stiff with

uncertainty. "He said he wanted to help her. But Papa locked them in together."

"No..." Tears welled in her eyes. "No, Julian. You don't understand." She gripped his hands. "Eliza—she's pregnant. She wrote it in her diary and your papa found out!"

"What does that mean—pregnant?"

" She's with child."

Julian's face paled, his wide eyes filled with fear and confusion. "No. Papa would never allow it!"

"Ben didn't just go back to help her. He returned to prevent this—to prevent her father from confining her, to rescue her. But he doesn't know how dangerous it is." Olivia ran to her father. "Daddy, Julian said that his papa has locked Ben in the room with his sister—daddy... don't let him die there!"

Clutching his daughter, Ethan frantically searched his mind for ways to save his son. He rushed to the scientists in a state of panic.

Working on the algorithms, Marlowe hunched over his laptop, his fingers flying across the keyboard. Despite his intense focus, a tremor in his movements betrayed the shock from the events. The realisation that, against all their previous theories, they had brought a historical figure into the future. It was a breakthrough—and a catastrophe—they had never prepared for.

"Theo, send me back—I need to save my son!" Ethan said, grabbing Theo's shoulders, his grip firm enough to shake him out of his concentration.

"I'm working on it. But we need to figure out the exact return point. I think it's the closet in his room, but if I'm wrong, you could end up in the wrong timeline. Who knows where—or when—you'd land?"

"Right," Ethan said, already heading for the stairs. "Let's do it."

Theo stepped in front of him, blocking his path. "It's not that simple, Ethan. We haven't pinpointed the correct—for lack of a better word—anomaly yet. Without it, the risk is far too great."

Ethan's jaw tightened, his eyes blazing with desperation. "I don't care! My son is in danger, Theo. Do something—now! Set up your gadgets in the closet and send me back!"

Theo frowned and hesitated. "I understand, Ethan, but we have to tread carefully. Sending Julian back as soon as possible is critical.

We don't know how long keeping him here might disrupt the historical timeline. The consequences could be... catastrophic." He handed Ethan a sleek recording device, its small red light blinking. "Take this with you. If we're attempting a dual transfer, we need to document everything. Any footage could be invaluable. Make sure you find your way to Olivia's—Julian's room by nightfall."

Ethan nodded and clipped the device to his shirt. "Fine. When I find Ben!"

"Understood. But remember, we'll only activate the gravitational field when the sensors detect significant fluctuations—our signal that you're near the wormhole's vicinity."

Without another word, Marlowe and Vince sprang into action, pulling out intricate devices and arranging them inside Ben's closet. The air buzzed with tension and the whine of machinery warming up.

Julian, standing a few steps back, stared wide-eyed at the flurry of activity. "What's happening?"

"They're setting things up to send you back home—to your time. Don't worry—you'll be safe," Olivia said.

"But what about your papa? Will he come with me?"

"That's the plan—just don't let go of his hand."

The faint glow of the equipment reflected in Julian's eyes as he nodded, clutching Olivia's hand. Meanwhile, Marlowe tightened the last bolt on the stabiliser, sweat trickling down his temple. "Ethan, get ready."

Ethan looked at Julian, his features softening. "I'll be right behind you, kid. You're not doing this alone."

The house shuddered as the machines powered up, signalling their high-stakes gamble with time.

"It's ready," Marlowe said, ushering Ethan and Julian to the closet. He gave a hesitant wave. "Godspeed!"

Ethan sat next to Julian on the floor, wrapping a protective arm around the boy's trembling shoulders. "It's okay. We've got this," he said, winking to mask his own nerves. Julian gave a small, hesitant nod, clutching Ethan's hand.

The air in the room seemed to thicken, charged with static electricity and smelling of ozone. The house lurched on its foundations, a low groan emanating from the walls as if the mansion itself protested against the strain. A lingering vibration rippled through the floorboards before everything fell quiet.

Theo stepped back, his knuckles white from gripping the doorframe. "It's done," he said, staring at the closet as the machines powered down.

Claire stood motionless outside the closet door, her hand hovering over the handle. She swallowed hard, then pushed it open. It was empty. She stumbled backward, a dismayed whisper escaping, "I... I didn't even say goodbye."

Theo appeared behind her. "If everything went as planned, they're already back in Julian's timeline. We've done all we can."

Claire's eyes remained fixed on the space, her thoughts racing with what-ifs. A subtle ozone odour lingered in the air, a ghostly reminder of the leap Ethan and Julian had taken. "What if something went wrong?"

Theo remained silent.

***

Julian flailed his arms, his stomach churning as though he had just fallen from a great height. The familiar scent of Eliza's bedroom—perfume and polish—filled his senses, grounding him.

"Ben's papa?" he said, twisting his head from side to side. But the room was empty.

Footsteps echoed from the hallway, growing louder with each step. Julian stiffened, his body rigid with dread. The door creaked open, and he tensed, waiting for something—or someone— terrifying to appear.

Instead, Isadora stepped inside. She moved with her usual grace, the soft rustle of her gown the only sound breaking the stillness. She stopped and looked at her son, her brow creased with concern.

"Julian," she said. "What is the matter, child? You look as though you've seen a ghoul. What are you doing in Eliza's closet?"

Julian wiped at his damp face with trembling fingers. "Nothing, Mama. I just feel a little... poorly," he murmured, his words trailing off before his stomach heaved. He vomited where he sat, a sour tang filling the air.

Isadora recoiled, her worry turning to dismay. "Oh, Julian," she said, exasperated. She turned to the hallway and called, "Fetch a maid at once!"

Kneeling beside him, she pulled a lace handkerchief from her sleeve and dabbed his forehead. "Julian, have you been sneaking into Cook's cakes again?"

Julian shook his head, staring at his soiled hands. "No, Mama," he said weakly.

The maid arrived a moment later, carrying a bucket and rags. Isadora stood, her tone brisk as she instructed, "Clean him up and deal with this mess. Then see that he's bathed."

"Yes, madam," the maid said, crouching to help Julian.

Isadora lingered for a moment, watching her son. "If something is troubling you, you must tell me," she said firmly. "You know I shan't tolerate secrets."

Julian briefly looked up at her. He wanted to speak, to explain the strange events that had shaken him, but no words came. He allowed the maid to guide him to the adjoining washroom.

Isadora smoothed her gown, casting a last glance at the mess on the floor. She sighed, exiting the room. Whatever had upset Julian, she intended to find out.

***

Ethan was lying on his stomach, then rolled over. Disoriented, he forced himself upright, his palms pressing against the damp. He jabbed a finger into his ear, trying to make sense of the muffled void where sound should have been—panic tightened his chest.

As his vision sharpened, the scene before him came into focus. He was on top of a dilapidated brick pile, overgrown with ivy that had been growing for decades. The realisation struck him—this was more than rubble. It was his house. Or what had once been his house!

A faint voice broke through the haze, calling to him from what seemed like a great distance. He swivelled his head, trying to locate the source, but his senses were dulled, sluggish. Then, without warning, his hearing returned in a sharp, almost painful rush. A bullet hissed past his ear, embedding itself in the bricks behind him with a dry, violent crack, sending up a spray of dust.

"Ethan! This way, and hurry!" The voice, now close, came from an old man crouched several metres away behind a broken wall. Adjusting the bandana over his face, he pulled its faded fabric taut against his nose and mouth. Tufts of grey hair escaped the edges of his head covering.

Ethan blinked, his thoughts struggling to keep up. "Who are you? How do you know my name?"

"There's no time for pleasantries," the man snapped, his weathered face set with urgency. "Get to cover!"

Another bullet sliced through the air, narrowly missing Ethan's shoulder. The sharp report of a distant explosion followed, shaking the ground. A plume of fire and smoke erupted several blocks away.

Without thinking, Ethan hurled himself forward, landing hard behind the crumbling wall. His mind reeled, a thousand questions vying for attention, but one thought drowned out the rest: something had gone wrong.

"What's happening?" he said, staring out in disbelief. Where lush green fields had once stretched endlessly, dotted with grazing sheep and whispering grass, now stood a war-ravaged city. Shell-ridden buildings loomed like jagged tombstones, their walls scarred by bullets and shattered by explosions. Fires raged among the rubble, spewing black smoke into a sky that had once been clear and serene. The crack of gunfire pierced the air, mingling with the distant rumble of artillery and the desperate shouts of unseen men. The acrid stench of burning rubble replaced the earthy scent of his farmland, and the ground beneath him quaked with each explosion. He flinched as another blast erupted nearby, a fiery plume of dust and debris where a peaceful meadow should have been. His mind reeled, struggling to reconcile the tranquil past he knew with the nightmare unfolding before him.

The old man didn't answer. Instead, he peered over the edge of the wall, scanning their surroundings. "We don't have time to chat. You're not safe out in the open—follow me!"

Ducking low to avoid a whistling projectile, Ethan sprinted after the old man, who moved with the surprising agility of a gazelle. The old man vaulted over shattered walls and piles of rubble with practised ease, his feet finding purchase where Ethan stumbled. The air was thick with smoke and dust, choking his lungs and stinging his eyes, but he pushed forward, his legs burning with every step. A deafening explosion erupted somewhere to his left, sending shards of stone clattering around him like hail.

Before he could react, something slammed into his side with brutal force, driving the air from his lungs. Pain lanced through his body as he crumpled to the ground, gasping and clutching his ribs. The edges of his vision blurred, the world spinning in a dizzying whirl of grey and orange light. He tried to rise, but his strength gave out. The shouts and gunfire around him faded into a dull roar, and then everything went black.

Ethan drifted in and out of consciousness, trapped in a nightmarish loop that offered no respite. The dreams came in fragments, strange and repetitive, each one more tormenting than the last. He was running through an endless void; the ground crumbling beneath his feet as he reached for Ben. His son was always just out of reach, his hand slipping from Ethan's grasp no matter how desperately he tried to hold on. Ben's cries echoed, growing fainter as he tumbled into the darkness, leaving Ethan grasping at empty air.

The scene shifted, dragging him into another dream. He saw his wife and daughter standing in the distance, their faces blurred by a hazy light. They were calling out to him, filled with urgency. He shouted back, his throat raw, but they didn't respond. He tried to move closer, his legs heavy as if wading through water, but no matter how hard he pushed forward, they remained far away. Their calls grew fainter, swallowed by a suffocating silence, and Ethan's chest tightened with helplessness.

He groaned as he regained consciousness, his head throbbing and his ears ringing from the blast. The world around him was a blur of smoke and debris, but he could make out the figure of the old man crouched at his side, his weathered face etched with concern.

"You're okay," the old man said. "It was just a concussion blast. You took a hard knock, but you'll live. Come on, we can't stay here—we need to keep moving."

Ethan blinked, trying to clear his vision as the old man helped him to his feet. His legs wobbled, and a wave of dizziness threatened to pull him back down, but the old man's grip was firm. "Stay with me," the old man commanded. "We're not safe yet."

CHAPTER 11: JULIAN

Julian eyed the smallest horse in the stable, his grip tightening on the wooden rail as memories surged back—the jarring fall, the bruises, and the sting of humiliation when one of the larger horses had thrown him during his first riding lesson. Since that day, he had avoided the stables, retreating to the comfort of his room where his tin soldiers waited, a predictable army he could control.

But this time was different. He needed a horse to reach the Whitfield family miles down the road. Ben and Eliza were in danger, and Julian couldn't bear the thought of failing them. The brief visit in the future had forced him to summon courage he hadn't known he possessed.

He glanced at the house, knowing there was no time to waste. With quiet determination, he stepped forward. The horse snorted and tossed its head; the motion reminding Julian of how much he had avoided this moment. He reached for the reins, his hand steady despite the doubt gnawing at him. If he was going to save them, he needed to start here—with the courage to climb back into the saddle and ride for help.

The horse reared onto its hind legs, its front hooves pawing at the air as if to ward him off, making Julian stumble backward into a pile of warm, fetid manure. A loud, piercing whinny burst from its throat, echoing through the stable, a sound laced with both alarm and warning. The horse's mane whipped with the sudden movement, adding to the spectacle of its hesitation and fear.

Daniel rushed to Julian's side, gripping the bucket of feed as he hauled him to his feet. "What on earth are you doing?" he asked, pulling Julian upright in one swift motion.

Julian grimaced, smearing manure onto his trousers. "I need to get to the Whitfield farm. Papa's locked Benjamin up with Eliza!"

"He's locked them up? When?"

"Last night," Julian said, scanning the stable shadows, as though his father might step out at any moment. "At least, I think it was last night. I wanted to come for help, but..." His words faltered, and he clamped his mouth shut.

"But what?" Daniel pressed.

Julian hesitated, his mind racing. He couldn't tell Daniel about the vision, the impossible future he'd seen—it would sound mad. "It doesn't matter," he said, straightening. "I just need to get to the Whitfield farm. Will you help me or not?"

Daniel studied him, his temple pulsing. "We'll have to hasten. If your father finds out..." He let the thought hang, grabbing a nearby saddle and tossing it toward the smallest horse. "You'll have to ride alone—I need to find my mama and tell her. Can you manage it?"

Julian inhaled. "I'll manage it!"

Daniel steadied him as he climbed into the saddle. "Hold tight, and remember—you're riding the horse, not the other way around."

As the horse shifted under him, Julian swallowed his fear and straightened. There was no turning back now.

He adjusted to the steady rhythm of the trot, each bounce in the saddle a little less jarring than the last. When he urged the horse forward, its pace quickened, and before long, they were galloping along the path. The wind tugged at his jacket and tousled his hair. A grin stretched across his face, wide and fierce, as exhilaration coursed through him.

The horse veered left, muscles surging as it chose its own path. Julian clutched the reins, almost toppling as his boots slipped from the stirrups. He scrambled to regain them, his chest tight with the rush of fear. A shaky laugh broke from him, but his grip faltered. The leather bit into his palms as he tightened his hold and leaned forward, steadying himself. He had never felt so alive.

The open air stretched before him, and for the first time, Julian felt free. He had spent so many hours cloistered indoors, retreating to the safety of his room, while others ventured into the world beyond. His mother's words echoed in his mind, warning him of risks and unseen dangers.

He straightened his back, his grip steady, his determination growing with each stride. Benjamin wouldn't have hesitated to take a chance like this. Julian had envied his courage—the way he faced everything head-on. No more excuses, Julian thought. No more hiding. If he wanted to be the type of person who could save Ben and Eliza, he would start here—with every gallop carrying him closer to the man he wanted to become.

As he approached the fields, he caught sight of Lily and Sam darting between the sheep, their laughter ringing out like a melody carried on the breeze. Julian raised a shy hand in greeting, the gesture small and tentative. How he wished he had friends like them—companions to laugh and play with, to chase through open fields.

The older Whitfield children, busy with their farmhouse chores, glanced his way. They exchanged confused looks but returned his wave with hesitant gestures before watching him ride past, curiosity etched into their faces.

Julian slowed the horse as he neared the farmhouse porch, unease creeping in. The thrill of the ride faded as he eyed the steps, wondering how he'd dismount without making a fool of himself. His stomach churned with doubt. What if he fell? What if they laughed?

"Master Julian?" Sarah's voice pulled him from his thoughts. She stood on the porch, wiping her hands on a dishcloth, her brow furrowed in surprise.

"Good day, madam," Julian said, straightening his back. Without thinking, he reached up to tip a hat that wasn't there. Realising his mistake, he dropped his hand, heat rising to his cheeks.

With newfound determination, he swung his leg over the saddle to dismount. But his boot caught in the stirrup, sending him spinning sideways. He landed with a thud, a puff of dust rising around him. For a moment, he lay flat on the ground, blinking at the bright blue sky above.

"Oh dear child, are you hurt?" Sarah said, dropping her rag and rushing to his side. She crouched down, pulling him to his feet and brushed the dust from his clothes.

"I... I'm fine, madam," Julian said, brushing at his trousers to help, though his pride stung more than his body. His eyes fell upon Lily and Sam, who, having paused their game in the fields, regarded him with amused, yet worried, faces. His cheeks burned again, but this time, he managed a sheepish smile.

"Well, you gave me a fright," Sarah said, smoothing her apron. "Let's get you inside. You look like you've had quite the adventure."

Julian nodded, patting the horse's neck before following her into the house. Despite the tumble, a small smile tugged at the corner of his mouth. He might have fallen, but he'd ridden here alone, and that was something he'd never thought he could do.

Sarah guided Julian into the sparse sitting room, where a narrow cot tucked against the wall revealed the dual purpose of the space. She gestured for him to sit on the well-worn armchair while she settled herself on a low wooden stool. The tension in her face deepened as she leaned forward, her hands clasping in her lap.

"What is it, child? Why are you here—do you know something about young Benjamin?"

Julian hesitated, his throat tightening as he tried to find the words. "Yes, that's why I've come," he said, brushing at the dust clinging to his sleeve. "Papa... he's locked Benjamin up. He's with my sister, Eliza, in a chamber down in the wine cellar. I didn't know where else to go. I tried to tell Mama, but she wouldn't believe me. She thinks Eliza's still in the city." He swiped his face against his shoulders, blotting the tears that threatened to fall.

Sarah's face reddened, and she gasped at the revelation. Fear for Benjamin's safety overcame her, his image flashing before her eyes. Her hands gripped the edge of the stool, her knuckles whitening. "I knew it," she said. "I told them he was too young for this—to be sent there alone. That's why I begged him to stay here."

Julian's hands fidgeted in his lap. "He's my best friend—and my sister. Please, I don't know what to do." He bit the inside of his cheek, fighting the urge to break down. His father's words echoed in his head, a constant reminder of his inadequacy. He wouldn't cry now, not in front of Sarah.

Sarah took his hands in hers. "You've been brave, Julian Braver than most grown men would be. And I won't let anything happen to Benjamin or your sister. You have my word."

Julian nodded, his resolve sharpening. "What do we do now?"

Sarah rose, resolute. "We get help. If your father's done what you've said, then we'll need more than just my family to make this right."

A faint vibration rattled her stool. Sarah frowned, lowering a hand to the ground as if to confirm the sensation. Her pulse quickened when she realised what was happening. The tremor swelled into a thunderous roar, the unmistakable drumbeat of hooves.

Through the front window, a storm of dust enveloped the air as horsemen came to an abrupt halt before the farmhouse. One rider, towering above the others, called out in a commanding baritone, "Julian!"

Julian shot to his feet, his face drained of colour. He clutched Sarah's arm. "Hide me—please!"

Before she could respond, Lily darted into the chamber from the back door, brandishing a stick, her eyes blazing with determination. Sam followed, a blend of curiosity and worry on his face.

"Mummy, do we fight?" Lily said, gripping the stick like a sword.

"No, Lily," Sarah said. She crouched to her daughter's level, locking eyes with her. "Take Julian and hide by the brook. Don't let anyone see you. Stay low and stay quiet."

Lily didn't argue. She seized Julian's hand and led him out the back without another word. The door creaked, then slammed shut.

Sarah smoothed the wrinkles from her skirt as she approached the front door. The air was thick with the earthy tang of horses and dust. She squared her shoulders and opened it.

"Lord Wilson," she said, holding herself steady. "What brings you to my doorstep today?"

The man atop the huge black stallion glared at her, his broad shoulders casting a shadow over the threshold. His horse pawed the ground, its wild eyes mirroring his temper.

"Where is Julian, woman? Do not try my patience with your falsehoods."

"Julian? I don't know what you mean. Is he missing?"

Ambrose Wilson leaned forward, his gloved hand tightening on the reins. "This is the horse he was riding," he said, motioning to the nearby chestnut gelding, its flanks marked by sweat. "Now, where is he?"

Before Sarah could answer, the rhythmic clatter of hooves drew everyone's attention. Martha appeared, riding astride a bay mare, her skirts hiked just enough to reveal the sturdy boots beneath. A determined yet calm look was on her face, her chin held high.

"I must apologise on behalf of my son," Martha said. "He took the horse for a frolic. I assure you, I shall punish him for his disobedience."

Wilson's dark eyes narrowed as he scrutinised her. His lips curled into a sneer. "Do you expect me to believe such a tale? Julian's mischief has brought enough grief to my household. If you see him, you will inform Lady Isadora. She is beside herself with worry."

Martha nodded gravely. "Of course, my lord."

Wilson lingered, studying the farmhouse as if it might reveal some hidden truth. Then, with a curt nod, he reined his horse around. The riders turned as one, the thunder of hooves fading as they retreated down the lane.

Sarah exhaled, her composure slipping. "Martha, we need a plan. This isn't over."

Martha slid from the saddle, brushing dust from her gloves. "Then we'd better think fast."

Daniel's horse skidded to a halt, its sides heaving, foam flecking its coat. He swung down, boots hitting the dirt with a thud. "What's going on? Was Lord Wilson looking for Julian?"

Sarah stepped forward, twisting her hands in her apron. "Daniel, go to the brook. Find Julian, Lily, and Sam. Tell Julian his papa's gone—it's safe to return to the farmhouse."

Daniel's jaw tightened. He glanced toward the brook, then back at Sarah. Without a word, he mounted his horse. The animal snorted, tossing its head as he urged it forward, hooves churning the soft ground.

Robert burst from the grain fields, his boots pounding the dry earth. He dabbed at the sweat streaming down his face, his shirt clinging to his back. Reaching the porch, he braced himself against the post, chest heaving. "What did that scoundrel want?"

Sarah's fingers trembled as she clasped them over her lips. "He was looking for Julian. The boy came to us for help. Ambrose has locked Ben up—with Eliza. That poor child must be beside himself."

Robert scanned the horizon, where the dust from Ambrose Wilson's posse still hung in the air. "That's it, then," he said, turning to Sarah. "It's a risk to the farm, to everything we've built. But I've got to confront Ambrose. Ben's in danger, and so is Eliza. We ride out as soon as Julian's back safe. That boy's been through enough. I won't drag him deeper into this."

Sarah nodded, her eyes glistening. She stepped closer, her hand brushing his arm. "Be careful, Robert. Ambrose isn't one to back down."

"Neither am I," he said, pushing off the post and heading for the barn.

The back door slammed open, banging against the wall. Sarah stepped into the kitchen, her eyes widening at the sight before her. "Good heavens, boys! You're soaked to the bone!" She grabbed two towels from the hook by the stove and draped them over Julian and Sam, rubbing their shoulders.

Lily stood by the table, stifling giggles behind her hand. "They jumped in the brook when Daniel came along."

Julian shivered, water dripping from his hair onto the floor. "We thought it was my papa," he said, his cheeks flushing as he stared at his boots.

Sarah shook her head, her hands darting to dry them off. "Let's get you warmed up as soon as possible. We need to get you back home before your papa tears the countryside apart." She placed a hand on Julian's shoulder. "Don't fret. Robert's going to help Ben, but we need to get you home first. Your papa's already on edge, and the longer you're gone, the worse it'll get."

Julian nodded, his teeth chattering. "I didn't mean to cause trouble."

"You didn't. You're a very brave lad for riding out here for our help," Sarah said. "But we've got to hasten. Come on, let's get you dried off and ready to go."

The kitchen felt warm, the scent of bread baking in the oven mingling with the dampness clinging to the boys.

As night fell, tranquillity enveloped the farm. A chorus of frogs and crickets rose from the fields, their song weaving through the warm night air. The horizon glowed as the moon climbed, its pale light spilling across the farmyard. Julian tugged on the last of his clothes, the fabric still warm from drying in front of the sitting room fireplace. Sarah had insisted they eat bowls of hearty soup while they waited.

Sarah led Julian to Daniel's horse and helped him climb onto the back, behind the saddle. "Take Julian the back way. Don't let anyone catch you. Drop him off at the boundary fence near the river."

Julian nodded. "I'll tell Mama and Papa I was playing by the river and fell asleep under the willow."

Sarah reached up and patted his hand, her calloused fingers warm against his skin. "You're a good boy—come back and visit. You are always welcome here."

Julian's chest tightened at her words. He managed a small smile, but inside, a deep ache stirred. He wished he could stay here, in this warm, bustling farmhouse, instead of the cold, echoing mansion he called home. His mama loved him, he knew that, but her love felt more like a cage than a comfort. She hovered, fretted, and worried, but she never hugged him, never said the things that made him feel like he belonged.

Daniel mounted the horse in front of him, settling into the saddle. "Hold on tight."

Julian wrapped his arms around Daniel's waist as the horse turned and moved, its hooves crunching on the gravel path.

Sarah stood in the moonlight, watching them go. Julian glanced back once, the farmhouse glowing in the distance. For a moment, he let himself imagine what it would be like to live there, to wake up to the smell of bread baking and the sound of laughter instead of silence. But the horse carried him forward, and the fantasy slipped away, leaving only the cool night air and the steady rhythm of hooves on dirt.

Daniel followed the river upstream to the boundary wall, keeping an eye out for any of Ambrose's men. He dropped Julian off near a grove of weeping willows.

Having thanked Daniel, Julian dashed between the willows, emerging on the other side. This time, he wanted to be seen. He needed to be seen. The mansion loomed ahead, its windows dark except for a faint glow from the kitchen. He slipped through the back door, the hinges creaking, and hurried across the polished floor, his damp boots leaving faint marks. The grand staircase stretched before him, its ornate banister catching the dim light. He took the steps two at a time.

Isadora clapped twice, slicing through the silence. "Where have you been?"

Julian froze, one foot on the next step. He turned to face her. She stood in the parlour's doorway, her arms crossed. "Mama, I... I fell asleep by the river."

"Do not deceive me, Julian!"

"Pray, do not be angry with me."

"Oh, Julian, you had me beside myself with worry. Your papa is out searching for you. He's been tearing the countryside apart. Get upstairs and into bed at once. I'll deal with your papa when he returns."

Julian nodded, relief flooding through him. He turned and hurried up the stairs, his boots clattering against the wooden steps.

Pounding at the front door echoed through the hall. Isadora strode across the foyer, brushing past the maid, who was hurrying to answer it. She opened the door, her eyes narrowing at the sight of Robert Whitfield standing on the steps, Caleb and Henry behind him. "What brings you here at this hour, Mr Whitfield?"

Robert doffed his hat, looking grave. "Apologies for the disturbance, Lady Wilson. Is his lordship at home?"

Isadora studied his face, noting the tension in his jaw and the fire in his eyes. "He's not. He's out with his men, searching... Can I assist you?"

"We've reason to believe he's locked a boy, Benjamin, and your daughter in the wine cellar."

Isadora recoiled, her lips curling in disbelief. "That's

preposterous! My Eliza is in the city, serving as a liaison for one of my husband's enterprises. Benjamin is here—he's with my son."

Robert exchanged a glance with Henry, then turned back to Isadora. "Pray, Lady Wilson, allow us to inspect the wine cellar. It will ease our concerns regarding the tales we've heard."

"This is outrageous!" Isadora snapped, lifting her chin.

Julian appeared at the foot of the staircase, his face pale but resolute. "Please, Mama. Benjamin's gone, and I'm dreadfully worried," he said, sorrow etching his youthful features. This was the moment he'd waited for—the chance to prove his friend and sister were prisoners in the basement. That day, Benjamin had pushed him into the secret passage, ensuring his safety while sealing his own fate. Julian couldn't shake the guilt that clung to him ever since.

Isadora hesitated. "Very well. Make it quick, before Lord Wilson returns." She led them down the hall to the cellar door.

Robert descended the narrow wooden steps, holding the lamp high. Its dim light skittered over racks of wine barrels and bottles. He scanned the room, searching for the hidden door Julian had described. There was nothing—just stone walls, the scent of aged oak lingering in the air.

Julian rushed to the far side of the room, his hands pressing against the cold stone. "The steps—they were here, leading down to the door!" he said in alarm.

Robert turned to him, his brow furrowed. "There's nothing here, lad." He looked at Isadora apologetically. "Forgive the intrusion, madam. We'll trouble you no further."

Julian dropped to his knees, his hands scrabbling over the wall. "Wait! Please! The steps, the door—they were here!" His eyes widened. "I can show you—through the coal room!"

"Julian, enough of these tales. Go to your chambers at once," Isadora said, her shoulders stiffening.

"Please, come and see," Julian insisted, grabbing Robert's hand and leading him to the coal room, its air thick with dust and the scent of aged wood. He pushed open a narrow door, revealing the chamber that housed the wine pool, and froze, his eyes widening. The pool, once a stagnant mess of fetid water and algae, now brimmed with fresh grapes. Inside, a group of maids stood with their skirts hitched, bare feet crushing the fruit. The rhythmic squelching had stopped, and they stared at Robert and Julian.

"Oh, no!" Julian's hands scrabbled over the rough stone, then fumbled against the wooden planks, searching for the hidden door. "Someone's covered it with planks!" he said, frustrated.

Lady Isadora's patience snapped. She seized Julian's arm with a firm grip and hauled him to his feet. "That's quite enough! Your stories have caused enough trouble. Go to your chamber and stay there."

Robert lingered, his eyes searching the room. He paused at the far wall, where a narrow airway vented the space. Almost hidden, dangling from the edge of the vent, was a rag—no, a shirt. Ben's shirt. He glanced at Julian, who was being dragged away by his mother, and gave a quick, knowing wink.

As the realisation dawned on Julian that Robert believed him, he stopped squirming. But why? How? His mind raced, but he forced himself to stay calm, to trust that Robert had seen what he needed to see. As Isadora pulled him from the room, Julian cast one last glance over his shoulder.

"Lady Wilson, might I have a stern word in private with Master Julian? He's caused me to neglect urgent work on my land, and I'd like to impress upon him the gravity of his actions," Robert said.

Disappointed, Isadora looked from Robert to Julian. She released his arm with a sigh. "Certainly. Please see yourselves out when you're finished."

Robert tipped his hat in acknowledgment, then guided Julian into the adjoining coal room, motioning for Henry and Caleb to wait outside. Once the door closed behind them, he placed his hand on Julian's shoulder. "Julian, your papa's built a wall, trapping them inside that chamber. It's a death sentence if they're not freed soon. You must find the key, break through those boards next door, and save them. Time's running out—God only knows how much water they have left." He paused, squeezing his shoulder. "Now, tell your mama I gave you a proper scolding. Make it convincing."

Julian's mind raced, his hands gripping the hem of his shirt. "I'll get Daniel to help," he said with determination.

Robert nodded, a flicker of relief crossing his face. "Good lad.

Now go. There's no time to waste."

Julian turned and hurried back to the main room, his heart pounding. He forced his face into a look of contrition as he approached his mother, his mind already spinning plans. Robert watched him go, his chest tight with worry. It was an impossible task for a ten-year-old, but Julian was their only hope.

Later that night, Julian crept barefoot down the grand staircase, the cold wooden floors sending shivers up his spine. The house lay silent, save for the occasional creak of settling timbers. He slipped into the kitchen, where Daniel waited, his face shadowed but alert. Robert had already briefed Daniel on the plan, and the urgency of their task hung heavy in the air. This time, they didn't need to navigate hidden passageways or risk being caught sneaking into the servants' quarters. As Ambrose's son, Julian could walk in, take the key, and if questioned, ask for warm milk to soothe his sleeplessness.

Daniel stepped forward and pulled Julian into a quick, tight hug. "You're a brave lad, Julian," he said. "We'll get them out." The gesture caught Julian off guard, but it filled him with a warmth he hadn't known he needed. For the first time, he felt a sense of belonging, of being part of something greater than himself. His shyness melted away, replaced by a steely determination.

"Take off your boots," Julian said. "We must be quiet." Daniel nodded, slipping off his boots and setting them aside.

Julian darted to the servants' quarters, his bare feet silent on the floor. He peeked into the head butler's office—it was empty. Spotting the board of keys, he quickly lifted the one for the room inside the wine cellar. He spotted a duplicate hanging just below it, and he grabbed that too, slipping it into his pocket.

"Wait in the coal room," Julian said. "I need to hide one of these keys in case something happens again and Papa throws them out or destroys them." Daniel nodded, disappearing into the shadows as Julian made his way upstairs to Eliza's chamber.

The door creaked as he pushed it open. The room smelled of perfume, a scent that brought a pang of longing for his sister. He scanned the space, searching for a hiding spot. His eyes landed on her dresser, and he remembered the secret compartments she had shown him years ago. Dropping to his knees, he crawled under, his fingers brushing the wood until he found the faint markings. He pushed on one side—nothing happened. With a soft click, a small compartment slid open when he tried the other. Julian placed the spare key inside, then clicked it shut again.

Like a ghost, he glided back downstairs, his movements silent. Daniel loomed in the coal room, his figure veiled in the dim light. Julian led him to the wall where the secret panel lay hidden. "These boards—we need to remove them."

Daniel nodded, his eyes scanning the room. He returned to the coal room and rummaged until he found an iron bar. He wedged it into the edge of the first plank, prying it loose with a soft groan of wood. The second board cracked as it broke, and Daniel froze, his head tilting as he listened for any movement from upstairs. "I'll try to be quieter," he whispered.

Every sound seemed magnified in the house's stillness. Daniel worked more carefully now. The boards gave way, revealing the dark outline of the hidden door behind them.

Ben lay curled on the old bedstead, his body aching from thirst and hunger. Eliza lay beside him, her arms wrapped tightly around his trembling frame, offering comfort to him—and herself. The air hung heavy, thin and stale, their lips cracked and dry from days without water. Ben's mind wandered, a dark thought taking hold: *When my daddy breaks down the wall, will he find one set of bones— or two?* He had spent what felt like an eternity searching for a way out, his fingertips raw from clawing at the corner, desperate to find a loose stone or a weakness in the wall. The stones held firm, and hope slipped away.

"I don't want to die," Ben said, his throat raw. "Not yet."

Eliza hugged him tighter, a tear slipping down her cheek. "Oh, sweet Benjamin. I'm so sorry you've been caught up in this. Papa is a cruel man," she said, kissing his cheek, masking her own fear with the need to comfort him.

"The lamp's nearly out," Eliza murmured, her eyes fixed on the flame. The thin layer of fuel at the bottom of the glass reservoir mocked them, a reminder of their dwindling time. Soon there would be eternal darkness.

A shiver ran through Ben, his body quivering against hers. He had never felt so helpless, so powerless. The light gave one last, feeble sputter before shrinking into nothingness, plunging the room into blackness. "Don't let go of me," Ben pleaded.

Eliza's arms tightened around him, her grip firm. "I shan't," she said, a tear slipping from her cheek into his hair.

They lay in the dark, long moments passing, ready to fall asleep—forever. Then, like a dream, the lock clunked. Ben sat up, his heart pounding, as the door creaked open, revealing the silhouettes of two figures. He blinked, unsure if angels had come for them.

"Benjamin? Eliza?" Julian's chest tightened, the sight of them splintering his heart as he broke the silence.

"Julian?" Ben said.

"Benjamin!" Julian rushed into the foul-smelling chamber, his arms wrapping around Ben in a fierce hug. He pulled back, his eyes darting to Eliza. She looked pale and frail in the dim light of the lantern Daniel held, his hand cupped over his nose to block the stench. Julian flung himself at Eliza, tears streaming down both their faces as they clung to each other.

Daniel stepped forward, holding out a bladder of water. Ben took it and handed it to Eliza first. She drank, the cool water burning her dry throat but soothing her parched body. She passed it back to Ben, who gulped it down, the relief immediate.

Daniel glanced around the chamber, his face a mask of disgust. *How could a father do this to his own daughter?* He thought, his stomach churning. The stench of dampness, filth, and decay overpowered him. He couldn't bear it. "Come on, we must go."

Julian nodded, helping Eliza to her feet while Daniel supported Ben.

Eliza's face twisted in disgust as she stared at the wall her papa had built to seal them away, to erase them forever. She knew hate was a sin, but she couldn't help it—she hated him. She looked at her brother and kissed his forehead. The once shy, spoiled boy had become their selfless saviour. How she loved him.

Daniel steadied Ben, who leaned on him with an arm around his neck for support. "I told you," Daniel said, his grip firm, exasperation tinged with admiration. "You're brave. But foolish. You should've waited."

Ben glanced at Daniel, a faint smile pulling at his lips, but he stayed quiet.

"I can walk myself now," Ben said feebly as they crawled through the secret door in the wine pool chamber and then into the coal room. The air felt cooler here, damp earth and old wood displacing the stifling stench of their prison.

"Up this way, through the coal chute," Daniel said. He reached out, helping Eliza and Ben climb the mound of coal. One by one, they emerged into the night, the sweet rush of fresh air filling their lungs like a balm.

"I'd best get back to my chamber," Julian said, hesitating at the chute's entrance.

"You'll need to come with us," Daniel said. "Your papa will know it was you who helped."

Julian's eyes lit up, and without another word, he scrambled up the chute.

Robert was waiting, his horse shifting beneath him. He had believed Julian's story, but seeing them emerge from the coal chute still left him stunned. He dismounted in one swift motion and moved to Eliza, lifting her frail body onto the back of his horse with gentle hands. Henry hoisted Ben onto his own horse, while Caleb helped Julian onto his.

Daniel mounted his horse but hesitated. "I'll ride back to my mother's cottage," he said. "I need to separate myself from this— to protect her." With a nod, he turned his horse and rode off into the night.

The three remaining horses ambled at first, their hooves quiet on the soft earth. But as they put distance between themselves and the house, the pace quickened, breaking into a gallop that carried them farther from danger.

Weak and hungry, Eliza leaned against Robert, finding comfort in his presence. She inhaled the crisp night air, as if drawing in the very essence of the freedom she had lost. Her hand drifted to her stomach, a silent prayer forming in her mind. *Please be okay.* The life within her felt fragile, but for the first time in days, she allowed herself to hope.

Two of Ambrose's men kept a distant watch on the group, their faces tight and giving nothing away. Briefly exchanging glances, they galloped back towards the estate, the sound of their horses' hooves disappearing into the distance.

CHAPTER 12: SANCTUARY AND SECRETS

Olivia opened the diary, flipping through its delicate pages. She searched for a new entry, any sign that her dad and Julian had arrived safely after being transported back in time. Two days had passed and still nothing.

Marlowe paced behind her, eyes darting to the makeshift monitors tracking gravitational anomalies. He scanned tirelessly for fluctuations that might signal someone stepping into the transference point. Since Julian's chaotic arrival in the present, the system had been silent.

She glanced at Marlowe and Colby. Grim-faced, they stared at the farmland—it had changed in impossible ways. Where there had once been open fields, a building now stood.

Colby stared at the hulking structure through the window. "It doesn't make sense. Buildings don't just appear."

Marlowe studied the building through his binoculars. "It's old—the place is a wreck, the windows shattered, rust everywhere. But we know it wasn't here before."

Olivia scrutinised the factory—a crumbling, brown-bricked monolith with jagged, empty windows. It loomed over the farmland, out of place, as though plucked from another era.

Colby looked at Marlowe questioningly. "What if the transference transcends time? What if it's pulling things from other timelines? Reshaping reality?"

Silence settled over them. Marlowe wiped his forehead. "No,

that's not it. I'm afraid Ben and Ethan might be unintentionally altering history."

Colby placed his hand against the glass, staring at the factory. "Then we need to stop it before it destroys more than history."

In Ben's room, Claire stared at the closet where she had last seen her husband vanish. Now, she spent her days confined to her son's bedroom, clinging to the fragile hope that both he and her husband might miraculously reappear from the past. The dream of turning their home into a charming bed-and-breakfast had twisted into something far darker—a living nightmare.

She clutched Ben's pillow to her face, inhaling his scent that still lingered. It was all she had left of him. Despite the silence and the impossible odds, she clung to one certainty: Ethan would find a way to bring Ben back. He had to.

"Mummy, look!" Olivia darted into the room, the door slamming against the backstop. Her face was alight with urgency as she thrust the diary forward. "Ben has written in the diary again!"

Claire froze, staring at the diary as if it were the Holy Grail. Her hands trembled as she took it, flipping to the page Olivia had showed. Her eyes scanned the familiar, uneven scrawl.

Olivia. Tell Mummy and Daddy I am okay. Julian and Daniel rescued Eliza and me after we had been locked up together for a long time. Before I come home, I need to help Julian and Eliza with something. I love you. Tell Mummy and Daddy I love them too. P.S. Julian said Daddy wanted to come back with him, but he wasn't here when Julian arrived.

She held the diary to her chest. Relief washed over her as she realised Ben was safe, sharply at odds with her growing dread about Ethan. Her vision blurred as a flush of panic surged through her body, spreading like wildfire.

"Olivia, when did this appear? Did you experience anything unusual? Did you hear anything?"

Olivia shook her head, her eyes reflecting the gravity of the moment.

Claire stormed up to Marlowe, jabbing her finger at the words in the diary. "Where is my husband?"

Marlowe took the diary from her, scanning the message. His mouth fell open, words failing him for a moment. He turned to Claire, then back to the diary, shaking his head. "I... I don't know. He should have been with Julian. They were together when the transference happened."

He looked at Vince, who had been observing from the corner. "Is it possible that only one of them passed through the wormhole while the other didn't?"

Vince crossed his arms, frowning. "It's not supposed to work like that. The energy signature was strong enough for both of them." He paused, glancing at the equipment. "But if there was interference... or if the wormhole fractured mid-transfer..."

"Are you saying my husband is missing? Stuck somewhere between timelines?"

Marlowe reached out as if to reassure her, but his words faltered. "I'm not sure, Claire. The process is... experimental at best. If something disrupted the connection—"

"Then we find out what went wrong! You fix this. You get him back."

Vince nodded. "We'll recheck the energy readings from the transfer and examine any anomalies. If there's even a chance Ethan didn't make it through, we'll figure out where he is."

**

Ben arrived back at the Whitfield's farm astride Caleb's horse, a smug grin spreading across his face. He was getting better at riding, and the thrill of it made the stolen moment even sweeter. But the satisfaction was short-lived. He hated sneaking around, yet he had to let Olivia and the others know he was all right.

Dismounting near the barn, Ben led the horse inside, its hooves clopping softly on the packed dirt floor. He fumbled with the saddle straps, the leather rigid under his inexperienced hands. Finally, he wrestled the saddle off, letting out a small sigh of relief.

"Where were you with my horse?"

The accusation startled him. Ben spun around, the saddle slipping from his grasp and landing with a thud. His eyes darted around the barn, searching for the source. For a moment, he wondered if it was his imagination. Then Caleb leapt down from the loft, landing with practised ease. A strand of straw dangled from his mouth as he stared Ben down.

"I just went for a ride." Ben said.

Caleb narrowed his eyes. "You went back to the Wilsons'. Why?"

Ben bent to retrieve the fallen saddle. "You wouldn't understand."

Caleb didn't respond. His silence was heavy, his piercing stare fixed on Ben as though trying to read the truth in his face.

Ben shifted uncomfortably under the scrutiny. "I had to do something important." But even as he spoke, he sensed Caleb wouldn't understand.

For a moment, Caleb remained silent and inscrutable. Finally, he tossed the strand of straw aside. "You'd best hope they didn't see you. You're going to get yourself into trouble—and not just with me."

"I didn't have a choice."

Caleb shook his head, then turned and strode out of the barn, leaving Ben alone with the horse and his thoughts. For a moment, Ben considered calling after him, trying to explain. But he let the silence linger, knowing no explanation would make Caleb understand.

Ben hated keeping secrets from Caleb. He had been more than just a companion—he'd been a source of steady friendship and comfort in an unfamiliar world. Caleb had opened up to him in a way few people did, sharing deeply personal stories about his past. He had described, in vivid detail, how the Whitfields had taken him in when he was just thirteen, alone and without a home.

Ben admired Caleb's resilience, his ability to forge a new life after losing everything. That made withholding the truth more difficult. He had trusted him, treated him like a younger brother, and here Ben was, dodging questions and keeping his thoughts to himself. It disturbed him, this betrayal, however unintentional. He didn't want to risk ruining the fragile bond they'd built. Caleb didn't deserve that—not after everything he had done to make Ben comfortable.

And yet, Ben couldn't bring himself to explain. The truth was too complicated, too tied to things Caleb wouldn't understand without knowing about the transference, the Wilsons, and the diary. Even if he didn't scoff or accuse him of lying, the risks were too great.

Ben was eager to learn about Eliza, who was still recovering in an outbuilding. His own strength had returned after a few days of Sarah's hearty meals and plenty of water, and he felt ready to act.

He called out to Caleb, who was feeding the pigs. "Who's that boy?"

Caleb trudged through the mud and grime, then vaulted over the fence with ease. He clapped an arm around Ben's shoulders and gave a friendly pat on his chest. "Don't you recognise your own friend?"

Ben narrowed his eyes, attempting to identify the boy by the outbuilding entrance. "Julian?—it's Julian!"

The initial confusion turned to amazement. Someone had cut Julian's once long, golden locks short, making his hair practical. He was no longer clad in the frilly, delicate clothes, but wore worn, sturdy farm clothes that had once belonged to the older boys and men of the farm. Julian, the rich, timid boy, now looked like any other regular farmhand.

Ben approached Julian and ran his hand over his cropped hairstyle. "What happened to your hair?"

Julian touched his short hair self-consciously, a small smile playing on his lips. "Sarah cut it. Easier to work with, and… well, I am no longer a milksop, am I?" Confidence threaded through his words, steadier than Ben remembered.

Ben couldn't help but laugh, clapping Julian on the back.

Ben made his way into the outbuilding. The dim light inside contrasted with the bright day outside, and there, on the side of her bedstead, sat Eliza. Her eyes lit up with recognition and joy when she saw Ben. He approached her, and they shared a long, comforting hug, Ben's relief palpable as he sensed her strength returning.

"Oh, Benjamin. I've news to share."

"What is it?"

"Alexander did not abandon me. If he understood Papa had misled him, I believe he would still love me. I've heard he's working for a blacksmith in London. Daniel has agreed to accompany me next week to find him."

Ben placed his hand over hers. "That's fantastic news. Will you go with Alexander if he asks?"

"Yes. But we'll need to be careful of Papa; he's a vengeful man. We'll have to go far away."

"What about Julian?"

"My dear, sweet brother will come with us if Alexander agrees. But I'm unsure of my mother's fate; she will die of heartache without Julian."

The burden of the situation was overwhelming for Ben. These decisions were far beyond his years, and it seemed a burden too heavy for anyone their age to bear. He could only hope they would all figure it out. His heart ached, not just for Eliza and Julian, but also because he was certain his own mother was worrying about him back home, in his own time.

Ben squeezed her hand. "We'll figure this out together. Maybe there's a way to keep everyone safe."

Eliza smiled, grateful for his support. "I hope so. I've thought about perhaps writing to my aunt in the countryside. She's always been kind and might offer us refuge, away from Papa's reach."

"That sounds like a plan. And what about your mother? Maybe she can come too?"

Eliza looked grim. "She would never leave Papa. But if we can convince her, perhaps… It's a lot to think about."

Ben nodded. "We should talk to Julian about this. He might have some ideas."

"You're right. Let's call him in. We need to be united in this."

Ben stood up to fetch Julian, understanding the gravity of the situation. As he stepped out into the sunlight, he was struck by the contrast between the warmth of the day and the cold reality of their plans.

Julian was in the pigpen, helping Caleb with the afternoon chores. Ben climbed the wooden fence, but his foot slipped, sending him tumbling down into the wet mud and grime with a squelch. Julian burst out laughing at the sight of Ben's muddied face emerging from the muck. With a playful glint in his eye, Ben reached out, grabbing Julian's boots, pulling him down into the mud with him. They both giggled, wrestling in the grime. Caleb, maintaining a safe distance, shook his head, laughing.

Ben's upward glance revealed two men on horseback, watching them with clear disdain, silencing their laughter. His stomach dropped as he recognised them as Wilson's men, in search of Julian.

Julian, rolling over, froze as he caught sight of the men, his eyes meeting theirs.

The rider eyed each boy, his disgust palpable. "What are you lads doing?"

Neither Julian nor Ben spoke, fear tightening their chests like a vise.

"We're looking for the Wilson boy, Julian. Have you seen him?" The man observed Julian, attempting to match the image of a country boy with his memory of someone more elegant.

Caleb, quick on his feet, stepped in, addressing the boys. "Arthur, Jebediah, stop your larking about. Get cleaned up!"

"Yes. Sorry," Ben said, pulling Julian to his feet before they both dashed to the nearby river. Over his shoulder, he saw the men talking to Caleb, who was pointing in a different direction, before they moved on.

Ben ran full speed into the river, his laughter returning, now tinged with relief. Julian was right behind him, splashing into the water. They washed off the grime in the cold, fresh river.

Ben scooped water onto Julian's back, washing the dirt from his shirt. "They didn't even recognise you!"

Julian managed a smile. "I suppose my new look fooled them. But we must be careful. They won't stop looking just because they didn't see me today."

They bathed, the river's babbling providing a temporary shield from the dangers that awaited beyond its banks. As they walked back to the farm, wet and somewhat cleaner, their laughter ceased.

Ben's heart dropped as he watched Eliza sprinting towards them, her face etched with panic. Behind her, a thick, black cloud of smoke billowed into the sky, a grim signal of something horrific unfolding at the farm. "Eliza, what's wrong?" Ben screamed.

Eliza was shouting, her throat raw as she held up her dress to avoid tripping over the uneven ground. "Run! Just run!" Her urgency was contagious, and it spurred Ben into action.

Ben, alongside Julian, who was already wide-eyed with fear, ran with Eliza. Their feet pounded the earth, the trio crossing the shallow river that marked the boundary of their innocent games, now a barrier between safety and the chaos behind them. As they ventured into the dense forest, piercing screams from the farm shattered the familiar harmony of their world.

"What's happening?" Ben choked out, his chest constricting with fear and confusion.

Eliza, not slowing her pace, tears streaming down her face, cried, "It's Papa. He knows the Whitfields helped me. He... he killed Robert!" Her words were like a knife to Ben's gut, slicing through the last threads of his childhood innocence.

Ben's legs failed him, and he sank to his knees, the situation too vast for his eleven-year-old frame to withstand. Was this all his fault? The thought that his actions might have led to this calamity overwhelmed him. "I have to go back! I have to help Lily and Sam."

Eliza, who had held them steady with her strength, turned back, determination and terror battling across her face. She grabbed Ben by the arm, pulling him to his feet with surprising strength for someone so frail. "Not now, Ben. If Papa catches you, he would... he would do the same to you!" She held back her panic. "Come on, we must keep moving!"

Julian, silent until now, grabbed Ben's hand, panic etched in his eyes. "Ben—come on!"

Together, they pushed deeper into the forest, the dense canopy above them casting shadows that matched the darkness of their hearts. Each step away from the farm seemed like a betrayal, but each step was also a step towards survival. The sounds of chaos faded behind them, replaced by the rustle of leaves and the distant, mournful call of a bird, as if nature itself was grieving for the innocence lost this day.

Eliza led them, her thoughts tangled with plans, fears, and the responsibility she carried—for the two young boys who looked up to her and for her unborn child. She knew they needed a haven, far from her father's control, where they could regroup.

Following a seemingly endless run, their lungs burning and legs aching, Eliza stopped, her face as pale as the risen moon. She lifted a thick layer of branches that concealed a small hollow in the earth, revealing a hidden refuge. "We can hide here," she said, ushering the boys into the cavity with a maternal urgency.

Huddled close together for warmth and comfort, they listened for any sound of their father or his men, or the dreaded barking of dogs that would betray their hiding place. The surrounding forest was silent, save for the occasional whisper of the wind through the leaves.

Julian, exhausted and scared, rested his head on Eliza's shoulder, seeking reassurance. "What are we to do now?" he asked, his words fragile, carrying the innocence of a child thrust into an adult's nightmare.

Eliza, still weak from her own ordeal but driven by necessity, kissed Julian's forehead. She took his hand. "We shall rest here until dark, and make certain no one is out looking for us. Then we'll make for London," she said, her eyes scanning the darkening sky through the gaps in their leafy shelter.

Ben shuffled closer to Eliza. "Why London?"

"To find Alexander. He's my—our only hope. Alexander, the love of my life. My father lied to him, told him I no longer wished to see him, that I didn't love him, especially after he learned I was carrying his child. That lie tore us apart, leaving me to face my condition alone, under my father's oppressive control. Now, I've no choice. I must find him."

As they waited for the black of night, Eliza's mind was a whirlwind of plans and fears. She knew London was far, and the journey would be perilous, especially in their current state. But Alexander, if she could reach him, had the means, the love, and perhaps the will to protect them. She prayed he would still believe in the love they shared, despite her father's deceit.

They sat in silence for a while, each lost in their thoughts, the only sounds the soft, rhythmic breathing of the trio and the occasional rustle of wildlife.

Eliza woke with a start, her heart racing as the morning sun cut slices through the protective branches of their makeshift shelter. "Benjamin, Julian. Wake up, we must go."

Julian awoke from a recurring nightmare where he was trapped in a burning farmhouse, the flames licking at his heels, with no escape in sight. He was thankful to be awake, yet the fear of what lay ahead clung to him like a shroud. He glanced at Ben, who was wiping the sleep from his eyes. The sound of Julian's stomach growling broke the silence of the morning. "I'm famished."

Eliza brushed leaves and twigs from her dress. "Come on, I think I know where we are. The Northcott farm should be near." She knew the Northcotts harboured a deep-seated hatred for the Wilsons, and in particular for her father, Lord Ambrose Wilson. She hoped, with cautious optimism, that this hatred would not extend to her and her brother.

Ben followed behind, peeling away the dried, caked mud from his clothes. Every so often, he would look over his shoulder, half expecting one of the Wilson men to catch up to them. Each step to London carried him further from the mansion and the possibility of returning to his own timeline, a thought that haunted him. Yet, his commitment to helping Eliza and Julian was unwavering; he loved them like his own family, the bonds of their shared plight tying them together.

Eliza's eyes lit up as the farm came into view through the trees. "There it is," she said. It was a small yet sustainable section of land with a modest house and fields stretching beyond.

Julian pulled Eliza down in fear of being seen. "What if they give us up to Papa?"

Eliza considered this, her mind racing.

Ben stood up. "I can go ahead, see if I can get some food for us. They wouldn't recognise me. I can claim to be an orphan."

Julian couldn't help but giggle, the tension momentarily broken. "You certainly look the part."

Eliza managed a small smile at their exchange, appreciating the moment of levity. "Stay here, both of you. I'll go first. If anything feels amiss, I'll return, and we'll devise another plan." She grasped the risk, but also understood their inability to proceed without nourishment.

As she crept towards the farm, Ben and Julian watched her, their hearts in their throats. The Northcotts, if they were kind, might provide the refuge they needed. If not, they would have to continue their journey with empty stomachs and heavy hearts.

CHAPTER 13: A CRUEL MASTER

Ambrose slammed his fist down on the table, the sound reverberating through the room and making his wife, Isadora, jump in her seat. "What do you mean, they weren't at the Whitfield farm? I had it on good authority the little orphan wretch was there, along with Eliza and Julian."

"He's only eleven years old," Isadora remarked, her eyes darting around the room, seeking a trustworthy ally among her husband's followers to protect the children from his harsh orders.

Ambrose stared at his wife with contempt, his lip curling in disdain. "Who's just eleven?"

"The orphan boy, Benjamin. Can you not leave him be?"

"It's he who put misguided notions into Julian's head. I'll see him hanged for that!" Ambrose's eyes flashed with a cold fury, revealing the depths of his cruelty. Isadora put her hand over her mouth, shocked at the venom in his words. He had always been a bitter man, but now, it was as if a demon from hell had possessed him. The revelation that he had locked their daughter up with Benjamin to erase them from history devastated her. How blind she had been to his true nature.

One man stepped forward, dressed in a red coat and chest armour. "My Lord, we searched the farm, and there was evidence of Miss Eliza and the boy. We burnt it to the ground as instructed. Robert Whitfield is dead, and we have his wife and children. What shall we do with them?"

Ambrose swept a beaker off the table. "Kill them!"

Isadora grabbed her husband's arm. "No! Their children are no older than Julian, mere babes."

Ambrose's face contorted with rage. "Why do you always undermine me, woman? Get out!"

Isadora's eyes silently pleaded with the guard as she left the room. She waited in the corridor, her heart filled with dread. When the guard appeared, she grabbed his arm in desperation. "Please... Not the children." The guard gave a slight, almost imperceptible nod before he left, leaving Isadora to wonder if her silent plea had found any mercy in his heart.

Back in the room, Ambrose turned his attention to a man dressed in black, a patch covering where his eye once had been. The man's presence exuded an arrogance and cruelty that matched, if not outweighed, that of Ambrose. He lounged back in a leather armchair, sipping red wine, the colour of which seemed to reflect the blood he was willing to spill for his employer.

Ambrose observed the dangerous man for a moment. "I want you to find my disobedient children before the news spreads. Use dogs if you must. Go to every farm in the district and offer rewards for their capture. Keep that boy, Benjamin, alive. I'll deal with him personally. One hundred pounds for the man who captures them alive!"

The man in black took one last sip of his wine, savouring it before setting the glass down with deliberate slowness. He stood up, his movements calculated, each step a reminder of the danger he posed. Before leaving, he paused at the door. "The price will be more."

Ambrose waved him off as one would an irritating fly, his mind already moving to the next phase of his plan. "Yes... yes." His gaze then shifted to the window, where he watched the progress on the gallows being erected outside. To the left, in a cage, a man beaten to the brink of recognition looked up; it was Henry, the farmhand suspected of aiding Eliza's escape. His bruised face and hollow eyes met Ambrose's, a living mark of the lord's cruelty.

Ambrose's mind was a whirlwind of vengeance and control. He envisioned the capture of his children, the public humiliation of Benjamin, and the eradication of any who dared to challenge his authority. The one-eyed man left the room with a bitter smile, his mind calculating the additional costs and the pleasures of the hunt. He had no loyalty to Ambrose, only to the riches he would gain, but in this moment, their desires aligned—a hunt for those who dared to escape the iron grip of Lord Ambrose Wilson.

Outside, with her back braced against the cold stone wall of the manor, Isadora kept her eyes fixed on the window above, waiting for her husband to turn away. The moment Ambrose's attention shifted, she darted towards the cage imprisoning Henry. His eyes, filled with a potent mix of hate and sorrow, met hers, and in defiance, he spat at her. Her hand trembling, Isadora took out a lace handkerchief and wiped her face, the fineness of the cloth stark against the brutality of the moment. She reached out, placing her hand on his, but Henry recoiled, pulling away in disgust.

Isadora glanced up at the window, then back to Henry, her eyes a tumultuous sea of sorrow and pain, tears having already carved paths down her cheeks. "Are you Robert and Sarah's farmhand?"

Henry was venomous with grief. "I am their son!"

Isadora's shock made her eyes widen. "Their son? Oh dear boy, don't let Ambrose find out. Make haste…" She fumbled with the cage's lock, her fingers clumsy with urgency but careful to keep her actions hidden from the men working on the gallows nearby. The key turned with a soft click, and she swung the door open just enough for Henry to escape.

"Why are you doing this?"

"You must save your family. Ambrose is going to kill them."

Henry, shocked to the core by the revelation, reacted with raw emotion. He lunged forward, gripping Isadora by the throat with hands calloused from farm work. Tears streamed down his face, his anger and grief colliding in that moment. But as quickly as he grabbed her, he pushed her away, his self-control just strong enough to keep his anger from turning on her. "He killed my father," his voice shattering with grief.

"Go!" Isadora rubbed her neck where his hands had been, her throat tender. "Forgive me."

Henry hesitated only for a second, then he bolted, his figure disappearing into the surrounding shadows. Isadora watched him go, her heart torn between relief and terror. She knew this act of defiance against her husband would have consequences, but the thought of those children, of her own children, pushed her to this desperate measure. She composed herself, tucking the handkerchief back into her sleeve, her mind racing with how to protect her own children from the man she once loved, now consumed by a darkness she could scarcely comprehend.

From a distance, the man in black watched, his silhouette a dark omen against the fading light, sitting astride his horse with an eerie stillness.

Desperate, Henry went to the barn where he found his imprisoned family. His heart raced as he saw the cages. His mother, Sarah, sprang to her feet the moment she laid eyes on him. She looked both relieved and anguished.

He grabbed a hefty rock from the ground, his hands shaking with both fear and determination, and bashed at the locks with all his might, but the metal held firm, refusing to yield to his frantic efforts. Blood soon stained his hands, and the rock slipped from his grasp as he struck again and again.

Sarah, seeing her son's futile struggle, reached out through the bars, her hands grasping his, stopping him. "Henry, listen to me. Save my babies. Get Lily and Sam and save them."

Henry's tears mixed with the blood on his hands as he looked back into his mother's eyes, the pain of failure and love for his family overwhelming him. "Where are they, Mama?"

"I don't know, but I fear for their safety. Henry, go now," she said. She knew the risk of sending her son away, but the thought of Lily and Sam, her youngest, out there in danger, was unbearable.

Henry nodded, understanding the gravity of his mission. He kissed his mother's hands, his eyes conveying a promise he intended to keep. With one last look at his mother and the other prisoners, he turned away, the world's troubles bearing down on his young shoulders.

Outside, the man in black observed Henry without moving to intervene. As Henry disappeared into the night, the man in black nudged his horse forward, a silent hunter in the darkness, his intentions as murky as the shadows he blended into.

At the house, the echo of a firm knock at the door interrupted the tension within. Ambrose, his face still flushed with rage from earlier, admitted one of his men, the urgency in the man's demeanour palpable.

"Sir," the man began, carrying the responsibility of important news, "we believe your daughter and son may be on their way to London."

Ambrose's reaction was immediate and violent; he struck the table with such force that the sound reverberated across the room, his anger palpable. "Alexander! Have all available men search for them on the roads to London. They must never meet again."

The man nodded, understanding the gravity of his orders. "Yes, my lord. I'll despatch riders to intercept them."

Ambrose's eyes were dark with fury and a twisted sense of justice. He paced the room, imagining scenarios in which he would regain control of his children, crush his daughter's defiance, and eliminate Alexander's threat. "Make it clear to everyone that anyone aiding them will share the same fate as the Whitfield family. I want this matter settled before it spirals further out of control."

The man bowed, acknowledging the orders, then turned to leave. Ambrose watched him go, his mind already plotting the next move in his chess game of power and retribution. He knew that sending men to London would not only hunt down his children but also send a message to all who dared to defy him.

CHAPTER 14: A FRAGILE SHELTER

Eliza crept forward, her steps cautious, torn between the decision to steal or to ask for help. She knew the deep-seated hatred that the Northcotts and most other farmers in the area harboured for the Wilsons, which posed a significant risk to both her and her brother. Perhaps it would have been safer if Ben had done this; his appearance was less likely to be recognised. But no, she reminded herself; she was the adult here. The sight of an old man interrupted her thoughts, his features weathered by time, holding a pitchfork. His sudden appearance made her jump in fright.

"Can I help you?" he asked.

Eliza stood erect, straightening her mud-stained dress, trying to regain some semblance of dignity. "Sir, might you spare some scraps for my brothers and I?"

Hidden in the brush, Ben's heart warmed at hearing her refer to him as her brother, but his senses remained alert to the potential danger she might be in. He gripped a rock, ready to charge if need be.

The man looked over her shoulder, peering into the trees. "Your brothers?"

"Sir, they are frightened. We are all scared, having escaped from a cruel master," Eliza looked back, signalling for the boys to come forward and show themselves. She hoped the honesty of their plight would appeal to the old man's compassion without revealing their true identity.

Ben and Julian emerged from the foliage, their faces smudged with dirt, their clothes torn from their hurried escape. Julian clutched Ben's hand, his eyes wide with fear but trusting in Eliza's lead.

Seeing their fear, the old man softened. "A cruel master, you say?" He lowered the pitchfork, the weapon now more of a staff than a threat. "And what made you run from him?"

Eliza paused in thought, weighing how much to reveal. "He wished to control our lives, to keep us locked away from the world. We had to leave to find freedom, to live as we choose." She was careful not to mention her father by name, fearing it might complicate matters further.

The old man studied her for a moment longer before nodding. "You're not the first to flee from a harsh master. Come, I'll see what we can spare."

Grateful, Eliza led Ben and Julian towards the modest farmhouse, each step feeling like a minor victory in their fight for survival. The old man, though still wary, seemed to understand the plight of those running from oppression, perhaps because he had his own stories of struggle against those in power.

The man ushered them inside to a warm, cosy kitchen where an old woman was standing over a stove, the air filled with the comforting aroma of freshly baked bread. "My name is George, and this here is my wife, Martha. Now, I rarely invite just anyone in, but you seem all right to me."

Martha put down her wooden spoon and approached the trio, her eyes filled with caring concern. She cupped Eliza's cheeks between her hands before studying the boys with the same maternal intensity. "You are beautiful children, under all that grime. What are your names?"

"My name is Ju…"

Eliza cut Julian off, her hand squeezing his arm. "Jude! And this is Arthur, and my name is Charlotte."

Martha glanced at the trio, her demeanour then softened into that of a mother. "Well, come on, children, sit down. I'll dish you up some rabbit stew and nice fresh bread I made just this morning."

As the three settled around the table, spoons clinking against bowls, George observed their manners. These were not simple orphan children; they bore an air of refinement. Despite the layers of dirt and grime, their skin seemed unblemished, hinting at a life far removed from hardship. He wondered if they were wealthy runaways, yet they carried none of the arrogance typically associated with wealth.

"How old are you all?" George asked, his curiosity piqued.

"Twelve, sir," Ben said, dipping a piece of bread into his stew.

Julian looked at Ben, puzzled. "I thought you were eleven?"

Ben's heart grew heavy as he thought about his family in another time. "It was my birthday a few days ago," he said, a realisation only hitting him hours earlier.

Julian, sitting next to Ben, wrapped his arm around his neck in a brotherly hug before returning to his meal.

Tilting her head, Martha looked from one child to the other. "You're not brothers and sisters?"

Ben realised his mistake and quickly corrected himself. "I'm an orphan."

Martha, touched by Ben's vulnerability, softened. "Well, you're safe here for now. No one will harm you under our roof." She watched as they ate, noting how they savoured each bite, their manners betraying their genteel upbringing even in this rustic setting.

George leaned back in his chair, his eyes thoughtful. "You've seen some trouble, haven't you?" he said, not pressing for details but offering them space to share if they chose.

"Yes, sir. More than we'd like to admit," Eliza said.

Just then, a loud banging on the door made the children freeze in horror. George, seeing their fear, guided them through a concealed trapdoor under the table's carpet, down a narrow ladder. Martha, with practised efficiency, gathered their unfinished dishes into a bucket, stashing them away. The door rattled again with another aggressive knock.

A large man pushed past George as he opened the door. "Why did you take so long to answer?"

Under the floorboards, Eliza held the boys close, noting Julian's fearful tremors against her. The floorboards creaked as the man walked around the kitchen above them. The floor muffled the adults' speech. Eliza hoped with all her heart that the old couple would not betray them, especially if they knew what had happened to the Whitfields' farm. The man lingered before the door thudded shut, shaking the house.

George opened the trapdoor. "You can come up now. It's safe."

He sat them back down at the table, Eliza still holding onto her trembling brother. For a long moment, he looked at them, his eyes searching for answers, trying to decide what to do. Then he pointed at Eliza, and said, "Eliza Wilson!"

"Sir, I beg of you. My father wishes me dead. He locked me in the cellar because…" She swallowed hard.

"Because you are unwed and with child," Martha finished, her features gentle, carrying no hint of judgment.

"How did you know?" Eliza whispered.

"Oh, child, a woman knows," Martha replied gently.

Eliza placed her hand on her stomach, her mind racing with the implications of her condition being known.

"You must be Julian, not Jude then," Martha said, cupping her hand under Julian's chin in a reassuring gesture.

Julian nodded.

Ben thrust his hand out, eliciting amusement from George as they shook. "I'm Ben…, Benjamin. Pleased to meet you."

Martha settled beside Eliza. "What are you children doing? You cannot run forever; your father is bound to find you."

Ben shivered, the fear in his eyes unmistakable, scaring even George. "He locked us in there to die. He built a wall in front of the room so no one could find Eliza and me."

George shook his head. "Come now, you're spinning a yarn. No parent could be that cruel."

"It's true, sir, I swear it," Julian said, recounting the rescue, detailing how the Whitfields had helped and the peril they now faced.

Martha, feeling sick from the story, enveloped the children in a long embrace. "You will stay here—we will hide you."

Eliza shook her head, gripping Martha's hand. "No, I thank you. My father is a cruel man. If he knew you had helped us, then... No."

"Please, reconsider. What about your brothers?" Martha urged.

Ben raised a finger. "I'm an orphan."

"Oh, fiddlesticks! You are a brother to these two," Martha declared.

Ben blushed as Julian nodded, placing a hand on Ben's arm.

For a moment, Eliza considered leaving the boys, but she knew Julian and Ben would remain in danger. She couldn't bear the thought of abandoning them, not knowing their fate, especially since they had risked their lives for her. "We need to find Alexander, the father of my unborn child. He's working in London. From there, we will start our new lives in a distant city, far from my father."

Martha leaned back. "Stay for a few days at least, rest up and regain your strength."

"The longer we tarry, the greater the peril we face. Papa will surely offer rewards, spreading falsehoods about us. You, too, will be in grave danger. No, we must depart at once, today, before nightfall."

"Well, if you insist. There is no time to lose. We must cut your hair," Martha declared firmly.

"What?" Eliza clutched her long tresses. "Why?"

"There are men searching for you, wicked men who would stop at nothing for coin. They seek a young woman and two boys. We must disguise you as a young man to throw them off the scent," Martha explained.

Ben slapped his forehead. "That's brilliant!"

Martha fetched a pair of shears from a drawer. "It shan't be forever, dear. Only until you find safety. We'll make you look like a lad who's known hard labour, not the daughter of a gentleman."

Eliza hesitated for a moment, then nodded. She understood the necessity. As Martha snipped away her hair, Eliza felt a peculiar sense of liberation. The weight of her locks, much like the burden of her past, was falling away. Meanwhile, George spoke with Ben and Julian, discussing how they might alter their appearances or manners to avoid drawing attention.

The boys' jaws dropped as Eliza emerged from the chamber, transformed and clad in George's old garments, expertly adjusted by Martha. Her once-familiar silhouette now resembled that of a young man, a cap shading her eyes, the jacket hanging just so.

Eyes wide, they took in the change. Eliza turned, revealing her disguise from all angles, her movements deliberate. "Now, we shall be a young man and two boys on the road to London," she said, mimicking a man as best she could, a thread of excitement weaving through her words.

Their nods were slow, the realisation dawning that they could blend into the throng of travellers as a group of boys. The shadow of Ambrose's pursuit seemed less menacing, armed with this new guise.

George's eyes spoke volumes of the dangers they would face. "You must keep your heads down. And remember, Eliza, you're 'Eli' now. Speak little, observe much, and let the boys do the talking when necessary."

Eliza acknowledged her new name, "Eli," with a resolute nod. Martha approached with a sack, placing it in Julian's hands. "Here. Some bread, cheese, a meat pie, and apples. 'Tis not much, but it should sustain you on your journey."

The group gathered their meagre belongings, including Martha's gift, the load of the provisions a clear sign of her support. Their departure was silent, filled with the unspoken promise of return if needed. George's firm handshake, and the way he squeezed Eliza's arm, spoke volumes. "Godspeed. And remember, if need be, you can always find your way back to us."

Martha watched Eliza and the boys depart with a heavy heart, her eyes misting over as she leaned against the doorframe of their modest farmhouse. She and George could not have children of their own, a fact that had always left a silent ache within her. The brief encounter with these young souls had reignited that longing, making her yearn for a child she would never have. Already, she missed them—their youthful banter, the spontaneous giggles, the way they filled the house with their energy. She wished she could wrap them in her comforting love forever, shielding them from the harshness of the world.

She didn't want to think about the dangers they were facing, especially the threat of Eliza's cruel father, Ambrose. His shadow was long and dark, capable of reaching even into the safest of havens. The thought of what he might do if he caught them made her stomach churn.

As the trio walked into the field, their figures growing smaller with each step, the boys turned and waved. Their smiles were bright against the backdrop of the golden field. She raised her hand, waving back, her gesture small but filled with all the love and protection she wished she could give them.

George, standing beside her, placed a comforting arm around her shoulders. "They're stout-hearted and they've got one another. They'll make it to London, mark my words."

Martha leaned into his embrace, drawing strength from his words, though she knew the journey would be fraught with peril. She watched until they disappeared from view, the horizon swallowing them up, leaving behind a quiet that felt too loud in their absence.

At that moment, she made a silent vow. If they ever returned, her home would always be a sanctuary for them, a place where they could find warmth, laughter, and the love she had in abundance, but no child to give it to.

Henry's horse snorted, its back glistening with perspiration. He surveyed the farm, now nothing more than a shambles. Ambrose's men had devastated everything they had built. The farmhouse was a smouldering heap of ash, the hogs slaughtered, and the horses gone. Only the outbuilding where Eliza and the boys had stayed remained intact. He bolted into the building, calling out for Ben, Julian, and Eliza. Inside, someone had ransacked the place, leaving it empty.

Outside, he cupped his hands around his mouth, shouting for Lily and Sam, fear clenching his heart for their safety.

Mounting his horse, Henry galloped across the river in search of them, his entire being consumed by trepidation.

Lily's eyes brimmed with tears at the sight of Henry. Clutching Sam's hand, she emerged from their hiding place. "Henry!"

Henry whirled around, dismounting in one swift motion, and rushed to Lily and Sam. He crouched, enveloping them in his arms. "Oh, praise the heavens."

Lily buried her tear-stained face into Henry's shoulder. "Where have you been?"

He hugged them closer, his hand stroking her hair. "I'm here now, hush, I'm here."

"How touching. My gratitude for finding the brats for me," the man in black said, dismounting and drawing his sword with a menacing grace.

Henry pushed his brother and sister behind him. "Run!" The siblings, eyes wide with terror, hesitated for a moment before bolting. He turned his attention to the man, rising from his crouched position, a rock gripped in his hand. "You vile cur! You slew my father, you locked away my family, and now you hunt helpless children."

The man in black flicked his sword, the metal glinting in the dim light, and laughed. "Those worthless whelps are only fit for the coal pits. As for you, I'd sooner see you dance at the end of a rope than dirty my blade. But either way, I'll have my coin."

Lily gripped Sam's hand as they ran, their feet pounding the earth. Behind them, there was nothing but silence, interrupted only by their own gasps for air. They entered the very hollow, its entrance shrouded in a canopy of leaves and twigs, that was used by Eliza and the boys the night before. Lily adjusted the branches and leaves as best as she could to hide them.

The man in black lunged forward with lethal precision, his sword scraping along Henry's side, slicing through fabric and flesh. Henry staggered, his hand flying to his side where warmth spread, wet and sticky with blood. With a desperate heave, he hurled the rock in his hand; the projectile whizzing past the man's face, missing his one good eye by mere inches.

Panic surged through Henry as he scanned the ground for another weapon, any weapon. The man in black laughed, a dark, mocking sound, as he swished his sword through the air, each swing bringing him closer. With no time to spare, Henry rolled to the side, his foot lashing out to sweep at the man's legs. The man stumbled, falling with a thud to the forest floor, his sword clattering out of reach.

In an instant, the man was back on his feet, his hand snapping the sword up just as Henry lunged for it. "Is that the best you can muster?"

Desperation fuelling his movements, Henry grabbed the nearest stick, swinging it like a club. The man in black reacted with a swift, slicing motion, cutting the stick in two with a casual flick of his blade. As the pieces fell harmlessly to the ground, he lunged at Henry, the tip of his sword aimed true.

Henry let out a pained moan, collapsing to his knees, his hands clutching his stomach where a fresh wound bled. The forest seemed to spin around him, the man's shadow looming large as he stood over Henry, sword raised for the last strike. A metallic tang of his blood mingled with the sharp scent of pine; the silence broken only by his ragged breathing and the ominous whisper of the sword cutting through the air.

Lily held Sam close, her arms wrapped around him as they shivered not just from the cold, but from sheer terror. Minutes stretched into what felt like hours, yet she clung to the belief that her big brother would triumph over the menacing figure they called *the man in black*.

A horse's familiar clip-clop broke the silence as it approached their hideout. Her heart leaped as she glimpsed the horse through the leaves; she knew its distinct markings well—it was Henry's horse. With a surge of hope, she and Sam scrambled from their hiding place, their eyes wide with anticipation as they looked up.

But the figure that emerged from the shadows of the trees was not Henry.

CHAPTER 15: THE ROAD TO LONDON

"At this rate, we shall soon have nothing left to sup upon," Eliza said, placing her arm over Julian's shoulder.

Julian bit into another piece of the pork pie, then held it up for Eliza. "I am still quite famished," he said. Eliza waved the pie away from her face, the aroma making her queasy.

As they navigated through the boggy fields, Ben surveyed their surroundings. A lone cow stared at them before returning its attention to the grass. "Eliza, are we going in the right direction?"

Eliza pointed at the sun, lowering in the sky. "Mark, where the sun sets? It's setting in the West, behind us. London lies to our East, this way. Remember to call me Eli; I am your brother now, not your sister."

Ben patted her back. "Oh yes, my apologies… Eli."

Eliza dropped to the ground on her knees, concealing herself behind the tall grass and weeds. Ben and Julian followed her lead without hesitation. She placed her finger to her lips. The boys nodded in silent acknowledgment.

A man on horseback had halted a group of travellers heading west on the dusty road, unaware that the children he sought were in a field, mere feet away. "We offer one hundred pounds for the capture of dangerous offenders—a girl and two young lads."

The man leading an ox cart, his appearance dishevelled, scratched his unkempt beard. "I saw those little rogues earlier, pilfering from my wagon—they were. I demand recompense for my losses."

"You shall receive your reward upon their capture. Lead me astray, and I shall ensure your head rolls," said the horseman.

The cart man, scratching his belly with dirty nails, reconsidered. "Perhaps... perhaps it was some other urchins."

The horseman grunted, then continued down the road in the same direction the trio was heading.

Eliza waited until the man was out of sight. "Come, we must put more distance between ourselves and the road."

The dishevelled man on the road spotted them running into the field. "Ho, there! Those are the brats!" he said, looking for the man on the horse, who was long gone. He chased after them but soon gave up, bending over out of breath. "Likely not them. Those were boy brats—those were."

After running what felt like forever, Eliza collapsed onto the ground, laughing. The boys piled on top of her, creating a tangled heap of limbs and giggles. She took Ben's face in her hands, their noses almost touching. "That was far too close for comfort."

Julian sat up and dug into his satchel, pulling out a biscuit. "Biscuit, or apple?" he asked, just as a raindrop hit him right on the nose. He looked up to see dark clouds rolling in from the West, turning the sky black. "Oh dear, not rain again!"

Ben held his hand out, watching as the rain fell. At first, it was nice, cooling them off after the hot day, but then it turned into a downpour, soaking them to the skin.

Eliza, drenched, got to her feet, helping her brothers up. "We must find somewhere to take shelter," she said. "Let's make haste before the storm worsens."

They looked around, squinting through the rain. To their left was a rundown old shepherd's hut, barely visible through the downpour. "There!" Eliza pointed. They ran for it, slipping in the mud all the way.

Once they reached the hut, they shoved the door open, glad to be out of the rain. It was dark and smelled like old wood, but it was dry. Ben shook off like a wet dog, while Julian laughed.

Leaning against the doorframe, Eliza watched the rain come down. "We'll have to wait this out," she said, her shoulders easing now they had shelter. "But at least we're safe from Papa for now."

Julian peeked out a tiny, broken window. "And who'd think to look for us in this wretched weather?" he said with a grin.

Eliza coaxed a fire to life in the hearth, the warmth spreading through the hut. The smell of herbs hanging from the beams filled the air as it heated.

Ben glanced around the hut, a slight frown on his face as he wondered if they were imposing on someone's home. "Who do you think lives here?" he asked, setting his boots close to the fire.

Before anyone could answer, the door burst open, slamming against the wall with a loud thud. A soaked man and his collie dog entered, water dripping from their coats. The sudden intrusion caused the trio to jump. First, the man's eyes fell upon Eliza, sitting at the table in wet clothes, then they moved to Ben and Julian by the hearth, their wide, frightened eyes meeting his. The collie shook itself dry, whining before lying down between Ben and Julian, at ease.

Shrugging off his jacket, the man shut the door and hung it on a peg. He turned back to the children, who were now motionless, waiting for his reaction. Without a word, he walked to a chest, pulled out some old, tattered towels, and tossed one to each of the boys, and then to Eliza.

Placing a pot of water on the hearth, he spoke, his voice husky. "Shep likes you. That means I like you. I reckon you lads needed a spot out of the rain. Name's Charles."

Ben stood up, placing the towel over his shoulder. "This is my younger brother, Julian, sir. And this is my older brother, Eli. My name is Benjamin. We didn't mean to…"

Charles raised a hand, cutting Ben off. "No matter. I often find stragglers using my hut for shelter. So long as you're not here to rob or wreck the place, you're welcome to stay till the rain lets up." He then directed his attention to Eliza. "Why's your younger brother doing all the talking, and not you?"

Ben pulled at his towel. "My brother is mute, sir. He can't talk. But he's brilliant."

Charles studied Eliza for a moment, the silence hanging heavy. He lit his pipe; the smoke curling upwards, his eyes never leaving her face. "Mute, eh?" he said, not sounding convinced. "Well, clever or not, everyone here seems to have a tale. And if you're wise, you'll keep your secrets as close as you keep dry."

He sat down at the table, pulling out a deck of cards from his pocket. "How about a game of cards to pass the time? No need for chatter in this one—just luck and a keen eye." His offer seemed to break the tension, giving them a way to distract themselves from their predicament.

Eliza nodded, grateful for the change of subject, and moved to join the game. Meanwhile, feeling more at ease, Ben and Julian warmed themselves by the crackling fire, uncertain whether this unexpected encounter would help or hinder their escape.

A few games into their impromptu session, Eliza displayed her cards to Ben and Julian, who sat on either side of her. Ben shrugged in confusion; the strange, old-fashioned card game was a mystery to him.

Charles threw his cards down, laughing as Eliza revealed hers. "You've won again," he said with a broad smile.

With a girlish squeal, Eliza clapped a hand over her mouth.

Charles stared at her, his eyebrow arching. "Mute, eh?"

Outside, the rain had tapered to a light drizzle. Ben didn't like the scrutiny in the man's eyes. "We need to go now, sir. Mama will be worried," he said.

Charles stood, calling to his dog. "You lads, *and young lady*, wait here. I'll be back shortly."

The door thudded shut, its finality echoing through the small room. A faint shuffle sounded outside, followed by a heavy clunk—wood against wood—then the rapid drum of hooves as a horse galloped away.

Eliza rose, alarm tightening her voice. "He's locked us in. I'm so sorry—this is all my fault. We must find a way out."

Julian struggled with his damp boots. "The window—it's too small," he said, eyeing the narrow, grubby opening.

They recoiled as Ben, with a determined look far beyond his years, grabbed the heavy iron pot and hurled it at the window. The pot shattered the glass and splintered the wooden frame with a resounding crash. "He's selling us out!" Ben said.

Eliza, her long limbs aiding her, manoeuvred through the jagged opening first, her hands brushing against the remaining shards. She winced at the slight pricks, but focused on clearing the way for her brothers. She reached back, assisting Julian, whose slight frame made the escape somewhat easier. Ben, though smaller than Eliza, still had to be cautious, his feet nudging out any remaining glass before he slipped through.

The air outside was cooler, the drizzle creating a mist that cloaked their movements. They crouched low, the wet ground squishing beneath their feet as they listened for any sign of Charles or his dog. Their escape was immediate; they dashed to the nearby treeline, their breaths fogging in the cool air.

As they reached the cover of dense foliage the forest swallowing them, Eliza whispered with urgency, "We must keep moving. If he's gone for help, we've little time to spare."

They moved through the underbrush; the wet leaves brushing against them, leaving trails of water that glistened in the low light. Their steps were careful, each footfall soft on the mossy floor. The forest was a labyrinth of shadows and whispers, but it provided them with the camouflage they needed. The trio navigated through the dense woods, their path marked by the occasional snap of a twig or the rustle of leaves, their minds racing ahead to their next move.

Worrying, Julian looked up. "Eliza, are we still headed the right way? We can't see the sun anymore."

Eliza paused, her stomach knotting as she surveyed the landscape. Before them, a wide, raging river, its waters churned into a frothy mess from the relentless rain. "I think so," she murmured, unsure. "But we must find a ford to cross… and quickly."

The distant sound of barking dogs seemed to pierce through the patter of rain. Ben squeezed Eliza's hand, his grip tight with panic. "We need to move now!"

Eliza dragged them along the riverbank, her eyes darting for any sign of safety. The roar of the river was deafening, a constant reminder of their dwindling options.

Julian's eyes caught the outline of a raft, half-sunken and battered, clinging to the riverbank, the water eager to pull it back into its deadly embrace. It was just large enough to hold them. "That raft—let's take it!" Desperation flashed across his face.

Eliza shook her head, her face set with fear. "No, it's too

dangerous. Look how fast the river's flowing!"

But the barking was no longer a figment of their imagination; it was real, and it was getting closer. Ben's senses were on high alert, his ears straining against the noise of the river. Julian, stopping dead in his tracks, turned back, his face pale. ' They're closing in."

A shiver ran down Julian's spine; he knew those barks could only mean one thing—bloodhounds. "Eliza, the raft—we've no choice! Dogs!"

Eliza's resolve crumbled as the sound of the pursuit grew closer, the barking now a menacing echo in the woods. She looked at the raft, then at the terror in her brother's eyes. With a sharp nod, she decided. "Very well, we'll take it. But be ready for anything."

They scrambled to the raft with desperate speed, the mud sucking at their feet. The wood was slick, the ropes on the verge of snapping, but it was their only shot at escape. Eliza pushed Ben and Julian onto it before getting on herself. They grabbed the single splintered oar, but the river was in control.

As they pushed off, the raft rocked, nearly capsizing. Eliza's arms flailed for balance, her command cutting through the water's chaos. "Hold on tight!"

The current grabbed them, thrusting the raft into a wild dance through the rapids. They dodged protruding rocks, the raft slamming against each one, water spraying over them, drenching them anew. Every moment was a battle against being thrown into the river, against the raft falling apart, against the dogs that were closing in.

The barking seemed to fade, but the peril of the river only intensified. The raft spun, threatening to tip with each new wave. "We mustn't let go!" Eliza's eyes remained fixed on the distant bank, their only hope of safety.

Terror and adrenaline surged through Julian as he gripped the worn ropes, his heart pounding. The raft hit an unseen rock beneath the river's surface, and, in a surreal moment, the force of the collision sent Julian into the air, his arms splaying as he fell into the frigid, relentless water.

Eliza and Ben's screams pierced the air, their hands stretching out in vain, fingers clawing at the space where Julian had been. They searched the river's chaos, their eyes wide with horror, every heartbeat a reminder of the precious life slipping away from them. The river seemed to mock their panic, another rock tearing their makeshift escape into splinters, sending them both into the icy embrace of the current.

Ben's heart pounded in his chest as the icy river water closed in around him. He was a strong swimmer, confident in his ability to navigate even the roughest currents, but the weight of his riding boots dragged him down like anchors. The water roared in his ears, a chaotic symphony of churning foam and rushing currents, as he struggled to keep his head above the surface. His lungs burned, each breath a desperate gasp that barely filled them before another wave crashed over him.

He kicked furiously, fighting against the pull of his boots, but the river was relentless. The water seemed alive, twisting and tugging at him with a mind of its own. His fingers fumbled with the buckles, numb from the cold and slippery from the water. Panic clawed at the edges of his mind, but he forced it down, focusing on the task at hand. *One boot at a time*, he told himself, though every second felt like an eternity.

Finally, the first boot came free, and he kicked it away, feeling a momentary surge of relief. But the second boot was stubborn, its leather straps tangled and unyielding. Ben's vision blurred as his lungs screamed for air. He twisted his body, pulling at the straps with all the strength he had left. Just as his fingers slipped and his strength faltered, the buckle gave way. He kicked the boot off and surged upward, his body lighter but still at the mercy of the river.

Before he could reach the surface, the current slammed him into a jagged rock. Pain exploded across his side as the impact tore through his shirt, ripping it to shreds and leaving his skin raw and bleeding. He cried out; the sound swallowed by the water, and for a moment, he thought he might black out. But the thought of sinking, of letting the river claim him, pushed him to fight harder.

With a final, desperate push, Ben broke through the surface. He gasped, the air rushing into his lungs like a lifeline. The world came back into focus—the grey sky above; the trees lining the riverbank, the sound of the water still roaring around him. He coughed, his body trembling with exhaustion, but he forced himself to keep moving. The river still had him in its grip.

As he struggled to stay afloat, he spotted Eliza nearby, her face pale and her arms thrashing as the current pulled her under. Without hesitation, Ben swam to her, his muscles screaming in protest. He latched onto her, his grip firm despite the water's relentless tug. "Hold on!" he shouted, his cry swallowed by the river's roar.

Ben dragged her to the riverbank, his chest heaving and his body trembling with exhaustion, but adrenaline surged through him, sharpening his senses. He stood on the side, his eyes scanned the churning water, searching for any sign of Julian. The river roared in his ears, its surface a chaotic swirl of foam, but Ben refused to look away. Every second felt like an eternity, every ripple a false hope. His hands clenched into fists, nails digging into his palms as he fought back the rising tide of fear.

Dread consumed Eliza as she called Julian's name, her throat raw from shouting, each cry a desperate plea to the universe to bring her brother back.

"There!" Ben cried, his shout cutting through the despair as he pointed to Julian's motionless form floating face down. He, with agonizing resolve, plunged back into the water. The swim to Julian felt like an eternity, his limbs burning, but his determination unwavering. He reached Julian, pulling him with every ounce of strength he had left to the bank where Eliza waited, her face a mask of anguish.

Eliza's cry was raw, cracking with sorrow, tears streaming down her face. "My brother… He's gone!" The words tore from her soul, filled with anguish and disbelief.

Ignoring her, Ben dropped to his knees beside Julian's lifeless body, his mind racing. His modern education kicked in, pushing aside the panic that threatened to overwhelm him. He had practiced this a few times in school, but now it was real—Julian's life depended on him.

With trembling hands, Ben carefully checked Julian's neck for a pulse, pressing his fingers against the cold, damp skin. Nothing. His stomach tightened, but he forced himself to stay focused. Leaning closer, he tilted Julian's head back, opening his mouth to check for obstructions. A trickle of water spilled out, but there was no sign of anything blocking his airway. Ben listened for breath, his own chest tightening as the silence stretched on. Julian wasn't breathing.

Time was slipping away. Ben yanked the remains of Julian's torn shirt up, exposing his chest. Positioning the heel of his hand in the centre of Julian's sternum, he interlaced his fingers and began compressions, pushing hard and fast. The rhythm came instinctively—thirty compressions, then two breaths. He repeated the cycle, his movements steady despite the fear gnawing at him.

The world around him faded—the sound of the river, the distant cries of the others, even the ache in his own body. All that mattered was the count, the rhythm, the hope that Julian would come back to them. Ben's arms were burning with the effort, but he didn't stop. He couldn't. Not until Julian breathed again. Each compression was a desperate plea for life, his actions standing in vivid opposition to the 19th-century world around them.

Eliza, utterly bewildered, tried to pull him away, her eyes wide. "What on earth are you doing?"

"Trust me!" Ben's conviction rang through his actions, a testament to his faith in science over superstition. He resumed the compressions, his count a mantra of hope. "Twenty-eight, twenty-nine, thirty..." He tilted Julian's head back, pinched his nose, and sealed his mouth over Julian's cold, blue lips, forcing air into his lungs. His own breath mixed with the taste of salt and the icy stillness of Julian's skin, but he didn't stop. Another breath. Another desperate plea for life. Then, in a moment that transcended time, Julian convulsed, coughing up water, his body jerking as he wrenched back to life. Ben, overcome with emotion, burst into tears, his arms enveloping Julian in a protective, loving embrace.

Overwhelmed with relief and disbelief, Eliza embraced the boys, her sobs filled with pure joy. She kissed Ben's cheek, her gratitude wordless but profound, before turning her attention to Julian, smothering him with kisses, her tears mingling with the river water on his face.

"What manner of sorcery is this?" she cried, her hands trembling with relief as she stroked Julian's wet hair.

Ben, his own heart still racing, looked into Eliza's eyes. "It's not sorcery, Eliza. It's CPR. I learned it... in my time." The words hung in the air, a bridge between two worlds, two times. They were all changed by this moment, bound by a love that had just proven stronger than the river, stronger than death itself.

Julian glanced between Ben and Eliza, his mind struggling to piece together the events that had just unfolded. "What happened?" he rasped, his words frail. He tried to support himself but collapsed, pain shooting through his arm. "Ow..."

Alarmed, Eliza rushed to his side, helping him sit up. 'What is it?"

Julian cradled his right arm against his chest, wincing. "It hurts dreadfully when I try to stretch it out."

Ben examined Julian's thin limp arm, gently pulling up the wet sleeve to assess the damage. "It's sprained, or maybe broken." Concern etched his face. He tried to rip the legs off his already torn trousers to make a sling, but the fabric resisted. *This isn't the movies*, Ben thought, frustration mingling with his concern. Then, his eyes landed on the food satchel, now useless for its original purpose. He emptied the soggy contents and, with gentle care, manoeuvred Julian's arm into it, fashioning a makeshift sling by wrapping the strap around Julian's neck.

Eliza watched with fascination, her respect for Ben growing. "You are a marvel to know such things, Ben."

Ben fought to keep his emotions in check, overwhelmed by the near loss of his best friend, no, his brother. His eyes were misty, but he blinked back the tears, focusing on the task at hand.

With Eliza's help, Julian stood, his eyes scanning the area. "I don't know how, but we've made it to the other side."

With the rain having ceased, Eliza took Julian's good hand in hers as they walked. The clouds parted, and the first twinkling lights of the evening reminded them of the vastness of the world and their small but fierce fight for survival within it.

Julian winced when he breathed in. "My chest hurts," he said, then looked down. "And where are our boots?"

"We'll have to find you both new boots—or brogues—and shirts as well. Yours are in tatters," Eliza said, glancing at Julian and Ben. She looked at Julian and recounted the events of the river.

"You were gone, Julian. The water took you under, and we thought we'd lost you. But Ben—he wouldn't give up. He pulled you out and..." Her chest quivered. "He brought you back."

Julian's face was pale, his eyes wide as he listened, his hand instinctively moving to his chest where the bruising ached with every breath. Ben stood beside him. "Your heart stopped," he said. "I had to perform CPR—it's a technique I learned to restart a heart. It's why your chest hurts now. I had to press hard, over and over, to get your blood flowing again. It's not pleasant, but it saved your life."

Julian winced, both from the pain and the staggering truth of what had happened. He looked at Ben, gratitude and disbelief mingling in his eyes. "I... I don't know what to say," he rasped. "Thank you. I owe you my life."

They walked in silence for a moment, each processing the trauma of what had just occurred. Ben's mind was a whirlwind of thoughts; he had saved Julian, but the fear of losing him had left a mark. Eliza felt a newfound gratitude for Ben, not just for his knowledge, but for the bond they shared, now stronger than ever. Julian, though in pain, felt awe for his friend, who had pulled him back from death's door.

Later that night, as they continued their journey, they came upon a small village. The spacious open farmland transitioned into more plots and built-up housing. The trio crossed a wide wooden bridge spanning another river.

Eliza paused on the bridge, leaning over the rail. "It's the Thames. We're drawing nearer to London."

Ben, standing beside her, rubbed his foot, the stones of the bridge cold and harsh. He wasn't used to walking such distances without shoes, and his feet were aching.

Eliza glanced at her brothers with concern. Both were in discomfort and pain, yet neither complained. "Come now, let's find you some brogues, shirts, breeches, and food. We'll pinch them if we must." Her brothers looked every bit like street urchins—dirty, dishevelled, and clad in torn clothes.

Julian stopped in front of a bakery, his eyes widening as he peered through the window at the display of cakes. His stomach growled in protest, a sharp reminder of how long it had been since he'd eaten. The bakery was long closed, its lights dim, and the door locked, but he couldn't help wondering if there might still be some scraps left from the day.

As if reading his mind, Eliza took both boys' hands, as if they were toddlers again, and pulled them into the alley between the shops. There, they found a bin full of the day's leftovers—bread crusts, stale cake, and other bakery discards. Without a second thought, they chased away cockroaches and pulled out their dinner.

"Good, isn't it?" came a murmur from the shadows, startling them. Toby, the homeless boy they would soon come to know, emerged, his eyes twinkling with mischief and understanding. He was making his own meal from the scraps.

Toby felt defensive when he first noticed them, but now, seeing their plight, his manner shifted to one of camaraderie. "Who might you be?"

"We mean no harm. We're merely passing through, seeking our way," Eliza replied, deepening her voice.

Toby noticed the smaller boys' bare feet. "I might be able to help with that." He gestured to a pile of discarded items at the end of the alley. "I've a knack for finding what folks toss out but can still use."

He led them to his small collection of brogues, some mismatched, some worn, but serviceable. Toby helped Ben and Julian find pairs that fit. "These won't win any fashion prizes, but they'll keep your feet from the cold."

As they fitted the shoes, Toby shared his story in brief, a faint levity in his tone despite the sombre content. The trio shared their tale, their friendship with Toby forming swiftly over shared adversities and the simple act of kindness he extended without hesitation.

Toby gave his only two spare shirts to Ben and Julian. They were dirty and ragged, too large for Julian, and hung open at the front, but they were still more than the boys had to their names. Julian, with his arm in a sling, simply draped his shirt over his shoulder, unable to wear it properly.

When they prepared to continue their journey, Toby offered, "I am acquainted with these streets as if they were the very lines upon my palm. I am able to guide you along the swiftest and most secure path to London." His offer was genuine, a chance for companionship as much as it was for helping them.

Grateful, they accepted, and thus, Toby joined them, becoming not just a guide but a new friend, his knowledge of the city's underbelly proving invaluable as they navigated the last, crucial leg of their journey to London.

Ben glanced at Toby, noticing that while he wasn't much taller, he carried himself with the wary air of someone who'd seen more than his share of hardships. "How old are you, Toby?"

"I'm fifteen, I reckon, or maybe sixteen," Toby replied, his eyes shifting to Eliza with a grin. "You fooled me, you know. I still can't believe you're a girl."

"You won't sell us out, will you?" Julian's expression tightened, a flash of pain and suspicion crossing his face. His arm throbbed, swollen from the injury.

Toby shook his head, a sincere look crossing his face. "Nah, what would I do with wealth? I'd rather have friends. Best you sleep here tonight; the law nabs loose orphan kids at night for the orphan home. They use those kids in factories or mines." He dipped his head to Julian. "They'd use you in a mine; they like the small ones for that."

A shiver ran through Julian at the thought. He had heard tales of child labour but had never given them much thought, nestled in the safety of his previous life. Now, the reality was too close for comfort. How he wished he could set all children free from such a fate.

In a conspiratorial whisper, Toby said, "We'll stay in this alley for now. It's hidden enough, and I know the best spots to avoid the patrols. We'll keep watch in shifts; you two get some rest." He pointed to where they could lie down, using the discarded rags and some old sacking he had collected.

Eliza, weary from their journey and the responsibility of her brothers, nodded in agreement. "Thank you, Toby. We owe you."

Toby shrugged off the gratitude, but his smile was genuine. "No debts here. Just looking out for each other." He made Julian a makeshift bed, supporting his injured arm.

As they settled down, the night's chill seeping into their bones, Toby kept watch, his eyes scanning the entrance of the alley with the vigilance of someone who knew too well the dangers of the night. Ben, lying beside Julian, spoke softly of home, of a time when things were simpler, his words a gentle balm for Julian's pain and fear.

Eliza, unable to sleep, watched Toby, marvelling at how someone so young could be so resourceful and kind. She thought of the contrast between their lives, of how privilege had once shielded them from such harsh realities. Now, in the dim light of the alley, with Toby as their guardian, they were all equals in their struggle for survival.

The night passed with the quiet sounds of the city, the distant clatter of carriages, and the occasional shout from a drunkard. But in their little corner, there was a bubble of safety, of camaraderie, where two siblings, a boy from another time, and a streetwise boy shared warmth, stories, and a silent promise to see each other through to the dawn.

The four awoke to the sound of a horse snorting. On its back was a man dressed in black, a patch covering one eye.

A toothless drunk, clad in little more than rags, stood next to the horse, pointing at the children. "There, I told ya! Now, where's my coin?"

CHAPTER 16: UNLIKELY HEROES

William gazed down at the two tatterdemalion figures huddled together. Their clothes clung to their thin frames, and their wide, fearful eyes reflected the faltering light of the dying sun. For hours, he tracked them, having taken the mercenary's suggestion to use Henry's horse as a lure. He couldn't shake the image of the mercenary's brutal decapitation of Henry. He, as his superior, had intervened just in time, ordering him away before he could find the younger children. The mercenary, the man in black, had sneered but obeyed, leaving him to finish the grim task alone.

William had no intention of delivering the children to Ambrose. He thought of Lady Isadora, of how she had clutched his arm in the manor's corridor. "I beg of you! Pray, do not allow him to lay waste to them. They are mere infants, innocent and helpless!" Her words had struck a chord deep within him, a chord that had long been silent. Lord Ambrose's madness knew no bounds, and he could no longer justify serving a man who revelled in cruelty. His own family—lost to the plague years ago—had hardened him, turning him into a weapon for hire. But this? This was a line he would not cross.

Lily clung to her younger brother, her heart pounding as she stared up at the imposing figure astride Henry's horse. The sight of the familiar steed had filled her with hope, but now that hope curdled into dread. The man was armoured, his face obscured by the shadow of his helm, and his presence radiated danger. At ten years old, she had already seen too much—the raids, the fires, the blood—but the thought of Henry's fate, so close and yet unknown, threatened to unravel her. Her brother buried his face in her side, his small hands gripping her sleeve.

William dismounted. He plopped on the forest floor, and the children flinched. He knelt before them, the ground cold beneath his knees. His face, weathered and scarred, was not unkind, but the intensity in his look revealed a history of violence and loss.

"Don't be afraid. I'm not here to harm you." He said.

Lily's grip tightened around her brother. Her voice trembled, but carried a defiant edge. "Where's Henry? Why do you have his horse?"

William hesitated, the onus of his guilt pressing down on him. "Henry… can't be with you anymore. But I made a promise to someone—to keep you safe. And I intend to keep it."

The younger boy peeked out from behind Lily, his tear-streaked face pale with fear. "Safe from what?"

"From the people who want to hurt you—from Lord Ambrose."

"Why should we trust you? You work for him." Lily said.

"I worked for him once, but not anymore. I've lost too much to stand by and let more innocent lives get hurt. You have my word—I'll keep you safe."

The forest stood in hushed stillness as the children studied him, their fear slowly giving way to a fragile hope. William extended a hand, his gauntlet glinting in the fading light. "Come with me. I'll take you somewhere safe."

Lily glanced at her brother, then back at William. After a long moment, she nodded, her hand reaching out to grasp his. Though burdened by her trust, a spark of long-lost purpose became apparent to William.

The sun dipped below the horizon, painting the sky in hues of amber and violet as William approached the Northcott farm. A faint smell of hay and wood-smoke, mixed with the rich scent of freshly turned earth, hung in the air. He had last visited with Ambrose's men, pretending to search for the children, though he knew they hid under the house's floorboards. Despite telling the couple who the children were, he hadn't revealed why they ran away. He had warned them that the children were in grave danger and urged them to protect them at all costs, ensuring the men outside remained unaware of their hiding place. Now, his purpose was different. Knowing the Northcotts would give their lives to protect the innocent, he had brought Lily and Sam to seek their help and shelter, shielding them from Ambrose's reach.

The farmhouse door creaked open as William dismounted, his boots sinking into the soft earth. At the entrance, a wary Mrs Northcott stood, her apron sprinkled with flour. She observed the children, then William, her eyes narrowing slightly. She stepped aside, gesturing for them to enter.

The interior of the farmhouse embraced visitors with a cosy glow, the fire in the hearth spreading warmth throughout. The wooden table sat crooked, its legs uneven against the floor. Beneath it, the carpet lay slightly askew, revealing the faint outline of a trapdoor. William silently acknowledged the Northcotts' courage. They had risked everything to protect Ambrose's children, defying a man who showed no mercy to those who crossed him.

Guarded, Mr Northcott appeared from the kitchen. He nodded at William, a silent understanding passing between them. They needed no words.

"They shall be quite safe here," Mrs Northcott said, kneeling before Lily and Sam, her hands gently brushing dirt from their faces. "No one shall discover them, not whilst we are here to guard them."

William nodded, the gravity of his decision settling on his shoulders. He had spent years serving Ambrose, his own bitterness and loss driving him to acts he now regretted. But the Northcotts had shown him a different path, one rooted in compassion and defiance. They had reminded him of the man he once was—or perhaps the man he could still become.

"Thank you." He turned to leave, the farmhouse door creaking shut behind him. The cool evening air wrapped around him as he mounted Henry's horse, the distant sound of crickets filling the silence. He glanced back at the farmhouse, its windows glowing in the gathering dark. For the first time in years, there was a sense of hope.

He nudged his heels lightly into the horse's flanks, urging it forward. His new personal mission crystallised in his mind: to protect Miss Eliza, Master Julian, and the strange orphan boy Benjamin. Despite his tender age of eleven, Benjamin had shown remarkable courage, risking his own life to save others.

The path ahead was uncertain; Lord Ambrose's reach was long, and his cruelty knew no bounds. Yet, as he rode into the dusk, William's resolve hardened. He would be their shield against the darkness, guiding them through the perils that lay ahead. With every step the horse took, William's determination grew, fuelled by the silent promise he made to keep these young souls safe, no matter the cost.

He had to find them!

***

Ethan ducked as a jet screamed overhead, its engines roaring like a wounded beast. Another followed close behind, the air splitting with the double boom of supersonic speed. The acrid stench of cordite, burning plastic, and decay clung to him, seeping into his pores as if the world itself were rotting. He trailed the old man through the shattered streets, once familiar grounds now reduced to a labyrinth of rubble and ash. Glancing back, he saw the ruins they had fled—crumbling skeletons of buildings silhouetted against a smoke-choked sky. The scene appeared ripped from a dystopian nightmare, a world unravelled.

Ahead, the old man spun. He raised a weapon. "Get down!" he shouted. Before Ethan could react, the shot rang out. Ethan flinched, throwing his arms over his head.

Behind him, a drone sputtered, its red eye stuttering as it struggled to regain altitude. The machine's metallic limbs twitched, its focus locked on Ethan. Panic surged through him, and he bolted, his lungs burning and legs screaming with every step. How could this old man move with such ease, as though time had spared him its toll?

The old man halted near the remains of a windmill, its structure broken and sprawled across the ground like a fallen giant. He checked the sky, then lifted a section of camouflage netting.

Beneath it lay a heavy, circular door, its surface pitted and scarred. "Get in, and hurry!" He gestured to the ladder that descended into darkness.

Ethan hesitated for only a moment before climbing down, the cold metal rungs biting into his palms. With a resonant clang, the old man sealed the door behind them, silencing the chaos above. The sudden quiet was unnerving.

Ethan had to crouch as he moved through the low, narrow tunnel. Pipes and wires snaked along the ceiling, their fittings brushing against his hair. The air grew cooler, the faint hum of fans replacing the distant thunder of explosions. The tunnel eventually widened, opening into a vast control room bathed in the glow of monitors and holographic displays. People moved with purpose, their fingers darting across keyboards as they plotted points on a floating three-dimensional map.

An older woman in a white lab coat stood at the centre of the room, her grey hair pulled into a loose bun. She turned, her eyes widening as they landed on Ethan. The clipboard she held clattered to the floor, forgotten, as she rushed to him. "You found him!" She threw her arms around him. "Daddy, I missed you so much."

Ethan staggered, his legs buckling beneath him. "Olivia?" The room seemed to tilt, the pressure of disbelief bearing down on him.

The old man stepped forward, his hand gripping Ethan's arm to steady him.

Ethan turned, his eyes meeting the old man's fading blue ones. "Ben?" he said.

Ben nodded. "It's me."

Ethan's arms tightened around them, pulling them close despite the years that had aged them beyond recognition. Tears streamed down his face, each one a testament to the love that had defined his life. Olivia and Ben clung to him as though they could bridge the chasm of time with the strength of their hold.

In that moment, the nightmare of reality outside receded, replaced by the warmth of a reunion that defied logic and time. Ethan held them, his children.

Eventually, they released their embrace, though their hands lingered, reluctant to let go. Ethan held Olivia at arm's length, his eyes searching hers. "How? What happened?"

Olivia guided Ethan into a quieter room, followed closely by Ben. She took her father's hands in hers as though he were the child and she the parent. "Daddy, do you remember the day the scientists tried to send you back in time with that boy, Julian?"

Ethan nodded, his brow furrowed. "That just happened. Not ten minutes ago. You were... you were just sixteen, and Ben—" His breath faltered as he glanced at his son. "Ben was only eleven. I don't understand."

Olivia's face softened. "There was an anomaly in the wormhole, Daddy. It sent Julian back to the 19th-century, but it flung you forward—to this future. We've been waiting decades for this day." She stood, her posture straightening as though bracing herself for what came next. "We've been working on a Quantum Temporal Conduit, built on the research of Dr Theodore Marlowe—"

"Quantum Temporal Conduit?"

"Time machine," Ben said.

Ethan nodded slowly, his mind racing to keep up. His eyes darted between them, filled with questions he couldn't yet articulate.

Olivia continued, "Something went wrong in history, Daddy. In the days after you disappeared and Julian went back, strange things started happening. An old factory, built in the early 1900s, materialised in the grazing field. More buildings followed, sprouting up like weeds. Before long, a village surrounded the entire mansion. The farmlands vanished, leaving us with only a tiny sliver of self-sustaining land. This all happened in a matter of weeks."

Ben interjected, "Long story short, Dad. We're trying to fix what I did. We think my interference in the past caused all of this— the wars, the dictatorship, everything."

Ethan's blood ran cold. "Dictatorship?"

"The world's not what it used to be. We're trying to warn the younger me before I—before he—makes a grave error in judgement."

Ethan's head spun, the room seeming to tilt around him. He struggled to process the flood of information, each revelation more staggering than the last.

Olivia continued. "That wormhole Ben fell into when he was

eleven—it wasn't a fluke of nature or some alien technology. A colleague and I created it twenty years after Ben's first travel date. We built the Quantum Temporal Conduit, and it... it 'blew' a hole, for lack of a better word, in the time continuum. It created an unstable wormhole spanning hundreds of years."

Ethan stared at her, his mind reeling. The pieces of the puzzle were there, but they refused to fit. "You're saying... you caused this?"

"Not just Olivia—me too," Ben said.

Olivia nodded, her face etched with guilt and determination. "Yes. And now we're trying to undo it."

The ground above them shuddered violently, sending a cascade of cement dust raining down from the ceiling. Instinctively, Ethan shielded his head, unlike Ben and Olivia, who stood still and impassive. Years of living in this war-torn reality had hardened them to the constant tremors of conflict.

Ethan straightened, brushing the dust from his shoulders, and turned to Olivia, concerned. "But how? How do we fix all of this?"

Ben exchanged a glance with Olivia before answering. "We wait. I made a mistake in the past—I inadvertently prevented Lord Ambrose Wilson from death. Because the timelines run parallel to one another, we need to go back and warn my younger self. But it has to be at the right moment. If I go back myself, it could create a paradox that might destroy the wormhole—and us along with it."

Ethan listened, his mind struggling to grasp the enormity of what Ben was saying.

"Daddy, Ben can't go back to warn himself. It would essentially erase him from existence. That's why we plan to send Grace," Olivia said.

"Grace?" Ethan glanced at the door Olivia was pointing to. There, standing in the doorway, was a young woman with striking features and an air of quiet confidence. Her presence lit up the room.

Ben took her lovingly by the hand. "Grace, meet your great-grandfather."

Ethan stood in silence, unable to utter a single word. Overwhelmed, he reached out to shake her hand, his thoughts spinning. But Grace stepped forward and embraced him instead, her arms wrapping around him in a hug that spoke of years of longing and connection. For a short time, the chaos of the world outside faded, giving way to the warmth of family.

Grace sat beside Ethan, her hand resting gently on his arm. "We've met before. Only briefly, though. Granny Olivia tried to send me back once, but we didn't account for the concurrent timeline. She's since repositioned the wormhole, but there was a miscalculation."

Olivia nodded with regret. "Daddy, remember the girl you thought you hit with the car, but it turned out to be a deer? That was Grace. We accidentally materialised her in the road, right next to that deer. When she saw our car about to hit her—she pulled herself back."

Ethan stared at Grace, his mind reeling. The memory came flooding back—the dark road, the flash of movement, the relief of realising he hadn't struck a person. His head pounded as the pieces fell into place. "That was you?"

Grace nodded, her eyes filled with empathy. "Yes. And now, we're going to try again—this time, to set things right."

Ethan looked from Grace to Olivia. "Grace's parents—where are they?"

Olivia's face crumpled, the heaviness of the question pressing down on her. A single tear escaped, tracing a glistening path down her cheek before she brushed it away with a trembling hand. "Killed. Years ago, in the war."

The words hung in the air, heavy and final. A pang of grief struck Ethan, not just for losing his grandchildren—people he had never known—but for the pain etched into Olivia's face "I'm so sorry."

"I remember a few things about them—the sound of my mother's laugh. The way my father used to carry me on his shoulders," Grace said, emotionally. "Granny Olivia and Uncle Ben have been my family since."

Ben placed a hand on Grace's shoulder. "We've done our best to keep her safe. But this world… it's not the one we wanted for her."

Ethan's chest ached as he regarded Grace, her youthful face

shadowed by a life marred by loss and conflict. He thought of the world he had left behind—a world where his children were still young, where the future had seemed full of promise. Surrounded by the wreckage of a fractured timeline in the dimly lit bunker, the full impact of his losses bore down on him.

Olivia inhaled, her shoulders straightening as she composed herself. "That's why we have to fix this, Daddy! Not just for us, but for Grace. For everyone. We can't let this future be the one that stays."

Ethan nodded. The grief and confusion still swirled within him, but beneath it all was a growing determination. He looked at Grace, then at Olivia and Ben. "Then tell me what I need to do."

Olivia tightened her grip on Ethan's hand, her eyes glistening with unshed tears. "We would love more time with you, but time is running out. Stop those scientists you invited in. They're interfering with the wormholes we're trying to control."

Ethan remained silent, his throat tight with emotion. He reached up, his fingers trembling as they brushed against Olivia's aged face. The lines etched into her skin told a story of years he had missed, of a life lived without him. "When I get back, I'm never going to let you go."

Olivia hugged him for a long while and kissed him on the cheek. "Let's get started. We'll send you back to your present while we work on sending Grace back at the right time. If Ben's calculations are correct, she'll arrive in the correct century to alert Ben and Eliza."

Ethan glanced at Grace, who stood nearby. "You... be careful."

"I will, and I'll make sure they listen."

Leaning in, Olivia whispered over the machinery's purr. "One last thing, Daddy, don't speak to young me—or anyone—about what you've seen here. We don't know how it might affect the future, or the past."

Ethan nodded, his throat tight when their eyes met. The enormity of the secret weighed on his chest, a burden he would carry alone.

Olivia stepped back, her eyes lingering on him for a moment longer before she turned to Ben. "Ready?"

Ben moved to a console, his fingers dancing across the

controls. The room resonated with energy as the machinery came to life, lights pulsing and screens displaying streams of data. "We're ready. Dad, you'll need to step into the chamber."

Ethan hesitated, his eyes lingering on Olivia and Ben. The thought of leaving them again, even to fix the past, tore at him. But he knew there was no other way. He squeezed Olivia's hand one last time, then released it and stepped into the chamber. The surrounding air crackled with static, and the drone grew louder, vibrating through his bones.

"We'll see you soon, Daddy. In a better future," Olivia said.

The surrounding light intensified, blinding and all-consuming. For a moment, Ethan was weightless, suspended between moments. Then, with a rush of energy, the world dissolved around him. He flailed, feeling as though he'd been tossed from a plane without a parachute. A blinding light seared his vision, accompanied by a deafening buzz that roared in his ears. His stomach lurched, and for a moment, the world spun in a chaotic blur of colour and sound. Gradually, his vision sharpened, the room coming into focus like a polaroid developing before his eyes.

Vince Colby sat on the edge of Olivia's bed, a melting popsicle dripping onto his hand, his mouth hanging open as he stared at Ethan. The scientist's face was a mask of shock, his usual confidence replaced by stunned silence.

Sixteen-year-old Olivia shot up from the floor where she'd been sitting beside Ben's bed. The house had shaken moments earlier, the walls rattling as if struck by an earthquake. She knew what it meant. Her heart pounding, she sprinted to her bedroom and froze in the doorway, her eyes widening at the sight of her father. "Daddy... Oh, Daddy!" She launched herself into his arms.

Ethan caught her, lifting her off the ground in a tight embrace. He buried his face in her hair, breathing in the familiar youthful scent. "Hey, baby girl." Emotion pressed through him, raw and unguarded. He kissed her forehead, her cheeks, her lips, her hair, as if trying to reassure himself she was real. "I'm never letting you go."

The sound of hurried footsteps echoed down the hall, and Claire burst into the room, her chest heaving from the sprint up the stairs. She skidded to a halt, her eyes locking onto Ethan. Tears welled in her eyes, spilling over as she rushed forward, wrapping her arms around both Ethan and Olivia. The three of them stood there, a tangled knot of relief and love.

Vince, still gripping his melting popsicle, broke the moment. "Marlowe! Get in here! It worked! Do whatever you did again—maybe we can pull Ben back too."

"Stop!" Ethan's cry cut through the clamour. He set Olivia down gently, then he strode to the equipment scattered around the room. Without hesitation, he began yanking plugs from the machines, the cords snapping free with each sharp tug.

Claire lunged forward, grabbing at his arms. "Ethan, stop! What are you doing? Ben is still stuck in the past!"

He turned to her, his hands cradling her face. His thumbs brushed away her tears as his eyes found hers. "Trust me." The urgency in his touch stilled her protests. He released her and continued dismantling the equipment, ignoring the scientists' frantic objections.

Marlowe appeared in the doorway, his face flushed with excitement and confusion. "What's going on? We need to—"

"Pack up your equipment, your gadgets, and your wires, and leave. Thank you for trying to help, but we've got it from here," Ethan said.

Claire stared at him, her hands trembling. "What about Ben?"

Olivia echoed her mother. "What about Ben, Daddy?"

Ethan turned to them. "We'll get him back, but not like this. Not with their help. Trust me."

A flash of lightning split the sky, its jagged brilliance illuminating the landscape for a split second. In that fleeting moment, the silhouette of yet another new building emerged, stark and imposing against the darkened horizon. It hadn't been there before. Towering over the former open fields, the building's sharp angles and strange design clashed harshly with the estate's familiar landscape.

Ethan stiffened, a gasp escaping his lips. The lightning faded, plunging the world back into shadow, but the image of the building burned in his mind. His stomach churned as the implications settled over him. The timeline was unravelling faster than he had realised, the past and future colliding in ways he couldn't comprehend.

Olivia stepped up beside him, her face pale as she stared out the window. "What are you going to do? How are we going to get Ben back without their help?"

Claire crossed her arms as if to shield herself from the unsettling sight outside. "It's happening more often now. Every time the wormhole destabilises, something changes. Buildings appear, roads shift, even the land itself seems to... rearrange."

Marlowe stepped forward, his hands outstretched in a pleading gesture. "Mr Wallace, you need us! You can't do this alone. What about your son—how will he get back?"

Ethan shook his head. "No. You don't understand. Please, pack your things and leave!"

Marlowe opened his mouth to protest, his face flushing with frustration. "But—"

"That's final!" Ethan's outburst cut through the room, sharp with exasperation. The force of his tone silenced Marlowe mid-sentence.

Claire stared at her husband, her heart pounding. She had never seen him like this—so decisive, so unshakable. The man standing before her was a stranger in some ways, yet undeniably the man she loved. She stepped closer, her eyes searching his face for answers. "Ethan. What happened? Where were you?"

Seeing her worry, Ethan's expression softened. He reached out, his hand brushing against hers, but he didn't speak. The burden of his silence spoke volumes, carrying with it a story too vast, too overwhelming, to put into words.

And a future he could never speak of.

CHAPTER 17: LONDON

Toby yawned and stretched as he got up, acutely aware of the danger posed by the man in black. He forced himself to act natural, as though he didn't have a care in the world, even as the mercenary's stare bore into him. Moving casually, he walked to the end of the alley and used a drain against the wall to relieve himself. As he finished, he glanced back at the mercenary, who sat motionless on his horse, watching intently. Toby raised an eyebrow, feigning nonchalance. "What is it you're staring at, sir?"

Ben, Julian, and Eliza joined Toby, directing three streams at the wall that flowed into the drain.

The mercenary struck the drunk man. "Drunken fool! I'm hunting a girl and two brats, not a pack of uncouth lads reeking of piss and ale." He turned and left, the drunkard begging for a few shillings.

With the mercenary gone, the four erupted in joyous laughter.

Eliza lifted the water bladder she had used as a makeshift boy part to fool the mercenary. "It worked! Toby, you're a bloody genius. He didn't even suspect a thing."

The baker shoved open the backdoor to the alley. A cloud of steam billowed out, carrying the rich, yeasty scent of fresh bread. He held out a golden loaf, its crust crackling as it cooled in the morning air. "Here, lads. Get this into you before it goes cold." Kindness was present in his gruff tone, yet his eyes flicked to the street, betraying a wariness of being watched.

Toby stepped forward, his hands closing around the warm loaf. "Thank you," he said, already tearing off chunks and passing them to the others. He glanced at Eliza, her face smudged with dirt, her cap pulled low over her eyes. "Eliza, we must move. If someone sees through that disguise, we're done for."

Eliza ate hungrily. "You must call me Eli, not Eliza!"

"Right. Sorry." Toby scanned the alley, his attention lingering on the entrance. "I'll get you to London, but we can't stay here. Finish up and let's be on our way."

Ben took his portion, the bread soft and warm in his hands. He bit into it, the flavour rich and comforting. His mind drifted to his mum's kitchen—the sizzle of bacon in the pan, the golden yolks of fried eggs, the buttery toast stacked high on a plate. The memory was so vivid he could almost smell it. He swallowed hard, the bread sticking in his throat. Without a word, he leaned into Julian. Julian smiled and leaned back into Ben.

The crisp morning air nipped at their faces, carrying the faint tang of wood smoke and the distant clamour of the waking city. Somewhere nearby, a cart rattled over cobblestones, and a dog barked, sharp and insistent. The alley itself was quiet, save for the soft sounds of chewing and the occasional shuffle of feet.

Eliza wiped her hands on her breeches, her eyes scanning the alley's mouth. "Let's go. Every moment we tarry brings us closer to being caught."

Toby nodded, glancing at the street. "Stay close and keep your heads down. We've a long way to go."

The group slipped into the shadows of the narrow passageway. Julian lingered, his gaze fixed on the baker's door, shutting out the kitchen's warmth. He flexed his arm experimentally, surprised to find he could move it again. It was still sore and stiff, but he straightened it, a glimmer of hope breaking through his weariness. "Benjamin, look," he said. "My arm—it's healing."

"Oh, thank goodness—it's not broken then," Ben said, helping Julian remove the makeshift sling.

They moved through the cobblestone streets, their footsteps echoing against the buildings that loomed on either side. Ben's eyes widened as he took in the architecture—the intricate carvings on stone facades, the timber-framed houses leaning precariously over the road, and the occasional grand structure with columns and arches that seemed to scrape the sky. He was walking through history itself, a living world he had only read about in books. Awe and disbelief, a dizzying mix, washed over him, leaving him breathless. He had come from the future, and yet here he was, surrounded by the very past he had studied.

Ahead, Toby and Eliza walked briskly, their heads bent close together as they debated their next move. "We'll begin at the docks," Toby said. "If Alexander's still in the city, that's where he'll be. Plenty of ships coming and going, plenty of places to hide."

Eliza's jaw tightened at the mention of Alexander's name. Her hand instinctively brushed her still-flat stomach, a fleeting gesture that betrayed the secret she carried. "He'll be at the forge. He always said he'd find work as a blacksmith if he had to. We'll start there."

Toby nodded, although his caution was clear. "If your father's men are watching the forges, it's a risk. We'll need to tread carefully."

Eliza's eyes hardened. "I don't care about the risk. Alexander deserves to know the truth—about me, about what my father did. He thinks I never wanted to see him again. I won't let that lie stand."

Ben fell back slightly, his arm slipping over Julian's shoulders. Julian responded in kind, his own arm around Ben's waist, a gesture of quiet solidarity. They walked like that, close and unspoken, their bond stronger than words. Ben felt a surge of gratitude for Julian, his best friend, his anchor in this strange world. He loved Julian and Eliza—they were like the brother and sister from this century. Together, they were a family, forged not by blood but by necessity and trust.

Busy streets bustled around them—vendors hawking their wares, children darting between carts, and the occasional horse-drawn carriage clattering past. The air was thick with the smells of baking bread, roasting meat, and the faint tang of the river nearby. The morning sun blazed, its warmth soaking into exposed skin and casting a golden glow over the scene. Ben breathed it all in, trying to memorise every detail: the hum of life around him, the heat on his face, the way the light caught the dust in the air. This was history, alive and real, and he was part of it.

Julian glanced at him, a small smile playing on his lips. "You're staring again."

"Can you blame me? This is… everything. It's incredible."

"Just don't get us killed while you're gawking."

Ben laughed, the sound swallowed by the noise of the street. "I'll try."

Up ahead, Toby glanced back. "Keep up, you two. We've work to do."

Ben and Julian quickened their pace, falling into step with the others, unwilling to let each other go.

Hours later, Ben's smile faded, twisting into a look of disdain as he took in the scene before him. The sun had passed its midday peak, but the sky had taken on an ominous hue. They had stopped at a bustling bridge, its wooden planks creaking under the weight of carts, horses, and pedestrians. Beyond the bridge lay London, sprawling and immense, its silhouette rising against the horizon like a beast of stone and smoke.

The city was impressive, yes, but also oppressive. A thick smog hung in the air, a murky veil that turned the sky a sickly grey and muted the sunlight to a faint glow. The buildings, once grand in their uniformity, now seemed drab and lifeless, their facades darkened by soot and grime. The streets teemed with people, but the filth beneath their feet was impossible to ignore. Sewage and animal waste flowed in rivulets down the gutters, merging with the murky waters of the Thames, which carried the stench of the city out to sea.

Ben wrinkled his nose, the acrid smell of rot and smoke assaulting his senses. He had learned about the squalor of 19th-century London, but nothing could have prepared him for the reality of it. The river, once majestic in his imagination, was now a sluggish, foul-smelling ribbon of filth, its surface littered with debris. He looked at Julian, standing beside him, his face mirroring his own grimness.

"Cheerful place, isn't it?" Julian said.

Ben shook his head, his disdain deepening. "It's like the entire city's drowning in its own filth. How do people live like this?"

Toby, standing a few steps ahead, turned to them with a wry smile. "You grow accustomed to it. Or you don't. Either way, it's home to more souls than you can count. And somewhere in that mess is Alexander."

Eliza stared at the city. Her face was unreadable. "We'll find him. No matter how vast or foul this place may be."

"All of you, hold hands," Toby said, cutting through the chaos of the crowded street. "You don't wish to be separated—or worse, snatched. You younger lads, stay close and don't let go of each other. They'll sell boys like you to the mines quicker than you can blink." His grip tightened on Eliza's hand. Eliza clutched Julian's hand like a lifeline, and Julian held Ben's, their small chain weaving through the throng of people.

Toby glanced back at Ben and Julian. "The fortunate ones end up as rich men's servants—scrubbing floors and cleaning outhouses. The rest? You don't want to know."

Ben shivered, his fingers tightening around Julian's hand. The streets were a nightmare—a sea of bodies pressing in from all sides, the air thick with the stench of sweat, sewage, and rotting food. He tried to focus on Julian's grip, but the crowd was relentless. A burly man reeking of alcohol and decay shoved past, his hip slamming into Ben with enough force to rip his hand from Julian's. Panic surged through Ben as he stumbled.

"Julian!" His shout vanished into the overwhelming noise of barking, shouting, and clattering wheels. He pushed through the crowd, his heart pounding, trying to keep his balance as hips and elbows jostled him from every direction. The press of bodies was suffocating, and he had to weave and duck to avoid being knocked over, the sea of legs and torsos closing in around him. The stench of the street was overwhelming—a nauseating mix of unwashed bodies, animal waste, and something far worse.

A cart laden with fish innards overturned in front of him, its contents spilling across the cobblestones in a slimy, reeking mess. Ben's feet slipped out from under him, and he landed hard in the putrid sludge. He gagged, struggling to sit up as the crowd parted around him, shrinking back in disgust from the foul morass.

"Julian!" he screamed, voice ragged with desperation, but the din swallowed it whole. He flailed, fighting to stand as the fish guts slicked his hands and knees, some of the slimy rot oozing inside his clothes, cold and clinging. Every move was a battle. Just as panic clawed at him, a hand seized his.

"Got you." Julian helped Ben up, dodging the slimy mess as best he could to keep the stench off himself. Ben's relief was short-lived as the smell hit him anew, and he doubled over, retching.

"Let's get out of here," Julian said, pulling Ben to the curb. Trembling, Ben stumbled after him, gagging at the stench clinging to his skin. He doubled over and retched again, his stomach heaving, but Julian kept a steady grip on him, urging him forward.

"Don't stop. We can't lose the others."

Ben nodded, swallowing hard as he forced himself to keep pace. The crowd thinned slightly as they reached the edge of the street, and Ben caught sight of Toby and Eliza waiting ahead, their faces etched with worry. Toby's eyes narrowed as he took in Ben's dishevelled state, but he said nothing, simply gesturing for them to keep moving.

"Stay close. Next time, you might not be so fortunate."

Ben gripped Julian's hand like a lifeline, his heart still racing as they pushed on into the labyrinth of London's streets. The city was a monster, he realised, and they were walking straight into its jaws. But as long as they stayed together, they might just press on without further mishap.

Toby yanked them into a quieter side street, away from the chaos of the major thoroughfare. The narrow lane offered a brief respite, though the stench of the city still lingered in the air. Ben leaned against a crumbling brick wall, gagging, his face pale and his hands trembling. "I... Aargh... It smells rotten," he said, wiping his mouth with the back of his hand. "I'd give anything for a shower right now."

Julian took a step back, wrinkling his nose as he sniffed his own hand, which had been gripping Ben's just moments ago. He grimaced. "I don't think it's going to rain soon," he said.

"Not that kind of shower," Ben said, though he was too miserable to explain further.

Eliza stood close by, looking disgusted. She wanted to comfort him, to pat his shoulder or offer a kind word, but the smell radiating from him kept her at arm's length. "Oh, poor Benjamin.

There must be some way to get you clean."

Toby, ever practical, scanned the alley and pointed to a narrow passageway beside the building they were leaning against. "There—a cistern. Come on." He led the way, his boots crunching over loose stones and debris. The others followed, glancing over their shoulders to make sure no one was watching.

At the alley's end stood a cistern, brimming with rainwater gathered from the rooftops overhead. Toby gestured to it. "Climb in."

Ben hesitated, guilt twisting his stomach. "But… this is someone's water. I'll ruin it."

Toby shot him a sharp look. "You'll ruin more than water if you don't get that stink off you. Now, in."

With a grimace, Ben hoisted himself over the edge of the cistern and plunged into the icy water. The shock of the cold forced a sharp gasp from his lungs, and he shuddered as the water seeped into his clothes, clinging to his skin like a second, slimy layer. Ben wasted no time stripping them off and tossing them over the edge of the cistern. The awful stench of rot overrode any sense of modesty, leaving little room for dignity. Soon, he stood waist-deep in the water, shivering but determined to rid himself of the foulness.

Toby didn't hesitate. He grabbed Ben by the shoulders and shoved his head under the water. Ben came up spluttering, his hair plastered to his forehead, but Toby was already scrubbing at his scalp with rough, hurried motions.

"Hold still," Toby muttered, though there was no real malice in his voice. His hands worked methodically, scrubbing at Ben's hair and back with an old piece of torn cloth.

Ben scrubbed at his arms and chest, the cold water turning his skin pink as he worked to remove as much of the filth as possible. Toby dunked the cloth into the water and handed it to Ben. "Here. Don't miss any spots. You smell like a week-old fish market."

The surrounding water turned murky, swirling with the remnants of his ordeal. He glanced up at Toby, who was watching him with a critical eye, and couldn't help but chuckle despite the chill.

"What?" Toby asked, raising an eyebrow.

"Nothing," Ben said, shaking his head. "Just… thanks. For this. For helping me."

Toby smiled, saying nothing.

As Ben finished scrubbing himself clean, Toby's sharp eyes caught sight of a clothesline strung between two buildings further down the alley. A few garments fluttered in the breeze, dry and clean. Without a second thought, he darted over, snatched a shirt, a pair of trousers and a tattered old towel, and returned to the cistern.

At the mouth of the alley, Julian and Eliza stood guard, their eyes scanning the street with sharp, anxious glances. The nearby sounds of the city—shouts, footsteps, the clatter of carts—seemed too close for comfort. "How much longer?" Eliza called, glancing over her shoulder. Ben was out and drying himself with the towel.

"Almost done," Ben called back, feeling liberated from the stench even though a faint fishy smell remained.

"Here," Toby said, tossing the clothes to Ben. "They're dry, at least. Better than nothing."

Ben caught the bundle and nodded gratefully. The clothes were slightly big—the shirt hanging loosely across his shoulders and the trousers baggy around his waist—but they were clean and comforting against his skin. Toby, meanwhile, had picked up Ben's discarded brogues and was scrubbing them with the rag, rinsing off the worst of the muck. He shook them out and patted them dry as best he could before handing them back.

"They're still wet," Toby warned, "but they'll have to do."

Ben slipped the brogues on, cringing slightly at the dampness but relieved to have something on his feet.

A door slammed open behind them. A man emerged, brandishing a broom like a weapon, his face twisted in anger. "Hey! What do you think you're doing with my water?" the man bellowed, his face red with fury.

Ben didn't need to be told twice. He took off running with the others, leaving the soiled clothes behind. Toby led the way, weaving through the maze of alleys, while Julian and Eliza followed close behind. Ben's brogues squelched with every step, but he couldn't help laughing as they ran—a wild, relieved sound that echoed off the walls.

The man's shouts faded behind them, and soon they were far enough away to slow down. Ben leaned against a wall, catching his breath. "Thanks," he said, grinning at Toby. "I feel almost human again."

Toby smirked. "Don't mention it. Just try not to fall into any more fish guts, all right?"

Eliza and Julian laughed, the tension of the moment lifting. Ben exhaled, his shoulders relaxing as the stress in his chest eased. His shoes, still damp, squelched with every step. As the sun dipped lower, stretching long shadows over the cobblestones, a distant sound reached them—a rhythmic clanging cutting through the city's bustle.

Ben's spirits lifted. "Eliza," he said, excitement lighting his eyes, "I hear an anvil. A blacksmith!"

Eliza's eyes lit up, and without a word, she took off running, her boots pounding against the stones. Ben and Julian exchanged a glance before sprinting after her, their exhaustion momentarily forgotten. They rounded a corner and skidded to a halt in front of a small forge. The glow of the fire spilled out into the street, and the sharp odour of hot metal filled the air. A greying man in a leather apron stood at the anvil, his hammer poised mid-strike.

Eliza's excitement carried her forward, and she nearly barrelled straight into the forge before the blacksmith stepped in her path, his hand shooting out to stop her. "Hey there, lad! Careful now. That there's hot enough to take your skin off, it is. What's the rush?"

Eliza barely registered his warning, her eyes scanning the forge. "Alexander?" she blurted out, hope twisting in her stomach. "Does he work here?"

The blacksmith frowned, lowering his hammer. "Alexander? Don't know no Alexander. Say," he added, squinting at her, "what's up with your voice? Hasn't cracked yet, has it?"

Eliza's heart sank, her shoulders slumping. "Thank you, sir," she said, forcing herself to stay polite. "Might there be any other blacksmiths in the city? Anywhere he might be employed?"

The man straightened, his eyes narrowing as he studied her more closely. He reached up and unhooked a sword hanging from the ceiling. "I say, you're that girl, aren't you? You're not a lad at all. They're searching for you, indeed they are."

Ben's stomach dropped. Without thinking, he grabbed Eliza's hand, his grip tight. "Run!" he shouted, yanking her back toward the street.

The blacksmith lunged forward, but they were already moving, their feet slapping against the cobblestones as they sprinted away. Eliza's heart pounded in her chest, her breath coming in short, panicked gasps. Julian was right behind them.

"Split up!" Toby shouted from somewhere ahead. "Meet at the old church by the river!"

Ben veered left, pulling Eliza down a narrow alley, while Julian stayed with Toby, disappearing into the maze of streets. The sound of the blacksmith's shouts faded behind them, but Ben didn't slow down. His lungs burned, and his damp shoes hurt, but he kept running, Eliza's hand still gripped in his.

They didn't stop until they reached the shadow of the old church, its spire looming dark against the twilight sky. Ben leaned against the wall, gasping for air, his clothes clinging to him once more—this time from sweat. Eliza slumped beside him, her face flushed and her eyes wide with fear.

"We'll find him," Ben said, though he wasn't sure if he was trying to reassure Eliza or himself. "We just have to be smarter."

Eliza nodded, her jaw tightening. "Next time, we shan't let anyone catch us unawares."

Toby and Julian came sprinting from another street, their faces flushed from exertion. They collapsed in a heap near Eliza. Toby, sprawled on the cobblestones, tilted his head back to look up at Eliza, a wry grin spreading across his face despite the exhaustion.

"Life is never dull in your company," Toby said. "Every day is an escapade—fleeing from blacksmiths, evading fish entrails, nearly being sold to the mines. What next? A duel with the king himself?"

"If it keeps us alive, I shall endure it," she said, her hands resting on her knees as she leaned forward, still panting. "But next time, perhaps we avoid the wrath of blacksmiths."

"I should welcome a day without running," Julian said, staring up at the darkening sky. "Or tumbling into something foul."

Ben chuckled. "I'll second that. Clean and boring sounds

perfect right about now."

Toby pushed himself up onto his elbows, his grin fading as he glanced around the shadowy street. "Cleanliness and tedium won't keep us alive," he said, his tone turning grave. "We must press on. That blacksmith shan't be the last to recognise you, Eliza. We need a scheme—and swiftly."

Eliza nodded grimly. "We shall find Alexander. But you're right. We cannot keep stumbling about like this. We must be more cunning."

Toby got to his feet, brushing dirt off his trousers. "Cunning and swifter. Let us quit the streets before someone else spots us. We'll devise our next move from there."

"As long as 'next move' doesn't involve more running," Julian said, half-joking.

"No promises," Eliza said, turning to lead the way. "But if fortune favours us, perhaps we'll find Alexander before anyone else finds us."

Eliza turned and looked up at the church, its weathered stone facade glowing in the fading light. The arched windows were dark, and the heavy wooden doors stood ajar, as if inviting them in. She squared her shoulders. "Let us seek refuge here tonight. It's safe, and perhaps they'll have something to eat—or at least a place to rest without looking over our shoulders."

Toby followed her gaze, his eyes scanning the building for signs of life. "Could be a suitable spot," he said cautiously. "Churches won't turn away the desperate. But keep your wits about you. Not everyone who hides behind a cross is a saint."

Julian stepped closer, his arms crossed against the evening chill. "I don't care if they're saints or sinners. As long as they've got a roof and a bite of bread, I'm in."

Ben nodded in agreement. His stomach growled loudly enough to draw a faint smile from Eliza. "Same here. I'd even settle for stale bread," he said.

Eliza led the way, her hand pausing on the rough wooden door, and glanced back at the others. "Stay close and let me do the talking. If anyone asks, we're travellers seeking shelter for the night. Nothing more."

Toby gave a curt nod, his hand resting on the hilt of the knife hidden beneath his coat. Julian and Ben fell in behind him, their eyes scanning the shadows that stretched across the churchyard.

Eliza pushed the door open, the hinges creaking. The church interior was dimly lit, illuminated solely by the weak candlelight on the altar and the last rays of sunlight streaming through stained glass. The air smelled of incense and polish, and the silence was heavy, almost reverent. A priest stood near the front, his back to them as he arranged something on the altar. Hearing their footsteps, he turned, mildly surprised.

"Good evening, Father," Eliza said. "We're travellers in need of shelter for the night. Might we rest here?"

The priest paused, his eyes lingering on their unkempt appearance. Then he smiled. "Of course, my children. The church is a sanctuary for all. Come in, and I'll see what we can offer."

Eliza stepped inside, the others following close behind. For the first time in what felt like days, she allowed herself a whisper of hope. For now, they were out of harm's way. And with a little luck, they might even find a moment of peace.

That night, they slept on the hard wooden pews of the church, their bodies weary from the day's chaos. Ben's exhaustion was so overpowering that not even the harsh surface could prevent him from dozing off quickly. He drifted into a dreamless sleep, his mind blank and his breathing steady.

Sometime later, a low rumble—distant thunder or perhaps the growl of a cart over cobblestones—jolted him awake. Outside, the faint shouts of drunkards echoed through the city, but inside, the silence felt almost sacred. Ben sat up, rubbing his eyes, and froze.

There, standing near the pulpit, was a figure—a woman, or perhaps a girl—dressed in a long white dress that seemed to glow in the dim light. Her hair flowed in soft waves around her shoulders, and she looked peaceful and composed. Ben blinked, unsure if he was still dreaming. He glanced at the others: Toby sprawled across a pew, Julian curled into a ball, and Eliza lying still, her face peaceful in sleep. None of them stirred.

The figure stepped down from the pulpit, her movements graceful. She raised a finger to her lips, signalling for silence, then gestured for him to follow. Ben felt no fear, no alarm—only a strange, inexplicable calm. He rose from the pew, his movements cautious, and approached her.

As he drew closer, she glanced over his shoulder at the others, ensuring they were still asleep, before turning back to him. Her eyes radiated warmth and compassion, hinting at a depth of wisdom beyond her age. Ben reached out, almost instinctively, and touched her face. He expected her to be a ghostly illusion, but her warmth grounded him in reality. She smelled clean, like fresh linen.

"Are you an angel?"

"No, Ben. But I came to help you."

"How do you know my name?"

"My name is Grace. You are my great uncle. My granny, Olivia, sent me."

Ben's legs gave out, and he sank onto the pulpit step, his mind reeling. Grace sat beside him, her presence steadying. He studied her face, searching for something familiar, and found it—the angle of her jaw, the shape of her eyes. She bore a resemblance to his family, to *him*.

"How did you know I would be here?" he asked. "Have I been gone so long?" The questions tumbled out, one after another, his thoughts a whirlwind. "How did you find me? What happened? Am I—"

Grace held up a hand, cutting him off. "I can't explain everything now. It's an endless story, and there's no time. I knew you would be here because you told me—in the future."

"I told you? Wait, how old am I when I told you? What happens to me? Do I—"

"Ben. I can't divulge too much. If I tell you, it could change history. Please, ask no more questions. Just listen." She drew nearer, her look grave. "A man in armour is looking for you. He's big, with a crest of the king on his chest. Ben, Toby is going to kill him, and you have the power to stop it—he is your... our only hope for the future. But do not tell Toby now. It will affect the timeline. Keep vigilant to his actions."

Ben's head spun, his heart pounding. "What? Who is he? Why would I—"

Grace grabbed Ben's hand, stopping him mid-sentence. She leaned in close, her voice dropping to a whisper as she shared more—names, events, things that might happen in the days ahead. She finished by telling him what to watch for, the signals that would mean it was time to return to his own timeline.

Having told him everything he needed to know, she pushed a button on the small device around her neck. The ground beneath their feet rumbled. Grace stood, her form beginning to shimmer, as if she were dissolving into the air. "Remember what I said, Ben. Trust yourself. And don't let fear guide you."

"Wait!" He reached out to her. But his hand passed through the empty air. She was gone, as if she had never been there at all.

Ben's mind was racing. Had it been a dream? A vision? He looked down at his hand that had touched her face. It still felt warm, as if her presence lingered. He glanced at the others, still asleep, undisturbed.

He stared at the spot where Grace had stood, her words echoing in his mind. A man in armour. A crest of the king. Toby. And somehow, it was connected to the future—his future, and hers.

He didn't know what to believe, but one thing was certain: he couldn't ignore what she had told him. Whatever was coming, he had to be ready.

CHAPTER 18: ALEXANDER

Alexander pounded the glowing metal on the anvil, each strike precise and deliberate as he shaped the red-hot iron into a wheel rim. The unfinished carriage stood nearby, its polished wood gleaming under the workshop's roof. It was a commission for the king himself, and Alexander took pride in his work, though his mind was far from the task at hand. Sweat dripped down his muscular, sun-browned arms, and he blew a stray tuft of hair from his face, the rest tied back in a loose ponytail. He plunged the rim into a barrel of water, the hiss of steam rising into the air as the metal cooled.

Every day, his thoughts drifted to Eliza. Her face haunted him—her laughter, her smile, the way her eyes had once lit up when she looked at him. But now, all he could remember was the last time he had seen her, the day she had turned on him so suddenly, so cruelly. He had gone to her, desperate to understand why she had sent him away, only to be met with snarling dogs and men on horseback, chasing him like a hunted animal. Her words echoed in his mind, sharp and cold: "I never want to see you again." Was it because of the child she carried? His child? The thought tormented him, but he had no answers, only the ache of a love lost.

The sound of footsteps pulled him from his thoughts. He turned, his hammer still in hand, to see a grubby-faced lad approaching from the road. Behind him stood three others, their faces wary and their clothes worn. The boy cleared his throat. "Alexander."

Alexander straightened, studying the group. He glanced at the youngest boy, who had spoken to him. There was something familiar about him, something that tugged at his memory. "Julian? Is that you?"

Julian took a hesitant step forward, his small frame trembling. "Yes."

Alexander's chest tightened, and he dropped his hammer, the tool clattering to the ground. He put his hands on Julian's shoulders, confused by the boy's attire. "Julian. What are you doing here? Where's Eliza? Is she—"

Before he could finish, the older boy stepped forward, his hands hiding his face, his shoulders shaking with silent sobs. Alexander frowned, his gaze shifting to the young man. There was something about him, something familiar, but he couldn't place it. The boy lowered his hands, revealing a face streaked with dirt and tears.

"Alexander, it's me." Eliza said.

At first, Alexander did not know how to react to this boy—this young man—nor did he fully comprehend the truth of the situation. He stared at the young man, his mind racing. The voice, the eyes—it couldn't be. But then he saw it, her eyes, the way her hands trembled as they reached up to touch her face. "Eliza?"

She nodded, tears streaming down her cheeks. "It's me, Alexander."

Alexander recoiled, his body stiff with shock and disbelief. "You sent me away. You told me you never wished to see me again. Why are you here now, dressed like this?"

Eliza stepped closer, her hands outstretched. "It wasn't me, Alexander. It was my papa. He lied to you, to both of us. He told you I hated you, but I never did. I love you. I've always loved you."

Alexander's chest was heaving with emotion. "I tried to contact you. I wrote letters, sent messages. But I never heard from you."

Ben stepped forward, unable to stay silent any longer. "Ambrose locked her in the cellar. Then he walled her in. He was going to kill her—and the child she's carrying."

Alexander's face darkened, his cheeks flushing with anger.

"That blackguard. He'll pay for this. I'll make him—"

Eliza grabbed his arms, her grip firm. "No, Alexander. He's a dangerous man. We can't fight him. But we can leave. We can go to the provinces, start a new life—a family. Just you, me, Julian, and our child."

Alexander stared at her, his anger warring with the love that had never faded. He pulled her into his arms, holding her as if afraid she might vanish. "Eliza. I've missed you so much. I thought I'd lost you forever."

"You never lost me," she said, her face pressed against his chest. "Not truly. And you never will."

Alexander cupped her face in his hands, his calloused thumbs brushing away the last traces of her tears. For a moment, he stared at her, as if committing every detail to memory—the curve of her lips, the way her eyes shimmered with unshed tears, the faint smudges of dirt that couldn't conceal her beauty. Then, unable to hold back any longer, he pulled her face to his and kissed her. It was a kiss born of longing, of months spent apart, of love that had endured despite the lies and the pain. Their lips met with a tenderness that deepened into passion, their arms wrapping around each other as if trying to close the distance that had separated them for so long.

Toby, standing a few feet away with Ben and Julian, rolled his eyes but couldn't suppress a grin. "Alright, that's quite enough of that." He stepped forward, covering Ben's and Julian's eyes.

"Hey!" Ben complained, his words muffled as he pushed at Toby's arm.

Julian giggled, squirming under his grip. "I'm not a child!"

Toby did not relent. "Some things are better left unseen, especially for you two." He looked at Alexander and Eliza, who were still embracing, and shook his head. "Give them a moment. They deserve it."

Ben and Julian continued to tug at Toby's arm, their giggles growing louder, but Toby held firm, his own laughter mingling with theirs. For a moment, the hardships of their journey dissolved, replaced by the joy of togetherness.

When Alexander and Eliza finally pulled apart, their faces flushed, their breaths uneven, Toby released Ben and Julian with a mock sigh of relief. "About time!" He crossed his arms. "We've got work to do, remember?"

Eliza, her cheeks still pink, reached for Alexander's hand. "He's right. We can't stay here. My father's men could be anywhere."

Alexander nodded gravely. "We'll leave tonight. But first, we need a plan. And supplies. I'm not letting anything—or anyone—come between us again."

A look passed between Ben and Julian, their earlier laughter fading as the reality of their situation settled back over them. Toby clapped a hand on each of their shoulders. "Don't fret. You've made it this far. You'll figure it out."

Toby's heart felt like a stone in his chest. Over the past days, he had grown to care for this ragtag group. They weren't just strangers anymore; they had become something like family to him, a word he hadn't dared to use in years. But now, as he stood there watching Eliza and Alexander reunited, Julian's eyes filled with optimism, and Ben's quiet determination, he felt a spark of hope. He didn't belong in their future, not really. His place was back in the shadows, in the alleyways, where he had always survived alone. The thought of returning to that life, of facing the cold, empty streets without them, made his chest ache.

"Well," Toby said, trying to sound casual, "my work here is done, I suppose. You've found Alexander, and you've got a plan. Good luck with the future." He forced a smile, but it didn't reach his eyes. He turned to leave, his feet dragging as if the ground itself were trying to hold him back.

Julian darted forward, his small hand clutching Toby's torn sleeve. "Wait! Why are you going? You can't just leave!"

Toby paused, looking down at the boy. Confusion and desperation etched Julian's face, his wide eyes pleading. Toby sighed and draped an arm over Julian's shoulders, pulling him close. "I need to return to my alley before someone pilfers my things. You know how it is—can't let the rats take everything." He tried to laugh, but it came out hollow.

Julian flicked a look at Eliza, who stood with her arms intertwined with Alexander's, her face soft with concern. Julian's eyes begged her to say something, to make Toby stay.

Eliza gave Alexander's arm a squeeze, then stepped forward.

She approached Toby, her hands reaching out to rub the sides of his arms in a gesture that was both comforting and grounding. "You can't go. You are part of our family now. One should never abandon family."

Toby faltered, struggling to contain the emotions threatening to spill over. His throat tightened, and he blinked, trying to hold back the tears, but they came anyway, welling up in his eyes despite his best efforts to hide them. He didn't trust himself to speak, so he said nothing. Instead, he pulled Eliza into a tight embrace, his arms wrapping around her as if she were the only thing keeping him grounded.

Eliza hugged him back with equal intensity, her hands pressing against his back. "You're not alone anymore, Toby. You don't have to go back to that life. Stay with us. We need you."

Toby's shoulders shook as he let go, the flood of loneliness and fear breaking over him. He had spent so long surviving on his own, trusting no one, relying on no one. But this—this felt different. For the first time in as long as he could remember, he felt like he belonged somewhere.

He pulled back, sweeping his tears aside, and looked at Eliza, then at Julian, Ben, and Alexander. "Alright. I'll stay. But only if you promise not to make me embrace anyone else. Once a day is my limit."

Julian laughed, sounding satisfied, and Ben cracked a smile. Eliza grinned, her eyes shining with tears of her own. "Agreed," she said.

Alexander stepped forward, clapping a hand on Toby's shoulder. "Welcome to the family. We're better with you in it."

Toby nodded, his heart lighter than it had been in years. For the first time, he allowed himself to believe that perhaps, just perhaps, he didn't have to face the world alone anymore.

Just then, the air split with a sharp, almost silent thwip as a crossbow bolt tore through the space between them. Before anyone could react, it struck Alexander in the shoulder, the force of the impact driving him to his knees. He grunted in pain, his hand gripping the metal shaft protruding from his flesh. Blood seeped through his fingers, staining his shirt a dark crimson.

"Alexander!" Eliza screamed in horror. She rushed to his side, dropping to her knees, cradling him in her arms. Her hands trembled as she brushed his hair back from his face, her eyes wide with panic. "Stay with me, Alexander. Stay with me!"

Ben, his heart pounding, scooped up a rock from the ground and spun around, searching for the attacker. His eyes locked onto a figure in black—a one-eyed man standing a short distance away, a cruel smirk twisting his face. Ben hurled the rock with all his strength, but it sailed wide, clattering against the wall behind the man. Before Ben could react, another man—a hulking brute with arms like tree trunks—grabbed him from behind, lifting him off the ground as if he weighed nothing. The brute reached out and seized Julian by the scruff of his neck, the boy's small frame dangling in his grip.

The one-eyed man laughed, a low, menacing sound that sent a chill down Toby's spine. He reached into his pouch and pulled out a handful of shillings, tossing them at Toby's feet. "A few coins for your trouble in helping us find Alexander and the brats. You've done your part, street rat. Now scram."

Toby's eyes burned with fury. He ignored the shillings scattered on the ground, his hands trembling. "Liar! You liar!" He lunged at the mercenary, his body moving on pure instinct, but the man was faster. A boot connected with Toby's jaw, the impact sending him sprawling backward. His head hit the ground with a sickening thud, and he lay still.

Ben screamed, writhing in the man's arms as he desperately tried to break free and help Toby.

The sound of hooves clattering against cobblestones filled the air as a prison wagon pulled by two horses rolled to a stop near the blacksmith's forge. The men in black wasted no time hauling Eliza, Alexander, Ben, and Julian into the wagon. They stripped off their brogues and shackled their ankles with heavy iron chains, the frigid metal digging into their skin. Eliza barely noticed. Her focus was on Alexander. She cradled his head in her lap, her fingers stroking his hair as she whispered soothing words to him.

"It's not as bad as it looks," Alexander said through gritted teeth. He tried to smile, though the pain was clear in his eyes. "Just a wee scratch. I've had worse."

Eliza's lips trembled as she fought back tears. "Don't you dare leave me! Not now. Not after everything."

The one-eyed man mounted, then rode his horse alongside the open prison wagon, his single bloodshot eye gleaming with malice. He leaned down and kicked the bars of the cage where Alexander lay; the sound rang out like a death knell. "Don't die yet, blacksmith. We've got a gallows waiting for you. Wouldn't want you to miss the fun."

Dazed and in pain, Toby stirred on the ground where they had left him. His vision blurred, but he could make out the wagon and the men loading his friends inside. Fear and adrenaline surged through him, cutting through the fog in his mind. He forced himself to stay still, playing dead until the men turned their attention elsewhere. Then, with a burst of energy, he scrambled to his feet and slipped into the adjoining alleyway, disappearing into the shadows unnoticed.

The wagon creaked as it moved; the horses pulling it forward with a steady rhythm. Eliza held Alexander close, her heart breaking as she watched the blacksmith's forge—the place where they had found each other again—fade into the distance. Ben gripped the chains imprisoning him, his mind racing for a way out.

Somewhere in the shadows, Toby ran, his feet carrying him as fast as they could, his only thought of finding help before it was too late.

Miles later, the prison wagon jolted to a halt, the sudden stop rattling the chains that bound them. Ben, his mind racing, reached over and shook Julian awake. "We're stopping," he said. "Maybe we can make a run for it if we can trick them into opening the back."

Julian pushed himself into a sitting position, the heavy iron shackles cutting into his ankles, leaving angry red marks. He winced as he shifted. "How, Ben? How do we get out of these things?"

Ben tugged at his own shackles. His stomach growled, and for a moment, his mind wandered to the comforts of his own time—milkshakes, hamburgers, and the simple pleasures he had taken for granted. He shook his head, forcing himself to focus. "I don't know yet."

Outside the wagon, the men were setting up camp. A fire crackled to life, its orange glow casting long shadows across the ground. The mercenaries removed the saddles from their horses, their laughter and rough voices carrying through the night air. One man passed around a jug, taking long swigs before handing it to the next. The smell of alcohol wafted toward the wagon, mingling with smoke and stale sweat.

Eliza sat huddled in the cage's corner, Alexander's head resting in her lap. She flinched as a man approached, his boots crunching against the dirt. He rapped his knuckles against the bars, the sound sharp and mocking. "You're a pretty little thing, aren't you?" he said, his eyes raking over her. "Even dressed like a lad, you're a sight. I'll be back later, and we can have some sport." He made a grotesque slurping sound and licked his lips, his intentions clear.

Alexander lunged forward, his chains rattling as he slammed his fist against the bars where the man stood. "You lay one hand on her, and I'll kill you myself!" The action sent a sharp pain radiating down his side from the crossbow wound, but he didn't care. His eyes burned with defiance.

The man laughed, a cruel, grating sound, and stepped back. "Big words for a man in chains," he taunted. "We'll see how brave you are when the noose is around your neck."

Meanwhile, Toby lay flat on his stomach in the long grass, his eyes fixed on the campsite. His mind reeled, trying to piece together a plan. How was he going to help his friends—no, his family? He couldn't let them down. Not now. He hoped they hadn't believed the mercenary's lie, that he had sold them out. The thought made his stomach churn.

His eyes scanned the campsite, searching for anything he could use. Then he spotted it—a crossbow leaning against a tree near the horses. Toby's mind raced—he'd have to move quickly and quietly. The fire and jug kept the mercenaries occupied. It was now or never.

He crawled forward, his body hugging the ground, every movement deliberate and silent. The crossbow was just within reach, but so were the mercenaries. One wrong move, and it would all be over.

Ben strained his gaze through the wagon bars, searching the

pitch-black night, until a jolt of relief hit him as he spotted Toby creeping through the shadows near the campsite. He nudged Julian, who was dozing beside him. "Julian, look. It's Toby. He didn't sell us out. He's here to help."

Julian blinked, rubbing his eyes as he followed Ben's stare. "I knew he wouldn't leave us."

Toby melted into the shadows. Laughter and song burst from the mercenaries gathered around the crackling fire, their words slurred and rowdy, a raucous symphony of the night. His eyes darted to the one-eyed leader, solitary and intent, sharpening his knife with slow, deliberate strokes. Toby's heart thumped in his chest as his eyes shifted between the men and the crossbow on the ground. He edged forward, each step calculated, the crunch of gravel under his feet barely audible.

Just as he reached out to grab the weapon, one man stood up, swaying from the drink. Toby froze. The man stumbled forward, muttering to himself. Toby rolled behind a thick trunk, pressing himself flat against the bark. The man stopped just a few feet away, and Toby's nose wrinkled in disgust as the sound of a stream hitting the ground reached his ears. He clenched his jaw, forcing himself to stay still as the man relieved himself, the acrid smell filling the air.

When the man turned and staggered back to the fire, Toby gathered his nerves and crept ahead. He avoided the wet patch on the ground, his face twisted in displeasure, and grasped the crossbow. His fingers tightened around the stock, and he checked the bolt, ensuring it was ready to fire.

From the corner of his eye, Toby spotted movement—a figure emerging from the shadows, clad in armour and carrying a sword. The man moved with purpose, heading straight for the back of the prison wagon. Toby's instincts kicked in, and he raised the crossbow, aiming for the man's head. His finger hovered over the trigger as he held his breath, then squeezed.

But before he could fire, a small, urgent plea came from the wagon. "Toby, stop! He's a friend!" Ben said.

Toby hesitated, his finger still on the trigger, as he glanced at the wagon. Ben clung to the bars, his eyes wide and pleading. "Don't shoot him! He's here to help us!"

The man reached the back of the wagon and began working on the lock, his movements quick and precise. Toby crept closer, keeping the crossbow trained on the man just in case. "Who are you?" Toby demanded.

The man glanced at Toby. "Name's William. I'm here to free Miss Eliza, Master Julian and Benjamin."

Inside the wagon, Eliza's eyes widened. "How do we know we can trust you?"

William didn't answer. Instead, he reached into his belt and pulled out a small, folded piece of parchment. He handed it through the bars to Ben, who unfolded it with trembling hands. The message was brief: "Trust him. He's your only hope. – Grace."

Ben looked up at William, then at Toby. "It's him," Ben said, his shoulders loosening with relief. "He's the one Grace told me about."

"Who is Grace?" Eliza asked.

"Never mind that now. Toby, please, trust me," Ben said.

Toby lowered the crossbow, though he kept it ready. "Very well. But if this turns out to be a trick—"

"It won't," William said. "Now, step aside. I'm getting you out of here."

The lock clicked, and the wagon door creaked as William swung it open. He unshackled them one by one and they climbed out, hurrying. Alexander leaned heavily on Eliza, while Julian and Ben stuck close together.

Toby kept watch, his eyes sweeping the camp. Their voices raised as they passed the jug. The mercenaries remained distracted.

"We've no time to waste—we must go now." Toby said.

William gestured toward the shadows. "Come with me. Stay close."

When they reached the mercenaries' horses, William worked swiftly, helping Eliza, Ben, and Julian onto one horse before lifting Alexander—pale and barely upright—onto another. Toby mounted a third, ready for any sign of trouble. Without a word, they set off, the sound of hooves muffled by the soft ground as they fled south.

After several miles, they arrived at a large encampment bustling with soldiers. The air was thick with noise—shouted orders, clanging metal, and the restless movement of horses. William led them to an area where the surgeons had set up their tents. He dismounted and eased Alexander to the ground, handing him over to the physician with a few quiet instructions. Alexander groaned but nodded faintly before being taken away. Toby followed, staying by his side.

William helped Eliza, Ben, and Julian down. His hands were steady, especially with Julian. As soon as Eliza touched the ground, she faced William. "I... I thought you were working for my pappa. Why would you help us?"

William met her eyes. "I worked for your father, Miss Eliza. For a time, I believed in his cause—or told myself I did. But I soon saw what kind of man he truly is. His cruelty, his greed, the way he tramples anyone in his path." His jaw tightened. "When I learned he meant to harm you... your mother begged me to protect you. She couldn't bear it. What your father has done to you, to Julian, to Benjamin—it's monstrous. I couldn't stand by and let it happen."

A wave of emotion surged through Eliza at the mention of her mother, but William continued before she could respond. "While I was looking for you in London, I met a young woman named Grace. She told me about you, about Alexander, about the boys—things no one else could know. I don't know who she is or how she knew so much, but I trust her. She's the one who led me to you."

The name Grace sent a shiver through Eliza. She glanced at Ben, who was already watching her with wide, knowing eyes. Julian looked between them, his face pale.

William pointed to the centre of the camp, where a grand tent stood, its fabric dyed in rich colours and adorned with the crest of the English crown. Two large soldiers, their armour gleaming in the firelight, stood guard at the entrance. Eliza hesitated, her grip tightening on both Ben's and Julian's hands. "When can I see Alexander?"

"Pray, soon. But first, there's someone you must meet," William said, leading them to the grand tent. Eliza, Ben, and Julian trailed close behind, their eyes scanning the camp's organised preparations for the upcoming battle.

As they approached the tent, the guards snapped to attention, their eyes scrutinising William and his companions before stepping aside to let them pass. William held the tent flap open and gestured for them to enter. Eliza braced herself, her pulse quickening, and stepped inside, pulling Ben and Julian along with her.

Inside the tent, the warm glow of the lanterns enveloped Eliza. Her eyes lifted to the walls, where rich tapestries hung, each one a silent storyteller. Then she noticed the large table in the centre, littered with maps and scrolls, each unfurled as if eager to share its tales.

Standing at the table, his back to her, was a man in fine robes, his posture radiating regal authority. As he turned, Eliza's heart skipped a beat; before her stood the King of England, his presence commanding the very air within the tent.

William stepped forward and bowed deeply. "Your Majesty, may I present Miss Eliza, Benjamin, and Master Julian."

The King smiled as he regarded them. "I've heard much about you. Your courage and trials haven't escaped my notice."

Eliza's knees trembled, and she tightened her grip on the boys' hands. She was at a loss for words, but one thing was certain: their lives were on the cusp of a profound change.

The King stepped forward. Eliza curtsied gracefully, despite her tattered and soiled attire. The King's eyes softened as he took in her appearance—the frayed fabric, the smudges of dirt, the way her boy's disguise hung loosely on her frame. A pang of remorse struck him as he considered how some of his own subjects could treat their children with such cruelty. Whispers of the mines her father operates, where he forces the frailest and most vulnerable children into gruelling labour, had reached his ears. It was a practice he abhorred, and he was drafting an act to abolish such exploitation.

"My dear," the King said, "your father's done you, your brother, and this young man a grave wrong. I'm deeply sorry for the suffering you've endured. Many of the men here are training and will return to their duties tomorrow, but I'll leave William and fifty of my finest soldiers to help you. They'll keep you safe and help you take back what's rightfully yours."

Eliza's eyes brimmed with tears, but she kept her composure, nodding gratefully. "Thank you, Your Majesty."

The King then turned to Julian. He bent to meet the boy's eyes, placing a gentle hand on Julian's dirt-streaked cheek. "And you, my brave lad, you'll be the man of your house now. It's a heavy burden, but I see strength in you. Look after your mother and run your household with fairness and dignity. You've got the heart of a leader, and I know you'll grow into it."

Julian's eyes widened. "I will, Your Majesty."

Finally, the King turned to Ben, who felt decidedly out of place amidst the opulence of the tent and the gravity of the King's presence. Ben's stomach churned with nervousness. "Benjamin," the King said, his gaze steady with admiration, "I've heard tales of your bravery and selflessness. For a lad—no, a young man—so young, you've proven yourself worthy in the eyes of your king."

A lump formed in Ben's throat. He had never imagined standing before a king, let alone being addressed in such a manner. The king's next words sent a jolt through him.

"Kneel," the king commanded, drawing his sword from its scabbard with a soft metallic ring.

Ben's heart pounded as he dropped to one knee, mimicking the gestures he had seen in stories and tales. The king stepped forward, the blade of his sword catching the light as he raised it. He laid the flat edge of the sword on Ben's right shoulder, then his left, and the top of his head. The weight of the blade felt both heavy and reassuring, a symbol of honour and trust.

"Arise, Sir Benjamin," the king said, his command ringing with authority and pride. "May you live your life with the same honour and courage you've shown in aiding Miss Eliza and Master Julian. You've proven yourself a true knight in spirit, if not yet in title."

Ben rose, his legs unsteady beneath him. He felt a rush of emotions—pride, disbelief, gratitude—all swirling together in a dizzying mix. "Thank you, Your Majesty," he said, his words trembling. "I… I won't let you down."

The king smiled, a genuine warmth in his eyes. "I know you won't." He sheathed his sword and placed a hand on Ben's shoulder. "You've already done more than most would dare. Remember this moment, Sir Benjamin, and let it guide you in the days to come."

Eliza and Julian watched in awe, their faces reflecting pure pride. William stood nearby, his arms crossed but a faint smile playing on his lips. The king stepped back. "You've all endured much, but your courage hasn't gone unnoticed. Rest now, for tomorrow brings new challenges—and new opportunities."

As the king turned, Eliza reached out and touched Ben's arm. "Sir Benjamin," she said with a teasing smile, yet filled with genuine admiration. "It suits you."

Ben laughed, his cheeks flushing. "I don't know about that," he said, rubbing the back of his neck. "But I'll do my best to live up to it."

Julian grinned, his earlier fear replaced by excitement. "You're a sir now, Benjamin! That's amazing!"

Toby, who had arrived earlier from the physicians, had been standing at the entrance of the tent. He stepped forward, clapping Ben on the back. "Looks like you've outdone yourself, lad," he said with pride. "But don't let it go to your head."

Ben smiled, his heart swelling with gratitude for his friends. They had been through so much together, and now, standing in the king's tent with a new title resting on his shoulders, he felt a renewed sense of purpose.

The king turned and looked at Toby. "And who is this young man?"

William stepped forward, clearing his throat. "This is Toby, Your Majesty. An orphan who selflessly aided in their safety. He turned down a large reward to protect them, even giving them the little he had to ensure their survival."

The king approached Toby and placed a hand on his shoulder. "Well then, you shall never want for anything again. A place in my service will always be open to you, should you ever have need of it."

Toby smiled and bowed his head. "That's mighty kind of you, Sire, and I thank you. But I've already promised my services to Miss Eliza and Alexander. I mean to keep that promise."

The king's smile widened, and he nodded. "Very well. You're a man of honour, Toby. Eliza and Alexander are fortunate to have you in their service."

Eliza slipped her arm around Toby's shoulders in a gesture of solidarity. "Sire, Toby isn't just our protector or servant. He's our equal and our friend. It's we who'll be in service to him."

The king's eyes sparkled with admiration as he looked at them. "Then you're all blessed to have one another. Such loyalty and friendship are rare treasures indeed. Godspeed to all of you. I'm sure we'll meet again."

Ben followed suit in bowing with the rest of them before turning to leave the tent. He followed William as he ushered them out of the king's tent, his mind still reeling from the events that had just unfolded. The cool night air was a welcome relief after the intensity of the meeting, and the camp buzzed with activity around them. William led them through the rows of tents. They reached a smaller tent soon after at the far end of the camp, its entrance flanked by two lanterns casting a warm, golden glow.

"You three lads can stay here tonight," William said, pointing to the tent. He then turned to Eliza. "Miss Eliza, your own tent is right next to theirs. It's smaller but private, so you can rest in peace. Alexander's doing well—the physicians say he's recovering. He'll be able to visit you before too long."

"Thank you, William—for everything," Eliza said, squeezing his hand.

William gave her a small, respectful bow before stepping aside to let her enter her tent. Ben, Julian, and Toby exchanged glances, their weariness overshadowed by curiosity. Ben pushed aside the tent flap and stepped inside, his mouth falling open in astonishment.

The tent was far more luxurious than anything they'd expected. To the side sat a large metal tub filled with steaming hot water, its surface shimmering in the lantern light. In the centre of the room was a rustic table laden with food—roasted chicken, fresh bread, ripe fruit, and even a small jug of what smelled like spiced cider. The sight made Ben's stomach growl.

At the far end of the tent stood three cots, complete with neatly folded blankets and plump pillows. On each cot lay a set of clean clothes, leather armour tailored to fit smaller frames, and a pair of sturdy new boots. Ben's eyes widened as he took it all in. "This... this is for us?" he asked, his mouth agape.

William chuckled, amused by their reaction. "It is. Consider it a reward for your bravery. Now, eat, bathe, and rest. You deserve it." With that, he gave them a nod and stepped out, leaving the three of them alone.

Ben didn't need to be told twice. He flew to the table, and grabbing a chicken leg, tore into it with gusto. The flavours exploded in his mouth—juicy, tender, and seasoned to perfection. Julian and Toby were right behind him, piling their plates with food. They hadn't had a proper meal in days. For a few blissful minutes, the only sounds in the tent were the clinking of plates and the occasional satisfied groan.

After eating his fill, Ben stood before the steaming tub. "Who's going first?" he asked, looking from Julian to Toby.

Julian, still nibbling on a piece of bread, shrugged. "You go ahead, Ben. You're the Sir now, after all," he said with a cheeky grin.

Ben rolled his eyes but didn't argue. He stripped out of his filthy oversized clothes, wincing at their state—stained, torn, and reeking of the residual smell of rotting fish and sweat—and tossed them out of the tent. Julian and Toby burst into laughter, their voices mingling in agreement as the clothes landed in a heap outside. Ben sank into the tub with a sigh of relief, the hot water a balm to his aching muscles. He leaned back, letting the warmth seep into his bones, and for the first time in what felt like days, he allowed himself to relax.

When he finally emerged, Toby and Julian took their turns, each savouring the rare luxury of a proper bath and soap. The tent filled with the sound of splashing water and occasional laughter, a brief but much-needed respite from the chaos of their journey.

Ben felt drained, and his muscles throbbed with pain. He rubbed his bruised ankles, then flopped onto a cot, his eyelids heavy. Julian and Toby followed suit, each claiming their own deliciously comfortable cot.

As Ben lay there, staring up at the tent's canvas ceiling, he felt a strange sense of peace. For now, they were out of harm's way and basked in the king's favour. But more than that, they had each other. Julian's soft snores filled the tent, and Toby's breathing was steady and deep. Ben smiled, his thoughts drifting as sleep claimed him.

In the adjoining tent, Eliza felt clean for the first time in weeks. The grime and exhaustion of their journey washed away. She stood in front of a full-length mirror, a luxury the king had ordered brought from his own tent to hers. The reflection staring back at her was almost unfamiliar—her skin glowed, her eyes sparkled, and the white silk dress she wore flowed around her, a garment fit for royalty. She dabbed perfume on her neck, a welcome change to the harsh smells of the last few days. Frowning, she tugged at her short-cropped hair, wishing it would grow faster.

As she adjusted the neckline of her dress, movement caught the corner of her eye. She spun to her left, her heart leaping as she saw Alexander standing in the doorway. His arm was in a sling, but his presence filled the tent, his eyes locking onto hers with the same intensity she remembered. He looked as handsome as ever, his rugged features softened by the warmth in his eyes.

For a moment, they stared at each other. Then, without a word, Eliza rushed to him, her movements careful to avoid jostling his injured arm. She threw herself into his embrace, her hands gripping the fabric of his shirt as if to assure herself he was real. Alexander's good arm wrapped around her, pulling her close.

Their lips met in a kiss that was both tender and desperate, a reunion that spoke of all the pain, fear, and longing they had endured. Eliza's fingers traced the line of his jaw, while Alexander's hand cradled the back of her head. When they pulled apart, breathless and smiling, Eliza rested her forehead against his.

"I thought I'd lost you," she said.

Alexander shook his head, his thumb brushing away a tear she hadn't realised had fallen. "Never again," he murmured.

Eliza smiled, her heart swelling with relief and love. For the first time in what felt like an eternity, she allowed herself to believe that everything might just be all right.

Still, the shadow of her father hung over her—a lingering presence that weighed on her thoughts, no matter how hard she tried to escape it.

CHAPTER 19: THE CONFRONTATION

From a nearby hill, William sat on his horse, watching Ambrose Wilson's manor. The sprawling estate loomed in the distance, its grandeur a vivid foil to the darkness of the man who ruled it. He glanced at Eliza, who sat atop a sleek black stallion beside him, with Alexander on her other side, his arm still in a sling but his posture strong and determined. Clad in the garb of a soldier, with a coat of leather for protection, Eliza was a striking figure—a blend of beauty and strength, her determination etched into every line of her face. Alexander, though injured, exuded a quiet resilience, his presence a steadying force.

"Miss Eliza," William said, "it is most advisable that you remain here. We shall exert every effort to apprehend your father without inflicting harm upon him. You have my solemn word."

A tempest of emotions raged across Eliza's face. She despised her father for his treachery—the lies that had poisoned her trust, the betrayal that had shattered her world, the cruelty that had nearly cost her life. Yet, despite it all, the thought of seeing him harmed, of blood being spilled by her hand or on her behalf, coiled like a serpent in her gut, tightening with every breath. He was a monster, yes, but he was still her father. The man who had once held her as a child, whose voice had lulled her to sleep, now stood as the architect of her deepest pain. The duality of it all—love and loathing, vengeance and guilt—left her torn, her heart a battlefield of contradictions. Alexander reached over with his good arm, placing a reassuring hand on hers. "We shall see this matter through," he said. "Together."

After a moment, Eliza gave a reluctant nod, her eyes never leaving the manor. "Pray… bring him to justice. That is all I ask."

William turned to the boys, each seated on their own horses. Toby, Ben, and Julian sat tall, their youthful faces set with determination. "You three," William said, his tone commanding, "remain here and guard your sister. No matter what may transpire, she is your foremost concern."

The boys exchanged glances, pride swelling in their chests. Though only Julian was Eliza's brother by blood, Toby and Ben embraced the bond as if it had always been theirs. They nodded in unison, their loyalty unwavering.

Behind them, fifty men stood ready, their horses restless but disciplined. The air was thick with anticipation, the quiet before the storm. A grim-faced officer approached William. "Sir, Wilson has more than a hundred men guarding the estate," he reported. "This shan't be an easy task."

The major, a seasoned soldier with a steely gaze, stepped forward. "Cowardly, untrained men," he said dismissively. "Most are in his service for coin and comfort, not loyalty or skill. We shall strike after sunset, when they are deep in their cups and ill-prepared. They shan't know what has befallen them."

William nodded, his jaw tightening as he surveyed the manor once more. "Then we shall bide our time. But when the moment arrives, we must act with swiftness and resolve. There is no room for error."

Eliza stared at the home she once knew. It no longer felt like a place of safety or comfort—it was a fortress of corruption, a symbol of everything she had fought to escape. Alexander's hand tightened on hers. "We shall prevail. No matter the cost."

Toby, sensing her unease, guided his horse closer to hers. "We stand with you, Eliza. Whatever may come, you are not alone."

Eliza managed a small smile. "I am deeply grateful. To all of you."

As the sun dipped below the horizon, the group prepared for what lay ahead. The night would bring battle, but also the chance for justice—and perhaps, for Eliza, a chance to find peace at last.

Under the cover of darkness, William stood before the assembled soldiers. "Men," he said, his eyes scanning the group, "we must proceed in utter silence. Leave the horses here—stealth is paramount. Our foremost duty is to liberate the family held in chains. We cannot allow Wilson to use them as hostages. I shall lead five men to secure their release. You others, be ready to advance should someone discover us. Five others shall remain mounted to pursue any who attempt to flee."

The men nodded in silent agreement. William selected the five most skilled soldiers, each trained in covert operations, and together they descended the hill toward the manor.

Using hand signals to communicate, William halted his team near a group of Wilson's men gathered around a fire. They were singing and drinking, their laughter carrying through the night. Beyond them, just inside the barn, stood a crude iron cage, its bars glinting in the firelight. In it, the Whitfield family huddled together—Sarah Whitfield, her teenage adopted son Caleb, and her daughter Maggie. William's heart ached as he marked the loss of Henry and Robert, knowing they had fallen victim to Ambrose Wilson's cruelty.

Too drunk to walk straight, one of Wilson's men stumbled from the fire to the garden where William and his team hid. The man stopped mere inches from one soldier, oblivious to the danger as he relieved himself. In one swift motion, the soldier silenced him; the man collapsed without a sound and was dragged into the shadows of the garden.

William gave the signal, and the remaining four soldiers took aim. With precision marksmanship, they released their arrows simultaneously, each finding its mark. The men around the fire fell silent, their laughter cut short.

"The rest of Wilson's men are asleep in a camp on the other side of the manor," William said. "Let us secure the Whitfield family's safety." He moved swiftly to the cage.

Inside, Sarah Whitfield flinched at the sound of the lock clicking open. She scrambled to the far corner of the cage, her arms wrapped protectively around Caleb and Maggie. "Stay back!" she cried. "Do not lay a hand upon my children!"

William crouched low, his hand outstretched in a gesture of

reassurance. "Mrs Whitfield, I am a friend. I have come to liberate you and your family, but you must remain silent. Time is of the essence."

Sarah's eyes widened, tears streaming down her face as she recognised the sincerity in his voice. "My babies, Lily and Sam— pray, tell me, are they safe?"

"Your children are well. Good, trustworthy people are sheltering your children on a nearby farm. Now, come. We must make haste," William said.

Sarah hesitated for a moment, her maternal instincts warring with her fear, before finally nodding. With trembling hands, she helped Caleb and Maggie to their feet. William guided them out of the cage, his eyes scanning the darkness for any sign of movement, his every sense on high alert.

"Stay close," he said. "We are not yet free of danger."

As they glided through the shadows, Sarah clung to her children, her heart aching for the family she had lost but grateful for the chance to save those who remained. William led them to the safety of the hill, his mind already racing with the next steps of their plan.

He returned to the manor, his plan clear: capture Ambrose Wilson without alerting his men. If he could take the man quietly, there would be a minimal loss of life—a goal William held firmly in mind. His men remained stationed outside, hidden in the shadows, ready to act if things went awry. William moved alone, slipping into the house through the coal chute. The cramped and filthy narrow passage offered him the stealth he needed.

Once inside, he navigated the corridors with care, moving past the servants' quarters and up a narrow staircase. The house was silent, the only sound the occasional creak of wood under his weight. As he reached the grand staircase, a loud groan echoed beneath his boot. He froze and listened. The house remained still.

Eliza had described the manor's layout in intricate detail, and William relied on his own memory to guide him. Moving silently, he reached the door to the master bedroom. Darkness shrouded it; only a faint glow from a fixed oil lamp in the hallway provided light. William drew his sword and flipped the weapon in his hand, ready to use the hilt to knock Ambrose unconscious.

He moved to the bed and pulled back the covers, raising his sword hilt, ready to strike. But the bed was empty.

"Looking for me, you blackguard?" Ambrose snarled from behind.

Before William could react, Ambrose lunged, striking him with the force of a madman. The blow sent William stumbling, his sword clattering to the floor. Ambrose's eyes burned with fury as he advanced, a dagger glinting in his hand.

Outside, chaos erupted as an ambush unfolded. William's men, positioned around the manor, fell one by one while arrows hissed through the air, striking from the shadows of the garden. One man gasped, clutching the shaft protruding from his chest. He tried to shout—to warn the others on the hill—but before he could utter a word, a blade slashed across his throat, silencing him forever.

Eliza sat atop her horse, her ears straining to pick up the distant sounds of chaos erupting from the manor. The clash of steel, the shouts of men, and the occasional scream carried through the night air. Her heart raced as she turned to Caleb, her tone clipped with urgency. "Something is amiss! You must get your family to safety—at once!"

Caleb nodded, his face pale, and guided his mother and sister away from the danger.

Ben sat frozen, his hands gripping the reins of his horse so tightly his knuckles turned white. He was terrified, more scared than he had ever been in his life. But he was a Sir now—Sir Benjamin—and the title rested on his shoulders like an unspoken duty. "I... I need to help."

Eliza turned to him, her expression softening despite the tension in the air. "Benjamin, you are helping. You swore to protect me, and that is precisely what you are doing."

Ben nodded, though his stomach churned with anxiety. He wanted to do more, like the knights in the stories he'd read, but the reality of the situation was overwhelming.

A horse burst from the shadows near the manor, galloping at full speed toward them. For a moment, Eliza's heart leapt—was it William? But as the rider drew closer, a chill ran down her spine. It was her father, Ambrose, his face twisted with rage.

"Ride!" Eliza's call rang out, urgent and raw. "Ride now!" She spun her horse, Alexander and the boys following close behind.

Ambrose rode hard, his eyes locked on his children. They had betrayed him—his own flesh and blood. Especially Julian, his heir, his only son. His betrayal burned like a brand, fuelling his fury.

A low boundary wall caught Julian's horse just as the others cleared it—a single hoof clipping the edge, sending the animal tumbling. The impact of the fall sent him flying from the saddle, hitting the ground with a sickening thud. Rolling, legs flailing, the horse narrowly missed him as it crashed down.

Ambrose cleared the wall with ease, pulling his horse to a halt beside Julian's crumpled form. He dismounted, his boots crunching on the dirt as he approached his son. Julian, dazed and trembling, looked up at his father, his face streaked with dirt and tears.

"You dare betray me, boy?" The venom in Ambrose's words struck like a lash. He seized Julian by the hair, dragging him to his feet. "My flesh and blood, my only son, turns against me? You sicken me, you wretched little cur!" He hurled Julian back to the ground, the boy landing hard on his side.

Julian scrambled backward, his hands raised to shield himself. "Papa, I beg you—" His words broke, barely a whisper, dissolving into a choked gasp. His heart pounded as he glanced at his horse, now lying motionless in the dirt, its leg twisted at an unnatural angle.

With a surge of adrenaline, Julian pushed himself to his feet and bolted, his boots kicking up dust as he fled. Behind him, Ambrose mounted his steed, his face a mask of cold fury. Julian's legs burned as he ran, but the sound of his father gaining ground spurred him on.

Ambrose drew alongside him in seconds, his horse's flank brushing Julian's shoulder. Without hesitation, Ambrose kicked out, his boot connecting with Julian's side. The impact sent the boy sprawling into the dirt, a cry of pain tearing from his throat. He skidded across the ground, his palms scraping against stones and dry earth.

Ambrose dismounted in one fluid motion, and he approached his son. Julian tried to push himself up, but a sharp pain in his ribs forced him back down. He looked up, his vision blurred with tears as his father loomed over him.

"You are a blight upon my name," Ambrose spat. He crouched down, seizing Julian by his hair and yanking him upright. "You are no child of mine. You are unworthy of bearing my name.' His grip tightened, shaking Julian as if to emphasise every word. 'You are naught but a failure, a blemish upon my legacy."

Julian's chest heaved, his throat tight with fear and shame. He longed to argue, to plead, but the words caught in his throat. Ambrose's eyes bore into his, filled with a hatred that made Julian's blood run cold. With a shove, Ambrose released him, letting him collapse back into the dirt.

"Rise," Ambrose spat, his mouth twisting, froth gathering at the corners.

Julian felt stones pressing into his skin as he lay there, his body trembling with exhaustion and pain. With a shudder, he pushed himself up, his muscles screaming in protest. He stood, swaying slightly, but met his father's glare with a glint of defiance. Tears trickled down his cheeks.

Ambrose drew his sword, the blade glinting in the moonlight. He raised it high, his face a mask of cold fury. Julian squeezed his eyes shut, bracing for the blow that would end his life.

But the blow never came.

Instead, an arrow pierced Ambrose's eye with a sickening thud. He froze, his sword slipping from his grasp as he staggered backward. For a moment, he stood there, swaying, before collapsing to the ground, lifeless.

Eliza stood a short distance away, her bow still raised, her hands steady despite the storm of emotions raging within her. She lowered the weapon, her eyes fixed on her father's body. This time, she felt no remorse. He had forfeited any right to be called a father.

Julian opened his eyes in time to see Ambrose fall. His body shook as he stared at the lifeless figure before him. Then his attention shifted to Eliza, who stood tall and resolute, the bow still in her hands. A sob escaped his lips as he pushed himself to his feet and ran to her, his legs carrying him as fast as they could.

Eliza dropped the bow and caught him, pulling him into a tight embrace. Julian buried his face in her shoulder, his tears soaking into her shirt. Eliza held him close, one hand cradling the back of his head, the other rubbing soothing circles on his back.

"Papa can never hurt us again, my sweet brother," she said. "We're free now. We're free."

Alexander dismounted his horse with difficulty, wincing as pain shot through his old wound. He gritted his teeth and pushed through it, running over to Eliza and Julian. With his good arm, he pulled them into a tight embrace, his heart swelling with relief.

Eliza and Julian clung to him, their tears mingling with the dirt and sweat on their faces. But their moment of relief was short-lived. A shadow moved, and they looked up to see a man in black wearing an eye patch approaching with his sword drawn.

The mercenary bared his teeth in a snarl, his eyes burning with cold fury. "You insolent brats. You've just cost me my wages. And I do not take kindly to such affronts."

Ben didn't hesitate. He urged his horse forward, positioning himself between the mercenary and his friends. His heart pounded as he raised a small dagger. "I'm so sick of you," Ben said, his chest heaving, a tremor in his words, but his stance unshaken. "If you want to get to them, you'll have to go through me first!"

The mercenary's single eye widened, but not at Ben. His attention shifted to the horizon behind them, where the sound of approaching hoofbeats grew louder. Fear flashed across his face as he caught sight of the king's soldiers riding into view. With a muttered curse, he yanked on the reins, turning his horse around and spurring it into a gallop.

Ben, unaware of the soldiers approaching from behind, stared after the mercenary, his body tense and trembling. He couldn't believe it had worked. "That's right," he called after the retreating figure. "You'd better run, or I'll stab you myself!"

Toby realised he had outpaced the group and doubled back. He reined in his horse beside Ben, a grin spreading across his face as he took in the scene. "You've done it, Benjamin! You sent that craven cur scurrying with his tail between his legs."

Ben straightened, a proud smile tugging at the corners of his mouth. "Yeah," he said, sliding the dagger back into its sheath. "I did, didn't I."

Toby chuckled, but didn't correct him. *Let the kid have his moment*, he thought. After everything they'd been through, Ben deserved to feel like the hero he was.

William rode at the head of the soldiers, his face pale and drawn. A knife wound bled through the makeshift bandage on his arm, and a large bruise swelled on his forehead. His eyes fell on Ambrose's lifeless body, and he gave a grim nod of approval before turning to Eliza.

"You have done what was necessary," William said, his words measured, the sorrow etched in his face. "He shall harm no one ever again."

"It is over," she said.

They rode down to the manor, the aftermath of the battle clear in every direction. The fight left broken weapons, scattered debris, and the bodies of the fallen littering the grounds. Soldiers moved methodically, clearing the dead and tending to the wounded. Eliza's stomach churned as she took in the scene, her heart heavy with the cost of their victory.

A gasp escaped her lips as she beheld the gallows—her father's creation—a grim reminder of the cruelty that pervaded this place. She dismounted, her legs unsteady beneath her, and stared at the structure in horror. Alexander followed close behind, his hand resting on her shoulder in silent support.

At the rear entrance of the manor, Lady Isadora stood, her hand to her mouth, weeping silently. She looked frail, her once-proud posture now hunched with grief and guilt. When she saw her children, her composure shattered. She cried out, "Julian!"

He flung himself from the horse, colliding with her in a fierce embrace, his face buried deep against her shoulder. "Mama," he choked, his words swallowed by her warmth.

Isadora clung to him, her tears flowing freely as she kissed his hair and face. "I am so dreadfully sorry... I am so sorry... I ought to have done more. I ought to have protected you."

Eliza dismounted, each step to her mother weighted with pain. Her lips tightened, her chest rising with a shuddered breath. "Why, Mama?" The words broke from her, raw and cutting. "Why did you allow him to do this to me—to us? How could you stand by and let him lock me away, let him harm Julian, let him destroy our family?"

William stepped forward and placed a hand on Eliza's shoulder.

"You must forgive your mother," he said. "Your father beat her more times than I can recount. She lived in fear, just as you did. It was your mother who sent me to find you. She only learned of your confinement in the basement after your escape. Every time she inquired after you, he punished her for it."

Eliza's anger faltered, replaced by a wave of sorrow. She looked at her mother—really looked at her—and saw the bruises, the hollow cheeks, the years of suffering etched into her face. "Oh, Mama," she said. She stepped forward and pulled her mother into a tight embrace, the first genuine hug they had shared since Eliza was a little girl.

For a long moment, they stood there, holding each other as years of pain and fear melted away. Julian joined them, his small arms wrapping around both his mother and sister. With a soft, understanding look on his face, Alexander observed from a distance.

After a while, William cleared his throat. "There is the matter of the king," he said, unrolling a scroll bearing the royal seal. The parchment crackled as he opened it, and he read aloud with authority: "His Majesty, the King of England, orders that Master Julian Wilson shall henceforth be lord of the Manor. Until he comes of age, Eliza Wilson and Alexander Hale shall serve as his mentors and advisors, overseeing the management of the companies controlled by the disgraced Ambrose Wilson. We decree that no orphaned child, nor any child, shall be subjected to labour in the mines. All children, regardless of station, are to receive an education equal to that of the wealthy. This decree is effective immediately."

William lowered the scroll and addressed Julian. "The king's orders are explicit. This estate, and its responsibilities, now belongs to you."

Eliza looked at Julian, who stood tall despite his youth, his eyes wide. She placed a hand on his shoulder. "We shall undertake this together," she said. "For the family we have lost, and for the future we shall build."

Alexander nodded. "And for the children who shall never suffer again."

Just then, the horses spooked, their ears flattening and their hooves stamping nervously against the ground. A deep tremor shook the earth, rattling the loose fittings of the manor both inside and out. Windows trembled, and dust cascaded from the ceiling. Ben felt a shiver as he recognised the signs Grace had alerted him to. This was it—his time here was over.

His chest tightened with anguish as he looked at Eliza and Julian, the two people who had become like family to him. The love he felt for them warred with the longing for his own family in the future. His heart ached at the thought of leaving them, knowing he might never see them again. But he had no choice.

Ben approached Eliza first and threw his arms around her, hugging her tightly. "I have to go now."

Eliza stroked his hair as she tried to soothe him. 'Where? Where are you going?"

"To my time," Ben said, drawing back sufficiently to meet her eyes. "I have to go back. I don't have a choice."

"No…" Julian cried, trembling with emotion. His brave façade crumbled, replaced by raw grief. "No… no…" he repeated, rushing forward and wrapping his arms around Ben. "You cannot leave us!"

Ben hugged Julian, tears streaming down his cheeks. His words broke, heavy and raw. "I don't want to," he said. "But I can't stay. I have to go back to my family, my time."

The house rattled again, another tremor shaking the ground beneath their feet. The air seemed to hum with energy, a strange, otherworldly force pulling at Ben. He knew he couldn't delay any longer.

"I'm so sorry, Julian," Ben said. His arms wrapped around Julian's neck. "I love you." He turned to Eliza, his eyes filled with anguish. "I love you too."

Julian couldn't speak, his throat too tight with emotion. He clung to Ben. Eliza's eyes glistened with tears, but she nodded, her strength unwavering even in the face of her own heartbreak. "Go," she said, composed despite the tears streaming down her cheeks. "We shall never forget you, Benjamin. Never. Thank you!"

Ben released Julian, his hands trembling as he stepped back. He gave them one last, lingering look, memorising their faces. Then, without looking back—afraid that if he did, he'd never be able to leave—he turned and ran through the manor, his footsteps echoing in the halls.

He reached Julian's chamber, his heart pounding in his chest. An eerie blue light bathed the room, and a faint distortion shimmered in the air, warping the surrounding space. Ben hesitated for only a moment, wiping the tears from his face with the back of his hand. He lingered for a moment, his chest aching with the sorrow of what he was leaving behind.

The house rumbled once more, the tremor stronger this time. Ben stepped into the distortion, the light enveloping him. For a moment, everything was chaos—a whirlwind of sound and colour. Then, as suddenly as it had begun, the world fell silent.

In the manor, Eliza and Julian stood frozen, the air heavy with the void left by their friend. The tremors had stopped, and the house was eerily quiet. Julian sank to his knees, his face buried in his hands, while Eliza knelt beside him, pulling him into her arms.

"He is gone," Julian said, wiping his eyes.

Eliza held him. "He is gone," she echoed. "But he shall forever remain with us."

Outside, the rising sun cast a golden light over the manor. The world felt different somehow, as if the fabric of time itself had shifted. But for Eliza and Julian, one thing remained unchanged: the love they carried for Benjamin, a bond that not even time could break.

CHAPTER 20: THE RETURN

Olivia awoke to a faint tremor rattling the house, the vibrations subtle but enough to pull her from sleep. She blinked against the bright morning sunlight streaming through her window, the golden rays casting warm patterns across her room. Something felt different—off. She stretched lazily, rubbing the sleep from her eyes, and then froze. From the corner of her eye, she caught sight of someone standing in her room, their figure silhouetted against the light.

Her heart leapt into her throat, panic surging through her. But as she turned her head, her fear melted into pure, unbridled joy. It was Ben. Her Ben. He stood there, dressed in strange, ancient-looking clothes—a 19th-century army uniform complete with a fitted coat, leather armour, and tall riding boots. The ensemble should have looked too large, too serious for a boy of twelve, but it gave him an air of unexpected maturity. The coat hugged his frame neatly, the leather armour adding a touch of ruggedness, and the boots made him stand taller, more confident. His face was still boyish, but there was a new determination in his eyes, a seriousness that made him seem older than his years. And then there was his smile—the same warm, familiar smile that had always been full of life, now paired with a newfound poise that made her heart swell with pride.

"Ben!" she screamed, the delight in her cry clear and bright. She flew out of bed, her feet barely touching the floor as she launched herself at him. Her arms wrapped around him with an intensity that spoke of weeks of worry and longing. "Oh, Ben, I've missed you so much!" she cried.

Ben staggered slightly under the force of her hug, but quickly steadied himself, his arms tightening around her. In that moment, everything he'd endured—the danger, the loss, the love of the family he'd found and left behind—rushed over him, suffocating in its intensity. He hadn't realised just how much he'd missed his own family, missed home, until now. Tears pricked at the corners of his eyes, but he blinked them away, holding her even tighter.

Olivia finally pulled back, her hands gripping his shoulders as she held him at arm's length. Her eyes scanned his face, taking in the changes—the new lines of maturity, the quiet strength in his eyes. "You look so grown up." She could sense it, even without him saying a word: her little brother had been through a lifetime of experiences in what had only been a few weeks.

Ben smiled, a little sheepishly, and said nothing.

Olivia's eyes filled with tears, but she smiled through them, her heart swelling with relief and love. "Welcome home," she said, pulling him into another hug. "Welcome home."

Ethan burst into the room, his heart racing at the sound of Olivia's scream. He stopped short at the sight before him: Ben, his son, alive and well, standing in the middle of the room. For a moment, Ethan could only stare, his mind struggling to process what he was seeing. Then, as if a dam had broken, Ben turned and launched himself into his father's arms, his legs wrapping around Ethan's waist like he was five years old again.

Ethan caught him instinctively, his arms tightening around Ben in a fierce embrace. Their cheeks touched, tears mingling. "Ben," he whispered with unbridled emotion. "My boy. You're home." He held Ben for a long moment, his hands trembling as they gripped his son's back. Then, pulling back just enough to speak, he called out with urgency, "Claire! Claire, come quick!"

Claire, still in bed, stirred at the sound of Ethan's voice. With every day Ben remained missing, her depression had swelled, her days blending into a fog of grief and despair. She had heard Ethan and Olivia's excited calls before—each time, her heart had leapt with hope, only to be crushed when it turned out to be something, or someone else. A strange new building appearing overnight, a diary entry in Ben's handwriting that hadn't been there before, or some other inexplicable phenomenon. Each time, she hoped, and each time, heartbreak followed.

But this time, Ethan sounded different. It wasn't the tone of someone who had found another clue or oddity—it was raw, emotional, and full of joy. Claire pushed herself up in bed, her heart pounding as she turned to the door. She hesitated, afraid to hope, afraid to be disappointed again. But then she heard Olivia, bright and tearful, and something inside her shifted.

The bedroom door creaked open, and there, standing in the entrance, was Ben. He looked taller, older, and more confident than she remembered, his clothes strange and almost regal. Behind him stood Ethan and Olivia, their faces glowing with happiness.

For a moment, Claire thought she must be dreaming. Her mind couldn't reconcile the sight before her with the reality she accepted. But then Ben stepped into the room, his eyes locking onto hers, and she knew this was real. "Ben? baby?"

Ben's heart ached at the sight of his mother, her face pale and drawn from weeks of worry. He crossed the room in a few quick strides and climbed onto the bed beside her. "Mummy, it's me," he said, wrapping his arms around her.

Claire clung to him, her hands gripping his shoulders as if afraid he might vanish again. Her face was wet with tears, her breath hitching as she buried her head in his chest, her body trembling with sobs she could no longer hold back. "My baby—my sweet boy. You're really here. You're really here." She repeated the words like a prayer, as though saying them aloud would keep them true.

She pulled back just enough to cradle his face between her hands, her thumbs brushing over his cheeks as if to reassure herself he was real. Her eyes, still brimming with tears, searched his face— every freckle, every curve, every detail she had memorised and missed so dearly. He was still Ben, her Ben, but something was different. There was a quiet steadiness in his face that hadn't been there before. The innocence of childhood had faded, leaving behind a maturity far beyond his years—one he should never have had to endure.

Overcome with love, she kissed his lips, then his nose, then his forehead—gentle, reverent touches that spoke of all the days she'd longed to hold him. When her fingers brushed the tears on his cheeks, she kissed those too, as if she could take away every hurt, every fear, every moment they'd been apart. "I've missed you so much," she whispered. "My brave, beautiful boy. I'm never letting you go again."

Ben didn't speak, but he didn't need to. The way he leaned into her touch, the way his hands clutched at her sleeves, told her everything she needed to know. He was here. He was hers. And no matter how much he'd grown, no matter how much the world had changed him, he would always be her child. He kissed her cheek. The guilt he had carried for putting her through so much pain weighed heavily on him, but in that moment, all that mattered was being home. "I'm sorry, Mummy," he said. "I'm so sorry."

Ethan and Olivia stood in the doorway, their arms around each other as they watched the reunion. For the first time in months, the house felt whole again, filled with a warmth and light that had been missing for far too long.

Olivia ran to her room and peered out the window, her eyes widening as she took in the view. The ugly old factory that had loomed over the farmland for years was gone, as were the strange, mismatched buildings that had been springing up like weeds. In their place stood a grand building, its brick façade weathered but elegant, as if it had stood there for centuries. Behind it, a group of boys jogged around a sprawling sports field, their laughter carrying on the breeze.

Ben followed his sister and peered out the window, his parents close behind. Ethan and Claire held hands, a rare and tender moment of connection after weeks of strain and worry. "That's new," Ben said, his eyes widening with surprise. "Isn't it?"

Ethan studied the building, his brow furrowed in curiosity. It stood on their land, which meant it could belong to them—but how? When was it built? His mind raced with questions. "Come on," he said. "I have to see this up close. Ben, you're staying with me. I'm never letting you out of my sight again." He reached for Ben's hand.

Ben smiled, his heart swelling with happiness as he took his dad's hand. Claire reached for his other hand, and together, the family walked across the field to the building. The air was crisp, the sunrise painting a golden hue across the landscape. A winding driveway branched off from the main road, leading up to the building through beautifully manicured gardens. Flowers bloomed in vibrant colours, and tall trees lined the path, their leaves rustling gently in the breeze.

As they approached, the building's grandeur became even more apparent. A clock tower crowned its main entrance. Above the arched doorway, engraved in bold letters, were the words: *1859 – Sir Benjamin Home for Boys*. Ben's mouth fell open, his eyes wide with disbelief. His family stared in stunned silence, taking in the sight.

The building was old, its brickwork weathered but impeccably maintained. Modern additions blended seamlessly with the original structure, giving it a timeless yet functional appearance. This place was not just a relic of the past, but a living, thriving institution.

Olivia stood behind her brother, her arms draped over his shoulders. She broke the silence, her eyes alight with wonder as she gently ruffled his hair. "Ben, what on earth happened back then? How did *this* come to be?"

Ben shook his head slowly, his mind racing. "I... I don't know."

Ethan squeezed Ben's hand. "Whatever it was, it's incredible. This place—it's a legacy, Ben. Your legacy."

Claire's eyes glistened with tears as she looked at her son. "This is beyond anything I could have imagined."

Ethan stood frozen, his eyes fixed on the grand building before him. The Sir Benjamin Home for Boys loomed like a monument, its clock tower casting a long shadow over the manicured gardens. As he stared, a strange sensation washed over him—a flood of memories that hadn't been there before, as if his mind was being rewritten.

Vivid images flashed through his thoughts: standing at the front of a classroom, teaching a group of eager boys mathematics; leading another class in accountancy, their faces bright with concentration. He saw himself in a bustling mess hall, children laughing and eating together, their joy infectious. Another memory surfaced—him consulting with contractors, pointing to blueprints for an extension to accommodate girls. The details were crisp, the emotions vivid, as if these moments had always been a part of him.

Ethan felt as if someone had given him the keys to this place and entrusted him with its management and legacy. The memories settled into his mind, not as something new, but as something that had always been there, waiting to be uncovered.

Two boys burst out of the dormitory, their laughter echoing across the courtyard. They ran toward the main entrance but skidded to a stop when they noticed Ethan. Grinning, they nodded respectfully. "Good morning, Dean Wallace," they said in unison. One of them glanced at Ben and added, "Hi, Ben!" before darting inside, their voices fading as the heavy doors swung shut behind them.

Ethan stared after them, his mind reeling. *Dean Wallace?* The title felt familiar, as if it had always been his. He turned to Ben in awe. "Did you... did you know about this?"

Ben shook his head, his eyes wide. "No, Daddy. I mean, I knew something had changed, but... not this. Not like this."

Claire stepped closer, her hand resting on Ethan's arm. Her eyes narrowed with concern. "What's going on?" she asked. "Ethan, you look like you've seen a ghost."

Ethan was trying to steady himself. "I don't know how to explain it," he said. "But it's like... like I've been here before. Like I've been a part of this place for years. I remember teaching those boys. I remember planning the expansions. It's all so clear, but... it's impossible. We have only been here weeks, not years."

Olivia, who had been quietly taking it all in, stepped forward. "Maybe it's not impossible," she said. "What if... what if this is part of what Ben did back then? What if he changed things—changed *us*—our history, without even realising it?"

Ben looked at his sister, then at his parents, his heart pounding. "I didn't mean to," he said. "I just... I wanted to help Eliza and Julian."

Ethan placed a hand on Ben's shoulder. "I am sure you did, son," he said, his voice brimming with pride. "I think you did more good than you could ever know."

Claire sat down on a garden bench, her legs feeling unsteady beneath her. Olivia joined her, the two of them sitting in silence as they tried to process everything that had happened. Claire's mind was spinning, a whirlwind of emotions and questions. She stared at the grand building before them, its clock tower standing tall against the sky. "Olivia. Do you think… do you think this is real? Or are we dreaming?"

Olivia reached over and took her mother's hand, squeezing it gently. "It's real, Mum. I don't know how, but it's real. And it's… it's amazing."

Meanwhile, Ethan and Ben stepped through the main entrance of the building, their footsteps echoing in the vast, polished marble hallway. The space was grand, with high ceilings and natural light streaming through tall windows. A staircase wound up to the left and right, its banisters gleaming with intricately carved woodwork. But it was the painting at the far end of the hallway that caught their attention.

Ethan was the first to see it; he gasped and froze. Ben followed his gaze, his eyes widening as he took in the larger-than-life depiction of himself. The painting showed Ben standing proudly in front of the old manor, his posture confident and his expression steadfast. He was wearing the same clothes he had on now—the outfit that had felt so out of place just moments ago.

Ben's heart raced as he stepped closer, his eyes fixed on the small silver plaque beneath the painting. The inscription read: *Dedicated to Benjamin Wallace—A Friend, A Companion, and A Brother.*

Ethan placed a hand on Ben's shoulder, his eyes softening with quiet wonder. "Ben," he said, "this… this is you." Ethan's grip tightened slightly. "You made a difference, son. You changed lives. This place, these memories—they're proof of that."

Ben stared at the painting, a lump forming in his throat. He thought of the people he had met, the friends he had made. It all felt so close now, as if they were just beyond the door, waiting for him to step outside and join them. But this painting, this building—they were real. They were evidence of the impact he had made.

As they stood there, the significance of the moment settled over them. The Sir Benjamin Home for Boys wasn't just a building—it was a legacy, a reminder that even the smallest actions could ripple through time and change the world in ways no one could have imagined.

That evening, after dinner and hours of catching up with his parents and Olivia, Ben wandered through the mansion. The familiar halls felt different now. The gory hunting paintings that had once adorned the walls, their grim depictions of death and violence, were gone. In their place hung vibrant, lifelike portraits of Eliza, Alexander, and Julian. Some showed them in moments of triumph, others in quiet reflection, and a few even included Ben and Toby, their faces filled with determination and camaraderie.

Ben paused in front of one painting, a laugh escaping him as he studied the image. It depicted him, dressed in rags, tumbling into an overturned cart of fish guts. The artist had captured the moment perfectly, from the look of shock on his face to the fish innards spilling everywhere. "I can't believe they painted this," he muttered, shaking his head with a grin.

He continued down the hall, his eyes scanning the other paintings. Each one told a story—a piece of the adventure he had lived through. There was one of Eliza standing tall and defiant, another of Alexander forging a sword, and even one of Toby grinning mischievously as he outsmarted a group of mercenaries. But it was the last painting that made Ben's skin crawl. It showed him sitting atop a horse, his posture protective as he shielded Eliza and Julian from the one-eyed man in black. The intensity in his own eyes, the determination in his stance—it was both awe-inspiring and unsettling.

Ben was so engrossed in the painting that he didn't hear Olivia approach. She put her arm over his shoulder, causing him to jump. "Sorry," she said with a laugh. "Didn't mean to scare you."

Ben exhaled sharply, his heart still racing. "You've got a knack for sneaking up on me," he said, trying to sound annoyed but failing to hide his smile.

Wonder filled Olivia's wide eyes as she gazed at the painting. "Was that really you, Ben? Did you really ride horses and fight?"

Ben nodded. "Yeah, I rode horses… I had to. But I didn't fight anyone. I would have if I needed to."

Olivia shook her head in admiration, her eyes shining with pride.

Ben thought about telling her everything—about Grace, the girl from the future who had guided him, about the battles they had fought, and the lives they had changed. But then he remembered Grace's warning: revealing too much could alter the course of history negatively. The secret burned in his chest, but he knew he had to keep it.

Olivia seemed to sense his hesitation. She nudged him playfully. "You've got that look again," she said. "Like you're keeping some big secret."

Ben forced a smile. "Maybe I am," he said teasingly. "But some secrets are better left untold."

Olivia rolled her eyes but didn't press him. Instead, she looped her arm through his and pulled him to the next painting. "Tell me about this one. And don't leave out any details."

As they walked through the mansion, Ben felt a sense of peace settle over him. The paintings were more than just art—they were a testament to the lives he had touched, the friendships he had forged, and the legacy he had left behind.

The next morning, Ben wandered through the gardens of the mansion, the air crisp and filled with the scent of blooming flowers. When they had first arrived, the gardens had been derelict—dry, lifeless, and overgrown. Now, they were a wonderland of colour and beauty, with vibrant flowers, neatly trimmed hedges, and winding paths that invited exploration. It was as if the land itself had been reborn. He turned and looked at the house. For a moment, he thought he saw Julian in Olivia's bedroom window, his small face pressed against the glass. But the illusion vanished as Olivia appeared, waving at him with a bright smile. He waved back, though his heart ached with a strange, unshakable sadness.

Ben turned his attention to the old graveyard, which still stood in its familiar place but was now well-maintained and cared for. Restoration efforts had made the inscriptions on the once cracked and weathered headstones clear and legible. He walked slowly among them, his fingers brushing against the cool stone as he read the names. Each one told a story—a life lived, a legacy left behind.

He stopped at a grave adorned with a large, graceful angel, its wings outstretched as if in eternal protection. The inscription beneath it read:

Eliza Wilson
1791–1864
Beloved Wife, Devoted Mother, and Faithful Friend.
Her strength and compassion shaped lives, her legacy endures in the hearts of those she loved.
A light in the darkness, her memory shines on.

Ben's heart grew heavy as he traced the letters with his fingers. Eliza had lived a long life, but the thought of her being gone was almost too much to bear.

Beside Eliza's grave was another, a smaller, older one. A stone statue of a boy mounted on a rearing stallion stood atop it, the figure frozen in a moment of youthful energy and courage. Ben's hands flew to his head in disbelief as he read the inscription:

Here lies Lord Julian Wilson
1800–1810
Beloved Brother and Unyielding Hero.
Taken from this world too soon, yet his courage and kindness endure eternally.
May his spirit find peace, and his memory live on in the hearts of those he cherished.

Ben fell to his knees, a cry escaping his lips. "Oh, no... no..." he said, his fingers digging into the earth as if searching for something solid to hold on to. He gripped the tombstone tightly, as if his sheer will could bring Julian back—weeping openly as he stared at the grave, the weight of Julian's loss crushing him.

He jumped up, his heart racing, and stared at the house. "I have to go back!" he said, his voice filled with desperation. "I can't let this happen—he can't die, not so young."

The words hung in the air, a promise and a plea. Ben didn't know how he would do it, or if it was even possible, but he knew he had to try. Julian's life—his laughter, his courage, his brother— was worth fighting for. And if there was even a chance to rescue him, Ben would.

As he stood there, the morning sun struggled to pierce the heavy veil of gathering storm clouds, casting an eerie, muted light over the gardens. Ben felt determination crystallise within him. He had faced impossible odds before, and he would do it again. For Julian and Eliza.

With one last glance at the graveyard, Ben turned and ran to the house, his mind racing with plans and possibilities. The past was calling him, and he was ready to answer.

CHARACTER GUIDE

The Wallace Family (Present Day)
Ethan Wallace – An architect and Claire's husband.
Claire Wallace – An illustrator who inherits Wilson House.
Olivia Wallace – Ethan and Claire's teenage daughter.
Ben Wallace – Ethan and Claire's eleven-year-old son.
Grace Wallace – Ben's niece from a dystopian future.

Other Key Characters (Present Day)
Penelope Marsh – The family lawyer.
Samuel – Wilson House's handyman.
Theodore Marlowe – A researcher studying Wilson House.
Vince Colby – Marlowe's research partner.

The Wilson Family (Past)
Lord Ambrose Wilson – Eliza and Julian's controlling father.
Lady Isadora Wilson – Eliza and Julian's mother.
Eliza Wilson – A young woman in love with Alexander.
Julian Wilson – Eliza's younger brother.

The Whitfield Family (Past)
Robert Whitfield – A farmer who helps Eliza.
Sarah Whitfield – Robert's wife.
Caleb Whitfield – Robert and Sarah's youngest adopted son.
Henry Whitfield – Robert and Sarah's eldest adopted son.
Maggie Whitfield – Robert and Sarah's adopted daughter.
Lily Whitfield – Robert and Sarah's young daughter.
Samuel Whitfield – Robert and Sarah's youngest child and son.

The Northcott Family (Past)
George Northcott – A farmer who offers shelter.
Martha Northcott – George's wife.

Other Key Characters (Past)
Alexander Hale – A blacksmith and Eliza's love interest.
Daniel – A stable hand and Martha's son.

Martha – The cook at Wilson House and Daniel's mother.

Toby – A streetwise orphan who helps Eliza and the boys.

The Man in Black / Mercenary – A dangerous man hired by Ambrose.

William – A soldier connected to the Wilsons and the King.

ABOUT THE AUTHOR

Robin Perks is an author whose extraordinary life experiences with Temporal Lobe Epilepsy (TLE) have profoundly shaped his creative vision and storytelling. Living with TLE since early childhood—though not diagnosed until the age of 40—Perks has navigated a world of vivid visions, altered states of consciousness, and moments of profound clarity. What once seemed like bewildering and isolating experiences have since become the foundation of his imaginative prowess and a deep understanding of the human mind.

For Perks, TLE is not merely a condition but a wellspring of creativity, offering a unique lens through which to explore the boundaries of reality, time, and perception. His personal journey—from confusion to understanding, and ultimately to empowerment—has transformed what could have been a limitation into a source of boundless inspiration. He intricately weaves this journey into his writing, particularly in his science fiction time-travel novels, where he invites readers to question the nature of existence and the fluidity of time.

Through his work, Perks crafts worlds that are as thought-provoking as they are captivating, drawing from his own experiences to create stories that resonate with authenticity and depth. His writing is a testament to the power of turning adversity into art, offering readers not only an escape but also a deeper connection to the mysteries of the mind and the universe

Robin Perks continues to explore the intersections of science, imagination, and human experience, proving that even the most unexpected paths can lead to extraordinary destinations.